# INTO THE GUNS

## ACE BOOKS BY WILLIAM C. DIETZ

IIIIIIIIIIIII AMERICA RISING IIIIIIIIIIIII
# INTO THE GUNS
IIIIIIIIIIIIIIIIIIIIIIIIIIIIIIIIIIIIIIIIIIIIIII

## william c. dietz

ACE
New York

ACE
Published by Berkley
An imprint of Penguin Random House LLC
375 Hudson Street, New York, New York 10014

Copyright © 2016 by William C. Dietz
Penguin Random House supports copyright. Copyright fuels creativity, encourages diverse
voices, promotes free speech, and creates a vibrant culture. Thank you for buying an authorized
edition of this book and for complying with copyright laws by not reproducing, scanning, or
distributing any part of it in any form without permission. You are supporting writers and
allowing Penguin Random House to continue to publish books for every reader.

ACE is a registered trademark and the A colophon is a trademark of
Penguin Random House LLC.

LEGION OF THE DAMNED is a registered trademark of William C. Dietz.

Library of Congress Cataloging-in-Publication Data
Dietz, William C.
Into the guns : the first America rising novel / William C. Dietz.
pages ; cm
ISBN 978-0-425-27870-3 (hardcover)
I. Title.
PS3554.I388I58 2016
813'.54—dc23
2015030798

First Edition: October 2016

Printed in the United States of America
1  3  5  7  9  10  8  6  4  2

Cover art by Paul Youll
Cover design by Sarah Oberrender
Book design by Kelly Lipovich

*I would like to dedicate this book to
Lieutenant Colonel Scot D. Pears, USA, Retired.
Thank you for your service to our country and your help with this book.
Strategic and tactical errors, if any, are entirely mine.*

# CHAPTER 1

||||||||||||||||||||||||||||||||||

*I am the Infantry . . .*
*I have won more than two hundred years of freedom.*
*I yield not to weakness,*
*to hunger,*
*to cowardice,*
*to fatigue,*
*to superior odds,*
*for I am mentally tough, physically strong,*
*and morally straight.*
*I forsake not . . .*
*my country,*
*my mission,*
*my comrades,*
*my sacred duty.*
*I am relentless.*
*I am always there,*
*now and forever.*
*I AM THE INFANTRY!*
*FOLLOW ME!*

—FROM THE INFANTRYMAN'S CREED,
UNITED STATES ARMY

## TACOMA, WASHINGTON

Sixty meteors entered Earth's atmosphere on May Day 2018. One of them swept in over North America at 1:11 P.M. PST. It was brighter than the sun and traveling at nearly sixty times the speed of sound. Because of the object's velocity and shallow angle of entry, it exploded above the San Juan Islands in Washington State.

The result was a flash of bright light, an expanding cloud of superheated gas and dust, and a powerful shock wave. Most of the meteorite's energy was dispersed into the atmosphere. But the remainder produced an explosion twenty to thirty times more powerful than the atomic bomb dropped on Hiroshima. The blast was felt hundreds of miles away.

|||||||||||

First Lieutenant Robin "Mac" Macintyre was walking toward the base exchange when she saw a flash of light out of the corner of her eye, heard a distant boom, and felt a wall of hot air hit her from behind. It threw her down. The ground shook for three seconds or so.

Mac did a push-up and was back on her feet in time to see a radio tower sway and fall. There was a resounding crash as the structure landed on a wood-frame building and cut it in half. Mac felt the force of the impact through the soles of her shoes. *What the hell's going on?* she wondered. *Did Mount Rainier blow? Did a plane crash nearby? No, a plane crash wouldn't knock the radio tower down.* Mac took off. She was off duty—and dressed in a tee shirt, shorts, and running shoes. Sirens wailed as aid units responded to calls, people ran every which way, and columns of smoke marched across the horizon.

Mac passed a chaplain as she rounded a corner. He was on his knees, head bowed, praying. *It's too late for that,* Mac thought to herself, as a thick layer of dust swept in to partially block the sun. *Something tells me that we're well and truly screwed.*

After crossing a grinder, Mac arrived at the company area where her platoon was waiting. Others were present as well, including Captain Paul Driscoll. The fact that he was dressed in camos came as no surprise since he was rarely seen in anything else. "I'm glad you're okay," Driscoll said. "We don't have orders yet . . . But it doesn't take a genius to figure out that the brass will come up with something for us to do. So draw weapons and get your platoon ready to roll."

"Draw weapons?"

Driscoll looked grim. "I'm just guessing, but some sort of civil unrest is a distinct possibility. Oh, and Mac, one more thing . . ."

"Sir?"

"Find something to wear. You look like a cheerleader on her way to a workout."

Mac made a face at him and went off to find Sergeant First Class Emilio Evans. He was her platoon sergeant and, if she was killed, would assume command until the army issued him a new lieutenant. Evans was five-five and typically stood on the balls of his feet as if to make himself look taller. He had brown skin, a round face, and a ready smile. "Good morning, ma'am . . . Is this some crazy shit or what?"

"It certainly is," Mac agreed. "Do you have any intel on what happened?"

Evans shook his head. "No, ma'am."

"Okay, how many people do we have at this point?"

"We're five short," Evans replied. "But three of them live off base. So they could be in transit."

"Yeah," Mac agreed although she had her doubts. The sky was a sickly-gray color, the light level had been reduced by half, and Mac could feel something gritty on her skin. Fallout from a nuke? If so, the entire platoon was going to die. But there was no point in saying that, so she didn't. "All right," Mac said. "I hope they're okay. Let's redistribute the people we have."

"Yes, ma'am. Been there, done that."

Mac chuckled. "Sorry, Emilio . . . That was stupid. Of course you have. Carry on. I need to find something to wear."

"Check the lockers in the maintenance bay," Evans suggested. "There should be some overalls back there." The ground shook, and they were forced to grab onto a Stryker vehicle for support. Soldiers swore, windows shattered on a building nearby, and a new crack zigzagged across the street. "We're havin' some fun now," Evans said, as the tremor faded away.

"If you say so," Mac replied. "See you in five."

Once inside the maintenance bay, Mac realized that it might be dangerous there. All sorts of stuff had spilled out of the wall lockers and onto the floor, including a stack of olive-drab overalls. Mac grabbed one labeled SMALL, and hurried to pull it on. By the time she returned to the vehicles, the platoon was armed and dressed in full combat gear.

Mac's vest was waiting for her. It weighed 3.6 pounds and was loaded with a .9mm pistol in a cross-draw holster, spare magazines, and a small first-aid kit. "The colonel is about to brief company commanders and platoon leaders," Evans told her. "Maybe *she* knows what's going on," he added hopefully.

Mac followed Driscoll over to the whitewashed headquarters building. The wood-framed structure dated back to WWII and stood slumped like an old soldier who could no longer stand at attention. Rather than run the risk that the building would collapse, the order was given to assemble in front of it. Somebody shouted, "Atten-hut!" as Wilson rounded a corner, and the soldiers came to attention.

Like Mac's father, Major General Bo Macintyre, and her older sister, Major Victoria Macintyre, Lt. Colonel Marsha Wilson was a West Point graduate. It was an honor Robin Macintyre had chosen to forgo, much to her father's disgust. Wilson was about five-eight and her back was ramrod straight. Mac scanned the other woman's face and didn't like what she saw. Uncertainty? Yes. But Mac could see something else as well. And it looked like fear.

"At ease," Wilson said. "I don't have the time to weasel word this," she announced. "So here's the straight scoop . . . It appears that a swarm of meteors hit the planet at a very high rate of speed. At least a third of them exploded over the oceans, but the rest detonated over land and caused significant damage. I'm sorry to inform you that Washington, D.C., took a direct hit."

The news was received with a chorus of groans followed by comments like, "No way," "Oh, shit," and "Those poor bastards."

One of Bravo Company's platoon leaders began to cry, and Mac knew why. The woman's husband was working at the Pentagon. *Had* been working at the Pentagon. And what about her own family? Where was her father when the poop hit the fan? And her sister? Mac felt an emptiness at the pit of her stomach.

"England, France, Italy, Romania, Turkmenistan, and China all took hits," the battalion commander said grimly. "But that isn't the worst of it . . . The Chinese thought they were under attack. So they launched a dozen intercontinental ballistic missiles from submarines out in the Pacific. Japan, South Korea, and Australia were targeted, along with certain locations in the United States. We believe Peterson Air Force Base was among them."

The news was so bad that none of them said anything as Mac sought to absorb what the words meant. Millions, perhaps billions of people were dead, and Peterson was the headquarters for NORAD (the United States Northern Command), as well as the Air Force Space Command. Both were hardened targets—but could they withstand what the Chinese had thrown at them? Only time would tell.

"The Chinese apologized once they understood the truth of the matter," Wilson said. "Not that it makes any difference. Our government has been destroyed—and our command structure has been decimated. So the general and his staff are on their own until someone wearing more stars shows up."

Mac knew Wilson was referring to the Joint Base Lewis-McChord's commanding officer, Lieutenant General "Rusty" Rawlings. A man who, unlike her father, had risen all the way from private E-1 to general. It was a long and nearly impossible journey.

"General Rawlings wants us to secure the base," Wilson informed them. "Civilians are trying to enter. Our orders are to stop them using the minimum amount of force required to do so." None of Mac's peers said a word as they made their way back to the company area where anxious soldiers were awaiting them. Now it was *their* turn to deliver the bad news.

Even though Mac prided herself on knowing each person under her command by name, she couldn't remember what area each one of them was from. But it seemed like a safe bet that each soldier had lost someone. Once the platoon was gathered around her, Mac delivered the news and eventually brought the briefing to a close with a lame, "I'm sorry." Some of the soldiers cried and turned to each other for support. A few stood motionless, their faces empty of all expression, while they sought to process what they'd heard.

PFC Wessel, AKA "the Weasel," started to giggle. "What the hell is wrong with you?" Specialist Sims demanded angrily.

"I'm from LA," the Weasel explained. "The Chinese nuked my ex-wife! There *is* a God."

Sims was staring at the other soldier in disbelief when Driscoll arrived. "Okay, people," he said in a voice loud enough for everybody to hear. "The CO wants us to establish a position west of the main gate on Division Drive. The MPs set up a traffic control post over there, and we're going to provide backup. Let's load up and roll out." His eyes roamed their faces. "I know this is hard,"

Driscoll added. "But you joined the army to do hard things. This is your chance to make a difference."

"You heard the captain," Mac said, as Driscoll left the area. "Let's roll."

Mac was in command of the battalion's scout platoon, which consisted of four M1127A2 Stryker RCs. The "RC" stood for "recon." Each vehicle was equipped with a .50 caliber machine gun, or a 40mm grenade launcher, and ancillary weapons as needed.

Crews consisted of a commander/gunner and a driver. A typical load out included a crew of two and a nine-person squad in back. But more people could, and frequently did, squeeze into the rear compartment. Archer Company's record was seventeen.

Mac chose to ride in the one-two vic (vehicle). She rarely if ever rode with Evans since that would put the platoon's entire command structure at risk. The rest of her tiny headquarters group consisted of Doc Obbie, the platoon's combat medic; Sparks Munroe, her radio-telephone operator (RTO); and forward observer Lin Kho. The weapons squad was crammed into one-two as well, which meant Mac was sitting knee to knee with Sergeant Brown. If the noncom was worried about the overall situation, she couldn't see any sign of it on his face.

The rear hatch produced a whining sound as it came up and locked into place. Now Mac was confined inside what amounted to a tin can where, though responsible for everything that happened to the platoon, she couldn't see. It was a helpless feeling, and one she would never get used to. The air was heavy with the sickly-sweet smell of hydraulic fluid. The truck produced a high-pitched, whining noise as it got under way.

The soldiers slumped sideways as the TC (truck commander) applied the brakes. That was followed by some backing and filling as he positioned the Stryker to fire on whatever targets might present themselves. As soon as the ramp went down, Sergeant Brown and his squad surged out to take up defensive positions around the first platoon's vehicles. But there wasn't any threat that Mac could discern. A group of citizens was gathered around a hastily created traffic control point (TCP)—but the MPs had the situation under control.

In addition to his military gear, Sparks was carrying a Sony pocket radio. He turned the set on and fiddled with the controls until he found a station that was still on the air. All of them listened intently as a field reporter described the way things looked from the top of Seattle's Queen Anne Hill. ". . . The top half of the space needle was sheared off . . . The wreckage fell toward the east—and is spread all over the place. Two of the buildings in the South Lake Union business complex were severely damaged, and one of them is on fire. The elevated section of I-5 can be seen through the smoke. It looks like a large section of it collapsed. Cars are scattered on the hillside and north–south traffic is blocked. Oh, no! *Another* section collapsed!"

"Turn it off," Mac said. "I can only take so much of that."

No one disagreed. Kho wiped her eyes. "My God, Lieutenant . . . When will it stop?"

Mac didn't know. And as the day progressed, it became increasingly obvious that no one else did either. By the time the sun set, it was completely hidden by a globe-spanning blanket of particulate matter. And, because the power was out, the only lights to be seen were those that belonged to a scattering of people with generators and the military. Sporadic gunfire began shortly thereafter. "What the hell are they shooting at?" Brown wondered out loud as he munched on a candy bar.

"Each other," Mac replied. "The people with generators shouldn't turn them on. Lights will attract trouble."

"What about *our* lights?" Brown inquired.

"Same thing," Mac told him. "It's only a matter of time."

That was the beginning of a long, nerve-wracking night. Gunfire was heard, fires could be seen in the distance, and by the time there was enough light to see by, a large crowd had gathered in front of the traffic control point. Some people had been driven out of their homes by looters. Others had been forced to abandon their cars on I-5 and were looking for a safe place to stay. But General Rawlings knew there were tens of thousands of such individuals out there—and a very real limit on how many refugees JBLM could safely handle. So he had chosen to dispatch medical teams, plus food and water, rather than let them enter the base.

But as two days morphed into three, the pressure was starting to build. As the amount of crime in the surrounding areas continued to increase, people wanted to enter the base for safety's sake. And Mac couldn't blame them.

A tall, thin MP had taken up a position in front of the barricades and was clutching a bullhorn. "Do not approach the barricade unless you are a member of the military and have ID to prove it!" the MP declared. "Please stay back."

A woman with two children approached him. Mac couldn't hear what was said, but could see the look of anguish on her face and saw the MP point. The woman was sobbing as she led her children back into the seething crowd. It was heartbreaking.

Macintyre heard a buzzing sound and turned in time to see a civilian helicopter appear from the south. It was flying low in order to escape the worst of the airborne grit and seemed to be following I-5 north. As an aid to navigation? In order to assess conditions on the freeway? Either possibility would make sense.

As the helo passed in front of her, Mac heard sporadic gunfire and realized that civilians on the freeway were firing on the aircraft!

*Why?* Maybe they wanted to punish someone for the situation they found themselves in even if that didn't make sense. Would her troops think the refugees were firing at *them*? Mac feared that the answer could be yes. "This is Archer-One actual," she said via the platoon net. "Hold your fire." They did, and the helicopter continued on its way, apparently undamaged.

The crowd in front of them continued to swell as more and more people left the freeway searching for assistance. Or had the crowd morphed into a mob? That was the way it appeared as a self-appointed leader elbowed his way up to the front of the assemblage and began to chant. "Let us in! Let us in! Let us in!"

The MP with the bullhorn tried to respond, but the mob shouted him down. Mac was about to notify Captain Driscoll when he appeared at her side. "Fire warning shots if they start to push through the barricade. If that doesn't work, shoot their leaders."

Mac was about to reply when a bullet blew the top of Driscoll's skull off. Blood and brain tissue sprayed sideways, and as Doc hurried to respond, the rest of them hit the dirt.

All sorts of thoughts flitted through Mac's mind. Had the sniper been waiting for an officer senior to her? Should she have ordered the platoon to dig in? Why wasn't Driscoll wearing his helmet? Private Hadley's voice cut through the muddle. "I have the bastard, Lieutenant . . . Just say the word."

Hadley was the platoon's marksman. "Smoke him," Mac ordered, and heard the Remington 700 fire a fraction of a second later. "Got him," the sniper said. "Over."

"Confirmed," his spotter echoed. "He was on the overpass at one o'clock. You can see the hole in the crowd. Over."

Mac looked, and sure enough, she could see a steadily expanding gap in the crowd of people who lined the rail. Unfortunately, there was no time in which to give the matter further thought as *another* voice came over the radio. "Brown here . . . Look west . . . Something *big* is coming our way. It's a front loader, and the bucket is raised to shield the driver."

Mac had to stand in order to see what Brown saw but was careful to use one-two for cover. A pair of binoculars brought everything in close. The machine wasn't big—it was HUGE! Stolen from a construction site? Probably. It looked as though criminals were trying to use the refugees as cannon fodder.

The loader was flanked by columns of motorcycles. The plan was obvious. Some sort of gang was planning to drive the machine through the TCP and head for the main gate. Once inside the base, they would go looking for heavy weapons. The kind they could use to take what they wanted. Judging from appearances, it looked as if the outriders hoped to flank the Strykers and get in behind them.

Did the man or woman in charge have some military training? Mac figured the answer was yes. She spoke into her mike. "Archer-One-Seven . . . Once the loader is fifty feet from the barricades, fire a burst of .50 cal over it. Archer-One-Four . . . If that plan doesn't work, put two rockets on the bastard. Stryker commanders are to engage the motorcycles if they attempt to flank us or charge the barricades. Over." Mac heard half a dozen clicks by way of a response.

People screamed and ran every which way as the loader and its escorts cleared the underpass and began to increase speed. The MP was still manning his post, his .9mm pistol raised, firing round after round at the charging machine. It was a gesture, but a brave one, and Mac was relieved when the soldier dived for the ground.

The sound of thunder was heard as the motorcycle riders revved their engines and spread out. Each man or woman had a passenger— and each passenger was armed. Mac heard the ping, ping, ping of bullets hitting one-two's armor as they opened fire.

Then the loader smashed through the barricades and someone

on Brown's squad fired a rocket at it. The missile struck the bucket and blew it away. The second rocket sped through the resulting gap and hit the cab. Mac saw a flash of light and heard the resulting boom as the machine jerked to a halt.

That didn't slow the bikers though . . . They kept coming. And that was when the remotely operated machine guns mounted on her Strykers began to chug. The subsequent battle lasted for less than thirty seconds. Once it was over, motorcycles and riders lay in a bloody sprawl out in front of the platoon's position. It was the first time Mac had been in combat. But rather than a sense of satisfaction—she felt sick to her stomach as she turned to Munroe. "Tell the captain what happened . . . I'm going forward to give Doc a hand."

Munroe stared at her. "Captain Driscoll is dead, Lieutenant . . . You're in command."

That was when Mac remembered the way Driscoll had been killed and turned to look at the body. The sight came as a shock. In command? It made sense since she was the company's XO (executive officer.) *But I don't want to be in command,* Mac thought to herself. *Hell, I don't want to be in the army.*

*Yet you joined,* the other her put in. *Not right away, like Dad wanted you to, but after goofing off for two years. Why was that anyway? To please the old bastard? To compete with your sister? Or because you couldn't think of an alternative?*

Mac forced herself to focus. The rest of Archer Company . . . Where was it? What had the other platoons been ordered to do? She spent the next half hour making the rounds.

Like the first platoon, the other two were positioned to prevent people from entering the base. But that wasn't all. Foot soldiers were patrolling the perimeter while the MPs searched for infiltrators, a number of whom had been placed under arrest. All of which made it impossible for the army to go out and help surrounding communities.

And that, according to a rumor Mac had heard, was the focus of a ninety-minute meeting between General Rawlings and a representative from the governor's office. A woman who, by all accounts, believed that *all* of JBLM's four-thousand-plus military personnel should be patrolling neighborhoods as far north as Seattle. But Rawlings called bullshit on that by pointing out that if the base were overrun, any work the troops managed to accomplish would be negated.

That was the way things stood as darkness fell, and orders came down for Archer Company's platoons to remain where they were. Mac ordered everyone to dig defensive fighting positions and stand four-hour watches. She was with the second platoon, eating an MRE, when Driscoll's replacement arrived. His name was Nick Hollister and he'd been taken off a desk job to lead Archer Company. Mac didn't have much respect for staff officers, but Hollister could talk the talk and clearly knew one end of a Stryker from the other.

Mac decided to take comfort from that as she completed the handover and hitched a ride to the spot where the first platoon was dug in. The power grid was down, but the spill of light from one-two's cargo compartment was sufficient to see by. Evans was there to greet Mac and provide a sitrep. "Everything's quiet," he assured her. "Everything except for some occasional sniper fire. But that's no big deal compared to what's happening on the other side of the freeway."

Mac turned to look west. No stars were visible because of the heavy cloud cover. But Mac could see the orange-red glow of what had to be a large blaze, and hear the intermittent pop, pop, pop of small-arms fire. No sirens though . . . Not a single one. After three days of chaos, the local police and fire departments had been neutralized.

Maybe the bad guys couldn't take JBLM. Not yet anyway . . . But they were free to rob, rape, and murder defenseless citizens. Some anyway. Although, with more than 300 million guns in the United States, others had the means to fight back.

That was the beginning of a long and mostly sleepless night. When dawn arrived, there was no sunrise as such. Just a gradual increase in the cold gray light that filtered down through thick layers of cloud. The air felt colder than it should have in May—and Mac wished she was wearing cold-weather gear. But that was in the BOQ with the rest of her belongings. So all she could do was clasp a hot mug of coffee with both hands and snuggle up to the heat that was radiating off one-two. That's what Mac was doing when a Humvee arrived and Captain Hollister got out. He had sandy-colored hair, a roundish face, and a spray of freckles across his nose. The same nose on which a pair of black-rimmed birth control glasses (BCG) rested.

Maybe Hollister was a PowerPoint Ranger, and maybe he wasn't. But he sure as hell *looked* like one. "Good morning," Hollister said, never mind the fact that it clearly wasn't. "Please ask the people who aren't on duty to gather around. Reliable information is still hard to come by, but I'll share what I have and ask you to brief the rest of the platoon later."

Mac was eager to hear the news no matter how iffy it might be—and knew the people in her platoon felt the same way. They were worried about their families and friends, some to the point where they were barely functional.

The soldiers came together on the east side of a Stryker, where they would be safe from snipers. "Okay," Hollister said as he consulted a printout. "Here's what the Intel people have been able to pull together. An object, widely believed to be one of at least a dozen meteorites, exploded over the San Juan Islands at approximately 1300 hours three days ago. The blast, plus the re-sulting shock wave, killed thousands of people. Earthquakes trig-gered by subsequent impacts caused additional deaths. Around the same time, a tsunami surged south through Puget Sound and laid waste to low-lying coastal areas. The Bremerton Naval Base and the Port of Seattle were destroyed."

That produced a chorus of groans. Hollister kept his eyes on the piece of paper. Because he was focused on the briefing? Or because it was difficult to maintain his composure? Mac suspected the latter. "The tidal wave surged south," Hollister continued. "And when it entered the Tacoma Narrows, the wall of water was a hundred feet high. The westbound span of the Narrows Bridge collapsed and dumped dozens of cars into the water. That means the channel is blocked, which will prevent ships from entering or leaving the port of Olympia until the Corps of Engineers can clear it."

Hollister looked up at that point. His expression was grave. "We still don't have a lot of information about the national or interna-tional situation other than what the colonel provided earlier. Once it comes in, I'll pass it along. In the meantime, we will continue to perform our duties.

"Unfortunately, Sea-Tac Airport was damaged by a quake—and very few planes are flying because of the particulate matter in the air. In fact, so much of the local infrastructure has been damaged that we have orders to escort thousands of civilians over Snoqualmie Pass to Yakima. A fleet of approximately forty buses is being as-sembled in Tacoma, and the convoy will depart at 0900 tomorrow morning. This platoon will take the point—and be responsible for scouting ahead.

"Your job will be to assess the condition of roads and bridges and provide the column with the kind of guidance that will enable it to keep moving. And that's critical. Because if the convoy bogs down, it might become difficult to keep the evacuees under control, and we'll be sitting ducks if criminal elements attack us. The second platoon will lead the column—and the third will bring up the rear. Platoon leaders will receive their orders by 1300 hours today."

Hollister looked at Mac. "In the meantime, you are to rotate your people back to their quarters, where they can shower, collect their winter clothing, and gear up. A platoon of Bradleys will relieve your platoon by 1600 hours. Once they do, swing by supply and pick up trailers loaded with MREs and water. We'll have a lot of mouths to feed. Do you have any questions?"

Mac had questions—plenty of 'em. Like, "How the hell can a recon platoon do its job while towing a frigging trailer?" But that sort of thing was best saved for a private conversation—or dispensed with altogether under the circumstances. "I'll get back to you, sir."

Hollister nodded. His expression was bleak. "Good. This is just the beginning. We're going to move two thousand people. But there are, or were, about 3.5 million people living in the Puget Sound area. Based on initial estimates something like 2.8 million of them are still alive. So our convoy will be the first of many as the government seeks to move at least eight hundred thousand residents east. I'm proud to say that Archer Company was chosen to lead the way."

Hollister made it *sound* good . . . But as a practical matter, Mac found it hard to believe that the authorities would be able to move that many people across the mountains two thousand at a time. What was that? Something like *sixteen thousand* busloads? Still, they were trying . . . And that beat the alternative.

||||||||||||

It was snowing in May. That was what Mac discovered when she rolled out of her rack and crossed the room to peer through the blinds. It was dark outside, but JBLM's emergency generators were running, and half of the streetlights were on. Mac could see individual snowflakes as they twirled down out of the black sky. Did that mean the weather had started to deteriorate? Because of the persistent overcast? Probably. And would this have a negative effect on crops? The answer was yes. According to one news report the so-called impact winter was going to have a devastating effect on agriculture, causing up to 25 percent of the human population to perish. That would be something like 3.5 billion people! A number so large, Mac couldn't wrap her mind around it. But there was nothing she could do other than help to the extent she could.

Mac had what was likely to be her last hot shower for days to come. It felt good, and she took her time. Once Mac was dressed, there were choices to make. Archer Company was supposed to return to JBLM in a matter of days. And maybe it would. But what if it didn't? Depending on what happened, she might never see her belongings again. So Mac placed the items of greatest importance into her "A" bag. That included all her winter clothing, two hundred dollars' worth of personal items purchased at the PX the evening before, and three framed pictures.

The first was of her mother. Some people said there was a resemblance, and Mac hoped they were right, because Margaret Macintyre had dark hair, intelligent eyes, and a softly rounded face. But unfortunately the woman in the picture had died of cancer shortly after her youngest daughter's tenth birthday. Mac missed her every day.

The second photo was of her father. The general was decked out in his dress uniform and looking into the camera with the implacable stare that he reserved for daughters who fell short of his expectations. Which was to say Mac, since Victoria excelled at everything.

And finally there was a picture of Victoria. It had been taken by one of Mac's friends and sent to her without Victoria's knowledge. In it, Vic could be seen kissing a helicopter pilot—the *same* helicopter pilot Mac had been engaged to at the time.

Had Victoria been in love with the man? Or had she taken him away just for the fun of it? To prove that she could? The answer could be seen in the fact that Vic dumped the pilot one week after Mac ended the relationship.

*Then why did you frame the photo?* Mac asked herself. *And, why keep it?* The answer was complicated. To remind herself that Victoria was a bitch? Certainly. Because it was the *only* image of Victoria she had? Maybe and maybe not.

Mac wrapped each picture in a tee shirt before placing them in the bag. The platoon wasn't supposed to take "A" bags because they were too large. But screw that. Mac had instructed Evans to let her people choose. Their "A" bag or a smaller "B" bag. The choice was up to them.

Finally, with her field gear on, her "A" bag in one hand and a rucksack dangling from the other, Mac left the BOQ. A flight of stairs took her down to a door and out into the frigid air beyond. A snowflake kissed her cheek. She didn't look back.

All four of Mac's Strykers were lined up and waiting. The so-called birdcages that surrounded the Strykers made them look big and ungainly but offered protection against rocket-propelled grenades. Each vic had eight wheels and was armed with light machine guns in addition to a .50 caliber machine gun or a grenade launcher.

The Engineer Squad Vehicle or ESV looked different from the rest, however. It had what looked like a bulldozer blade mounted up front. But rather than use the machine for clearing mines, which it was designed to do, Mac planned to move stalled cars with it.

Something they'd do a lot of. It hadn't been easy to get the ESV, though . . . Hollister had been cynical, and Evans was on record saying that the last thing they needed was "a fucking anchor." But Mac had prevailed in the end, and the ESV had been brought in to replace her fourth truck.

After handing her gear to a private in one-four, Mac went looking for Captain Hollister. He was with the second platoon. "Good morning," he said, seemingly oblivious to what lay ahead. "How's the first platoon? Did everyone report for duty?"

Mac hadn't thought to ask but knew Evans would have told her if someone had gone over the hill. "The people who were MIA yesterday still are," she replied. "But the rest of the platoon is here."

"Good," Hollister replied. "Two members of the second platoon are AWOL, along with a soldier from the third. All of them have families who live off base."

Mac winced. It made sense given how bad things were. An effort was under way to bring dependents inside the wire—but that could take weeks. And how would families fare in the meantime? Had she been in their place, Mac might have done the same thing. "Yes, sir. I understand."

"Okay," Hollister said as he offered a printout. "Here's the plan. Take your platoon to the Tacoma Mall parking lot, where the buses will be waiting for you. Then you'll lead the column up I-5 and onto Highway 18, which will take you to I-90. From that point, it will be a straight shot up and over the pass. I will ride with the second platoon at the head of the column. Do you have any questions?"

"Yes, sir," Mac said. "Odds are that at least one of those buses will break down. What then?"

"That's a good question," Hollister answered. "We will have *forty-two* buses. Two more than we need, plus a fuel tanker, and a wrecker following along behind the column."

"That's awesome," Mac said, as she gave Hollister points for planning. It looked as if the ex–desk jockey had a clue. Thank God.

The sky was starting to lighten as the first platoon led Archer Company down Forty-first Division Drive to I-5. Mac was riding in one-two, with her head and shoulders sticking up through the forward air guard hatch. There were two reasons for that. The first was that she wanted a clear view of what was taking place—and the second had to do with her incipient claustrophobia.

So Mac was in a good position to see the Bradleys, the aid station, and the recently established food-distribution point. Two six-bys were parked next to it, and soldiers were busy unloading boxes of MREs for the people lined up to receive them. The line stretched west and under I-5 to the neighborhood beyond. MPs were patrolling the column to prevent people from jumping the queue—and that was critical to keeping the situation under control.

It was cold, though . . . And most of the folks in line were wearing winter coats or had blankets draped over their shoulders. Mac waved at them, and most waved back. That boosted her spirits. The feeling was short-lived, however, as one-two pulled up the ramp and onto the freeway. There was enough light to see by then, and I-5 was strewn with cars, RVs, and trucks. An Apache helicopter roared overhead and disappeared to the south. God help anyone who fired at it.

Having determined the situation to be relatively safe, Mac ordered the ESV to take the lead. Then, with the blade lowered, it began to push cars out of the way so that the other trucks could follow. Most of the abandoned vehicles had been looted. So smashed windows and open doors were a common sight. Items the thieves didn't want lay strewn on the highway. There were a lot of brightly colored toys.

The process went slowly at first. *Too* slowly. But as the ESV's driver continued to gain confidence, the pace quickened. That, plus the fact that there were occasional open spaces, meant that the rest of the column could travel at a steady 5 mph. Bodies lined the route, and the crows covered them like black shrouds. As the ESV approached, some of the birds were so full, they were barely able to take off.

There were signs of life, however, including pet dogs that didn't know where to go and refugees who came in all shapes and sizes. Some, like a disheveled businessman, were on foot. But there were bicyclists, too . . . Plus people on horses and a steady stream of heavily laden motorcyclists traveling in both directions. Mac tracked them with the machine gun mounted forward of the hatch, but none posed a threat.

It took an hour to make what should have been a fifteen-minute trip. The snow had tapered off by the time they arrived at the mall. The parking lot was strewn with items looted from the stores and later rejected. Dozens of people were picking through the castoffs, searching for shoes that fit them, a jacket for a child, or something to eat.

As the company entered the parking lot on the east side of the Tacoma Mall, Mac saw that while some of the stores were intact, about a third of the complex lay in ruins. According to Hollister, the two thousand people who were going to take a bus ride east had been chosen from roughly five thousand people camped in and around the mall. Were they looters? Hell yes, they were. Although the line between thief and survivalist had started to blur.

A lottery had been held to determine who the "winners" would be—assuming that the people who boarded the buses were better off as a result. But would that occur? The final outcome was anything but certain. As one-two came to a stop, Mac saw that the last passengers were passing through a security checkpoint before boarding the buses. That's where they were required to temporarily surrender their weapons or remain in Tacoma. A commonsense precaution that was intended to prevent violence along the way.

Some of the buses were yellow and had the words TACOMA SCHOOL DISTRICT painted on their flanks. Others were the property of Pierce County Transit and Greyhound. "Archer-Six to Archer-One," Hollister said over her headset. "Send some people out to verify that each and every bus has a full tank of diesel. Over."

Mac's estimate of Hollister's competence went up another notch. "This is One. Roger that, over."

Evans had already dispatched a squad to do Hollister's bidding by the time Mac ducked down into the cargo area and exited through the rear hatch. It took the better part of an hour to check all of the buses, top off tanks, and get the riders settled.

Meanwhile, *more* people had arrived at the mall, and some of them were pissed. Why weren't *they* on one of the buses? Hollister tried to explain, but many of the newcomers refused to listen, and the situation had started to get ugly when Mac received orders to move out. "Clear the way," Hollister told her. "The second will lead the convoy out—and the third will provide security until the last bus is clear."

Mac returned to one-two and her position in the front hatch. The ESV led the rest of the platoon out of the parking lot, over I-5, and onto the freeway. That stretch of highway was depressingly similar to what they'd experienced earlier. But things went smoothly until they arrived at the point where an overpass had collapsed onto the freeway, blocking all the northbound lanes.

Mac radioed a warning to Hollister and ordered her vehicles to execute a U-turn. Even though it took fifteen minutes to reach the last exit, they still arrived before the column did and were able to

lead it down a ramp onto a frontage road. It took them north under
the portion of the overpass that was still standing.

After that, the column crept through the maze of stalled cars,
RVs, and trucks that littered the highway—until it arrived at the
junction with I-90 northbound. Even though the communities on
the east side of Lake Washington could lay claim to businesses
of their own, Microsoft's campus in Redmond being a good example, the suburbs north and south of the freeway owed their
existence to Seattle. And prior to the impact, many of the people
who lived on the east side had been forced to make the difficult
commute across one of two floating bridges each day. How many
of them had been trapped downtown? Or been killed in the after-
math? Thousands at the very least.

The population began to thin as they passed through the town
of North Bend and entered the foothills beyond. And, because there
were fewer wrecks to deal with, there was less work for the ESV's
driver to do. So as Mac's platoon began to pick up speed, they were
able to get out in front of the column, where they were supposed
to be.

Vehicles passed going in the opposite direction every now and
then. Traffic consisted of motorcycles for the most part, but there
were cars and RVs, too. People who were trying to hook up with
their families—or folks who'd been caught on the east side of the
mountains when the poop hit the fan. Maybe they'd be happy to
return home, and maybe they wouldn't. Some waved, and Mac
waved back. Thickly treed slopes began to press in from the right
and left, and snowcapped peaks appeared in the distance. They were
tall and stood shoulder to shoulder, as if to bar all further progress,
and their flanks were bare where rockslides kept the native evergreens
from growing. Mac had been taught to fear such places because of

the possibility that enemies could fire down on her Strykers. That seemed highly unlikely in this case—but even the remote possibility of such a thing made her feel uncomfortable.

The road curved back and forth as it crisscrossed the Snoqualmie River and continued to gain altitude. And they were about ten miles east of North Bend when they came to a line of cars and the bridge beyond. Or what *had* been a bridge before the earthquakes dumped 70 percent of it into the river below. The ESV came to a stop, as did one-two, and Mac was happy to exit the Stryker and stretch her legs.

Motorists who had been stalled there hurried over to see what the soldiers were going to do, and Mac sent Evans to explain. A short walk took her to the point where she could see white water breaking around the crumpled remains of a sixteen-wheeler and a fully submerged SUV. There was no way in hell that the Strykers or the buses would be able to cross what remained of the span.

The westbound lanes of I-90 were another matter, however. They rested on their own bridge, which, for reasons unknown, remained intact. So Mac sent soldiers over to force westbound traffic into the right-hand lane. That freed the ESV's driver to doze a path across the median. Once that task was complete, it was a relatively simple matter for him to drive the ESV across the bridge, angle over, and reconnect with I-90 eastbound.

The buses would have to proceed slowly, as would the civilian cars that were waiting to follow, but they would make it. The convoy caught up with the recon platoon just as the second crossover was completed. Hollister thanked the first platoon for doing a great job—and Mac couldn't help but feel a sense of satisfaction.

Had it been possible, Hollister would have ordered the column to drive all the way across Snoqualmie Pass without stopping to rest. But it was well past 1400 by then, and his civilian charges were not only hungry but in dire need of a bio break. Not to mention the fact that three of the buses were experiencing mechanical problems. So like it or not, Hollister had to call a stop and chose the Bandera State Airport as the place to do so.

Bandera wasn't much as airstrips go, even emergency airports, which it was. The two parallel runways were convenient, however, since they were close to I-90 and would allow the column to park in a tidy line. Not a good idea in a combat environment—but okay for the situation they found themselves in. Mac was appalled by what she saw as one-two followed the ESV onto the airstrip. Wreckage was strewn the entire length of the southern runway—and the remains of a two-engine plane could be seen at its far end. A commuter flight perhaps? On its way to or from Spokane? Something like that. Perhaps it was in the air when the meteor exploded. And maybe the shock wave or the airborne dust forced the pilots to attempt an emergency landing.

Whatever the reason, the landing hadn't gone well—and Mac could see bodies scattered around as Evans drove east. "Sergeant Kallas, take your people out and cover those bodies," Mac instructed. "The kids on our buses have seen enough bad things today. Let's use the ESV to scoop out a grave."

Meanwhile, MREs were unloaded from the trailers, and people fanned out to find places where they could sit and eat. A few complained about the food but not many. Food was scarce, and the evacuees knew it. Some could be seen stashing meal components in pockets.

The mechanics attached to Archer Company were able to fix a couple of buses. But the process consumed twice the amount of time that Hollister had allotted—and it was 16:35 by the time the convoy got under way again. A bus that the mechanics hadn't been able to repair was left behind.

After that, it was a matter of following the steep road up through a succession of curves toward the ski area located at the top of Snoqualmie Pass. Some of the heavily loaded buses, especially those on loan from the Tacoma School District, had a difficult time of it. That reduced the convoy's progress to little more than a crawl.

The air was getting colder, and it had started to snow. Not just a little, but a lot, as they passed the skeletal ski lifts and began the trip down the east side. Getting that far was a major accomplishment. And as the waters of Lake Keechelus came into view on the right, Mac was beginning to think that they'd make it to Cle Elum by nightfall. Steep cliffs rose to the left of one-two as the road rounded the north end of the lake and turned south.

Boulders, loosened by the succession of tremors, lay scattered on the surface of the road. The ESV could push the smaller ones out of the way—but heavy equipment would be required to move the big boys. Fortunately, there was sufficient room to drive around or between them. Mac felt someone tap her on the leg and looked down to see Private Adams's boyish countenance looking up at her. "Coffee, ma'am," he said. "Just the way you like it."

Mac said, "Thank you," and was reaching for the metal mug when the Stryker began to pitch and roll. Adams fell sideways, and Mac was forced to grab both sides of the hatch for support. That was when she realized that she was feeling the effects of an earthquake. Mac was still in the process of absorbing this when Hollister shouted over the radio. "Rockslide! Coming down on us! Gun your engines!" Mac looked straight up and waited to die.

# CHAPTER 2

||||||||||||||||||||||||||||||||||||||||||

A journey of a thousand miles begins with a single step.

—CHINESE PHILOSOPHER LAOZI

TAMPICO, MEXICO

United States Secretary of Energy Samuel T. Sloan was standing on the uncertain surface of a floating solar farm as the meteor shower fell. Sloan, along with a delegation of Mexican officials, was on the raft to symbolically throw the switch that would send a surge of solar-generated electricity to the east coast city of Tampico a couple of miles away.

The purpose of the project was to provide the town with a source of renewable energy, help revitalize the crime-ridden community, and strengthen the often testy relationship between the United States and Mexico. And the fact that most of the equipment involved had been manufactured in California didn't hurt. So that's what Sloan was doing when the meteor flashed overhead. It was brighter than the sun and traveling so fast that it broke the sound barrier. The resulting boom was loud enough to be heard from miles away.

The object was visible for only a few seconds before it disappeared over the eastern horizon. Then the officials saw a flash and heard what sounded like a *second* clap of thunder. That was followed by an upwelling of *what*? Steam? Sloan wasn't sure. But one thing was for sure . . . One helluva big wave could be coming their way, and Sloan didn't plan to be standing on the solar farm when it arrived. And judging from the speed with which the Mexicans were boarding their patrol boat, they shared his concern. Sloan turned to his sole bodyguard, an ex–special ops type named Brody. "Let's haul ass." A blast of hot air hit the farm, causing the rafts to rock back and forth. Sloan struggled to remain upright.

Brody had a full face and was one size too large for his tan suit. "Roger that . . . Follow me." Brody was out of shape, but he knew his stuff, and rather than allow Sloan to travel on the navy patrol boat with the Mexican officials, the contractor had insisted that they have transportation of their own. The fiberglass fishing boat wasn't fancy, but it was equipped with a *huge* outboard, the kind that could be used to run drugs when its owner needed some extra cash.

The Mexicans were casting off when the fisherman started his engine and, under orders from Brody, opened the throttle all the way. Sloan was forced to hang on as the narrow hull cut a straight line through the water and left the larger craft behind.

As Sloan looked back, he saw that an ominous-looking cloud was spreading across the eastern sky even though it was still sunny in Tampico. Sloan was starting to question his own judgment. What would Mexico's Secretary of Energy think about the haste with which the *norteamericano* had fled? A Televisa news crew had been present to tape the ceremony. Would they play footage of Sloan speeding away? And would CNN get ahold of it? Should that happen, Sloan would be held up to ridicule, and that would reflect on the president.

That was what Sloan was thinking as the fisherman reduced power, the boat slid in through light surf, and Brody fished a wad of money out of his pocket. "Here," he said, as he gave the fisherman a fifty. *"Muchas gracias."*

If the fisherman was grateful, there was no sign of it on his sun-darkened face as he killed the engine. Sloan heard a whining noise as the prop left the water and the bow slid up onto the wet sand. A gang of boys ran out to steady it. "Let's haul ass!" Brody said as he vaulted over the side. "If a wave comes, there's no telling how far inland it will go."

Sloan jumped over the side and followed Brady up the mostly empty beach. The big man was nearly out of breath by the time they made it to the street. A black SUV was waiting for them twenty feet away from a dilapidated taco stand.

Had Sloan been the Secretary of State, the vehicle would have been guarded by a team of people from the Diplomatic Security Service. But the Secretary of Energy didn't rate that kind of protection—so Brody had been forced to hire a vehicle and driver from the local limo company. It had tinted windows and was extremely shiny. "Stay back," Brody instructed, as he slipped a hand into his jacket.

As Brody went to inspect the vehicle, Sloan took a moment to scan his surroundings. Tampico had been a burgeoning tourist town a few years earlier. But that was before two drug cartels began to fight over it. Citizens were assassinated in broad daylight, grenades were thrown into crowded bars, and the population of three hundred thousand lived in fear

Sloan turned just as Brody pulled the SUV's back door open and was thrown backwards by a blast from a shotgun. Brody's body hit the street with a thump, and he lay there staring sightlessly into the sun. Sloan stood frozen in place as a man with long black hair got out of the SUV. He was dressed in a neon-pink shirt, black trousers, and silver-toed cowboy boots. A pair of empty shell casings popped out of the double-barreled weapon and fell to the ground as he broke the shotgun open. *"Buenos días, Señor Sloan,"* the man said conversationally. "Get in the truck."

The bastard knew his name! It was a kidnapping then . . . What would a high-ranking American official be worth? Nothing really, since the government wouldn't pay, but maybe the Tampico cowboy wasn't aware of that. Or maybe he knew and didn't believe it.

All of that flashed through Sloan's mind, followed by the impulse to run. He circled the SUV in an attempt to use it for cover. Then he took off. Thanks to the adrenaline in Sloan's bloodstream, plus the fact that he was a competitive runner, he got off to a fast start. His goal was to put as much distance between himself and the man with the shotgun as he could. Maybe the Tampico cowboy would hold his fire. After all, what good is a dead hostage? Unless . . .

Sloan felt the pellets strike his back a fraction of a second before he heard the BOOM. He stumbled, caught his balance, and continued to run. Sloan had grown up on a farm in Nebraska and, like all farm boys, knew a thing or two about shotguns. The fact that the man in the pink shirt was firing birdshot, rather than buckshot, meant he had a chance. Especially after sixty feet or so, when the spread produced by the short-barreled weapon would grow even wider.

As if to prove that point, the cowboy fired again—and if any of the shotgun pellets struck Sloan, he didn't feel them. He was running west on the Avenida Álvaro Obregón. The thoroughfare consisted of two lanes divided by a median. Shabby stores lined both sides of the street where they waited for tourists who were unlikely to appear. But where *were* the shop owners? Gone. And no wonder . . . A man with a shotgun was chasing a gringo . . . Why hang around?

Sloan spotted some taller buildings up ahead and forced himself to run faster. He didn't dare look back over his shoulder because that might cause him to break stride. He could hear the roar of an engine though—and knew his pursuers were about to catch up.

Sloan was desperate to get off the street, so he made a sharp left and ran toward an open doorway. Then, as he slipped into the shadowy interior, Sloan realized he was inside what had been a shopping arcade back before the gangs seized control of the city. A dry fountain marked the center of the inner courtyard, and a frozen escalator led to the floors above. Sloan took the trash-covered stairs two at a time.

He stepped onto the walkway that circled the second floor, and when sunlight touched his face, Sloan looked up to see blue sky through a hole in the roof. Then, worried about what the Tampico cowboy was up to, Sloan hurried over to a shop on the north side of the building.

The inside walls were covered with graffiti, drug paraphernalia lay scattered about, and the single window was open. As Sloan looked down, he saw that the SUV was parked out front. The cowboy was standing next to the vehicle, staring east. *Why?*

Sloan turned his head to the right, where he saw the oncoming wave. It was at least fifty feet high and coming fast! Sloan could see that dark shadowy objects were trapped inside the wall of water and realized that some of them were boats.

The tidal wave ran up the beach and broke over the row of shops that fronted the gulf. Most of the structures were obliterated, and it seemed safe to assume that the people inside were dead. The cowboy had entered the SUV by that time, and it was pulling away. But not quickly enough, as the rampaging water surged up the street and under the vehicle. The SUV rose, lost traction, and began to float. The water had traveled as far as it could by then . . . And as it flowed back to the gulf, the truck went with it.

Would the gang members be carried out to sea and killed? Sloan hoped so.

His mind raced as he followed a second escalator down to the ground floor. Now that he had time to think about it, Sloan realized that the kidnapping attempt had been planned days, if not weeks, in advance, and had nothing to do with the disaster. Was the attempt to kidnap him over? Maybe . . . But maybe not.

That meant it would be stupid to return to his hotel because that was where gang members would look first. So what to do? The obvious answer was to call for help. But first Sloan felt an urgent need to shed his power suit and attempt to blend in.

The plan wasn't perfect, but it was better than nothing, and as Sloan continued west on the Avenida Álvaro Obregón, he was on the lookout for any sort of store that would sell men's clothing. After what he estimated to be a mile or so, Sloan spotted a small mom-and-pop *tienda* off to the right. The front window was filled with lots of brightly colored sports outfits and a sign that read, *"Ropa para el hombre activo."* ("Clothes for the active man.")

As Sloan entered, he could tell that the proprietors were surprised to see him and not sure what to expect. But after he spoke to them in Spanish, they hurried to help. Once in the changing room, Sloan made use of the mirror to examine his wounds. There were three of them—and it would have been nice to dig the pellets out. But that wouldn't be possible without help. Fortunately, the bleeding had stopped, and by wrapping the bloody dress shirt inside his jacket, he was able to conceal it.

Sloan left the *tienda* wearing a ball cap, a pair of wraparound shades, and a shirt with an enormous soccer emblem on it. The rest of his outfit consisted of Levi's and a pair of Nike knockoffs. Sloan stuffed the business suit into the first trash can he passed. Now, with the disguise in place, Sloan felt a good deal more secure. The next thing he needed to do was to make contact with his office in D.C. Or, failing that, the embassy in Mexico City. Either one of which would send help.

For the first time since early that morning Sloan removed his cell phone from a pocket and attempted to make a call. What he got was a recorded announcement. *"Lo sentimos. El servicio telefónico no está disponible en este momento. Por favor, inténtelo de nuevo más tarde."* ("We're sorry. Telephone service is not available at this time. Please try again later.")

Sloan swore. It seemed safe to assume that the meteor, assuming that was what he'd seen, was responsible for the outage. So he wasn't going to get any help—not in the short term anyway. What to do? Sloan looked around. There were a lot of people on the street, and sirens could be heard in the distance. None of the other pedestrians was paying any attention to him, and that was good.

Maybe he should find a second hotel, check in, and hole up. Once cell service was restored, he would call for help. But how sophisticated was the criminal network that ran Tampico? The clothes had been purchased with cash, so there was very little of it left. What would happen if he used a credit card? Would gang members come on the run? And even if they didn't, would a hotel accept a card they couldn't verify?

Sloan concluded that it would be stupid to use a card until he knew the answer to at least some of those questions. He needed a goal though . . . Something to do. Head for the airport? No. The General Francisco Javier Mina International Airport was located at the heart of the city, and planes could normally be seen taking off and landing around the clock, and the ominous-looking sky was empty.

So what to do? He figured the next step was to find a place to hide, stay there until nightfall, and move under the cover of darkness. But in which direction? The obvious answer was north, to the good old US of A. Texas was only three hundred miles away! It felt good to have a plan—even if the details were a bit vague.

Sloan had passed a number of vacant buildings during his walk. Some were grouped in clusters, and leaning on each other for support, while others stood in splendid isolation. The Hotel Excelsior was one of the latter. He'd passed it earlier, and as Sloan approached the building for the second time, he knew it was the one. Not because it was inherently safer somehow—but because the Excelsior's faded glory appealed to him. The ten-story hotel had two Mission-style towers and was adorned with rows of high-arched windows, ornamental iron balconies, and peeling white paint. Down on the ground floor, there were two verandahs, one to the left of the main entrance and one to the right. What had once been carefully manicured trees were huge now and surrounded by trash. A sad sight indeed.

In spite of the plywood nailed across the front door, Sloan felt sure there was a way in. And sure enough . . . As he circled the building, he came to a crude staircase. It consisted of a crate pushed up against an old dumpster. After climbing up onto the top, Sloan was able to step through an empty window into the hotel's kitchen.

Everything of value had been stolen by then, so the only things that remained were the enormous stove, a concrete prep table, and lots of trash. Were people living there? That was a distinct possibility, and Sloan knew he was taking a chance. Light filtered in through arched windows as he passed through the dining room, entered the lobby, and spotted the reception desk. The air was thick with the smell of urine. From there, it was a short walk to a marble staircase, which remained elegant, in spite of how filthy it was and the mindless obscenities that had been spray-painted onto its walls.

Sloan followed the stairs up to the mezzanine floor. That's where the bar had been . . . And Sloan could imagine people sitting at tables and looking into the lobby below as they had a drink. Even though there were lots of rooms on the floors higher up, Sloan preferred to stay low, where he would know if people entered the building and would be able to escape more easily. With that in mind, he circled the mezzanine, looking for a spot to take a nap. He chose a corner where a previous "guest" had been kind enough to place a large piece of cardboard on the floor. It was dusty but otherwise clean.

So Sloan lay down, curled up into the fetal position, and allowed his thoughts to wander. The coast. He would return to the coast. It might be difficult to find a boat that hadn't been damaged by the tidal wave, but he would try. And assuming that he found one, he'd row or sail it north. And if that plan failed, he would walk. Three hundred miles divided by fifteen miles per day equaled twenty. That was how long it would take. Okay, twenty-five, just to be safe. But one way or another . . .

Sloan woke to the sound of machine-gun fire off in the distance somewhere. He sat up and looked around. It was dark, and only the slightest bit of light was leaking in through the windows—a sure sign that the power was off. The firing stopped. Sloan stood and checked his watch. It was time to get going. A task that would be more difficult without streetlights. *Why didn't you buy a flashlight instead of tacos?* Sloan asked himself. *Because I'm an idiot,* came the response.

Sloan took a few steps, tripped, and nearly fell. That was when he remembered the flashlight app on his cell phone and turned it on. A blob of light preceded him down the stairs. Once Sloan was outside, he had to turn the light off or run the risk of attracting trouble. The moon was up, thank God, which meant there was enough light to navigate by. And that reminded Sloan of the compass on his phone. All he had to do was check it occasionally to stay on course.

Sloan tried to remain in the shadows as he began what promised to be a five- or six-mile hike back to the gulf. The same five or six miles he'd walked earlier that day. But that couldn't be helped. What was, was. Now, as Sloan's night vision continued to improve, he could make out glimmers of light in some of the buildings that he passed. Battery-powered lanterns perhaps, or candles, mostly hidden lest they attract predators. And they were out and about. More than once, Sloan had to seek cover as headlights appeared and a pickup loaded with gun-wielding men roared past. Gangbangers? Yes. On their way to participate in one of Tampico's never-ending turf wars.

The sky was lighter and it had started to rain by the time Sloan entered the flood zone. There wasn't much to see at first. But it wasn't long before he found himself in among smashed cars and damaged buildings. Objects of every sort were strewn about, including hundreds of plastic jugs, a sizeable section of fishing net, a motorcycle helmet, brightly colored toys, a seaweed-draped sofa, a straw hat floating in a puddle, and a scattering of identical knapsacks. From a cargo container? Probably. They were navy blue and adorned with the Adidas logo. Sloan took one for himself. It was wet but would dry out once the rain stopped.

Then, as Sloan entered the area immediately west of the beach, he saw a navy patrol boat. It was big, at least sixty feet long, and looked like a beached whale. Was that the vessel his fellow officials had been on? Quite possibly.

He paused to look up. The rain had slackened a bit—and the sun was no more than a dimly seen glow. What if a semipermanent haze kept the normal amount of sunlight from reaching the ground? The solar industry would suffer . . . But that was the least of it.

Crops would fail all around the world, and millions, if not billions of people would starve. It was a horrible thought, and all Sloan could do was hope that his worst fears wouldn't come true.

Sloan turned onto the Corredor Urbano Luis Donaldo Colosio and followed it north.

An hour passed. And about the time the rain stopped, and people began to emerge from their homes, Sloan came across a rusty bicycle. It was leaning against a fence—and was too good an opportunity to pass up. After a quick look around, Sloan climbed aboard and pedaled away. The terrain was flat, and he made good time.

The highway was headed west, so Sloan turned right onto the Boulevard de los Ríos, which took him north into an industrial area. A car sprayed him with water as it passed, but Sloan was so wet he barely noticed.

Eventually, he spotted a convenience store that was still open for business and hurried to seize the opportunity. Assuming his theories were correct, the local *tiendas* would start to run out of goods or be overrun by looters soon. So it was important to buy what he could.

Sloan parked the bike out back, circled around to the front door, and went inside. He had the equivalent of $168.00 US and was determined to spend every peso of it before merchants stopped accepting government currency. The store's interior had a homey feel—and the shelves were well stocked. Sloan filled a basket with two Bic lighters, a large pocketknife, a plastic cup, a small cooking pot, and the sort of prepackaged foods that are light and easy to prepare. He topped the load off with a large bottle of water.

If the woman behind the counter was curious, she gave no sign of it as she rang up the purchases. It didn't pay to ask questions . . . Not in the city of Tampico. She had long pink fingernails, each of which was decorated with a finely drawn gold cross, and they seemed to dance over the cash register's keys. As the proprietress handed Sloan the bill, he saw that the total was a third more than what he'd expected. And when he asked her about it, she shrugged. "Prices have gone up."

"Since yesterday?"

"*Sí.*"

Sloan sighed, removed a third of the food from the basket, and asked her to total it again. The second bill came in slightly under what Sloan had—so he bought a map and three crispy taquitos. After loading his purchases into the damp knapsack, Sloan went out back to eat. Judging from the trash that lay strewn about, other people ate there all the time. He was hungry, and the taquitos were gone in no time.

The next hour and a half was spent pedaling north to a bay called Puerto de Altamira. An access road took him east past the bay and onto land that bordered the east–west ship channel. Because the terrain was low and flat, the tidal wave had been able to sweep across it without encountering any resistance. Multihued shipping containers with names like MATSON, SEALAND, and MAERSK were scattered like abandoned toys.

And crowds of people, many with pickup trucks, were swarming around the containers, taking what they could. Sloan gave them a wide berth as he continued on his way. The air was thick with the smell of rotting sea life, a rusty freighter sat high and dry, and Sloan saw a body lying facedown next to a pile of debris.

Then Sloan spotted the yacht. It was at least fifty feet long and lying on one side. And there, secured to the deck just aft of the streamlined cabin, were two red kayaks! A kayak would be perfect for paddling up the coast. Sloan did a 360, looking for other scavengers, and saw that two men were working on a fishing boat. But they were a thousand yards away—and were busy patching a hole in the boat's hull.

Thus encouraged, Sloan made his way up to the yacht and lowered the bike to the ground. Then came the task of climbing in over the downside rail and making his way up to the spot where the brightly colored watercraft were waiting for him. After considerable effort, Sloan managed to cut one of them loose. The plan was to lower it gently to the ground, but once the kayak was free, it fell.

Fortunately, the surface below the yacht was dirt rather than cement, and no significant damage was done. The kayak was about ten feet long, weighed about forty pounds, and came with a hard, plastic seat. That meant it was intended for recreational use rather than touring, but beggars can't be choosers.

The only thing he lacked was a paddle. Was that stored inside the yacht somewhere? If he entered the yacht, Sloan feared that looters might take the kayak. But a kayak without a paddle was worthless, so there was no choice. It was difficult to move around inside the boat, but after ten minutes of searching, Sloan found two collapsible paddles that were stored in a side locker. He took both along with a coil of line and some canned goods.

Once outside, Sloan was relieved to find that the kayak was right where he'd left it. After placing the paddles and his other belongings in the cockpit, he had to haul the kayak across open ground to the slate-gray water beyond.

The biggest problem was figuring out a comfortable way to carry it. Sloan carried it like a suitcase for a while. Then, when that grew tiring, he hoisted it up over his head. But being a desk jockey, he couldn't maintain that position for very long.

Finally, after fifteen minutes of effort, Sloan made it to the water. It was choppy and littered with floating trash but a welcome sight nonetheless. Sloan's plan was to follow the coast north, paddling at night and hiding during the day. And that should be possible given all the inlets, bays, and lagoons that lay along the coast.

After stuffing his gear into the watertight compartment located aft of the kayak's cockpit, Sloan replaced the lid and checked to make sure that it was on tight. Then it was time to drag the fiberglass hull down a muddy bank and into the ship channel that led out into the Gulf of Mexico. After laying one of the paddles across the hull, Sloan stood astride the kayak and walked it out into the ship channel. As soon as the tiny boat was afloat, he sat down while bringing his feet up and in.

Then it was time to start paddling. A breeze was blowing in from the east, which forced Sloan to paddle harder than he would have preferred. But after a sustained effort, he managed to propel the kayak past a half-sunken ship and into the open sea.

He was paddling into the waves at first, but the moment he turned north, water slapped the side of the low-lying craft and threatened to swamp it. In order to prevent that, Sloan had to cut the waves at an angle and tack back and forth.

As hours passed, the beach was his constant companion. Any huts that had been on it were gone now . . . And the only people Sloan saw were occasional fishermen in small boats. Most waved, and he waved back.

Finally, as the light began to fade, Sloan knew it was time to go ashore on a deserted stretch of beach. Once on dry land, he could see where the high water had swept up and inland. Pieces of plastic had been left hanging in the scrub that lined the shore, but the hardy bushes seemed none the worse for wear. After locating a clearing about a hundred feet inland, Sloan went back for the kayak and dragged it up and out of sight. Then he cut a branch and returned to the water, where he backed up the beach and erased his footprints.

Overkill? Maybe, and maybe not. The cartels had been running drugs up that coast for a long time. Would the current set of circumstances bring drug traffic to a stop or cause it to grow? Sloan didn't know and wasn't about to run any unnecessary risks.

Once it was dark, Sloan built a small fire, which he used to prepare a simple dinner. Plain though the meal was, it tasted good and served to remind him of the fact that he'd have to find more food and ways to replenish his water supply. The beaches were littered with plastic bottles, but how to fill them? That would require some planning.

After gathering driftwood and constructing a rudimentary shelter, Sloan curled up and managed to sleep in spite of the insects that continually bit him. When morning came, he rose, enjoyed a cup of instant coffee, and wondered why he hadn't been smart enough to buy toothpaste. The day passed slowly, and he gave thanks for the ever-present clouds. The heat would have been unbearable without them. Finally, after what seemed like an eternity, evening came and it was time for his much-anticipated dinner. Once his stomach was full, Sloan put the fire out and dragged the kayak down to the water.

Thus began what would be a pattern for days to come. Paddle at night and sleep during the day. During that time, Sloan mastered the art of stealing food from fishing camps, looting crab pots, and night fishing. And so it went for nineteen days. During that time, Sloan became stronger and leaner. He still had a couple of pellets in his back. But the wounds had healed, and there were no signs of infection. And that was all he could ask for.

As the twentieth night began, Sloan felt a rising sense of anticipation, knowing that if he hadn't entered US waters, he would soon. Moonlight filtered down through broken clouds to frost the surface of the gently heaving sea. He was enjoying the beauty of that when he heard a distant rumble and felt a stab of fear.

It wasn't the first engine he'd heard. Two days earlier, the steady thump, thump, thump of a diesel engine had announced the presence of a dimly lit fishing boat that passed within a hundred feet of the kayak. But *this* sound was different. The throaty roar belonged to a cigarette boat or something similar. Not the sort of craft a fisherman would use.

So Sloan had reason to be afraid as the noise passed him on the right and sent a succession of waves his way. That made it necessary for him to turn into the other boat's wake or risk being swamped. But the danger had passed, or so it seemed, until a powerful spotlight split the night. Had someone seen something as the boat passed him? That's the way it seemed as the blob of light swung left, right, and nailed him. The voice was amplified. *"Levante sus manos— y mantenerlos allí!"* ("Raise your hands—and keep them there!")

*Shit! Shit! Shit!* Sloan dug his paddle into the water in an attempt to escape the light. But it followed him, and Sloan heard a burst of gunfire. White geysers shot up all around him, and there was a thump as one of the bullets punched a hole in the hull. Cold liquid squirted into the cockpit and Sloan struggled to get out. Then the boat was there, looming above him, as a silhouette leaned over to look down at him. *"Tirar los peces en. Vamos a ver lo que tenemos."* ("Pull the fish in. Let's see what we have.") The journey was over.

# CHAPTER 3

||||||||||||||||||||||||||||||||||||||

And the platoon is the truly characteristic component of
an army; it is the lowest unit habitually commanded by a
commissioned officer; it is the real and essential fighting
unit, whose action conditions that of the other arms and
formations; it is a little world in which the relations
between the led and the leader, the men and their
commander, are immediate, actual, continuous, and
entirely real.

—MAJOR M. K. WARDLE

## NEAR YAKIMA, WASHINGTON

Mac was familiar with the dream by then and knew she was dreaming it but couldn't escape. For what might have been the twentieth
time, she stood in the hatch and stared upwards as hundreds of
tons of rock slid down the side of the mountain to obliterate the
second platoon and half of the buses. One moment, they were there,
and the next moment, they weren't. At least a thousand lives had
been lost in the blink of an eye. But Lieutenant Robin Macintyre
and her platoon were spared. *Why?* Because, that's why.

Mac awoke as she always did, with a scream trapped in her
throat and her heart pounding. How long would the dreams go
on? *Until they stop,* the voice answered. *Deal with it.*

Mac eyed her wristwatch. The time was 0436, and the alarm was set for 0500. But she wouldn't be able to get back to sleep, so why try? Mac turned on the bedside light, pushed the sleeping bag down, and swung her feet over onto the cold floor. The baseboard heater was working but couldn't counter the chill.

Mac swore, grabbed her robe, and made the trip to the bathroom. The platoon and a collection of other lost souls were headquartered at the Vagabond Army Airfield just outside the city of Yakima. It was a small facility that was normally part of the Yakima Training Center. However, most of that command's personnel, munitions, and fuel had been loaded onto vehicles and sent east to reinforce Fairchild AFB in Spokane.

Captain Hollister had been killed in the rockslide. His death left Mac in charge and made her responsible for the orders Hollister had been given. That meant Mac was supposed to establish a refugee camp adjacent to Vagabond and prepare to receive more convoys of people even though the east–west highway was blocked, and she lacked the resources necessary to do so. A problem she had repeatedly emphasized via radio but to no avail. JBLM's answer was always the same: "We've got a lot of irons in the fire right now . . . We'll get back to you."

So all Mac could do was secure the base and wait for something to happen. In her capacity as interim CO, Mac had ordered a specialist to fire up Vagabond's emergency generator each day between 0400 and 0600. That gave everyone a chance to shower before they went on duty or after they came off it, as well as being an opportunity to charge batteries and run power tools.

After taking a hot shower and completing her morning rituals Mac put on her winter uniform and stepped out into the driving sleet. With her head down, she hurried over to the Flight Control Center. The lights were on as Mac entered the office and stamped her feet on a mat. After the generator went off, the headquarters staff would fire up the woodstove that Platoon Sergeant Evans had "borrowed" somewhere. That, plus some lanterns filled with helicopter fuel, would get them through the rest of the day. "Good morning," Evans said as he raised a mug by way of a salute.

"What's good about it?" Mac demanded as she shed her coat and made her way over to the coffeepot. They still had coffee, but for how long?

"Cinnamon rolls," Evans said smugly, pointing to a tray. "Private Brisby made them. Who knew he could cook?"

"I'm in," Mac said as she went to help herself. "Have we heard anything from JBLM?"

Evans made a face. Mac asked the same question every morning. "Yes, ma'am. But nothing good. The gangs launched another attack—and our people had to pull back again."

Mac felt her spirits fall. That was what? The *third* pullback? JBLM was getting smaller each day. And since I-90 had been closed by the rockslide, and a self-proclaimed warlord had taken control of east–west Highway 410, there was no way for JBLM to reinforce her. Meanwhile, the chickenshit CO of Fairchild AFB refused to intervene without permission from above. That made Mac angry, but she couldn't say so without harming morale. So she didn't. "Okay, what's on the agenda?"

"After making the rounds, you're supposed to meet with Mr. Wylie," Evans told her.

"Oh goody," Mac replied. "That will be fun."

Evans laughed. "Better you than me."

Mac sipped her coffee. Yakima had a city council, and one of the council members was called the "mayor at large." But City Manager Fred Wylie actually ran things, and he was a huge pain in the ass. "Okay," she said. "I'll leave after my rounds."

After consuming the rest of her roll, and a second cup of coffee, Mac went out to check in with what? Could it be called a platoon? Or was it a company now? Not that it mattered. The ritual began with a visit to the small building that housed the ready room. That's where the pilots and their crew people met each morning.

Mac thought of them as orphans, meaning people who had been at Vagabond when the poop hit the fan, or drifted in since, looking for a unit to belong to. Tim Peters and copilot/gunner Jan Omata were excellent examples. Their Apache AH-64 had been grounded due to mechanical problems when their platoon flew out on April 30. And were still there on May 1, when the meteors fell. So for the moment, at least, the warrant officers belonged to her.

The sleet was cold and wet as it hit Mac's face. She hurried past a couple of sheds to what everyone called "the Shack." It was toasty inside thanks to the huge heater that had been "reallocated" from one of the hangars. The walls were covered with photos of helicopters, old and new, a detailed map of the training center, and a tidy bulletin board. The newest item on it was over a month old. Five people were seated around the Formica-covered table and all of them stood as Mac walked in. It was an honor generally reserved for high-ranking officers, but Mac was all they had. She said, "At ease," and waved them back into their chairs.

"Good morning, ma'am," Peters said. "Have you got any news for us?"

Peters was a lanky six-two and liked to wear his hair high and tight. He had piercing blue eyes, a firm jaw, and an easygoing personality. He also had a strong desire to fly rather than sit around playing soldier. "I'm sorry," Mac replied. "Just the same old, same old. The people at JBLM were forced to fall back again. And we don't have anything new from Fairchild."

The news produced groans of disappointment. "That sucks,"

Omata said. Mac liked the pilot and felt sorry for her at the same time. Her family was in San Francisco . . . And, like so many people, Omata had no idea what had become of them.

"Yeah, it does," Mac agreed. "But hang in there . . . Something will break soon."

"Really? You think so?" Grimes inquired. He was a mechanic and a member of the Apache's ground crew.

"Yes, I do," Mac lied. "In the meantime, I really appreciate the way you folks have pitched in. Speaking of which, I have to be in town at 0930. So Mr. Peters will be in charge."

"I plan to give everyone a raise, a strawberry ice-cream cone, and their own unicorn," Peters announced.

"I'm glad to hear it," Mac replied. "I don't need a unicorn, but some ice cream would taste good."

The sleet found her skin as Mac left the Shack and caused her to swear. Each Stryker was housed in its own storage building, all separated by a fire lane. Two trucks were on guard duty at any given time—and the rest could roll on five minutes' notice. After checking in with the Stryker crews, Mac made her way to the tiny dispensary, where a navy doctor named Pete Hoskins and medic "Doc" Obbie were waiting.

Hoskins and his wife had been in Yakima visiting her parents when the meteors struck. And, since he couldn't reach his duty station in San Diego, Hoskins reported to the heliport. Obbie stood as Mac entered, but Hoskins outranked her and didn't.

Hoskins was a serious-looking man with graying hair, wire-rimmed glasses, and the precise movements of a bird. His report was as predictable as the morning sleet. It seemed there had been a few minor injuries in the last twenty-four hours, two soldiers had colds, and 80 percent of the base's personnel were clinically depressed. "Including *you*," Hoskins said pointedly, "even if you won't admit it."

"Thanks," Mac said. "I feel so much better now . . . Please keep up the good work." Hoskins crossed his arms, and Obbie grinned.

Corporal Garcia and the Humvee were waiting as Mac left the dispensary. The vehicle came with the base and allowed Mac to travel without using one of the trucks. The heater was running full blast—and it felt good to get in out of the cold. Sparks Munroe was seated in the back, along with Private Atkins, who would man the fifty should that be necessary. "We're headed downtown," Mac announced. "But let's pull a 360 first."

Garcia nodded. "Yes, ma'am." It took less than ten minutes to circle the tiny base. They paused occasionally to check in with the truck commanders and the soldiers who were guarding the perimeter. They were cold, but in reasonably good spirits, and looking forward to a hot meal. Once the tour was complete, Garcia drove the Humvee west on Firing Center Road to I-82. The pavement was wet, and slightly slushy, but no challenge for the all-wheel-drive vehicle. Visibility was limited, and there wasn't much to see other than a few widely separated homes.

Once on the freeway, and headed south, Mac was struck by how light the traffic was. They passed horse-drawn wagons on two occasions, and Mac wondered what that implied. Were people running out of fuel? Or were they hoarding it? Both, most likely; and things were bound to get worse. And, according to what Sparks had been able to pull in from ham-radio operators, conditions were similar elsewhere in the country.

Garcia turned onto 823 a few minutes later and followed it into Yakima. It had been a pleasant city, but the clouds were so low that it felt like they might smother the city, and very few people were out on the streets.

Like the Vagabond Army Heliport, the city had been forced to limit power to a couple of hours per day, and the electricity wasn't scheduled to come on until 1800 hours. That was devastating for the business community, which had been forced to lay people off. And if people couldn't buy things, they would eventually try to take them. Then what?

The question went unanswered as Garcia turned off North Second. Wylie's office was located in a complex that was surrounded by parking lots and deciduous trees. Mac noticed that in spite of the fact that it was summer, all of them had shed their leaves.

The Humvee came to a stop, and they got out. Mac turned to Atkins. His job was to guard the vehicle. "Keep your eyes peeled," Mac cautioned. "And holler if you see anything suspicious."

Atkins's face was nearly invisible thanks to cold-weather gear and a pair of goggles. She saw him nod. "Yes, ma'am."

Mac led the tiny detachment into the building's lobby, where two bored-looking cops were waiting to receive her. That was new and a sure sign of trouble. "I'm Lieutenant Macintyre," she told them. "I have an appointment to see Mr. Wylie."

One of the policemen consulted a clipboard. His breath fogged the air. "Right . . . You can go up. But you'll have to leave the sidearm and the soldiers here."

"That isn't acceptable," Mac responded. "Please inform Mr. Wylie that I attempted to see him. Have a nice day."

"Whoa," the second man said. "There's no need to get your panties in a knot . . . I'll check with Mr. Wylie's assistant."

Mac waited while the policeman mumbled into a radio and wasn't surprised when the verdict came in. "Sorry," the cop said stiffly. "But we have to be careful these days . . . And just because someone's wearing a uniform doesn't mean much. You can go up."

Mac thanked him and followed a series of hand-printed signs past the elevators to a door marked EXIT. A flight of stairs led up to the second floor and another fire door. It opened into a hall that led past the restrooms to an open area and a dozen cubicles. The room was lit with jury-rigged work lights. And while the air wasn't warm, it wasn't cold either, thanks to a pair of space heaters.

Wylie's assistant was there to receive the visitors. Her name was Martha Cobb. She was a pleasant-looking woman with nicely styled hair, chiseled features, and a confident manner. "Lieutenant Macintyre! It's nice to see you again. Mr. Wylie is in his office. Would you care for tea or coffee?"

"It's good to see you as well," Mac replied. "I'd love a cup of coffee—and I'm sure my men would appreciate some as well."

"I'll take care of it," Cobb promised. "Please follow me."

Mac removed her jacket as Cobb led her past the cubicles to the corner office where Wylie was waiting. He was a big man with thinning hair, beady eyes, and a pugnacious jaw. He circled the desk in order to shake hands. Mac felt his hand swallow hers and felt lucky to retrieve it. "Good morning, Lieutenant," Wylie said, "and thanks for coming. Please, have a seat."

"It's my pleasure," Mac lied, as she took a seat at a small conference table. "What can I do for you?"

Wylie was direct if nothing else. "Don't be coy, Lieutenant. You know what I need . . . And that's fuel."

"The vast majority of the training center's fuel was taken east," Mac reminded him. "But yes, I have some. Not enough to solve your problems though . . . And, once orders come in, we'll need what we have."

"That's the same line of bull you gave me last time," Wylie said as he stared at her. "When will those orders come?"

"I don't know."

Wylie placed a pair of beefy forearms on the table. "Let's be honest, Lieutenant . . . The whole country is belly-up! So there's a good chance that those orders won't arrive. And, while you sit on that fuel, the citizens of Yakima are suffering."

"I'm sorry," Mac replied. "I really am. But let's keep this real. Yakima would run through my fuel in less than a week. It's a drop in the bucket compared to what you need."

Wylie had just opened his mouth to speak when Cobb entered, carrying a tray and two cups. "There you go," she said cheerfully. "Please help yourselves to cream and sugar."

Wylie thanked her and waited until Cobb had left the room before speaking again. His eyes were like chips of coal. "Listen, Lieutenant . . . I'm tired of playing footsie with you. Either you give 80 percent of your fuel to Yakima—or I'll send the police over to take it away from you."

Mac stood. Her voice was cold. "I would advise against that, Mr. Wylie . . . If you send your police to attack Vagabond, we will kill them. And who will protect you then?"

And with that, Mac took her jacket and left the office. Cobb looked concerned as Mac strode past her, and both soldiers stood. Mac paused to let them gulp the rest of their coffee before leading them to the stairs. The meeting was over.

In the wake of the face-to-face with Wylie, Mac had no choice but to put her tiny command on high alert. An observation post was established on the east side of the freeway, some of the platoon's fighting positions were reinforced, and command-detonated mines were placed at key points around the perimeter.

But after three days without an attack, Mac began to relax. Then, on the fourth day, something remarkable occurred. The clouds parted—and the sun appeared! Mac felt better, and so did her troops, all of whom shed at least one layer of clothing—and went looking for opportunities to work outside. Even the normally dour Dr. Hoskins had a smile on his face.

So morale was up when the distant drone of a plane was heard, and the soldiers peered into the sky. All they could see was a dot, and a momentary glint of reflected light. Eventually, the dot morphed into a single-engine plane. It was boring in from the west, and that alone was enough to raise Mac's spirits. Maybe, just maybe, someone had been sent to replace Captain Hollister! And that hope grew as Omata broke the news. She was tracking the plane with a pair of binoculars. "It has air force markings," she said, "and it's turning our way!"

The sound of the engine grew louder as Mac turned to Peters. "Get on the horn," she told him. "See if you can make contact."

Peters entered the Flight Control Center as Omata continued to eyeball the incoming aircraft. "It's a T-41 Mescalero," the pilot said. "I learned how to fly in the civilian version. Uh-oh . . . I see what could be bullet holes."

Peters was back. "The pilot isn't responding, Lieutenant."

Mac turned to Evans. "Find Hoskins and take some people down to the airstrip. Roll the crash truck. The pilot could be wounded." Evans shouted orders as he ran.

Now Mac could see the white-over-blue prop plane more clearly as it circled the base. "He's checking us out," Omata observed, "trying to make sure that we're military."

That made sense given current conditions—and Mac continued to watch as the plane turned into the wind. "He's going to land," Omata predicted, and she began to run. Mac was right behind her.

The runway had never been long enough for anything other than light planes. That was one of the reasons why Vagabond had been redesignated as a heliport. But Mac figured that if any plane could land there, the Mescalero could. The trainer was about fifteen feet off the ground as the women arrived at the edge of the runway.

Everything looked good at first, and Mac thought the Mescalero was going to make a textbook landing, when the right wingtip came down. It hit the ground, threw the plane into an uncontrolled loop, and razor-sharp pieces of metal flew through the air as the prop shattered. The officers hit the dirt, and metal screeched as the fuselage skidded to a halt.

Both women were up and running as the crash truck roared in to foam the wreckage. Omata was the first to duck under the left wing and jerk the door open. A man was slumped over the controls, and as Mac got closer, she saw holes in the roof.

Omata cut the pilot free from his harness and began to pull him out. The seat was soaked with blood, and the pilot was clearly unconscious as they lowered him to the ground.

Dr. Hoskins arrived seconds later, closely followed by Obbie. "Good work," the doctor said. "Now get the hell out of the way."

Mac and Omata backed away as the man was lifted onto a stretcher and carried to the waiting Humvee. "Shit," Omata said feelingly. "Did you see that? The poor bastard had at least two holes in him."

"Hoskins will patch him up," Mac predicted, and hoped it was true. "Search the cockpit. Recover what you can. Maybe we can figure out who this guy is—and what he was up to. We'll meet in Flight Control thirty from now."

"Yes, ma'am," Omata responded. "I'm on it."

Mac spent the next half hour supervising the cleanup, with help from Peters. Then she went up to Flight Control, where a number of items were laid out on a table. The collection included an AWOL bag, a laptop, a cell phone, a folding knife, a wallet, and some pocket litter.

"I got some of this stuff from Doc Obbie," Omata explained. "And the rest is from the plane. The pilot is an army unmanned aerial vehicle operator named Staff Sergeant Nick Esco. He's stationed at JBLM."

"Okay," Mac said. "Good work. Is that all?"

"No," Omata said as she pointed to a pink envelope. "He had a girlfriend named Karol."

"*Had?*"

"She dumped him two weeks prior to the meteor strike."

"And she told him in a letter?"

"That's affirmative."

"What a bitch . . . All right, find your boss and tell him I would appreciate a low-level reconnaissance of the area."

Omata's face lit up. 'You're clearing us to fly?"

"Yes, I am."

Omata produced a whoop of joy and nearly bowled Evans over on her way out of the building. He looked at Mac. "Why so happy?"

"She gets to fly."

Evans shook his head. "Rotor heads . . . They're crazy."

The Apache lifted off half an hour later, circled the base, and went looking for trouble. That was useful, but the true purpose of the mission was to keep the pilots sharp and to boost their morale.

Shortly after the helicopter's departure, Mac went to check on Sergeant Esco. The dispensary was well lit, and the air was warm. Hoskins was sitting in the tiny waiting room drinking a cup of coffee. He nodded. "Thanks for the power . . . I could operate by lanternlight. But I don't want to. A bullet punched through Sergeant Esco's right thigh, and another was lodged in his right buttock. Both projectiles came up through the bottom of the cabin. No wonder he crashed . . . The poor bastard was bleeding to death."

Mac sat down. "And now?"

"And now he's all patched up," Hoskins informed her. "Obbie's with him. He's a good hospital corpsman, by the way . . . You're lucky to have him."

"We are," Mac agreed. "Although we call them medics."

"Who cares?" Hoskins responded. "He's good. That's the point."

"Roger that," Mac said. "I appreciate the feedback. So when can I speak with Sergeant Esco?"

"When he wakes up," Hoskins said. "I'll let you know."

"Good," Mac replied. "And thanks . . . We're lucky to have you as well." And with that, she left.

Mac was sitting in the Flight Control Center fretting about the unit's quickly dwindling supply of food when she heard the helicopter clatter overhead and come in for a landing. If it hadn't been for the MREs stored at Vagabond, the platoon would have run out of food weeks earlier. It was a perplexing problem, and one that became increasingly acute with each passing day.

Mac's thoughts were interrupted when the door opened, and a blast of cold air flooded the room. The generator was off, and the stove provided what warmth there was. Evans sat with his back to the rest of the room. He said, "Hey, close the fucking door," before turning around to look.

"That's 'close the fucking door,' *sir*," Peters said with a huge grin.

"My bad," Evans conceded, as Peters trooped in. "I should have known. Only a pilot would be stupid enough to leave the door open." Peters flipped him off, and both men laughed.

"So what's going on out there?" Mac inquired.

"Not a helluva lot," Peters said, as he plopped down. "Unless you're into mining trucks."

"Mining trucks? What *kind* of mining trucks? And where were they?"

"*Big* honking mining trucks," the pilot replied. "On the other side of the river. They're parked next to a convenience store. Omata has gun-camera footage, but we'll need some juice in order to show it to you."

Evans looked at Mac, she nodded, and he left. Once the generator was purring, it took five minutes to download the footage. There wasn't much to see at first . . . Just some widely separated homes.

Then the helo crossed both the freeway and the Yakima River. That was when four gigantic trucks became visible. Metal canopies jutted out over their cabs, and as the Apache circled, Mac saw that a steel balcony was mounted on the front of each vehicle.

Pickups looked like toys compared to the big beasts, and people were like ants, as they ran in every direction. And that raised an important question. Why would people run unless they had something to hide?

Mac had seen such trucks on TV and knew they were associated with open-pit mines. But there weren't any open-pit mines nearby. None that she knew of. And that raised a second question: Why were the big mining machines parked next to a convenience store located a short distance from Vagabond? Then it came to her. The ore haulers were part of Wylie's plan to attack the base! Mac felt a sudden emptiness at the pit of her stomach. "Can you give me some magnification? I'd like to have a closer look at the cabs on those trucks."

Omata could and did. The video was grainy but sufficient to confirm what Mac already suspected. By welding steel plates to the balconies that fronted the truck cabs Wylie's people had been able to provide the drivers with a modicum of protection. Was the armor thick enough to stop a .50 caliber slug? Probably. Could the Apache destroy the haulers with Hellfire missiles? Of course. But what then? What armament they had for the helicopter was already hanging on it. And once that was gone, the unit would be SOL if faced with an even greater threat.

Plus, there was the weather to consider. Mac was well aware of the fact that a lot of things can go wrong when an attack helicopter is forced to fly below five hundred feet, and visibility is limited to a couple of miles. And the clouds were moving back in. Evans was staring at the video. "Holy shit . . . Those bastards are getting ready for war."

"Yes, they are," Mac agreed. "It looks like they plan to roll in, crash through the fence, and level the base. Then they'll take our fuel. Wylie was serious."

Peters stared at her. "So what are we going to do?"

"We'll attack," Mac said without hesitation. "We have no choice. Now they know that we know—so they'll come for us as soon as they can." She turned to Evans. "Get everyone ready . . . I want to roll by 0400."

Evans was on his feet. He looked grim. "Yes, ma'am." Then he was gone.

There was a lot to do, and when the pilots left, Mac was all alone. *You're an idiot,* she told herself. *You should have sent patrols across the river. The fact that the weather cleared, and the rotor heads saw the trucks, was dumb luck.*

*I didn't think Wylie would follow through,* the other her objected. *Plus, it would be easy for a patrol to get cut off that far out.*

*Excuses won't cut it,* the first voice said harshly. *Get your shit together.* Mac stood. A mistake had been made, and she wasn't going to repeat it.

None of the soldiers slept that night. There were trucks to perform maintenance on, weapons to clean, and a wide variety of contingencies to plan for. The Apache was a good example. Rather than commit the gunship to the fight, Mac placed it on standby. It was her ace in the hole . . . A weapon she'd call on if necessary but only if forced to do so.

At 0305, Mac returned to her quarters to gear up. As she was getting ready, she came across the .9mm "Baby" Glock her father had given her when she graduated from high school. Some of her friends received jewelry, trips, and, in one case, a car.

But her gift was the pistol and lessons at the local range. It seemed stupid at the time—and her friends felt sorry for her. But now, as she prepared to go into combat, there was something comforting about the way the handgun felt in her hand. Was her father alive? There was no way to know as she slid the weapon into its holster.

The troops were loaded and ready by 0330. But before they left the base, Mac wanted to get one last report from Forward Observer Lin Kho. Private Hadley had been sent along to provide security, and the two of them were hidden in a cluster of trees just east of the convenience store, where they could put eyes on the mining trucks. They were equipped with night-vision goggles, so very little would escape their notice.

Mac was standing in one-one's forward hatch as she spoke into her mike. "Archer-Six to One-Ten. Do you read me? Over."

"This is Ten," Kho whispered. "I read you five by five. Over."

"We're ready to roll . . . Give me a sitrep. Over."

"You were correct," Kho replied. "It looks like the trucks are preparing to depart. About twenty police officers are present, along with roughly thirty civilians, all of whom are armed. Hold one . . . Some of the cops are climbing up onto the roof canopies. They have bipod-mounted machine guns. Over."

"Roger that. Is there any sign of Wylie? Over."

"There's a guy who's walking around shouting at people," Kho answered. "Over."

"That sounds like him," Mac said. "Tell Bravo-Two-Two to take the shot if he gets one. Then run like hell. Over."

"This is Two," Hadley replied. "Roger that. Out."

"All right," Mac said. "Withdraw toward the overpass if you can . . . We're on the way. Out." Then, speaking to the truck commander, she said "Let's roll."

Strangely, given their size, the Strykers were extremely quiet. So much so that when first deployed to Iraq in 2003, people referred to them as Ghost Riders. Mac heard a high-pitched whine as one-one began to pick up speed and felt the cold air press against her face.

Rather than barrel straight down Firing Center Road, the three-vehicle column took a less direct route that zigzagged through back roads and went cross-country at times. Mac would have preferred to divide the platoon in two, with each team following a different route, but she had to leave a truck at the base just in case. And since the engineering vehicle was the most ungainly of the four—it made sense to leave that truck behind with a squad of soldiers and her orphans.

"This is Bravo-Two-Two," Hadley said in her ear. Mac could hear heavy breathing and knew the sniper was running. "The guy with the big mouth is down—and five or six civilians are chasing us. The cops have dogs, and they're closing fast. We're looking for a place to make a stand. Out."

Mac swore under her breath. *Dogs.* She hadn't anticipated that. What else had she failed to think of? "This is Archer-Six actual. Roger that, Two . . . We'll be there soon. Over."

The Stryker produced a noise reminiscent of a city bus changing gears as it slowed, rounded a corner, and began to pick up speed. The overpass was directly ahead, and Mac could hear the steady bang, bang, bang of Hadley's rifle interspersed with three-round bursts from Kho's M4. They were making their stand. "This is Archer-One actual," Mac said. "Bring one-two up alongside one-one, so we can put the maximum amount of firepower downrange. Three will guard our six. Over."

Mac heard a series of double clicks as two pulled up next to one and three started to slow. As they passed a burned-out car, Mac saw Kho wave. From that point, it was possible to follow a line of dead bodies west. Mac didn't feel so much as a bump when 16 tons of truck rolled over a dog and two dead humans. The bodies were evidence of the skill with which Kho and Hadley had handled themselves, and Mac felt proud of them.

That was when a pair of bright lights came on. They were

unusually high off the ground and at least twenty feet apart. With a sense of shock Mac realized that one of the monster trucks was coming straight at her! An impression that was confirmed when a cop lying on top of the dump truck's metal canopy opened fire. And being up high, he had an advantage. "Button it up!" Mac ordered, as she dropped into the vic. "Archer-One actual to One-Two. Put the AT4 team on the ground and kill that truck. Over."

Meanwhile, one-one's gunner was using the Stryker's remote-weapons system to fire the truck's fifty. Mac could hear the thump, thump, thump of outgoing rounds and wished she could put eyes on the target. "This is One-Two," Sergeant Ralston said. "We're in position. Stand by. Over."

Even though Mac was inside a Stryker, she could hear the explosion as the AT4's high-explosive projectile hit the truck. A combination of curiosity and claustrophobia drove her up through the hatch to stand on the seat. A glance was enough to confirm that the rocket launcher had done its job. The front of the gigantic hauler was wrapped in flames, and civilians were bailing out of it. "Kill the runners," she ordered, and watched as tracers found the fugitives.

The slaughter wasn't something that Mac enjoyed. But it had to be done in order to protect her people and the base. Then it was over, and Mac felt a brief moment of satisfaction in knowing that the other haulers were too large to pass the burning wreck.

But the feeling was short-lived as Evans spoke over the radio. He was in charge of the base, and his voice was calm. Mac heard an explosion in the background. "This is Archer-One-Seven. We're taking mortar and small-arms fire from the south. I have two KIAs and a WIA. Over."

Mac felt surprise mixed with anger. *Mortars? Maybe they got them from a National Guard unit,* Mac thought to herself. Not that it mattered. She had to stay focused. The force protecting the base consisted of the ESV, a squad of infantry, and the five-person air crew. That was a small contingent of defenders. What orders had been given to the attackers? Were they trying to pin the soldiers down while they waited for the ore haulers to arrive? Or were they prepping the base for an infantry assault? There was no way to be sure.

Mac faced a choice. She could send one or more vics back to reinforce the base, thereby weakening the force located on the overpass, or she could order Evans to counterattack, using the ESV. That would involve sending an unsupported Stryker out to fight by itself. A definite no-no under normal circumstances.

Still . . . It seemed safe to assume that the locals weren't trained or equipped to tackle armor—and that meant that the vic would have a good chance against them. *Assumptions get people killed,* the voice told her, but Mac chose to overrule it. "This is Six . . . Send the ESV after the bastards. And tell Tillis to keep moving, so they can't put mortar fire on him. Over."

"Roger that," Evans replied. "Over."

Having made what might be a fateful decision, Mac had to let go and turned back to the situation in front of her. There were three additional monster trucks to disable or kill. "This is Archer-One . . . Let's put the rest of our boots on the ground. Once everybody is clear, one-one will lead the way, followed by one-two and one-three. Watch those intervals. Over."

The first squad was riding on one-one, and Mac followed them out into the cold night air. By the time the second and third squads had deassed their trucks, one-one had entered the narrow gap that lay between the burning truck and the bridge. Truck Commander Lamm was forced to put a set of four tires on the sidewalk to get through. The rest of the Strykers followed with squads one, two, and three bringing up the rear.

Mac had to jog in order to keep up with one-three, and the rest of the platoon followed her example. She positioned herself to the left of the vic in order to see past it and ensure that the way was clear. A couple of minutes later, one-one cleared the bridge and began to close on the parking lot that Mac had seen earlier. Then she realized that the surviving ore haulers were spread out. As one-one passed between two of the behemoths, Mac felt a sudden sense of alarm. Something was wrong . . . But *what*?

The answer came in the form of a massive explosion as the truck on the far right was transformed into an orange-red ball of flame. It rose like an obscene balloon, which popped a hundred feet off the ground. Mac came to a halt and ordered her troops to do likewise. The smoke made it impossible to see. Sparks gave her the mike. "One-one? One-two? This is Archer-Six . . . Report. Over."

"This is one-one," came the halting reply. "One-two was caught in the blast. It's gone."

Mac felt her heart sink. It wasn't the truck . . . Fuck that. Evitt was dead, plus his gunner, and Evans's people. All to defend a base that nobody cared about. Mac felt nauseous but couldn't throw up because people were counting on her. She forced herself to speak. "One-one and one-three will destroy the remaining ore trucks. As soon as that's accomplished, the rest of the platoon will move in and mop up."

The remaining vics were taking machine-gun fire but nothing big enough to matter. One of the ore haulers took off, or tried to, but didn't get far as one-one's vengeful gunner poured fire into the truck. It didn't take long for a tracer to find a fuel line and spark a fire. Mac heard a thump as flames appeared, and the behemoth ground to a halt.

Meanwhile, one-three's gunner was firing his 40mm grenade launcher at the remaining truck. It seemed to wilt as blast after blast hit the cab, engine compartment, and gigantic tires. Then it, too, was gone as the fuel tank blew—and one-three's commander uttered a whoop of joy. Sergeant Ralston ordered him to "Cut the crap."

Mac grinned. "Come on!" she shouted. "Follow me . . . Let's get the rest of them!"

Machine-gun fire was coming from in and around the convenience store. Bullets dug divots out of the parking lot as Mac zigzagged forward. She was using cars and pickups for cover, and that wasn't the brightest plan, since it was safe to assume that some of the vehicles had fuel in their tanks. And there was the possibility of another IED. But Mac was hating rather than thinking, so none of that occurred to her.

When a smoke grenade landed in front of the store, she charged through the fog, firing bursts from the M4. Then she was through the front door and inside. Mac saw shadowy forms turning her way and fired at the one off to her right. She saw the man stagger as the .223 rounds hit him but knew better than to watch because the other targets were still in motion. Each person was part of a race to see who would live and who would die.

Mac switched to full auto and held the trigger back as she sprayed the woman in front of her with bullets. The bitch fell, but it wasn't going to be enough. A *third* defender had Mac dead to rights and was about to fire. That was when Mac heard a loud boom to her left, and saw half of the man's face vanish. The force of the blast turned him around, and he collapsed. Mac couldn't believe her good fortune, and turned to see Sparks work the action on his twelve-gauge pump gun. The RTO spit on the floor. "Asshole."

Mac laughed and took note of how shrill it sounded. After thanking the RTO for saving her ass, Mac turned her attention to the things that had to get done. First, she ordered the remaining Strykers to provide security. Then she sent the first squad out to retrieve intelligence. That included electronic devices, documents, IDs, and pocket litter.

While they took care of that, Mac made the rounds with the second squad. Their job was to collect all of the weapons and ammunition that were lying around. Later, once the unit returned to base, the pile would be divided into two categories: keep and destroy.

Finally, after confirming that Hadley's dead man was none other than Fred Wylie, Mac ordered the unit to pull out. She rode in one-three on the way back and understood why the mood was so somber. A battle had been won, but the price of victory had been high. Two men had been killed, and not only killed, but obliterated. Not so much as a dog tag had been found in the blast zone. It was depressing as hell, and all of them were silent as the vic rolled onto the base.

The good news was that one-four had been able to find and eliminate both of the insurgent mortar teams. One-four's gunner had taken one group out while Tillis ran the other team down. They were holding the tube between them and running south when the vic caught up and crushed them. Some riflemen were killed subsequent to that—but Evans figured that a dozen of the bastards had survived.

Unfortunately, none of this could make up for the two people who'd been killed during the initial mortar attack. And as an orange disk rose in the east, and the bodies were lowered into what Private Wessel callously referred to as "a double wide," it was Mac's duty to say a few words. Her throat felt tight, and she wished there had been time to prepare something.

"We're gathered here to say good-bye to our comrades. Men who stood by their country in its darkest hour, who fought to keep it alive, and died protecting their fellow soldiers. We're going to miss them . . . And keep them alive with the stories that we tell. May God take and keep them."

Once the service was over, and the grave was filled in, half of the soldiers were sent to grab some sleep while the rest stood guard. And that included Mac, who flipped a coin with Evans and won. After a hot shower, she crawled into her bag and fell asleep. And when her alarm went off two hours later, it seemed as if only seconds had passed.

The generator was off, so the best Mac could do was to wash her face and brush her teeth prior to shuffling over to the Flight Center, where Evans was waiting to be relieved. After two cups of coffee and an MRE, Mac went to visit the dispensary. Dr. Hoskins was there to introduce Staff Sergeant Nick Esco. The noncom had sandy-brown hair, green eyes, and a ready smile. Mac saw him wince as he got up off a pillow. "Good morning, ma'am . . . The doctor tells me that you helped to pull me out of the Mescalero. Thank you."

"Warrant Officer Omata got to you first," Mac told him, "so it was a team effort. You're lucky to be alive. We saw lots of bullet holes. Some of which were in you."

"Yeah," Esco said wryly. "A whole lot of bad guys were shooting at me as I took off from JBLM, and believe me, there's nothing worse than getting shot in the ass. It's embarrassing."

Mac chuckled. "Yes, I suppose it is. But what you did took a lot of guts. Were you a pilot before you joined?"

Esco shook his head. "No, ma'am. Even though I'm a drone pilot, I had never flown a *real* plane until I took off from JBLM."

Mac allowed her eyebrows to rise. "That's amazing . . . And you flew over the mountains?"

"I followed Highway 410 most of the way . . . People shot at me as I flew over Chinook Pass."

"Yeah," Mac said. "We heard that a warlord controls it. I hear that travelers have to pay him in order to travel back and forth. So why come here? You could have gone anywhere."

"Sergeant Poole is my cousin . . . Maybe the only family I have left. So, given the way things are going, I'd like to join your outfit."

Poole was in charge of squad two—and a good man. Mac nodded. "Welcome to the platoon. Tell me, what's going on at JBLM? Why can't we reach anyone?"

Esco stared at her. "You haven't heard?"

Hoskins spoke for the first time since making the introductions. "No," he said, "she hasn't."

There was a hollow feeling in Mac's stomach as Esco looked at her. What was that in his eyes? Sympathy? Pity? She wasn't sure. "JBLM was overrun," Esco said. "They call themselves 'the People's Army,' but that's bullshit. All they are is a consortium of gangs that came together to loot the base. We fought them for more than a month, but they grew stronger, and we had to fall back. Hundreds of our people were killed. Eventually, it came down to a choice between bombing most of Tacoma or pulling out. And we were about to do that when a mob broke through the perimeter. We fought, but not for long . . . All of us had been ready to go for days, so all I had to do was grab my AWOL bag and run. The Mescalero was parked near the building where I worked, so I took it. End of story."

Mac turned so that the men couldn't see the tears, wiped them away, and knew that Esco was wrong. The loss of JBLM and all that it stood for wasn't the end of the story. It was the beginning.

# CHAPTER 4

||||||||||||||||||||||||||||||||||||||||

The liberties of our country, the freedom of our civil
constitution, are worth defending against all hazards:
And it is our duty to defend them against all attacks.

—SAMUEL ADAMS

**OFF THE EAST COAST OF MEXICO**

After twenty days spent paddling up Mexico's east coast, Sloan
knew that if he wasn't in American waters, he'd arrive there soon.
The moon was playing hide-and-seek behind broken clouds, and
there were moments when it looked as if he were dipping his paddle
into molten silver.

But the otherworldly moments came to an end when Sloan heard
the sound of powerful engines and felt the first stirrings of fear. He
didn't want to have contact with *anyone* . . . Especially drug runners. Fortunately, the kayak was so low in the water, it would be
difficult to see. When the speedboat passed him, Sloan had to turn
into its wake or run the risk of being capsized. As he completed the
maneuver, a powerful spot came on, swept the surface of the water,
and nailed him. The voice was amplified. *"Levante sus manos—
y mantenerlos allí!"* ("Raise your hands—and keep them there!")

*Shit! Shit! Shit!* Sloan dug his paddle into the water in a frantic attempt to escape. The light followed, and Sloan heard a burst of gunfire. Geysers of water shot up all around the kayak. Then there was a thump as a bullet passed through the hull. That left Sloan with no choice but to roll out as cold seawater flooded the kayak. Suddenly, the boat was there, looming above Sloan, as a black silhouette peered down. *"Tirar los peces en. Vamos a ver lo que tenemos."* ("Pull the fish in. Let's see what we have.")

Sloan had no choice but to cooperate as strong hands reached down to pull him up. Sloan heard one of the men address the helmsman in English. "Hey, Bob . . . Turn the bow into the waves. She's rolling like a pig."

Sloan grabbed onto a seat as his feet hit the deck and the boat lurched. "Are you Americans?"

There was barely enough moonlight to see by. A man looked at him and grinned. "Hell no," he said. "We're Texans! Who are you?"

"My name is Sloan . . . Samuel T. Sloan, the United States Secretary of Energy."

"Do you have ID to prove that?" the man inquired.

"No," Sloan admitted. "It was in the kayak."

"That's one possibility," the man agreed. "Or, and this seems more likely, you belong to a drug cartel. Cuff him, Hank."

Sloan could see their uniforms by that time along with their disk-shaped badges. Texas Rangers perhaps? It didn't matter. All he could do was allow himself to be chained to an eyebolt and wait for the nightmare to end.

Finally, after what seemed like an eternity, night surrendered to day—and Sloan spotted a smudge of land. The United States? Yes, he thought so, and felt a renewed sense of hope. After going ashore, the authorities would free him. With that out of the way, he'd contact his staff. Would the president want to speak with him? Probably . . . Then he'd call the assisted-care facility to check on his mother.

That's what Sloan was thinking as the gunboat rounded the south end of Padre Island. Sloan had been there numerous times and knew the area well. The boat slowed as they neared the Coast Guard station.

Once the gunboat was moored, Sloan was escorted up a ramp to a one-story building. A woman with two children stared at him. That was when Sloan remembered his bushy beard, ripped clothes, and bare feet. None of which would add to his credibility.

After being led through the scrupulously clean lobby, and past a reception desk, Sloan was escorted down a hallway to the holding cells located in the back of the building. The civilian clerk laughed when Sloan said he was the Secretary of Energy but wrote it down anyway. Then it was time to answer questions pertaining to his criminal record, health, and identifying marks if any.

Once the booking process was complete, and mug shots had been taken, an officer placed Sloan in cell 002. The six-foot-by-six-foot enclosure was equipped with metal bunk beds, a freestanding toilet, and a small sink. What light there was came from the single fixture located over his head—and a narrow gun-slit-style window. He heard a clang as the door closed. "Hey, dude," the man in the next cell called out. "You got a smoke?"

"No," Sloan replied. "I don't."

"Then fuck you," the man said. "I hope you die." Sloan was home.

||||||||||||

After a day of questioning by a variety of people, Sloan was given an airline-style personal-hygiene kit and allowed to shower and shave. Then he was required to don orange overalls that had the word PRISONER printed across the back. A pair of canvas slip-ons completed the outfit. After that, he was left in his cell to think and worry. Eventually, Sloan went to sleep. There were dreams . . . Lots of dreams. And all of them were bad.

When morning came, he received a breakfast that consisted of a cup of coffee, an orange, and some sort of egg McMuffin thing. He couldn't get it down.

Shortly after breakfast, Sloan was removed from his cell and taken out through the front door. The Coast Guard station had a small helipad. And as Sloan was escorted along a walkway, he saw that the civilian version of a Huey was sitting on the concrete slab, with its rotors turning. Two men were waiting for him. Both wore Glocks, blue polo shirts, and khaki pants. Who were they? There was no way to know, as the man with the flattop and aviator-style shades pointed at the open door. "Get in!" He had to shout in order to be heard over the helo's engine.

Sloan had no choice but to get in. The interior was set up to transport cargo—but fold-down seats were bolted to the bulkheads. Once he was seated, the second guard was there to secure his seat belt. The helicopter took off two minutes later. There weren't any doors. That meant that the slipstream could enter the cabin and pummel Sloan's face. He turned to the man with the flattop. "Where are we going?"

When the man smiled, his lips pulled away from a set of teeth that were shaped like white tombstones. Then he held a finger up to his lips as if to shush a child. That was that.

Time crawled by. Sloan could see out through the starboard door, but there wasn't much to look at. Just the dull gray water of the gulf, a few fishing boats, and an occasional glimpse of an oil rig in the hazy distance. The monotony combined with the drone of the engine put Sloan to sleep. And when he awoke, it was to see verdant vegetation below. Trees mostly, but marsh grass, too, and lots of water. Freshwater from the looks of it—that filled lakes, ponds, and hundreds of serpentine channels. A swamp! They were flying over a swamp . . . But *where*? The southeast corner of Texas seemed most likely since it was only a few hours from Padre Island, and the sun was behind them.

A flock of birds took to the air as the helicopter lost altitude and skimmed the treetops. Sloan couldn't see what lay directly ahead. But as the helo entered into a wide turn, an oil rig appeared. The blocky superstructure was three stories high and sitting on a steel barge. Though barely legible, the name HUXTON OIL could be read on the side of the rig, and that was interesting—since the Texas-based company was one of the largest in the world. Or had been anyway. Judging from how rusty all the running gear was, the derrick mounted on the bow hadn't been used in a long time.

Such were Sloan's thoughts as the Huey settled onto the circular pad affixed to the barge's stern. "Get out," Flattop shouted, as he pointed at the door.

Sloan pressed the release on his seat belt and stood. Two women stood waiting on the cluttered deck. Both had black hair, dark skin, and were dressed in blue overalls. One held a Taser barrel up, with her index finger resting on the trigger guard. "Welcome aboard, Secretary Sloan," she said. "Please follow Molly . . . Mr. Godbee wants to meet you."

Sloan took note. They knew his name! Finally . . . But why was he being held against his will? Out in the middle of a swamp? Hopefully, Godbee would tell him.

Sloan had no choice but to follow Molly under a platform, past a blowout preventer, and up a set of steel stairs to the deck above. A walkway gave access to a large office, which was surprisingly clean and tidy.

A man rose from his desk and came forward to meet Sloan. He had a limp, which forced him to use a tree-root-style cane. His clothing consisted of a tasteful Hawaiian shirt and white slacks. "Welcome to the *Belle Marie*, Secretary Sloan . . . It's a strange name, don't you think? This rig was never pretty. My name is Walter Godbee, and I'm in charge here. You can remove Mr. Sloan's cuffs, Molly. Please don't do anything unpleasant, Mr. Sloan . . . Lucy doesn't like troublemakers." Sloan looked at Lucy. The Taser was still in her hand.

"Understood," Sloan said, as the cuffs came off. "So why am I here?"

Godbee smiled. "This is a repository of sorts. A place where individuals like yourself can be stored."

"By Huxton Oil?"

Godbee shrugged. "What difference does it make? You're here, and you're going to remain here, and that's what matters. My staff and I will do what we can to make your stay tolerable. As for *you*? Well, I suggest that you consider the serenity prayer by Reinhold Niebuhr: 'God grant me the serenity to accept things I cannot change, the courage to change the things I can, and the wisdom to know the difference.' And this, Mr. Sloan, is something that you cannot change. Take Mr. Sloan to his cabin, ladies. I'm sure he'd like to shower after his journey. Oh, and Mr. Sloan . . . Don't waste your time trying to seduce Molly or Lucy. They play for the other team."

Sloan followed Molly out of the office and up another flight of stairs, to the third deck. From there, it was a short trip to the hatch labeled CABIN 3.

The mechanism on the outside surface of the hatch was common to larger vessels that had watertight doors. It consisted of a wheel and four spoke-like "dogs" or rods that could extend to hold the slab of steel firmly in place. The chances of breaking out? Zero.

Molly turned the wheel, waited for the dogs to clear, and pulled the door open. Then she stood to one side, so Sloan could enter. The cabin was nicer than he had expected. The bulkheads were covered with light green paint. The full-sized bed was nicely made and topped with two large pillows. There was an easy chair, too . . . And a side table. A small bathroom could be seen through an open door.

"Your dinner will arrive at six," Lucy told him. "I hope you like fish." And with that, the women withdrew. Sloan heard a series of clanking sounds, followed by near silence.

The cabin boasted a single curtain-covered window. Sloan went over to peer out. He could see bars and mangrove trees beyond. *Okay,* he thought to himself. *I'll find another way to escape.* The next fifteen minutes were spent exploring the nooks and crannies of his cabin. There were two orange jumpsuits in the dresser, both of which had the word PRISONER on the back and would make it that much more difficult to evade capture should he manage to escape. No, *when* he escaped.

A radio was sitting on the table next to the chair, and it worked! That meant he could listen to the news once he managed to find some. The only station he could get was playing country-western music at the moment. Where were the rest? Off the air as a result of the meteor impacts? Maybe.

A closer inspection of the bathroom turned up a set of toiletries, and that led him into the shower, where he spent ten glorious minutes under a powerful stream of hot water. Sloan felt clean and reinvigorated as he put a fresh jumpsuit on. He was about to fiddle with the radio when the hatch opened.

Molly entered first. She was carrying a linen-covered tray. Lucy came next with the Taser at the ready. She was about five-eight or so, and in good shape. But Sloan had four inches on her and was in tip-top condition after weeks of paddling. So, if he could get behind Lucy, Sloan felt sure that he could take her down. *Will take her down,* he told himself. *And soon, too.*

After placing the meal on the table, Molly withdrew. That was Lucy's cue to back out through the door. There was a metallic clang as the hatch closed.

The catfish dinner was excellent, but it went largely unappreciated because of the newspapers that had been delivered with it. There was a week-old copy of the *New York Times*, complete with coffee stains, and a two-day-old copy of the *Dallas Morning News*. Sloan read both of them from front to back as he hoovered up every scrap of information he could get. And that included the ads because the kinds of goods and services being offered made their own statement about postimpact America. Cold-weather clothing was popular . . . As were Mason jars, tools, and backup generators.

Tears ran down Sloan's cheeks as he read the latest assessment of what it would take to rebuild Washington, D.C. Had his mother been killed? Probably. And his staffers? Yes . . . Unless they'd been on vacation or something. And the president! He was dead, along with thousands of other government officials. The vice president had survived though . . . and, according to the *New York Times*, was hard at work trying to get the nation back on its feet.

But that's where things got interesting. After reading the *Dallas Morning News*, Sloan had the impression that many, if not most, Southern politicians were unhappy with the president's ambitious reconstruction plans. They objected to "higher taxes," "big government," and "too much regulation."

Sloan was a creature of Washington, D.C., and recognized the rhetoric as being part of the long-standing philosophical divide between conservatives and progressives. Except now there seemed to be some ominous undertones. Prominent civil and business leaders talking about "more self-determination," "state's rights," and "local autonomy." One even went so far as to raise the possibility of secession! Was it vote-getting rhetoric? Or the real deal? It was impossible to tell from where he was. One thing was for sure, however: The person or persons in charge of Godbee's "repository" wanted to keep him in the loop. *Why?*

Sloan put the papers aside to finish his meal. The food was cold by then, but he ate it anyway, and was polishing his plate with a chunk of corn bread when Molly came around to collect it.

The next three days were spent eating his fill, getting a lot of sleep, and watching Godbee's "ladies" come and go. During that time, Sloan was careful to follow every order they gave him without offering any pushback. The plan was to convince them that he wasn't a threat. Then, on the fourth day, Sloan made his move. He had chosen to escape at dinnertime, when there would be only a few hours of daylight remaining. That would help him to hide.

That was the theory, anyway. Although Sloan was well aware that the swamp was full of creatures that could find him even if humans couldn't! Still, he preferred to take that risk rather than sitting around waiting for who knows what.

So there he was, hiding behind the hatch when Molly pushed it open. She was holding the dinner tray with both hands. And as Molly entered the cabin, she could see that the bathroom door was ajar and hear the rush of water in the shower. That was the same scenario she'd seen for the past two days, except that Sloan wasn't in the bathroom this time.

Lucy followed Molly into the room. She was carrying the Taser barrel up as usual. Sloan brought the toilet seat up and around. It glanced off the side of Lucy's head, and the force of the impact knocked her down.

One down and one to go! Sloan felt a sudden surge of confidence as he went after Molly. But, as fast as he was, Molly was even faster. The spin kick struck Sloan's right temple and sent him reeling. He was still trying to recover his balance when a flurry of kicks and blows put him down. So there he was, lying on his back, when Lucy loomed over him. Blood ran down the side of her face—and the Taser was pointed at his chest. "No!" Sloan croaked. "Don't . . ."

Lucy smiled as she pulled the trigger. Sloan jerked spasmodically as fifty thousand volts of electricity surged through his nervous system and caused his muscles to lock up. Then, as he lay helpless, the ladies began to kick him. The blows continued even as the effects of the Taser began to wear off. Sloan saw Molly pull her foot back, and saw the boot come at him, but that was all. The world ceased to exist.

## FORT HOOD, TEXAS

The Concho sanction had been successful if somewhat messy, and there had been little to no blowback thanks to the efforts of a New Order sympathizer inside the *Dallas Morning News*. Her header read: "Gang-style massacre in Richardson." And that was enough to point most people in the wrong direction.

Now, as Victoria drove south on Interstate 35, she saw a steady stream of National Guard vehicles going the other way. There were trucks loaded with troops, platoons of Strykers, and tank transporters all headed north where they had orders to "restore law and order." But, depending on how things went politically, Victoria knew there might be more to it than that. Much more.

After passing through Temple and Killeen, Victoria arrived in Fort Hood. Rather than stop by her condo, she drove straight to the base. The traffic lights were working, which meant that the power was on. And no wonder since the base had a very high priority.

Victoria was dressed in civilian clothes. But, when the corporal on the gate saw the sticker on the BMW's windshield, he threw Victoria a salute. "Good afternoon, ma'am . . . ID please." After comparing the picture on the card to her face, the corporal waved her through.

Victoria had been stationed at Fort Hood for more than a year and knew the base well. The sports car seemed to drive itself to III Corps headquarters. The modernistic building consisted of two squares connected by a central triangle. Victoria drove past it, parked at the rear of the complex, and got out. The sun was an angry-looking disk that was barely visible beyond a brooding mass of low-hanging clouds. Thunder rumbled in the distance.

Victoria's heels made a clicking sound as she entered the building, showed her ID, and made her way through a maze of offices to the one her father occupied. He had two jobs at the moment. The one assigned to him by the Pentagon before it was destroyed and one reflected by the title on the door. That was INTERIM COMMANDING GENERAL. But everyone who was anyone knew that "interim" would disappear if the decision was made to secede and the New Confederacy came into being.

Bo had always been a conservative, and other conservatives knew that. So, when Southern elites began to discuss the possibility of a nation based on conservative principles, they'd been quick to approach him. And his oldest daughter was proud of that. As for Robin? Her views lay on the other side of the political divide.

Victoria entered a large reception area and made her way over to the fortresslike desk that barred the way. Mrs. Walters, Bo's longtime civilian secretary, looked up from her computer. "Good afternoon, Major Macintyre . . . The general is in a meeting at the moment. It should be over in ten minutes or so."

Walters was fortysomething, blond, and well-groomed. She was also efficient and extremely loyal. Was Walters more than a secretary? Victoria assumed so and understood the necessity. Her mother had been dead for a long time. "Thank you, Mrs. Walters . . . I'll wait."

Other officers were waiting as well. Half a dozen of them. And none were very happy when a clutch of colonels left the office, and a civilian was ushered in ahead of them.

General Bo Macintyre was sitting behind his desk as Victoria entered and didn't bother to get up. True, they were at work, but Victoria knew it wouldn't make any difference if they weren't. Hugs, kisses, and all the rest of the emotional claptrap so important to her mother and sister weren't part of Victoria's relationship with her father. He nodded. "Nice job in Dallas, Major . . . Morton Lemaire sends his thanks. It looks like he'll take over as the New Confederacy's first CEO if things go that way."

Victoria sat in one of four guest chairs. "Not Mr. Huxton?"

General Macintyre shook his head. "Huxton is too old and cantankerous. The public wouldn't like him. But enough politics . . . We have a problem, and you're the solution."

Victoria looked him in the eye just as he had taught her to do when she was three. "Yes, sir. What's the problem? Another situation like the one in Dallas?"

"No," her father replied. "Are you familiar with the Space X launch site near Brownsville?"

"No, I didn't know there was one."

"Well, there is. It was built to provide the Space Exploration Technologies Corporation with the capacity to launch their Falcon 9 and Falcon Heavy launch vehicles on a moment's notice."

"And?"

"And the Zapata drug cartel took control of the facility two days ago. There wasn't much to stop them, just some rent-a-cops, and they went down in a matter of minutes."

Victoria frowned. "But why?"

"We aren't sure," General Macintyre replied. "But here's an educated guess. A man named Felipe Cabrera runs the cartel. And if the reports are true, he has plans to reshape it."

"Into what?"

"Into a narco state," her father answered. "A narco state with its own communications, weather, and spy satellites. All launched and controlled from Brownsville. According to sources in Mexico, Cabrera sees this as the perfect opportunity to grab what he wants. He captured the port facility as well."

"Okay," Victoria said, "that's a serious problem. But what's he got? Some gangbangers armed with assault rifles? We'll throw a battalion of troops at him, send in some gunships, and boom! End of problem."

"If only it were that easy," General Macintyre replied as he raised a remote. "Take a look at this." The video had been captured by a drone. The facility consisted of a circle divided into quadrants by crisscrossing streets. Notable features included clusters of small buildings, fuel tanks, and four spindly com towers.

Judging from what Victoria could see, the Zapatas were equipped with personnel carriers that had once been the property of the Mexican army, a variety of SUVs, and three pieces of towed artillery. Bulldozers and backhoes were being used to construct defensive barriers. And, as Victoria watched from above, a Zapata fired an RPG at the airborne camera. It missed. Then, as the UAV turned east, Victoria saw something that caught her by surprise. "Holy shit . . . What's *that*?"

"That," her father said, "is the destroyer ARM *Netzahualcoyotl* D-102, formerly known as the USS *Steinaker*. She was commissioned on May 26, 1945, and transferred to Mexico on February 24, 1982. And, based on her presence in this video, we can assume that the Zapatas seized control of the ship subsequent to the meteor strikes and intentionally ran her aground."

The last part was certainly true. As Victoria watched the video, she could see that the destroyer's bow was way up on the beach—and that put her within a thousand feet of the Space X launchpad. "But *why*?" she wondered out loud.

"We figure that the Zapatas lack the skills and resources necessary to keep the *Netzahualcoyotl* at sea," General Macintyre said. "Maybe they killed too many of the crew or maybe anything. So they ran her ashore. And the reason for that is mounted on the ship's bow. See that butt-ugly turret? That's a Russian-made Kashtan antiaircraft weapons system. The Russkies gave it to the Mexican navy a year ago in hopes that they'd buy some.

"It boasts *two* six-barreled 30mm rotary cannons and 9M311 launchers, equipped with four ready-to-fire missiles. They're fed by a reloading system that contains thirty-two missiles in ready-to-launch containers. And the whole thing is controlled by an integral scanning and targeting system. The basic idea is to throw so much ordnance into the air that nothing can get through it. And that's why we aren't sending any Apaches in to hose the place down. As for long-range artillery and surface-to-surface missiles, they would erase the facility . . . And we might need it later on."

As if to illustrate the problem, the Kashtan turret swiveled toward the camera and fired. The screen went black, and as it did, Victoria understood Cabrera's plan. The destroyer was there to prevent air attacks while work on the fortifications was completed, and the gang leader brought more AA weapons in from the south. It was a brilliant example of guerilla warfare. There was a sardonic smile on his father's face. "Nifty, huh?"

"Yes, sir," Victoria answered. "And my orders are?"

"Take the launch facility back and hold it until you're relieved."

Victoria stood. "Yes, sir. Is there anything else?"

"Yes," General Macintyre said as he made a steeple with his fingers. "Teach the Zapatas a lesson they'll remember. It's only a matter of time until the Northerners attack us. We need to lock the back door now."

"I'll take care of it," Victoria promised, and with that, she left the room.

## BROWNSVILLE, TEXAS

Prior to the meteor strikes Brownsville, Texas, had been a major economic hub for shipping, a center of manufacturing, and home to a lot of poor people. The air was heavy with moisture as the task force rolled into town, and Victoria thought it might rain. Two days had passed since the conversation with her father, and most of it had been spent gathering the resources necessary to carry out her mission. The column consisted of two Abrams tanks, some smaller vehicles, and a long line of trucks.

The Zapatas had been using captured artillery to shell the city—and columns of black smoke were rising up ahead. Fortunately, the local National Guard unit, the Brownsville Police Department, and a makeshift army of citizens had managed to hold the northern part of the city. Victoria was counting on her tanks to clear the way to Highway 4, where Task Force Snake would turn east.

Victoria was riding in the back of a specially equipped com truck, sitting elbow to elbow with a tech sergeant as the vic's tires bumped over the pieces of debris that lay on the pavement. An array of screens were positioned in front of them, and thanks to the video provided by no less than *three* drones, Victoria could see what lay ahead.

As her convoy pushed through a barricade manned by cheering

locals, she saw that the enemy was falling back. They had some RPG-29s and the capacity to call for artillery support, but they didn't know how to do it effectively. As a result, howitzer shells began to fall around the convoy, but none of them were on target.

Explosions threw dust and debris into the air, and Victoria could hear the rattle of small-arms fire, as the Zapatas tried to slow the juggernaut that was smashing through their lines. Those efforts failed as the tank commanders opened fire with their 105mm guns, and squads of infantry rushed forward to claim contested ground.

Because the effort was going well, Victoria felt free to turn her attention elsewhere. "Snake-Six actual to Sky-Hammer," she said. "Do you read me? Over."

"This is Sky-Hammer actual. I read you five by five. Over."

"Destroy the bridge. Over." The bridge Victoria was referring to was the B&M Bridge over the Rio Grande river. Without it, the Zapatas couldn't bring vehicles into Brownsville and would have to retreat on foot if at all.

"Roger that," Sky-Hammer replied. "Keep your heads down. Over."

The MGM-140 Army Tactical Missile System was more than sixty miles away when two guided missiles flashed out of the boxy launcher and vanished into the low-hanging clouds. Victoria watched via one of the drones as both rockets hit the B&M Bridge at midspan and exploded. A large gap appeared as the smoke cleared. Mission accomplished.

"We're coming up on the exit for Highway 4," the tech sergeant announced.

"Got it," Victoria replied. "Tell the driver to pull over, so I can switch vehicles. And keep me informed."

"Yes, ma'am. Watch your six."

Victoria was wearing a full combat rig as she left the com truck.

She was carrying an M4 carbine. A couple of dune buggy–like Desert Patrol Vehicles had been tagging along behind the com truck, and both pulled up alongside it. Sergeant Cora Tarvin was driving one of the buggies, with Private Roy Poston riding shotgun. Corporal Jimmy Gatlin was behind the wheel of the other. A pair of retro goggles protected his eyes. "Good morning, ma'am . . . Fancy meeting you here." All three were members of Victoria's special ops team.

Victoria slid in beside Gatlin. A pintle-mounted 7.62 machine gun was located in front of her. Victoria strapped in, ran a radio check, and held on as the DPV took off. Open country, which was to say tank country, lay to either side of the two-lane highway. There wasn't much to see other than grass and an occasional bush.

Gatlin could literally run circles around the tanks if he chose to but knew better than to enter their line of fire. That forced him to go more slowly than he would have preferred. It wasn't long before some obstacles appeared in the distance. Three trucks were positioned to block the highway. Why? So the gringos would drive between the vehicles, or circle around them. But the tank commanders were smarter than that. They fired, cars exploded, and IEDs went off. Debris was thrown high into the air, only to come twirling down again.

Gatlin uttered a personal war cry and stomped on the gas. The DPV surged forward, bumped through the ditch next to the road, and turned, so Victoria could fire on the men who were hidden next to the ambush site. Hot casings flew sideways as she fired the 7.62. Bodies fell, the DPV bounced over one of them, and Victoria felt all powerful until an RPG exploded twenty feet ahead of them. Gatlin swore as a fragment of metal hit his left hand, and blood began to flow.

Then it was time to turn east again and catch up with the tanks. Victoria took a moment to check the screen mounted between them and saw that they were about to enter Bola Chica Village. That was where the Space X control center was located. The Zapatas had control of it but not for long. The plan called for the trucks to drop two platoons of infantry outside the village, and Victoria expected them to take it back in less than an hour. In the meantime, she, along with the rest of the task force, would continue to the launch site. Unfortunately, the Russian Kashtan system would be waiting for them when they arrived.

According to the literature, the turret could engage shore targets. But did the people manning the weapons system know that? And what were they doing? Had the Zapata techs been ordered to sit there and scan the sky for Apaches? If so, they might waste time deciding what to do when ground targets appeared. Time her tanks could use to attack. That was Victoria's plan, and she was staking lives on it, hers included.

The tanks were rolling east at their top speed of 45 mph, and Victoria wished they could go faster. But that was impossible. So all she could do was hold on as the DPV bounced across open country south of the tanks. The second dune buggy was doing the same up to the north.

As the tanks began to close in on the launch site, Victoria gave orders for the drones to swing wide rather than run head-on into the metal hail that the Kashtan battery could throw up. Then she got on the horn to the captain in command of the trucks following behind. "Snake-Six actual to Bravo-Six. Order your drivers to pull over and unload your troops. Bring them forward but use cover. There's no telling what that weapons system is going to do. Over."

The infantry officer already had his orders, but Victoria didn't know him personally, so she wanted to make sure he understood the need to hang back at first. Because if the people in the turret *were* prepared to engage shore targets, the 30mm rotary cannons would rip the troops to shreds. "This is Bravo-Six," the officer replied. "Roger that, over."

"There it is!" Gatlin shouted over the engine noise, as a thicket of radio towers appeared up ahead. Victoria was thrown against her harness as he turned the wheel to avoid running into a marshy estuary. Victoria spotted the grounded ship as the DPV bounced onto the road, and Gatlin put his foot down. The destroyer's bow was higher than it should have been because of the upward slope of the beach. And that was a good thing because it meant the 30mm cannons couldn't be brought to bear on the launch site!

But the feeling of jubilation was short-lived as the Kashtan battery came to life and fired two missiles. They flashed out of their tubes, accelerated away, and were soon lost in the low-lying clouds. *They're gone,* Victoria told herself. *The tanks are too close for the rockets to hit.*

That was when a missile fell from the sky and landed on top of the lead tank's turret. There was a massive explosion, and the M-1 was transformed into a pile of burning scrap. A series of secondary explosions destroyed what remained of the machine. Victoria had been wrong, *terribly* wrong, and she felt a sense of shame.

The next missile missed the second tank but not by much. And the near miss blew a storage shed to smithereens. The tank commander was firing by then, and Victoria saw a flash as one of the 105mm shells hit the destroyer's bow, but it wasn't enough. *Two* missiles fell on the Abrams in quick succession, all but obliterating the sixty-ton machine.

Most of Victoria's offensive capability had been destroyed—and she felt her stomach flip-flop as she shouted into the mike. "Get in close! They won't be able to put missiles on us there . . . See the ladders? We'll do this the hard way."

Gatlin was driving around the road that circled the facility. Tires screeched as the DPV entered a controlled skid. Then he jerked the wheel to the right and launched the patrol vehicle up and over the dune that lay between the facility and the beach. The DPV took to the air, landed hard, and threw sand as Gatlin stood on the brake.

Victoria hit the harness release as the second dune buggy stopped next to them. "Everybody out!" she ordered. "Follow me!"

Geysers of sand jumped up all around Victoria and Gatlin as they ran, and the men on the destroyer's main deck fired down on them. But in spite of Victoria's order, Poston had chosen to stay behind. He brought the vehicle's pintle-mounted 7.62mm machine gun to bear on the men at the railing and fired a long, sweeping burst. Zapatas fell like tenpins. And that gave Victoria and Gatlin the opportunity to reach the extension ladders that stood against the ship.

*More* defenders appeared as the threesome began to climb, but the newly arrived Zapatas were forced back, as Poston continued to fire. Victoria felt the ladder tremble under her boots and paused to lob a grenade up onto the deck above. She heard a loud bang, followed by a scream.

Gatlin had made it to the top of his ladder by then, and when Victoria glanced over at him, she saw the bloody bandage on his left hand. He'd been wounded, and she'd forgotten. But there was no time for guilt as he fired his pistol one-handed, and a Zapata fell back out of sight. Then Victoria was up and over, with Tarvin right on her heels as both women arrived on the bloody deck. Bodies lay everywhere . . . And when one of them moved, Victoria put three bullets into it.

Gatlin was ahead of them at that point, having climbed a ladder closer to the bow. He kept his back to the superstructure as he made his way forward. Rather than step out into the open, he took a peek around the corner. "The turret is all buttoned up," he announced over the radio.

"Then let's open it up," Poston said, as he arrived. "This should do the trick."

Victoria saw that he was carrying a satchel charge. She watched him set the timer, step up, and sling the pack around the corner. Would the explosion destroy the turret? Or destroy the turret *and* the ordnance stored below? If so, that would kill them all.

There were two seconds of silence followed by an explosion so powerful that it shook the entire ship and nearly knocked them down. But there were no secondary explosions. And, after congratulating herself on being alive, Victoria went forward, ready to fire. There weren't any targets. The Kashtan turret was little more than a smoking lump of twisted metal. "She-it," Gatlin said happily. "That was sweet."

"This is Snake-Six actual," Victoria said into her radio. "We need a medic on the ship—and I mean *now.*"

Gatlin looked at the bloody ball of gauze as if seeing it for the first time. He frowned. "The bastards blew my fuck-you finger off . . . It's down in the DPV. God damn it, what'll I do now?"

It wasn't funny, not really, but all of them laughed. And they were still laughing when a perplexed medic came up over the rail. It was only later, after the site was secured, that Victoria allowed herself to think about the dead tankers. She felt the need to cry but didn't . . . "Good soldiers never cry." That's what her father told her the day she fell off her bike . . . And there hadn't been any tears since.

SOUTHEAST TEXAS

More than two months had passed since the disastrous escape attempt. The first two weeks had been spent trying to recover from the severe beating that Sloan had received. The doctor who was brought in confirmed that Sloan was suffering from a concussion and had to put in seventy-two stitches to close all of his cuts.

Sloan had been restricted to his cabin during his convalescence. Now, with cuffs on his wrists and chains on his ankles, Sloan was allowed to make ten circuits around the deck each day. Molly led the way, and Lucy brought up the rear, with her Taser at the ready.

Yes, he might be able to vault over the rail, but what then? It would be impossible to swim without the use of his hands and feet. Plus the *Belle Marie*'s cook had orders to dump the galley slops over the side, a practice guaranteed to keep a cadre of alligators close by.

So each day was nearly identical to the last. Get up. Shave. Eat. Exercise. Eat. Listen to the radio. Eat again. Read the newspapers and go to bed. On and on it went until Sloan settled into a never-ending state of depression.

As for *why* Sloan was being held, that remained a mystery, as were the fates of the other prisoners who came and went. Sloan rarely caught a glimpse of them but assumed that when the Huey arrived, it was bringing a person in or taking one out.

So when he heard the helicopter arrive on the morning of the sixty-fourth day of his captivity, Sloan assumed it was business as usual and saw no reason to interrupt his push-ups. He was halfway through a set of thirty squats when the hatch opened. But, rather than Molly and Lucy, two men entered the cabin. Sloan recognized Flattop and Short Guy right away. Both were armed. "Grab a jumpsuit," Flattop ordered, "and put it on. You're going for a ride."

Sloan felt a stab of fear. Did that mean he was going for a gangster-style ride? Or a *real* ride? The kind where you're alive at the other end.

It took a couple of minutes to put on a fresh jumpsuit and a pair of sneakers. "Hold your hands out," Flattop instructed. There was a click as the cuffs closed.

"You know the drill," Short Guy said. "Do what you're told, or we'll stomp you. Do you have any questions?"

"No."

"Good. I'll lead the way." Sloan had no choice but to follow Short Guy out of the cabin, down to the main deck, and over to the helicopter pad. Shortly after the passengers climbed aboard the Huey, its rotors began to turn, and the chopper took off. It skimmed the treetops for a while and gradually gained altitude. That was when Sloan allowed himself to relax a little. He hoped that the Huey was taking him somewhere to meet with someone. That would be a whole lot better than a bullet in the back of the head.

Time dragged. But eventually Sloan saw farms through the side doors, soon followed by towns and sprawling suburbs. And then, as the helicopter turned, Sloan caught a glimpse of what he recognized as downtown Houston! And there, off to the right, was the skyscraper called Huxton Tower. His duties as Secretary of Energy had brought him to Houston on a frequent basis, and the building was a very visible element of the skyline. It seemed to grow as the chopper closed in on it. Then the high-rise was below them as the Huey settled onto the roof. *Finally*, Sloan thought to himself. *This will be interesting*.

The rotors slowed and came to a stop as Sloan was ordered to get out. A short walk took them over to a cube-shaped structure, where Short Guy led the way into a beautifully furnished lounge. There were two elevator doors, and Short Guy pushed the DOWN button. Thirty seconds passed before the lift arrived, and Flattop gave him a nudge. Sloan took the hint.

The doors closed, and Sloan watched a blunt finger push the button labeled 72. They arrived on the seventy-second floor seconds later. The doors opened onto a tastefully furnished lobby, and as Sloan stepped off, he could see the wide-eyed look on the receptionist's face. Sloan thought that was odd until he remembered that he was wearing handcuffs and an orange jumpsuit! Not something she saw every day.

The receptionist continued to stare at him as she reached for the phone. Sloan couldn't hear what was said—but the conversation was short. "Take him in," the woman said, and Sloan was led to a huge door that was embellished with a hand-carved H.

It opened into a large office. Four people were seated at a conference table made out of some exotic hardwood. Sloan could see an executive-style desk, windows, and the cityscape beyond the glass. All of those present turned to look his way, but only one of them rose to greet him. Matt Rankin had a high forehead and partially hooded eyes. "Hello, Sam . . . I'm glad you made it back from Mexico." Rankin turned to the security men. "Remove the cuffs and wait outside."

Sloan had met Rankin before and knew him to be Huxton Oil's CFO. So what the hell was going on? The cuffs were removed, and the security men left. "Come over to the table," Rankin said. "I'll make the introductions. Let's start with my boss, Fred Huxton."

Sloan had seen Huxton's picture on the cover of *Time* magazine but never met the tycoon face-to-face. He knew that the legendary oilman had taken the small drilling company left to him by his parents and turned it into a global brand. The oil baron had thinning hair and implacable eyes. A walrus-style mustache hid most of his mouth. He made no attempt to rise or to extend a hand. "Welcome to Houston, Mr. Sloan . . . Or should I say, 'Mr. President'?"

Sloan frowned. "'*Mr. President*'? What do you mean?"

Huxton laughed. "Well, I'll be damned . . . He doesn't know! The Yankee bastard is President of the United States, and he doesn't know!"

Rankin cleared his throat. "I guess you haven't heard . . . President Wainwright had a heart attack and died yesterday afternoon. And *you*, believe it or not, are the next person in line for the presidency."

Sloan struggled to assimilate it. Wainwright dead . . . Still another blow to the struggling nation. He was still processing what the president's death meant when a *third* man came around the table to shake hands. "I'm Morton Lemaire . . . I don't believe we've met."

As Sloan shook Lemaire's hand, he realized that he was talking to the governor of Florida. "I heard you paddled three hundred miles to get home from Mexico," Lemaire said. "That took balls."

Then the only woman in the room rose to greet him. "Yes," she said, "it did. I'm Maria Perez." She had black hair, brown eyes, and a firm handshake. Sloan was so dazed that it took him a moment to remember that Perez was the governor of Texas.

"It's a pleasure to meet you," Sloan said. That wasn't true, of course, since Perez had been very critical of the president's energy policies. Especially those related to carbon emissions. Maybe he could convince her to . . . Then Sloan remembered. The president was dead, and carbon emissions were the least of his worries.

"Please," Perez said as she gestured to an empty chair. "Have a seat."

Sloan sat next to Rankin. His thoughts whirled as his brain struggled to assimilate the information he'd been given—and apply it to the situation that he found himself in. He was still attempting to sort things out when Rankin spoke. "I'm sorry, Sam . . . Please allow me to explain . . . After we lost the president, Congress, and what's estimated to be 30 million people, everything ground to a halt.

"And don't forget . . . The Pentagon was destroyed as well . . . So even though some senior officers survived, they were scattered around the country and lacked a central command structure. That led to disagreements. And while they squabbled, bases like Fort Bragg in North Carolina, Pendleton in California, and JBLM in Washington State were overrun by heavily armed gangs.

"Meanwhile, Vice President Wainwright was sworn in as

president. And within a matter of days, she began to put forth reconstruction plans that would not only bankrupt the nation but override state's rights and restrict personal freedoms."

"She wanted to implement gun-control laws," Huxton put in. "She claimed it was a way to combat lawlessness, but that's ridiculous. You've read the papers; you know what's going on. If citizens don't defend themselves, no one will."

Sloan *had* read the papers and now he knew why he'd been allowed to do so. Huxton and his cronies had been well aware of the fact that he was next in line for the presidency, and had been keeping him on a shelf in case he might come in handy! And in the wake of President Wainwright's death, they were dusting him off. Not only that, but according to what he'd read, Huxton was correct. For the moment anyway. There was a lot of lawlessness, and millions of people were on their own. So Wainwright's push for gun control had been premature.

"So," Huxton continued, "that's why *we*, which is to say a group of about thirty people in and out of government, have been trying to assemble a substitute government here in the South. One that is better equipped to deal with things the way they really are. But before we pull the trigger on that effort, we thought it would be a good idea to have a chat with you. Now, I reckon you're pissed . . . And I get that. I would be, too. But, if you can put the anger aside, you'll see that there's an opportunity here. An opportunity to lead the nation back to greatness. But we need the right man."

"That's right," Governor Perez said. "No offense, Mr. Sloan, but the people haven't had a chance to vote for you. So, even though you inherited the presidency—you may or may not be the right man for the job."

There it was. A clear declaration of intent. The people seated at the table were going to vet him. Never mind the fact that they had no legal right to do so. And if they didn't like what he said? No problem. They were the only people who knew that he was alive. "I see," Sloan replied. "So tell me about 'the right man.' What would he be like?"

"That's a good question," Huxton replied. "The right man would take a look around and realize that while the highly centralized federal government crumbled, the corporate infrastructure survived. *Why?* Because it was more self-sufficient, widely dispersed, and better met the needs of the people. And the right man would not only take inspiration from that—he'd build a *new* government based on the principles of personal initiative and responsibility. Or, put another way, he would create a new order for a new reality."

The last phrase would have been perfect on a bumper sticker— and Sloan got the feeling that the planning Rankin had referenced was pretty far along. "I think you'll agree that the devil is in the details," Sloan temporized. "How would the new government work?"

"Shareowners would own the country," Huxton replied. "And each shareowner would express his or her wishes by voting the number of shares they happen to own."

"Everyone would receive a hundred shares off the top," Rankin explained, "and could sell them, or buy more in a free market."

Sloan looked from face to face. "Does that include corporations?"

"Of course it does," Perez answered. "Corporations are people . . . The Supreme Court made that clear."

"I see," Sloan said. "Aren't you afraid that corporations, and the oligarchs who own them, will seize control of the new order by acquiring millions of shares?"

Huxton shrugged. "The free market will rule . . . Everyone who chooses to participate will receive annual dividends they can spend on the services they believe are most important. And by voting their shares in blocks, lesser shareowners can still have a significant impact on what happens."

Sloan felt a rising sense of anger. Not only was the plan illegal . . . The conspirators were planning to seize control of the country for their own benefit! "So the right man will serve as a front for the new order?" he demanded. "A democratic face for the largest power grab in history?"

Huxton made a snorting sound as his eyes swung around. "It's just like I told you . . . Sloan is one of *them*. We're wasting our time."

"Is that right?" Rankin demanded. "Are we wasting our time?"

Sloan paused to consider it. Maybe they were correct . . . Maybe some sort of structure was better than none. And, if he was part of the new order, he could work to change it from the inside. But his inner voice refused to go along. *What a load of crap! They won't listen to you . . . They'll tell you what to say—and you'll be forced to say it.*

Sloan knew the voice was correct—and knew what had to be said. "Yes, you're wasting your time. If I'm the president, then it's my duty to preserve, protect, and defend the Constitution of the United States. And by that I mean the one written in 1787, not a *new* constitution intended to further the interests of the wealthy."

Lemaire broke the ensuing silence. "You're one stupid son of a bitch," he said contemptuously.

Sloan heard a noise and turned to see the security men enter the room. How they had been summoned wasn't clear. "Put Mr. Sloan on the chopper," Huxton ordered, "and take him back to the *Belle Marie*. We'll figure out what to do with him later."

The words had an ominous quality, and Sloan rose from his chair. "Don't bother," Flattop said. "Unless you want to feel a lot of pain."

"Extend your wrists," Short Guy instructed, and Sloan had no choice but to obey. The cuffs felt cold as they came into contact with his flesh. It would have been a good time to say something cool, but the best he could do was try to keep the fear from showing and resist the temptation to beg. Sloan heard one of the conspirators laugh as he was led away.

Once they were out in the reception area, Sloan was forced to board the same elevator he'd ridden before. And by the time they reached the roof, the Huey was ready to depart.

The helicopter took off, banked away from the skyscraper, and flew east. All Sloan could do was let the slipstream buffet his face as the ground sped by below. The landscape was dry at first. But that began to change roughly twenty minutes later as the aircraft flew over part of the Piney Woods that covered most of east Texas. Eventually, the trees surrendered to the streams, rivers, and bayous that bordered the state of Louisiana. That was when the aircraft began to lose altitude and continued to do so until it was flying just above the treetops. Channels passed by below, as did stagnant ponds and small lakes.

Where was the *Belle Marie*? Five or ten minutes ahead? Yes, and once aboard, Sloan knew he would never have a chance to escape.

Short Guy hit the release on his seat belt and stood. The reason for that wasn't clear, but it gave Sloan an idea. What happened next was more the result of an impulse than careful planning. Short Guy was framed in the door as Sloan hit his release and charged forward. The maneuver wouldn't have been possible with Flattop. He was too tall. But Short Guy was short . . . And that made it possible for Sloan to bring his handcuffed hands down over the security officer's head. Then, with Shorty trapped in his arms, Sloan threw himself out through the open door.

A multitude of thoughts flashed through his mind. *Hang on to him! He has the key to the cuffs! Pray for water . . . I don't have time to pray . . .* Then they hit, and hit hard. The force of the fall drove both men deep under the surface of the water.

Sloan's eyes were open, but the swamp water was so thick with vegetable matter that he couldn't see. Short Guy was struggling by then, and no wonder . . . While Sloan had known what was coming and taken a deep breath, the other man hadn't. That's why he was flailing around.

Of course, Sloan needed air, too . . . How long could he hold out? Long enough to kill the security officer? Sloan pulled the handcuffs tight under Shorty's chin and pulled back. A sharp elbow connected with Sloan's gut, and a large gulp of precious air was lost. A man was going to die. But which one?

# CHAPTER 5

||||||||||||||||||||||||||||||||

When in doubt, do something.

—HARRY CHAPIN

**SOUTH OF YAKIMA, WASHINGTON**

It was a cold, wintry day in August as the convoy rolled onto Highway 82 and the soldiers began the thousand-mile journey to Arizona. The Humvee was out on point, about half a mile forward of the other vehicles, and Garcia was behind the wheel. Mac sat next to him, with Sparks and Kho in the back.

Mac had no way to know what *they* were feeling—but her emotions were evenly divided between excitement and fear. On the one hand, it felt good to do something, *anything*, after such a long period of relative inactivity. The decision to leave Vagabond hadn't been made lightly.

After giving the matter a lot of thought, Mac had concluded that it didn't make sense to remain at the airfield while their supplies dwindled away to nothing. So she'd called a meeting. It was held in a hangar and, with the exception of those on guard duty, the entire unit was present. "Here's the deal," she told them. "Gangs are in charge of JBLM, we're still cut off, and the locals are likely to take another run at us pretty soon.

"Rather than sit here and wait for that to happen, I think we should go south where, according to what the ham radio operators have to say, the weather is a little warmer. Plus there's a pretty good chance that we'll be able to acquire additional supplies along the way.

"Will such a trip be easy? Hell no. Will we make it to Arizona? I think so . . . But there aren't any guarantees. Do you *have* to go? No. Anyone who would like to leave the unit and go their own way is free to do so. I will provide you with written orders that might or might not shield you from charges if you happen to encounter the *real* army somewhere.

"But be advised that the officer in command could charge you with desertion . . . And that goes for those who follow me—since we'll be acting without orders.

"Finally," Mac said, "I want to make it clear that if you remain with the unit, military discipline will continue to apply. Because without it, we will lose unit cohesion and the ability to fight effectively. And make no mistake, we *will* have to fight. Do you have any questions?"

There *were* questions. Lots of them. And when the three-hour session came to a close, four people decided to go looking for loved ones while the rest chose to stay. And they, plus a handful of dependents, like Dr. Hoskins's wife, were aboard the column of vehicles that was following the Humvee.

Mac's thoughts were interrupted as the Apache roared overhead. Peters and Omata were under orders to scout ahead—and provide air support if necessary. But only for short periods of time. Evans had been able to "requisition" three tankers . . . But only one of them was carrying JP8 for the helicopter. So the pilots had orders to conserve fuel by landing short of Kennewick, Washington, and the National Guard armory located there. Had it been looted? There was only one way to find out.

Meanwhile, the situation on Highway 82 was what Mac expected it to be. There wasn't a whole lot of car traffic. But motorcycles whizzed by from time to time, bicyclists weaved in and out between the wrecks, and heavily laden pedestrians were a common sight. A man on a John Deere lawn mower passed them half an hour into the journey. He waved, and Mac waved back. Most people were less friendly. They needed help and weren't getting any.

Columns of gray smoke wafted up from modest homes to merge with low-hanging clouds as they passed the town of Union Gap. The smoke was a sure sign that the power was out, and the locals were burning wood to stay warm.

But that wasn't all . . . Many houses had been fortified, or were in the process of being fortified, which suggested that crime was on the rise.

What would society be like in six months? Mac wondered. And how would her unit survive? "Flyby-One to Archer-Six," Peters said. "Over."

"This is Six," Mac replied. "Go. Over."

"We just flew over Sunnyside. The highway is clear for the most part although there are a lot of wrecks, and an IED could be hidden in any one of them. Over."

"Roger that Flyby . . . Anything else? Over."

"There's one thing," Peters replied. "A lot of pedestrians are walking south on 82 . . . And more people join them at each ramp. Oh, and most are wearing white."

Mac thought about that before pressing the TRANSMIT button. "How many constitutes 'a lot'? Over."

"Hundreds," Peters answered. "Maybe a thousand in all. Over."

"Keep me informed," Mac said. "Over."

Peters delivered a double click by way of a reply.

It wasn't long before Mac began to see the people Peters had mentioned. That was when she realized that they'd been there all along, hiking down the highway in small groups and wearing white. Not from head to toe . . . But by way of a headband, a scarf, or a waist sash. And most of them were armed.

So what *was* she looking at? A pilgrimage of some sort? And did it represent a threat? The obvious answer was "yes," as more people poured onto 82, and the Humvee became an island in a river of humanity. "What do you think?" Kho demanded. "Should I go upstairs and get on the fifty?"

"No," Mac replied. "Not yet anyway. We'll go with the flow for the moment."

Mac examined her map. The Columbia River ran east to west up ahead. If they stayed on the freeway, they could cross it south of Kennewick near Umatilla, Oregon. But where were the pilgrims headed? The city of Kennewick seemed like the most likely answer, but it was never a good idea to assume anything.

Mac turned to Kho. "When I tell Garcia to stop, I want you to get out and gather some intel. Chat with some pilgrims. Find out where they're headed and why. Go with her, Sparks . . . And stay within a hundred feet of the Humvee."

Both of them nodded, and Kho said, "Yes, ma'am."

Mac ordered Garcia to stop so the soldiers could get out. Then she went topside where she could keep an eye on them and fire the fifty should it come to that. Fortunately, it didn't. The soldiers returned ten minutes later, and Mac left the gunner's position to hear Kho's report. "They belong to what sounds like a cult," the observer reported. "A woman called the Lady of Light is in charge and gets her orders from a group of so-called space masters.

"It seems that although most of the Hanford nuclear facility is shut down, the part that's still operational came under the cult's control two weeks ago. The people we spoke to believe that once the space masters bring all of Hanford's reactors back online, a new civilization will be born."

Mac looked from Kho to Munroe and back again. "You're shitting me."

"No, ma'am," Kho replied. "These people are serious."

It would be foolish to follow the pilgrims into Kennewick. Mac realized that now. She looked at the map. There weren't that many bridges across the Columbia. The nearest alternative was a hundred miles west at a town called Maryhill. The detour would cost the unit time and fuel. But it was either that or try to bullshit her way past thousands of cult members. The choice was no choice at all. She turned to Munroe. "Put out the word. We're going to turn off the freeway onto 221 south. The exit is about five miles ahead. And," Mac added, "tell everyone to pay close attention to what's going on. These people are batshit crazy."

## PENDLETON, OREGON

Master Sergeant Rollo Smith peered out through a shattered window. He could see his breath, and snowflakes fell out of the gunmetal-gray sky as he stared north. National Guard headquarters, Pendleton, Oregon, was located adjacent to the city's tiny airport. And that made sense since the unit had three Chinook helicopters and some UAVs.

*No,* Smith told himself, *that isn't accurate. We had three Chinooks . . . Back before the takers towed one of them away and forced us to destroy the others.* When was that anyway? Three days ago? Time didn't have much meaning anymore. The only things that mattered were pride and duty. No pack of civilian assholes was going to steal the unit's supplies! Not so long as Smith was vertical. And not while he had orders to hold the base.

*Where's Major Elkins?* Smith wondered. The answer was obvious. Five days after the meteorites struck, Elkins and the rest of the unit had been dispatched to deal with civil unrest in Portland. They hadn't been heard from since. That meant they were . . . *No!* Smith told himself. *Don't think it. You're tired, that's all.* And that was true.

The takers had attacked twice during the night—but his force of nine men and women had managed to hold them off. *Again.* The bastards didn't like to attack during the day, and there was a good reason for that. The machine guns on the roof could cover every inch of the surrounding ground. As for darkness, well, the bad guys liked that better. But not a *lot* better because of the night-vision gear that Smith's people had. *They're wearing us down, though,* Smith thought to himself. *From thirteen to nine. It's just a matter of time.*

"Breakfast is served," a voice said, and Smith turned to discover that Private Anne Renke was standing behind him. She handed him an MRE. "It's your favorite," she added. "Beef brisket." Smith knew that she'd gone digging for it, or arranged for a trade. Not to suck up, but to make him feel better. Something she did for everyone.

"Thanks," Smith said as he sat on an ammo crate. "How's it going? Are you okay?"

"I could use a shower," Renke answered. "But so could you."

Smith laughed. And that was Renke's talent, since she was a piss-poor shot and didn't have any tech skills to speak of. The Guard was a part-time job for her . . . A way to make money for college. Now she was in the shit, and holding up damned well, all things considered. "Go take a nap, Private. They'll be back."

"Sure thing, Sarge," Renke said, and turned away. An empty casing rattled away from a boot as she entered the hall.

Smith waited until Renke was gone to put the MRE on the floor and lean against the wall. He closed his eyes. *The Alamo,* Smith thought to himself. *We're in the fucking Alamo. And that's where John Wayne died.* Then he fell asleep.

## MARYHILL, WASHINGTON

According to Kho, who'd been there before, the tiny town of Mary-hill, Washington, was named for the wife and daughter of a wealthy businessman named Sam Hill. And after following the north bank of the Columbia River west, the column was going to cross the Sam Hill Memorial Bridge and enter Biggs Junction on the other side.

Mac knew that the old bridge was clear because Esco said it was. But as the column paused to take a bio break, she eyed the other side of the river through a pair of binoculars. There were no signs of trouble. The trip down Highway 221 to 14 had been un-eventful. And although hundreds of pilgrims had passed the convoy going east, while the soldiers went west, there weren't enough fa-natics to represent a threat. And even now, there was a one-way stream of white-clad travelers coming her way across the bridge.

Mac lowered her glasses. They were about a hundred miles from Pendleton, Oregon. They'd been forced to bypass Kennewick, and the armory there, but what about Pendleton? Could they get sup-plies there? Mac felt a surge of impatience as she turned to Munroe. "Pass the word . . . The break's over. Let's cross the bridge."

## PENDLETON, OREGON

The clouds were the color of an old bruise as Smith brought a pair of binoculars up to his eyes. A bitter wind was chasing pieces of trash across the airfield, but there were no other signs of movement. And despite Smith's expectations to the contrary, there hadn't been any attacks during the night. *Why?* Had the takers given up? Smith *wanted* to believe that but didn't. No, he decided, the person or people in charge of the gang were getting ready to try something new. The possibility frightened him. They knew how many people he had, or *didn't* have, and how each one of them was deployed. That's why Smith figured the bastards were going to throw something different his way. Something calculated to take advantage of the unit's weaknesses. Of which there were plenty. "Oh, shit," Corporal Cassidy said over the radio. "Look north . . . What *is* that?"

Smith swung his glasses to the right and saw a Greyhound bus emerge from behind a hangar. Sheets of metal had been fastened to the boxy vehicle.

"I see a semi," Renke added, "coming in from the west. Over."

"And a school bus is headed our way," Haskins added.

Smith's suspicions had been confirmed, but the noncom took no pleasure in being right. The makeshift armored vehicles were meant to divide the defenders' fire, bulldoze their way through the base's defensive wall, and deliver a shitload of men into the compound. And when that happened, his soldiers would die.

"Okay," Smith said. "They plan to divide our fire and get in close. But we have an app for that. Let's feed those bastards some rockets. Then, if any of them close in, man the fifties. Over."

"Got it, Sarge," Cassidy said. "I'm gonna kill me a bus."

Smith felt a sudden surge of confidence. Maybe, if enough rockets hit the targets . . .

"Uh-oh," Private Weller said. "*More* assholes are coming out to play."

Weller was correct. A dozen fast-moving cars, pickups, and SUVs had appeared on the airfield and were darting back and forth to distract the soldiers and divide their fire even more. "Ignore them," Smith instructed. "Go for the big boys."

Cassidy was standing behind a waist-high wall of sandbags off to Smith's right. He had an AT4 on his shoulder and was aiming at the Greyhound. There was a flash of light followed by a loud report as the 84mm rocket flew downrange. Smith saw an orange-red explosion as the HEAT round hit the front of the bus and produced a loud boom. The behemoth coasted to a stop. Smith waited to see if passengers would exit, and none did. The takers knew how vulnerable they'd be out in the open.

"Give them a second helping," Smith said, as he turned to survey the airfield. He felt a sense of panic. Things were happening quickly, he was losing control, and he didn't know how to reacquire it. Smith swore as a rocket missed the semi and sailed off into the distance. "Shit, shit, shit!"

Renke spoke in his ear. "Aircraft inbound at two o'clock. Over."

Smith turned to look. What the hell? Did the takers have a plane? Were they going to drop a barrel bomb on the building? Once the glasses came to bear, Smith realized that he was looking at an Apache gunship! What felt like liquid lead filled the pit of his stomach. If the bastards had an attack ship, the whole unit was SOL. "I have radio contact," Private Tubin announced. "I'm patching the pilot through."

"Flyby-One to ground unit, Pendleton," a male voice said, as the Apache passed overhead. "Give me a sitrep. Over."

Smith felt a sudden sense of hope! "This is Master Sergeant Rollo Smith, Detachment 1, Company B, Forty-first Special Troops

Battalion. We're under attack by a criminal gang that's trying to capture our weapons. Over."

"Roger that," the voice said, as the helicopter circled the airport. "What's the army motto?"

Smith swallowed. It was a test . . . To make sure that he was the real deal. "This we will defend."

"What animal does West Point use as a mascot?"

"A mule."

"What does FUBAR mean?"

"Fucked-up beyond all recognition."

"Thanks, Sergeant . . . Keep your head down. Your people did a nice job. We'll tidy up. Over."

A reedy cheer went up from the beleaguered building as the Apache went to work. A Hellfire missile struck the school bus and blew it to yellow smithereens. Then the machine's copilot went to work with the helo's minigun. Geysers of asphalt and soil chased the smaller vehicles across the field and overran a black SUV, which disappeared in a bright orange explosion. The surviving vehicles fled in a desperate effort to escape the killing zone. Only one of them made it. The battle was over.

After circling the airfield a couple of times, the Apache came in for a landing next to the carcass of a burned-out Chinook. Smith was there to greet the copilot as she dropped to the ground. The rotors continued to turn, so she had to shout. "My name's Omata . . . Warrant Officer Peters is going to remain at the controls in case the bad guys counterattack."

"It's a pleasure to meet you, ma'am," Smith said. "You saved our butts. Thank you. How big is the relief force?"

"There is no relief force," Omata told him. "We're attached to Archer Company, First Battalion, Second Stryker Brigade. Our outfit was cut off after the meteor strikes. The company's CO is a first lieutenant named Macintyre. She'd like to bring the company here and lager up for the night. Would that be okay?"

"*Okay?* That would be wonderful," Smith said. "Strykers . . . I like the sound of that. The bastards won't mess with us tonight."

Omata smiled. "No, Sergeant, they won't."

Smith removed a glove and extended a big paw. Omata's hand disappeared. "Welcome to Pendleton, ma'am . . . I have some scotch stashed away—and the drinks will be on me."

|||||||||||||

Archer Company took some sniper fire as it entered Pendleton. But there weren't any casualties, for which Mac was grateful.

As a consequence of being cooped up inside the Stryker, Mac didn't get to see anything until the column arrived and one-two came to a stop. Once the ramp was down, Mac made her way out and onto the tarmac. She was inspecting the burned-out helicopter as two people came forward to greet her. "This is Sergeant Smith," Omata said. "Sergeant Smith, this is Lieutenant Macintyre."

They shook hands, and Mac liked what she saw. Even though Smith hadn't shaved in days and was filthy to boot, his military bearing was intact. He had beady brown eyes, a hatchet-shaped nose, and a pugnacious jaw. "It's a pleasure," Mac said. "I'd put you and every member of your unit in for a medal if I could."

"Thanks," Smith replied. "But based on what Warrant Officer Omata tells me, we're cut off."

"That's what I thought at first," Mac told him. "But 'cut off' implies that a command structure still exists. And I'm not sure that it does."

"Let's go inside," Smith suggested. "It's warmer there."

"That sounds good," Mac replied. "But I want the tour first . . . And I'd like to meet your people."

"Yes, ma'am," Smith said. "Follow me."

After touring the area, and pausing to chat with each one of Smith's soldiers, Mac allowed herself to be steered inside. By the time they sat down in Major Elkins's office, she had a pretty good idea of how the weeklong battle had been fought. The lights flickered every now and then. "So," Mac said, "thanks for the hospitality."

Smith shrugged. "You're welcome, ma'am. But you're army, we're army, so what's ours is yours. Especially since you're the ranking officer here."

"That's true," Mac said. "Sort of. But I can't assume anything. Not the way things are."

Smith stared at her. "You want our supplies. And you came here to get them."

Mac nodded. "We did."

"But you aren't going to take them?"

Mac smiled thinly. "I hope you'll give them to me."

Smith frowned. "Tell me something, Lieutenant . . . Let's say that I give you everything there is to give . . . What will you do with it? And more importantly, what will you do with my people?"

"We're headed south, Sergeant . . . To Arizona, where if the ham-radio reports are correct, the weather is a tad better. That's the first objective. Then, once we find a place to hole up, we'll try to survive."

"For what purpose?" Smith demanded. "To wait for orders that may not come? And, if they do come, might instruct you to do something stupid?"

Mac had been thinking about that. And now, for the first time, she put her thoughts into words. "That's a good question . . . I don't think it should be up to me alone. Each person should have a vote even if that isn't very military.

"That said, I think we have to adapt if we're going to survive. All of us have seen what the gangs can do. And they're just getting started. Once the easy pickings are gone—how long before they take control of towns? And battle each other for turf?"

"Not long," Evans said darkly. "It may have begun. Who knows what's going on in Kennewick."

"Exactly," Mac agreed. "And in the absence of law enforcement, there will be a need for soldiers who can defend the people who can't defend themselves. But, in order to do that, we'll have to charge for our services. Otherwise, our vehicles will run out of fuel—and our troops will starve."

Smith frowned. "*Mercenaries?* How is that different from becoming a gang?"

"Yes," Mac replied. "I guess the word 'mercenary' would apply. But my notion is this . . . Rather than operate the unit as a business—we would run it as a self-sustaining nonprofit. The mission would be to keep our soldiers alive, feed their families, and help other people to the extent that we can."

"You've been thinking about this," Smith put in.

Mac shrugged. "For a few weeks."

"You're serious about the vote? And the mission?"

"Absolutely. Although it needs to be understood that army-style military discipline will prevail. A democracy won't work. So once a person joins, they will be expected to serve out the length of their contract."

"I'm in," Smith said, "assuming you want me. My wife passed away sixteen months ago, my son is stationed in Germany, assuming he's alive, and the weather sucks. Arizona sounds good."

"I want you," Mac said. "More than that, we *need* you."

"Thanks," Smith said. "One last thing . . . I outrank Evans here, but I don't want the number two slot. I'm a supply sergeant by trade . . . And correct me if I'm wrong, but you're going to need supplies, plus some son of a bitch to keep track of them."

Mac laughed. "I do, Sergeant. The job is yours."

"Good," Smith said. "A lot of our stuff went west with the major. And we had to expend some ammo fighting the takers. But I've still got quite a stash. Not to mention plenty of JP8 for your Apache."

"That's good news," Mac said. "*Very* good news since we've been burning through what we had. Let's set up a meeting with the people who are off duty—and a second one for later on. Some or all of your people may elect to stay here."

The meetings took place over a period of twenty-four hours and went the way Mac expected them to. All of those who had decided to stay with the company understood the need to become what Mac called "nonprofit mercenaries" and voted for it. And although none of Smith's soldiers objected to the concept, three of them expressed a desire to stay with family members in Pendleton.

Mac understood that and authorized Smith not only to let them retain their personal weapons but to give them a supply of ammo in lieu of severance pay. She also gave each soldier a letter explaining the decision she'd made, and taking full responsibility for it, even though it seemed unlikely that the "real" army was going to show up in Pendleton anytime soon.

There was a party to see them off, and to welcome twelve family members who were going to accompany their soldiers to Arizona. Even though the company already included a few civilians, Mac hadn't given the issue of dependents much thought until then. And the fact that she had eighteen more mouths to feed put a lot of additional pressure on her. It couldn't be helped though . . . Not if her troops were to enjoy normal lives in Arizona. And, truth be told, Mac knew that soldiers with families to defend would fight that much harder.

Some of the civilians joining them had useful skills. The group included a nurse, an auto mechanic, and an elementary school teacher. And with school-age children to care for, her skills would become increasingly important.

The civilians wanted to bring truckloads of belongings, not to mention their personal vehicles, and Mac couldn't allow that because each additional car or truck would require fuel and maintenance.

And there was another issue to confront as well . . . As the column grew longer, it would be increasingly hard to defend. So Mac was grateful when Smith issued a detailed list of what people could bring, forced them to package their belongings in shipping crates, and put all of their personal belongings on a moving van. Problem solved, for the moment at least.

Meanwhile, there were military stores to deal with, including a considerable quantity of weapons, ammo, and fuel. All of which were welcome. Once the company's tankers were full, Mac sent the Apache out to find more fuelers. And when the pilots located them, Evans took two squads of soldiers out to "requisition" the additional trucks from a local oil company.

Mac felt guilty about that but had no way to pay for them. Not yet. Later, once the unit had some money or the equivalent thereof, she planned to buy vehicles rather than steal them.

Two days later, Mac was going over a list of to-dos when there was a knock on the door. She was sitting at Elkins's desk and turned to see that Master Sergeant Smith and Staff Sergeant Esco were standing just inside the doorway. "Come in," she told them. "Take a load off. Esco's wearing a big smile. What's up?"

"*Drones,*" Esco replied. "Sergeant Smith has *four* of them! Two Ravens and two Shadows. They're still in crates, but once we put them together, we'll be able to use them for scouting missions. And that will save a lot of JP8."

Mac knew that Tier I UAVs like the hand-launched Raven had a range of six miles and could stay aloft for sixty to ninety minutes.

Tier II UAVs, such as the Shadow, could go farther and stay up longer. And Esco was correct. Although the Apache *could* scout ahead, it would not only burn a whole lot of fuel but announce their presence. There was a potential problem, however—and Mac addressed the question to Smith. "If I'm not mistaken, the Shadows would require a launcher . . . Do we have one?"

Smith grinned. "You're pretty smart for an officer. Yes, ma'am, we have one. It's mounted on a trailer. We'll haul it behind the Humvee. That'll add to the length of the column, but it'll be worth it."

"I agree," Mac said. "Let's assemble one of each. Have we got the necessary know-how?"

"The Raven will be easy," Esco predicted. "They come in a couple of cases—and I could probably do it by myself. As for the Shadows, I've flown them but never been required to assemble one. The Apache's ground crew said they'd be willing to pitch in, though—and we have the necessary manuals."

"How long will it take?"

"Two days," Smith replied. "Assembly's only half of it. We've got to test the drones and train up."

Mac felt a rising sense of frustration. She wanted to get on the road as soon as possible but knew how valuable the UAVs would be. "Okay, go for it. But two days max . . . We need to amscray before something big and ugly comes this way."

"Yes, ma'am," Esco said as he stood. "We'll be ready."

The sergeants left Mac to stare at the opposite wall. A picture of the president was mounted there. He looked confident as he stared into the camera. *One nation under God,* Mac thought to herself. *Not anymore.*

# CHAPTER 6

||||||||||||||||||||||||||||||||||||

The American people abhor a vacuum.

—THEODORE ROOSEVELT

**SOUTHEAST TEXAS**

Swamp water churned, and arms thrashed as the men fought. Sloan's handcuffed hands were positioned in front of Short Guy's throat, and as he pulled them back, the connecting chain bit into the security officer's throat. *Die, son of a bitch, die!* Sloan thought to himself.

But Sloan's lungs were on fire . . . And as he began to lose consciousness, he had no choice but to give up and kick with his feet. Their heads broke the surface together. And, as Sloan struggled to suck air into his oxygen-starved lungs, he found himself in the powerful downdraft caused by the Huey's whirling rotors.

The downward pressure flattened the water around him but started to ease as the helicopter drifted sideways. That was when Flattop appeared in the open doorway above. Geysers of water jumped up in front of Sloan as the man opened fire. Sloan felt Short

Guy jerk as a 9mm round struck his body. Holy shit! Flattop didn't care who he hit.

Sloan tried to take Short Guy with him as he ducked below the surface. It didn't work. All Sloan could do was slide in under the other man and use the security officer's body as a shield while he kicked his feet and struggled to breathe. Fortunately, they were close to shore, which meant Sloan was able to tow Short Guy in under the thick foliage that hung out over the water.

The chopper vanished from sight as Sloan felt mud under his shoes and attempted to stand. But that wasn't possible without lifting his arms up off Short Guy first. Once on his feet, Sloan saw that the other man's face was blue. Had he been dead *before* Flattop shot him? That's the way it looked because the bullet hole was in Short Guy's left shoulder. Sloan looked up through a tangle of branches as the helicopter passed overhead. Then it was gone. Would Godbee send people to find him? Hell yes, he would.

After securing a firm grip on Short Guy's collar, Sloan dragged the dead man up onto the muddy bank. His hands shook as he searched the security officer's pockets. The key, he needed the key, and was thrilled to find it in a pants pocket.

It took three tries to get the key into the lock and turn it. Then, as the cuffs fell away, Sloan felt a profound sense of relief. He could use his hands freely now . . . And that felt wonderful.

Sloan set about the task of recovering everything else the corpse had to offer. That included Short Guy's Glock, an extra magazine, and a pocketknife. There was a wallet, too . . . With 118 bucks in it! Plus a photo of a little girl. She was smiling. Sloan swore. Short Guy was a father—and his daughter was never going to see him again.

That was the moment when Sloan realized he was a killer. Not a pathological killer, he assured himself, but a killer nonetheless.

He felt a terrible sense of guilt. But there was fear, too . . . Fear of being caught. And that was enough to get him moving.

It would have been nice to take the other man's clothes and rid himself of the jumpsuit, but there was no way that Short Guy's duds were going to fit. So Sloan pushed the body out into the water, where it soon sank below the surface.

Did the Huey pilot have an exact fix on the spot where the two of them hit the water? That seemed unlikely. So by getting rid of the body, Sloan hoped to make it that much more difficult for searchers to find the starting point.

*Think,* Sloan told himself, as he used a piece of driftwood to erase his footprints. *What should you do next?* The answer was obvious. Put a lot of distance between himself and the spot where he was standing. *But how?* He couldn't swim from place to place. Not without winding up inside an alligator. *I need a log,* Sloan concluded. *Anything that will keep me up out of the water.*

That realization began a search that took him halfway around what turned out to be an island. People had been using the swamp for a long time, so plenty of plastic bottles and chunks of styrofoam were washed up along the shoreline. But it wasn't until twenty minutes into the search that he located a section of what had been a dock. It consisted of three planks nailed to crosspieces. A raft!

But when Sloan pulled it down into the water, he soon discovered that the planks weren't enough to support his weight, which meant that they were partially submerged. Not only that, but his feet were hanging off one end and might look good to a hungry gator.

That couldn't be helped, however. Sloan had to get going and do so quickly. Darkness was still hours away—and Godbee would send boats to find him. Sloan chose the tallest tree on the far shore as his target and began to paddle. It was easy at first. But then, as the adrenaline started to fade, his arms began to tire. All Sloan could do was grit his teeth and keep on.

Eventually, the trees grew taller, details became clear, and the tall marsh grass took him in. As the bottom came up, Sloan stood, pushed the raft in farther, and made his way onto the shore. And not a moment too soon. Sloan *heard* the airboat before he saw it . . . He hurried to find a place to hide, remembered the footprints he'd left behind, and went back to smooth them over. He was barely out of sight when the propeller-driven boat appeared.

There were three men in the boat. One sat on a raised seat with the rudder stick in one hand and his foot on the gas. The others were up front, rifles at the ready. Water surged away from the squared-off bow as the driver cut power, and the riflemen used their scopes to search the shoreline.

All Sloan could do was hunker down and wait. According to Short Guy's Rolex, only ten minutes passed before the engine noise increased, and the airboat departed. But it seemed like an eternity. Sloan felt a sense of relief as he watched it go. But that emotion was short-lived. He needed to do something, but what?

It was tempting to choose a direction and start walking or wading. But that would consume valuable calories, and for what? Chances were that he'd find himself standing in a similar spot two hours later, and with darkness closing in.

No, Sloan decided, it made sense to stay where he was for the night. He'd been a Boy Scout. So he was familiar with the bow-and-drill method of starting a fire, and he knew how difficult the process could be, even in the backyard.

That's why he decided to build a debris shelter before tackling anything else. There were plenty of fallen branches to choose from, and while going out to gather them, Sloan discovered that he was on a narrow finger of land that jutted out into a lake.

After half an hour or so, Sloan had a large pile of construction materials. The next hour was spent turning them into a small but serviceable hut.

The light was starting to fade as he went to work on a fire. The raw materials had been set aside during the hut construction process— and included a green branch, a stick, fireboard, drill, and socket. With dry tinder at the ready, Sloan turned the branch into a bow by adding one of his shoelaces. The drill consisted of a stick, a concave rock that would serve as a socket, and a piece of dry driftwood for the fireboard.

A legion of mosquitoes began to feast on Sloan as he went to work. And when darkness fell, he was still working, with only a single wisp of smoke to show for his efforts. Eventually, after what might have been an hour, he gave up in disgust.

When it started to rain, Sloan left the hut to tilt his head back and drink as much as he could. Then it was time to go back inside and watch the lightning zigzag across the sky. It lit up the point the way a flashbulb would . . . But that was comforting in a way because it allowed him to see his surroundings for a moment.

As the thunder died away, Sloan was left to sit in complete darkness as the swamp dwellers came out to eat and be eaten. Sloan heard a cacophony of grunts, what sounded like human screams, and the occasional splash out in the pond. There were hoots as well and, way off in the distance, the intermittent barking of a dog. And that was interesting because dogs usually live with people. Those sounds, combined with the constant whine of the mosquitoes, meant that Sloan didn't get a wink of sleep.

When daylight returned, it did so gradually as if reluctant to chase the night away. Sloan was hungry by then, his skin was raw from scratching bites, and he was shivering. Not a good start to the day. *Get up,* Sloan told himself, *and move around. You'll feel warmer then.*

That's what Sloan was thinking about when he heard the distant but unmistakable sound of a chain saw. It was coming from what he thought of as the east, so he dashed across the point to try to get a fix. He was facing a body of water, and the sound seemed to be coming from a point beyond an extremely tall tree, which would give him something to aim at.

Thus began a long, torturous day. It was difficult to steer a straight course as he traveled through a maze of channels. On two occasions, it was necessary to slide off the raft and duck under the surface of the water as the Huey passed overhead. And Sloan saw numerous boats but always in the distance. Were they searching for him? Or did the speedy outboards belong to swampers, who were out doing whatever swampers did? There was no way to know.

All Sloan could do was head from one reference point to another and try to keep the sun behind him. At one point, he tried to *will* the person with the chain saw to start the machine up but with no success. Finally, hungry and exhausted, Sloan was forced to stop. As the light began to fade, he went ashore and set about the business of gathering materials and building a second hut. A water moccasin slithered away at one point, but the process went more quickly than it had the day before, and Sloan was grateful for that.

There were two potential sources of water, the stuff straight out of the swamp and what could be found in puddles. Sloan was desperately thirsty by that time and decided to take a chance on a pool of rainwater. He took care to filter it through the fabric of his undershirt and into a plastic Coke bottle that had washed up onto the beach. Of course, that was something of a joke because thousands of evil microorganisms might be living in the bottle—or could pass through the weave of his shirt. But it was the best he could do.

After slaking his thirst, Sloan sat down in front of the hut determined to start a fire. But after assembling another bow-and-drill set, and working for what must have been half an hour, he was forced to give up again. The long, cold night began, complete with the usual symphony of nerve-wracking noises.

After what seemed like an eternity, Sloan woke to the realization that he had fallen asleep at some point, the sun was up, and he could hear a chain saw! He burst out of the hut, launched the raft, and began to paddle. The noise stopped after ten minutes—but the sound was enough to restore his morale.

Splash, pull, splash, pull . . . The work went on and on. There were times when Sloan had to veer off course and circle an island before homing in on whatever tree he was using as a target. He saw alligators from time to time . . . But none were close.

As the hours passed, Sloan fell into something akin to a trance. His chest was raw by that time, and his shoulders were on fire, but he was only dimly aware of the pain as the battle continued. Finally, as Sloan rounded a point of land, he saw something that caused his heart to leap. A long pole was sticking up out of the water—and a length of bright pink surveyor tape was tied to the top of it! And another marker could be seen farther on! It didn't take a genius to realize that the carefully placed poles would lead him somewhere. To the person with the chain saw? That seemed like a good bet.

But Sloan knew how vulnerable he was. Maybe the person at the other end of those markers would help him. But it seemed more likely that they'd take one look at the orange jumpsuit and turn him in. And, in the wake of Short Guy's death, that would be the equivalent of a death sentence.

As Sloan passed the first marker, and closed in on the second, he prayed that no one would happen along in a boat. Because if they did, he'd be at their mercy. Yes, there was the Glock to turn to, but he wanted to avoid that.

To improve his chances of escaping detection, Sloan propelled his raft in under the bank of thick foliage that hung out over the water. It was dark under the greenery, and he would be hard to see there. The next half hour or so was spent working his way into a well-marked side channel. That led him into the lagoon, where a shabby houseboat was moored. It was positioned up against a muddy bank, with a plank to serve as a footbridge.

Sloan stopped paddling at that point and was careful to stay under the foliage. He could see the flat-bottomed skiff that was secured to the houseboat and the motor on the stern. That was his way out *if* he could steal it. And what other choice did he have? He couldn't throw himself on the mercy of a complete stranger who, assuming he had a gun, might take one look at the orange jumpsuit and open fire. Where was the swamper anyway? Inside? Or out in the mangroves?

Sloan learned the answer about fifteen minutes later when a man and a hound dog emerged from the trees adjacent to the houseboat. The swamper's head was bald, but he had a bushy beard to make up for it and was naked except for khaki shorts and rubber boots. He'd been fishing, judging from the pole that he carried in one hand and the bucket that dangled from the other.

The dog was dashing to and fro, sniffing the ground, and pausing to pee every now and then. The plank bounced as the pair made their way aboard the houseboat and disappeared inside. *The dog is a problem*, Sloan decided, *but darkness will fall in a few hours. Maybe I can steal the boat without making any noise.*

It wasn't much of a plan. But it was all he had. So with at least four hours of daylight left, Sloan had no choice but to lie on the raft, let the mosquitoes have their way with him, and drift in and out of consciousness.

Eventually, he woke to discover that it was dark. Sloan eyed the Rolex. It was five to ten, and he could see a square of buttery light through a window, which suggested that the owner was up and about. With that in mind, Sloan resolved to paddle in closer, but not *too* close, and wait for the light to go out. Once the man was asleep, he'd make his move.

Water gurgled as it swept along both sides of the raft, and Sloan gave thanks for the chorus of swamp sounds. Taken together, they were more than enough to cover his approach.

When Sloan was about fifty feet away from his objective, he brought the raft to a halt with some stealthy back-paddling. At that point, he could hear country-western music emanating from what he assumed to be a battery-powered radio.

Sloan felt a stab of fear as a door opened, and the man emerged. Because the swamper was backlit, all Sloan could see was a silhouette. There was the distinctive rasp of a zipper followed by the unmistakable sound of water hitting water as the man emptied his bladder into the lagoon. That was followed by a throaty growl as the dog emerged to test the night air. "Whatcha smell, boy?" the animal's owner inquired. "You got a coon?"

The dog yawned and went inside. Sloan released a long, shallow breath and was surprised to learn that he'd been holding it.

The door slammed, the light went out shortly thereafter, and Sloan had the darkness to himself. After counting to five thousand, Sloan paddled in next to the skiff. It would have been impossible to enter the boat from the water without making a commotion. But with the raft for support, he managed to enter the boat with a minimum of fuss.

The next step was to free the skiff from the houseboat and,

thanks to Short Guy's knife, Sloan had the means to cut the painter. The houseboat was so close that he could reach out and touch it. So Sloan put both hands on the hull and gave a push. The boat slid out into the lagoon stern first and coasted to a stop.

At that point Sloan had a fresh set of problems to deal with. Which way to go? And how to proceed? Would the motor start easily? And, even if it did, would he run aground in the darkness? Sloan feared that he would, and set about the process of deploying the oars. The oarlocks rattled but couldn't be heard over the racket being made by the creatures of the night.

Sloan had the oars out and was pulling away when the dog began to bark. Because of *him*? Or in response to something else? There was no way to know. A light appeared inside the houseboat, the door opened, and a powerful beam shot out to probe the lagoon. It missed the skiff at first but soon came back to pin the boat in its glare!

Sloan was momentarily grateful for the light because it told him which way to go. The man shouted at him and waved a fist before ducking into the cabin. Then he was back with a rifle. But, because the swamper had to hold the weapon *and* the big flashlight, his aim was off. Geysers of water jumped up around the skiff as Sloan pulled with all his might.

Then the houseboat was gone as the skiff entered the main channel. Sloan permitted himself a whoop of joy. The rifle shots, plus his celebratory shout, were enough to silence the denizens of the darkness for a moment. But they were in full cry seconds later. Sloan laughed out loud. He was alive . . . And he was free!

As Sloan pulled on the oars, darkness ruled the swamp, and ominous noises could be heard from all around. He couldn't see. So it wasn't long before the skiff ran into what proved to be a tangle of mangrove roots—and Sloan decided that it would be foolish to continue on. After securing the boat to a branch, he searched it for food. That was difficult in the dark, but the cooler produced two cans of beer, one of which went down straightaway.

The alcohol entered his bloodstream quickly, and Sloan was feeling light-headed when he found a large ziplock bag. It contained a Bic lighter, a Hershey bar, and a grimy map. Sloan didn't fully appreciate the find at the time, however, because he was too busy consuming the candy bar. It was the best thing he'd ever tasted.

After that, all he could do was stretch out on the middle seat with his feet sticking out over the side. A rain poncho served to protect his upper body from insects and conserve heat. What followed was a long, uncomfortable night spent drifting in and out of sleep as the night creatures conspired to keep him awake. And those moments were spent worrying.

What if the swamper had *another* boat hidden away? Or possessed the means to summon help? Sloan hadn't rowed far . . . No more than half a mile. So was the man closing in? Preparing to shoot him? And who could blame the swamper if he did?

Sloan wished there was some way he could compensate the man for the boat but couldn't think of one. As soon as there was enough light to see by, Sloan consulted the map. And he was sitting there, wishing for a compass, when the sun appeared! Not for long . . . But the brief glimpse was enough to get oriented.

The motor had its own integral gas tank, which was half-full. Sloan hoped that it, plus the fuel in the two-and-a-half-gallon auxiliary tank, would get him to neighboring Louisiana.

The motor started with a single pull of the rope and ran smoothly as Sloan followed pole markers to what he thought was an eastbound channel. It was a dead end. Fifteen minutes had been wasted going in, and fifteen minutes had been wasted coming out, not to mention some precious fuel.

Thus began a frustrating day. But by the time the light began to fade, Sloan had found his way into Stark's North Canal and entered Black Lake. During the journey, he had seen vehicles driving along the tops of dikes and spotted boats in the distance. That's why he was wearing the poncho over the jumpsuit. Not only was it an obnoxious shade of orange; it had the word PRISONER printed across the back and would leave no doubt as to his status. Sloan needed to find clothes and food. His stomach growled in agreement.

As the sun set, Sloan beached the boat in a hidden cove and built a fire for warmth. Ironically, given the fact that he had a fishing boat, there wasn't any gear in it.

In hopes of finding something edible along the shoreline, Sloan removed his shoes and began to wade through the mud. A long shot, or so he thought, until he stepped on what felt like a rock. But the rock *wasn't* a rock! It was a fine specimen of *Corbicula fluminea*!

Sloan knew that because the so-called Asian clams had a propensity to clog intake pipes and were the bane of power plants. As Secretary of Energy, he'd been in charge of the effort to eliminate them.

Sloan was tempted to eat the clams raw . . . But, rather than risk it, he resolved to steam them instead. He brought double handfuls of the bivalves over to the fire he had started using the Bic, placed carefully chosen stones in among the coals, and went out to gather additional driftwood. Fifteen minutes later, Sloan placed six shells on top of the improvised cooking surface and waited for them to open.

It didn't take long. As soon as a clam was ready Sloan was there to grab the shell with a pair of rusty pliers and remove it from the fire. As he ate, Sloan washed the clams down with sips of lukewarm beer. It was one of the best meals he'd ever had. And for the first time in days, he went to sleep feeling full, mostly warm, and free from fear.

When Sloan rose the next morning, he was hungry but filled with hope as he launched the boat. Fuel had started to run low by then . . . So Sloan kept an eye out for a boat or fishing camp that might yield what he needed.

He hugged the south end of Black Lake because, according to the map, that would allow him to reach the Intracoastal Waterway through a connecting channel. There was an industrial complex on the right. Sloan gave it a wide berth, knowing that there would be people around.

Channels ran every which way at the southeast corner of the lake, and Sloan lost the better part of an hour making wrong turns. Finally, after starting over, he fell into company with a small tug. It had a barge in tow and was headed east. To the Intracoastal? Probably. So Sloan followed along behind. The tug entered the larger waterway an hour later, and that was Sloan's cue to turn left, knowing that the Intracoastal would take him north to the city of Lake Charles, Louisiana.

There was a lot of boat and barge traffic on the waterway and, much to his surprise, some of it was clearly recreational. What about fuel? Why did everything look so normal? It didn't make sense. Most of the traffic was commercial, however, so he ran the boat along the eastern shoreline, where there was less chance of being hit. Even so, some of the larger vessels produced wakes so powerful that Sloan had to turn into them. That was a worrisome waste of both fuel and time.

Meanwhile, the little five-horse was about to run out of gas because all of the fuel in the auxiliary tank had been transferred to the motor by that time. So when a pontoon boat appeared up ahead, Sloan took notice. It was a yacht in all truth but riding on pontoons rather than a conventional hull, which created a lot of deck space. The boat was moored to a pair of trees and seemed to be deserted. But maybe the owner was inside taking a nap. With that in mind, Sloan gave a shout. "Ahoy there! Is anyone home?"

Having heard no response, Sloan pulled over in front of the larger craft, tied the skiff to a sapling, and called out again. After a minute or so, he jumped the gap. The door to the cabin was in front of him and a handwritten sign was posted in the window: MECHANICAL PROBLEMS . . . BACK SOON.

That meant the owner could return at any moment. Sloan felt his heart beat faster as he took a rock out from under his poncho and broke the window. After knocking the remaining shards of glass loose, he reached in to open the door. *Be quick,* Sloan told himself. *Get in and get out.*

Broken glass crunched underfoot as Sloan entered and went straight to a nicely equipped galley. A canvas tote was stored in a cubbyhole, and after dumping half a dozen cans into it, Sloan remembered to grab a pot, plus a pair of salt and pepper shakers. The bottle of Riesling was an afterthought.

Then he went forward. A closet was located next to the head—and Sloan had lots of clothes to choose from. He appropriated a pair of jeans, two tee shirts, and a Tommy Bahama jacket. They went into a nylon knapsack along with two pairs of boxers and some black socks. *Hurry,* Sloan told himself, *don't screw around.*

Blood was pounding in Sloan's ears as he grabbed a box of Kleenex to use as toilet paper and returned to the galley. Then with a bag in each hand, he went outside and jumped over to the riverbank. After placing the loot in the skiff, Sloan grabbed the auxiliary gas tank and returned to the yacht.

The pontoon boat was equipped with a pair of humongous four-cycle outboard motors. That meant they, unlike the five-horse, could use straight gas. But if Sloan could find a quart of oil, he could add some to the fuel—and use it in the little motor.

Sloan went to the stern, where he opened storage lockers until he found part of what he needed. That included a well-equipped toolbox and half a quart of Honda Marine engine oil. The next step was to open a deck hatch and access the plastic tubing that ran every which way. The last thing Sloan wanted to do was cut a fuel line.

Sloan spent three minutes isolating a water line, clamped it off, and cut a section free. After dividing the hose in two, he set about the process of siphoning gas into the auxiliary tank. A skill perfected on the family farm. The process seemed to take forever, and Sloan felt jumpy. Was the distant speedboat turning his way? No, thank God, but the next one might.

Finally, the auxiliary tank was full. Sloan removed the tubes, screwed the cap onto the tank, and lugged it over to the side of the boat. After heaving the heavy container across the narrow strip of open water, he followed. Then he carried the container to the skiff, put it in, and cast off. No way in hell was he going to sit there and refuel the motor when the pontoon boat's owner could arrive at any minute.

Sloan felt guilty as he got under way—and refused to make excuses for himself. He knew what his father would say: "Stealing is wrong regardless of the circumstances, son . . . You need to make it right." But Sloan *couldn't* make it right . . . And he could feel the weight of his father's disapproval as he motored north.

Sloan glanced back over his shoulder from time to time, fearful that a vengeful yacht owner was after him. When a side channel opened up on the right, he took it. The bottom came up quickly, but the skiff drew very little water and entered without difficulty.

As the waterway curved to the left, Sloan realized that he was circling a small island. That was good since there were lots of trees on it, and they would screen him from the Intracoastal.

The moment a small cove appeared, Sloan cut power, pulled the outboard up out of the water, and rowed to shore. The hull made a scraping sound as the bow ran up onto a gravelly beach. Then it was a simple matter to ship the oars, get out, and wade ashore.

The next hour was spent taking a bath and donning clean clothes. Sloan got rid of the orange jumpsuit by digging a hole and burying it. As soon as that was accomplished, he built a small fire, knowing that if someone happened along, he'd look as innocent as a man with a scruffy beard could.

Sloan's loot included a can of stew. After dumping it into the stolen pot, he was forced to wait. To kill time and slake his thirst, he opened the bottle of wine. And, lacking a corkscrew, he made quite a mess of it. *I should have selected a red,* Sloan thought to himself as he pried the last chunk of cork out. *To go with the stew.*

Sloan's stomach rumbled ominously as he took the bubbling brew off the fire and went to work. He ate, using a cooking spoon and pausing occasionally to take sips of wine.

Once his stomach was full, Sloan was faced with a choice. It was midafternoon, so perhaps he should remain on the island and get an early start the next morning. But the sooner Sloan arrived in Lake Charles, the sooner he'd be able to travel north, where he hoped to find some support.

With that in mind Sloan put everything back in the boat, poured water on the fire, and rowed out to where he could start the motor. The channel led him into the main waterway, where he fell in behind a heavily loaded barge. With the motor running full out, Sloan could keep up—and was content to do so as day gave way to night.

Clusters of lights appeared, marking the locations of small communities and signaling the fact that the power was on. How could that be? But what was, was.

Finally, after an hour or so, Sloan made the decision to go ashore. He was tired and concerned lest the motor run out of gas while on the Intracoastal. And the last thing he wanted to do was to try to refill the internal tank in the dark. He saw some lights and took aim at them.

Fifteen minutes later, Sloan arrived at a small town. He had some money, but should he spend it? Especially in a little Podunk town where strangers would stick out. No, Sloan decided, it would be best to hold out for a larger town.

The waterfront park was equipped with picnic tables and metal barbecues. There was no way to know how the local police force would look on overnight camping, so Sloan chose the spot farthest from the parking lot, hoping to escape notice.

There wasn't much firewood to be had, but Sloan managed to scrounge enough fallen branches to build a small fire and heat a can of chili. That, along with what remained of the wine, was sufficient to warm his belly.

After washing up, Sloan put on every piece of clothing he had with the rain poncho on top. Then, with no good place to sleep, he was forced to hunker down on a much-abused cushion that was enough to keep his butt up out of the water in the bottom of the boat. The incessant moan of a distant foghorn, the occasional barking of a dog, and a sudden rain shower kept him awake. The night seemed to last forever.

Dawn came eventually. But with no dry firewood, Sloan left as soon as there was sufficient light to see by. He figured he was north of Moss Lake and likely to reach the city of Lake Charles by evening.

The sky was blue for once, and Sloan hoped that was a good omen, as an endless succession of whitecaps marched down from the north. Spray exploded sideways as the boat smacked into the waves, and droplets of water flew back to wet his poncho.

There was no warmth to be had from the wan sunlight. All

Sloan could do was sit in the stern and shiver, as the tireless five-horse pushed him past Prien Lake and into Lake Charles.

It was necessary to refuel shortly thereafter. Sloan had to hurry as waves hit the skiff broadside and threatened to swamp it. But he got the job done. And it wasn't long before Sloan saw two office buildings and a TV tower on the horizon. The city of Lake Charles! He was close.

Forty-five minutes later, Sloan could see the town's mostly low-lying buildings and a well-developed waterfront. And that raised a question: Where to leave the boat? The obvious answer was with other boats—in the hope that no one would notice it for a while.

It took about fifteen minutes to find a small marina, collect his scant belongings, and walk away. Maybe the authorities would be able to trace the boat back to its rightful owner via the registration decal on the bow. Sloan hoped so. The marina was located near the intersection of Bor Du Lac and Lakeshore Drives.

As Sloan entered town, he was surprised to see how many people were marching about, waving flags, and shouting slogans. A man carrying a Confederate flag was flanked by picketers armed with "New Order" signs.

Meanwhile, a hundred feet away, those waving American flags had the support of a costumed flutist who was playing "Yankee Doodle Dandy."

Most of the bystanders were cheering for the Confederates, so it appeared that Huxton and his friends were making progress. Having failed to recruit him, what would they do next?

But politics would have to wait. Sloan had more pressing problems to deal with. Thanks to Short Guy he had enough money for some basic toiletries, a decent meal, and a night in a cheap hotel.

He awoke feeling hungry. But before Sloan went looking for

breakfast, he wanted to take full advantage of the shower and the opportunity to shave the scruffy beard off.

Sloan had no choice but to put the same clothes back on. Clean now, for the most part anyway, he made his way to a nearby café, where he ordered the "Sunrise Special." It consisted of two strips of bacon, two eggs any style, and two pancakes—plus all the coffee Sloan could consume. He ate every bite and consumed three cups of coffee.

Then it was time to hit the streets and look for an affordable way out of town. The first thing Sloan noticed was the number of people on the streets. And the way they were congregated around various speakers. By listening in, it soon became apparent that a referendum was under way. Should the state of Louisiana secede? Or remain with the "old" government, which, according to the propaganda being bandied about, was intent on subverting the Constitution on behalf of "the takers." Takers being those on social security and public assistance.

That was bullshit, of course, and some of the "patriots" stood up to say so. One such person was a thirtysomething black man wearing a well-cut business suit. He was standing on the bed of a bunting-draped pickup truck and holding a bullhorn up to his mouth. "This is the time to rally *behind* our country," he told a small crowd, "not to tear it down. Do you really believe that rich people are going to look after your interests? Of course they won't . . . The only thing they care about is themselves! That's what 'security through self-reliance' means. It's another way of saying, 'I have mine, and you can kiss my ass!'"

The man might have said more . . . But a dozen men armed with baseball bats chased the onlookers away. They lined up along both sides of the truck and began to rock it back and forth. Sloan took a look around. Where were the police? Deliberately missing in action. The beleaguered speaker had little choice but to jump off the back of the vehicle and run. Two thugs gave chase, caught up with the man, and hauled him around a corner.

Sloan pushed his way through the crowd. There was a construction site to his left, and he paused long enough to grab a four-foot length of two-by-two from a pile of scrap, before continuing on. The Glock was at the small of his back, but Sloan wasn't planning to use it unless forced to do so.

When Sloan rounded the corner, he saw that the thugs had the man down, and were kicking him. Their backs were turned, and that was fine with Sloan, who came up behind them. After planting his feet, he took a swing. He felt the impact of the blow as the stick hit the man's head. The thug fell as if poleaxed and lay motionless on the ground.

As the second attacker turned, the two-by-two was falling again. Sloan missed the thug's head and struck his shoulder. The man uttered a scream as the force of the blow broke his left clavicle. He stumbled away, fell, and lay moaning on the ground.

The patriot was back on his feet by then, dusting his suit off. The kick was an afterthought. "Asshole."

"Come on," Sloan said. "Let's get out of here."

"Recommendation accepted," the other man said. "'The better part of valor is discretion.' *Henry IV, Part 1*, act 5, scene 4. Reginald P. Allston at your service."

"You're an actor?" Sloan inquired, as they hurried away.

"An amateur," Allston replied. "I make my living as an attorney."

"I liked your speech," Sloan told him. "That took balls."

"Thanks. And you are?"

"Samuel Sloan."

Allston frowned. "The name sounds familiar."

"I was the Secretary of Energy until recently," Sloan replied.

"If you say so," Allston replied.

"No, really, I was."

"*Was?*"

"Well, according to what I've been told, the president, which is to say Marilyn Wainwright, had a heart attack and died. And, since all of the officials who outranked me were killed, I'm the president."

Allston laughed. "That's absurd. You're delusional."

Sloan stopped, causing Allston to do likewise. He wanted the attorney to take him seriously. But *how*? Then he saw the building on the opposite side of the street and realized that the solution was waiting inside. "Can I call you Reggie?"

"Everyone does."

"Good. Follow me, Reggie . . . I'm the President of the United States, and I can prove it."

The sign on the front of the building read, CARNEGIE MEMORIAL LIBRARY. Once inside, Sloan led Allston to the information desk, where a young woman with purple hair looked up at him. "How can I help you?"

"Where are the periodicals located?"

"Prior to the meteor strikes, most people went online to access periodicals," the woman said, as if explaining the concept to a child.

"But you have copies stored here, right?"

"In some cases, yes."

"How about the *New York Times*?"

"We have copies predating the meteor strikes if that's what you mean . . . But the *Times* has been added to the proscribed list, so if the paper still exists, we won't be able to obtain new copies."

"*Proscribed* list?" Allston demanded. "What's that?"

"It's a list of publications that the state legislature considers to be counterproductive," the librarian replied expressionlessly. Did she approve or disapprove? Sloan would have been willing to put money on the second possibility.

"That's censorship," Allston said. "And it's a violation of the First Amendment to the United States Constitution."

"You aren't in the United States," the woman countered. "You're in the state of Louisiana."

Sloan was afraid that Allston was about to deliver another speech and hurried to cut him off. "Thanks for your help. Where can we access the periodicals that you still have?"

The librarian pointed, and Sloan escorted Allston back through the stacks to a corner of the library. A sign said PERIODICALS, and four terminals were located immediately below it. "I appreciate what you did for me," Allston said. "But I don't have time for this."

"Five minutes," Sloan said. "That's all I need."

"Okay," Allston said reluctantly. "Five minutes. Then I'm out of here."

Sloan sat down, worked his way through a menu, and selected *"New York Times."* Then he entered a date. The article he wanted was on page one above the fold. "There," Sloan said, as he stood. "Take a look."

Allston sat down. And there, right in front of him, was a photo of Sloan standing next to the President of the United States. The headline read: "New Secretary of Energy Sworn In."

Allston looked at Sloan and back to the screen. "Holy shit . . . It's *you!*"

"Yes, it is," Sloan agreed. "And, assuming that all of the people who outranked me were killed, then I'm the president."

"Hell yes, you are," Allston said enthusiastically, and hit PRINT. A printer began to whir, and Allston was there to receive five copies of the article as they slid into the tray. "Do you realize what this means?" he demanded. "We can prove who you are! And we can pull the country back together. That's what you want, right?"

"That's what I want," Sloan assured him. "I want to restore the government."

"Then I'm with you," Allston assured him. "Come on . . . Let's see what those bastards did to my uncle's truck."

Sloan followed Allston past the reception desk and outside. Sirens could be heard, and greasy black smoke was spiraling up into the sky. And when the men rounded a corner, they could see that the pickup was on fire. The police were nowhere to be seen, but an aid unit was pulling away, and firemen were working to extinguish the flames. "Uh-oh," Allston said, "Uncle Leo's gonna be pissed. Come on, let's get out of here."

"Where are we headed?" Sloan inquired, as they hurried away.

"We're going to rent a car," Allston answered. "And drive it to Shreveport."

Sloan knew that Shreveport was to the north, so there was no reason to object. It took the better part of an hour to find a rental agency and complete the necessary paperwork, all the while wondering if someone would recognize Allston and refuse to serve him. No one did. The attorney had to pay half the fee in advance and used silver coins to do so. Sloan made a note to learn more about them later. As soon as they were in the car, Allston made his way onto Highway 171 and drove north. "We're going to meet with some friends of mine," Allston said. "They saw this day coming—and are ready to fight."

"Sounds good," Sloan said. "Where are they?"

"They're going to meet at a location in the Ouachita National Forest," Allston replied. "And I was planning to join them there. So," he continued, "how did you wind up in Lake Charles?"

Sloan told him about Mexico, about paddling north, and being held prisoner. And when it came to the meeting in Houston, Allston was incredulous. "So they *knew* who you were? Damn, that's amazing. So what happened?"

Allston listened intently as Sloan told him about jumping out of the Huey, stealing the boat, and making his way up the Intracoastal. Allston shook his head in amazement. "You are one persistent son of a bitch, Mr. President, and that's a good thing."

The highway took them through Moss Bluff and Gillis before transforming itself into Highway 190. Then, just north of De-Ridder, Highway 171 signs appeared again. From that point on, it was a straight shot up through Leesville and Mansfield to the city of Shreveport.

But what should have been a three-hour trip was transformed into a four-hour pain in the ass, as Allston was forced to deal with a succession of military convoys all headed north. "Eyeball those markings," Allston said, as they passed a column of olive drab trucks. "Do you notice anything?"

"Yes, I do," Sloan confirmed, as he eyed the wind-whipped Confederate flags that were flying from aerials, and the handwritten words on doors. They read, ARMY OF THE NEW CONFEDERACY. And the meaning was clear. At least some of the military had broken away and aligned itself with the South.

"The bastards are moving quickly," Allston observed.

"Yes, they are," Sloan agreed. Was it too late to catch up? The thought frightened him.

They entered Shreveport half an hour later. "This is home sweet home," Allston said. "I need to drop by my apartment—and you need everything. You only get one chance to make a first impression. That's what my daddy told me—and you look like a bum. So we're gonna go shopping. How 'bout it, Mr. President? Is that okay with you?"

"Yes," Sloan answered. "Thanks. I'll pay you back."

"Good," Allston replied. "I'd hate to sue the POTUS." Both men laughed.

Sloan had been to Shreveport once before but only briefly. He recognized the Regions Tower, however, if not the lesser buildings that surrounded it. Allston guided the car through the streets with the expertise of a native—and it wasn't long before they entered an area called Country Club Hills. "This looks like a nice neighborhood," Sloan observed. "What kind of law do you practice?"

"Alternative Dispute Resolution."

"Which means?"

"Which means trying to resolve disputes through the use of mediation, arbitration, and old-fashioned common sense."

"And it pays well?"

"Very well . . . And that's why I can afford to pimp the president out. Or at least I think I can. Businesses won't accept credit cards anymore, but I have a supply of new coin."

"New coin? What's that?"

"Look in the bottom of the cup holder . . . You'll find some new coins in there."

The strange-looking coins were made of silver, and had the likeness of a man on both sides. No, as Sloan looked more closely, he realized that he was looking at the Libertarian icon Ayn Rand! A dyed-in-the-wool believer in the sort of free-market, laissez-faire capitalism that the fortunate few loved but would leave everyone else to beg on the streets.

And sure enough, the words SECURITY THROUGH SELF-RELIANCE could be seen chasing each other around the rim of each coin. Sloan felt a rising sense of desperation. Huxton and his friends were issuing money, while the President of the United States was trying to make his way north. Sloan sighed. There was so much bullshit to counter and so little time to do it in.

Allston's home was located in an attractive five-story apartment building. We'll have to leave the car out here," the lawyer explained, as they pulled into visitor parking. "I have a single slot, and my car is in it."

"Your sports car."

"Damned right my sports car . . . And it's a righteous ride. Come on."

Allston's two-bedroom apartment was on the top floor and looked like an ad for Restoration Hardware. "Nice," Sloan said, as they entered, "very nice. And you aren't married."

Allston frowned. "How could you tell?"

"Someone left a bra hanging on the telescope."

"Oh that," Allston said dismissively. "It's a good thing that Mom didn't drop by. Okay, do what you need to do, and we'll leave in ten."

It was thirty minutes later when they left. Allston chose to drive his BMW 2-series sports car rather than the rental car. It was dark by then, but the lights were on, and there was plenty of traffic. "Okay," Allston said. "We're headed for the mall, and if things go the way I hope they will, a lot of people are going to meet you during the coming months. And since you're a farm boy, not to mention a man of the people, you should dress accordingly. That's why we're going to buy you a couple of ball caps, a barn coat, plaid shirts, Levi's, and hiking boots. Some camping gear would come in handy, too, since we'll have to hoof it up north."

They were inside the mall by then. The lights were on, but the crowd was thin. "Did you say 'we'?" Sloan inquired.

"I'm going with you," Allston said.

"What about the law practice, the apartment, and the BMW?"

"Screw that stuff," Allston replied. "Our country comes first."

Sloan stopped, forcing Allston to do likewise. The younger

man had short hair, a high forehead, and wide-set eyes. Sloan extended his hand. "Thanks, Reggie. And congratulations."

Allston had a firm grip. "'Congratulations'? For what?"

"For being appointed Attorney General of the United States of America . . . That's subject to confirmation of course—but we'll cross that bridge when we come to it."

Allston grinned. "Momma's gonna be proud."

After two hours of shopping, and dinner at a chain restaurant, they returned to the apartment. Allston pointed the way to the guest room. "Make yourself at home and grab some sleep. You may hear me going in and out. I have a lot to do, including stashing my personal records in a safe place."

"So you won't be back?" Sloan inquired.

"Not until we win the war," Allston replied.

"You think it will come to that?"

"I think it's under way," Allston said.

The foreboding words were still echoing through Sloan's mind as he carried his new possessions into a nicely furnished guest room and set about the business of removing tags. Then it was time to pack everything he wouldn't need the following day.

After brushing his teeth, Sloan took a shower and went to bed. It was comfortable, and he was tired. Sleep claimed him. It was still dark when Sloan heard a knock on the door. "Get up, Mr. President," Allston said from the hallway. "You have work to do."

Sloan rolled out of bed, entered the attached bathroom, and spent the next twenty minutes getting ready. It felt good to put on clean clothes. He was tying the laces on his boots when Allston entered. "Good morning . . . Are you ready to go?"

"Yes. How 'bout you?"

"It was tough saying good-bye to Mom. Fortunately, there's plenty of family to look after her."

"Good," Sloan said. "Did you tell her about the new job?"

"Yes, but she doesn't believe it. Hell, *I* don't believe it."

"I know how you feel," Sloan said as he hoisted the new back-pack off the floor. "Let's get going."

Rain was falling from a lead-gray sky, and the occasional clap of thunder could be heard off in the distance, as the men placed their packs in the Beemer's tiny trunk. "What about the rental car?" Sloan wanted to know.

"I told my uncle to come over and take care of it. And I gave him my furniture," Allston replied. "He isn't happy, mind you—but I hope to make it up to him later."

Allston departed Shreveport on Highway 3. It turned into 29 as it left Louisiana and entered Arkansas. They had breakfast at a restaurant in Bradley before making their way north through Lewisville to the town of Hope.

After a pit stop, Allston followed I-30 up to Arkadelphia, where he left the interstate for Highway 8. "This will take us into the Ouachita National Forest," he predicted. "And that's where we'll ditch the car."

Sloan looked over at him. "That's gotta hurt."

Allston's eyes were on the road. "I don't want to talk about it."

Sloan nodded. "Got it."

Allston had a map, which he gave to Sloan. "X marks the spot, Mr. President. We'll walk from there."

Sloan looked up from the map to the rain-smeared windshield. There were forests of oak trees, the occasional glimpse of a lake, and streams that flowed under the highway. About ten minutes passed before Sloan spotted what he was looking for. "There it is," he said. "Walker Road. That's where we turn right."

Allston made the turn, and Sloan eyed the map. "Watch the odometer," he advised. "We're supposed to drive for ten miles and turn off onto a road marked by a large boulder."

"Got it," Allston replied. The gravel road forced him to keep the speed down, but it wasn't long before they hit the ten-mile mark and saw a garage-sized boulder up ahead. And there, what looked like a wide path led off into the woods.

Allston turned onto it but the BMW had very little ground clearance, and it wasn't long before he had to pull over and park. "This is as far as we can go," he announced. "Everyone out."

Once the trunk was open, Sloan got into the rain gear acquired the day before. Then he shouldered a pack. Allston did likewise. "I left the doors unlocked and the key in the ignition," he said. "Who knows what the authorities will make of that."

The next two hours were spent following trails that frequently split into *more* trails, forcing Sloan to repeatedly consult the hand-drawn map. Was it accurate? He hoped so because they were wasting a lot of time and effort if it wasn't.

In spite of the rainy weather, others were out and about as well. Because according to the calendar, it was summer and time to go camping. Something the locals were determined to do regardless of the circumstances. The men exchanged greetings with other hikers as they continued to follow a succession of well-trod paths in a generally northeasterly direction.

The terrain, which had been flat to begin with, began to slope upwards as time passed. And Sloan could see a mountaintop ahead. Unlike most ranges in the United States, the Ouachitas ran east and west instead of north and south.

At one point, the Ouachitas had been as tall as the Rockies. But erosion had taken a toll over thousands of years, and once-craggy peaks had been reduced to softly rounded summits. And that's what Sloan could see in the distance.

As they followed the map off a well-established trail, and up through stands of red, black, and white oak trees, Sloan saw some loblolly pines to one side, flanked by native shrubs. Sloan had begun to feel the climb by then. His breath came in gasps, his shoulders ached from the weight of the pack, and his boots felt as if they were made of lead. Allston was suffering, too. "How much farther?" he inquired, as they paused to rest.

Sloan consulted the map. "See the rockslide? And the cliff beyond? The cave is located at its base. Assuming we're in the right place."

"I hope we are," Allston said fervently. "Let's get moving."

It took a long time to negotiate the rockslide. The scree was loose and had a tendency to slide, which forced the men to scramble. So a climb that should have taken half an hour lasted twice that long. But, eventually, they arrived at the top of the slope, where a cluster of pines marked the base of the cliff. "We're there," Sloan announced. "Or we should be. Come on."

As Sloan led the way to the pines, he felt as if something, or someone, was watching him. And sure enough, when he looked up, Sloan saw an eagle circling above. "Put your hands on your head," a voice said. "And turn around."

The sentry had been hidden behind a pile of boulders. He was a middle-aged man with wire-rimmed glasses and an AR-15. It was aimed at Sloan and wavered slightly. "Don't shoot him," Allston said as he arrived. "He's one of us."

As the man turned to look at Allston, the assault rifle turned with him. That gave Sloan the perfect opportunity to pull the Glock and fire. And that, he realized, was the problem with a volunteer military force. Especially if they had to fight trained soldiers like the ones who'd gone over to the New Confederacy. "Reggie!" the man said enthusiastically. "It's good to see you."

"Likewise," Allston replied. "Sam . . . This is Frank Garrison. He's a gentleman farmer, a cutthroat bridge player, and a stamp collector. And that's why he wants to reconstitute the government. So there will be new stamps."

Garrison chuckled and was careful to point his weapon at the sky as he came forward to shake Sloan's hand. "It's a pleasure to meet you, Sam . . . Any friend of Reggie's is a friend of mine."

"The pleasure is mutual," Sloan assured him while he shook a callused hand.

"The entrance is up there," Garrison said as he removed a walkie-talkie from a pocket. "I'll let 'em know that you're coming."

Sloan heard the sound of Garrison's voice as Allston took the lead. The entrance to the cave was concealed by bushes that had clearly been planted there. A vertical crevice opened onto a passageway that led into the mountain. Sloan had to bend over to make his way forward—and felt the pack scrape on the ceiling as he did so.

The passageway delivered them into a dimly lit cave. What illumination there was came in through a hole in the roof combined with the light from a small fire and two battery-powered lanterns. They threw shadows onto the wall as people gathered around.

Allston was quite popular, as evidenced by hugs and the enthusiastic manner in which the others received him. Then it was time for introductions. Cindy Howell presented herself as a marathon runner, a high school science teacher, and a future bomb maker. Sloan got the feeling she was looking forward to blowing things up.

Lester Jenkins was AWOL from his job as a deputy sheriff. The combination of brown skin and light blue eyes made his face memorable—and Sloan marked him down as a man who would be useful in a fight.

Sam McKinney was the strong, silent type, who, according to Allston, had spent eight years in the army and left it to care for his gravely ill wife. It wasn't clear what happened thereafter—but his presence seemed to speak volumes.

Doyle Besom was fortysomething, at least twenty pounds over-weight, and wore his hair Ben Franklin–style. He'd been a public-relations manager before leaving his job to join the patriots.

Finally, there was Marsha Rostov who introduced herself as Deputy Commissioner of the IRS. She was short, dumpy, and had eyes like lasers. Sloan knew the type. He figured Rostov for a pro-fessional bureaucrat who, thanks to hard work and political acu-men, had risen as high as one could go without being a political appointee.

And while it was tempting to dismiss her based on appearances, Sloan knew that could be a costly mistake. It was reasonable to assume that Rostov knew everything there was to know about collecting taxes, and the government was going to need money. Where was the commissioner anyway? Dead or alive? Sloan did his best to turn on the charm. "Ms. Rostov! This *is* a pleasure. I know the commissioner . . . Did she survive the strike on D.C.?"

"It's hard to be sure," Rostov replied cautiously, "but there hasn't been any word of her. Have we met? You look familiar."

"And that brings me to Sam's status," Allston interjected smoothly. "I forgot to mention the fact that he was the Secretary of Energy back on May 1. And, in the wake of President Wain-wright's death, that makes him President of the United States."

Rostov blinked. "Holy shit . . . Really?"

"Really," Allston replied. "It seems safe to assume that if a more senior official had survived, he or she would have come forward by now."

That led to a spirited discussion, in which Besom took the role of cynic. "We need a new president, that's for sure," he said. "But how do we know this man is who he claims to be?" Besom turned to Sloan. "No offense . . . But have you got a driver's license or something?"

"I was in Mexico when the meteorites struck," Sloan said. "And I lost my ID during the trip north."

"How unfortunate," Besom said.

"I suggest that you take a look at this," Allston said, as he removed a piece of paper from a coat pocket. There was a rustling noise as he held it up for people to look at. Jenkins made the article readable by aiming a flashlight at it. Then he read the headline out loud. "'New Secretary of Energy Sworn In.'"

"That's where I saw him!" Rostov exclaimed. "On TV! Testifying in front of Congress."

All eyes turned to Sloan. McKinney was the first to speak. "Congratulations, Mr. President. The job won't be easy."

Sloan felt the full weight of the presidency settle onto his shoulders. "Thank you . . . And no, it won't. The people down south have a big head start."

"That's for sure," Jenkins agreed. "Take the defense towers for example. Once they're complete, a curtain of steel will divide North from South."

Sloan frowned. "Defense towers? Tell me more."

So Jenkins told him. The rebels were building what amounted to a high-tech Maginot Line that was going to run east–west between the northwest corner of Texas and Norfolk, Virginia. And according to patriot sympathizers who were working on the project, the towers would be connected by fiber-optic cable, topped with landing pads for helicopters, and armed with missile batteries. The idea being to wall the South off from what the New Order stalwarts called "the takers."

"But there's more to it than that," Jenkins added. "According to the New Order's propaganda machine, the profligate Yankees will run out of fuel soon. And once they do, their cities will go dark. That's when the barbarian horde will head south in an effort to seize control of the so-called Confederacy's oil reserves. Except they aren't the Confederacy's oil reserves, they're *our* oil reserves since they belong to all of us."

Sloan felt something heavy land in the pit of his stomach. Of course! He should have thought of it. *Would* have thought of it if he hadn't been so busy struggling to survive. The Strategic Petroleum Reserve fell under *him*. Or it had in his role as Secretary of Energy. And the last time he'd seen a report, there'd been something like 700 million barrels of oil stored in five locations, all of which were located down south! That equated to roughly forty days' worth of oil for the predisaster United States. Of course, that period of time could be greatly extended through conservation measures and by dividing the country in half!

Especially since the Southern states were producing energy using a variety of technologies including solar and wind. In fact, despite its reputation for relying too heavily on an oil-based economy, Texas was producing a lot of energy via wind and solar. So much so that they might be able to get along without the petroleum reserves as long as they didn't have to share with the North. What did that imply? Were Huxton and his cronies planning to keep some of the oil for emergencies and sell the rest? Taking the money for themselves? Sloan wouldn't put it past them. "I want to see one of the defense towers firsthand," he said. "And I need to go north."

McKinney nodded. "Yes, sir . . . We'll leave first thing in the morning." The war had begun.

# CHAPTER 7

||||||||||||||||||||||||||||||||||||||

The mercenary captains are either capable men or
they are not; if they are, you cannot trust them, because
they always aspire to their own greatness, either by
oppressing you, who are their master, or others contrary
to your intentions; but if the captain is not skillful, you are
ruined in the usual way.

—NICCOLÒ MACHIAVELLI

**BOISE, IDAHO**

Mac was standing in the Stryker's air-guard hatch looking back
as the convoy rounded a curve. The column consisted of a Ford
pickup with a fifty in back, the Humvee with the UAV launcher in
tow, a Stryker, two fuelers, a six-by-six loaded with dependents, a
moving van carrying their possessions, a second Stryker, a fueler
filled with JP8, a U-Haul loaded with supplies, a second armed
pickup, and another U-Haul. A Stryker brought up the rear. Each
vehicle had a number, a radio, and two qualified drivers. Radio
procedure wasn't perfect, but it was improving, and Mac figured
the entire group would have it down before long.

The unit was just north of Boise. *Why?* Because the city was on
the way to Arizona, that's why . . . Although Mac had a secondary
motivation, which was to visit the family farm even if that wasn't
fair to the others since they couldn't direct the column to *their* homes.

The Macintyres hadn't lived there full-time. Not during Mac's lifetime. But her father had been raised on the farm and kept the place after his mother's death. Most of the land had been sold off by the time he inherited it. But ten acres remained, including the four-bedroom farmhouse that sat perched on a rise. And that's where most of Mac's summer vacations were spent.

Her father hadn't been there much. That bothered her sister but was fine with Mac, who came to dread his unannounced visits. Bo Macintyre liked to sponsor competitions. There were shooting contests, family fishing derbies, and long-distance runs. And, since Victoria won most of them, Mac grew tired of competing. Not just for whatever silly prize her father offered, but for his affection.

Nothing was said. Colonel, and then *General*, Macintyre was too disciplined for that. But everyone knew. Victoria was his favorite. So Mac formed a close bond with her mother. And that had a downside because Margaret Macintyre had grown tired of military life, and longed for stability. That put pressure on her marriage to Bo. The result was a chasm, with Victoria and her father on one side—and Mac and her mother on the other.

Yet Mac still cared about her father, and her sister, too, for that matter. So if one or both of them were at the farm, she wanted to stop by. Even if it meant granting herself a privilege not available to others. Mac's thoughts were interrupted by a voice in her ear. "Roller-One to Roller-Six."

"Roller" was the name Mac had given to the convoy—and "One" was the number assigned to the first vehicle in the column. It was an armed pickup driven by Corporal Garcia. "This is Six actual," Mac said. "Go. Over."

"There's a roadblock up ahead and no obvious way around it. Over."

"Roger that," Mac replied. "Hit the brakes. Six to all Roller units . . . Pull over, but keep your eyes peeled and your engines running. I'm going forward. Over."

Mac was riding in the Stryker designated as Roller-Three. It pulled out and around the Humvee before coming to a stop next to the pickup. Mac climbed up on top of the Stryker to get a better view. A large construction site was visible in the distance, and her binoculars brought everything closer. Lots of heavy equipment could be seen. What were the locals doing? Working on a highway? No, they were building a wall! A defensive wall, like the ones used to protect ancient cities. Had they been attacked? Or were they preparing for the possibility of an attack?

Mac's thoughts were interrupted as two A-10 Thunderbolts roared overhead and circled the city. So much for her dreams of capturing the Air National Guard assets stationed at Gowen Field. The unit's aircraft and their supplies were already under someone's control. She moved to make room for Sparks Munroe. "Get Peters on the horn," she instructed. "Tell him to lie low . . . Tell him that a couple of Hogs are circling the city." Sparks nodded and went to work.

"A delegation is coming out to meet with us," Garcia announced as he peered up at her.

Mac could see them through the glasses. She nodded before climbing down. Sparks followed. Once on the ground, Mac said, "Okay, time for a chat. But be ready just in case." Both men checked their weapons.

It was a typical postimpact day, which was to say gray, cold, and windy. Pieces of litter skittered across the highway as Mac and her soldiers went forward to meet the townsfolk. The local delegation included two men armed with AR-16s, and a woman decked out in a white fur coat. That would have been politically incorrect months earlier, but things had changed since then. Staying warm had priority now—and to hell with how a person went about it. A pair of shiny, knee-high boots completed the look. Mac felt dowdy by comparison.

"Good morning," the woman said, as both groups came to a halt. "My name is Pam Scheemer—and I'm the mayor of Boise." Scheemer had well-plucked brows and rosy cheeks.

"I'm Lieutenant Robin Macintyre," Mac replied. "It looks like you're building a wall. Were you attacked?"

"No," Scheemer replied. "Not yet. But, with no one to protect us, it's just a matter of time."

Mac looked up as one of the A-10s circled to the south. "No one to protect you?"

"We have our local guard unit," Scheemer acknowledged. "But they live here. Where's the rest of the military?"

"I'm sorry about the lack of support," Mac replied. "I wish we could help . . . But we were cut off from our unit. And the ham operators claim that President Wainwright is dead. So we're traveling to Arizona."

Scheemer frowned. "On orders from the army? Or to suit yourselves?"

Mac was formulating a response when Sparks Munroe stepped in. "We call ourselves Mac's Marauders, ma'am. And we plan to fight for those who need help."

"For money," Scheemer said contemptuously.

"To survive," Mac replied. "You have homes, and we don't, so we're looking for a place to live. If you'll let us through, we'll be on our way. It's as simple as that."

Scheemer was silent for a moment. "All right," she said finally. "But keep your word. The A-10s will eat you for lunch if you don't."

"Yes, ma'am," Mac replied. "I'll keep that in mind."

Scheemer nodded and tugged her fur collar up around her face.

"I think it's going to snow," she said to no one in particular. Then she turned and walked away. Mac looked up, and sure enough, snowflakes were beginning to fall.

The roadblock consisted of two semi-tractor-trailer rigs parked trailer to trailer. Diesel engines rattled, and black smoke jetted up from chromed stacks, as the trucks pulled away from each other. About two dozen locals were there to watch the convoy pass through the resulting gap. A Humvee was stationed on the other side. The FOLLOW ME attached to the back end said it all.

In spite of the agreement with the mayor, Mac knew they might be entering a trap. And since she couldn't call on the Apache for help, she was blind. Or thought she was until a familiar voice came over her headset. "Roller-Two-One to Roller-Six. The Raven is up and feeding video. The route is clear. Over."

Mac was standing in the back of Roller-One at that point just forward of the fifty. Sparks was at her side. Even though Esco hadn't been ordered to launch a drone, he had taken it upon himself to do so. "Well done, Two-One. Over."

Mac turned to Sparks. "Tell Peters to take off, circle west, and approach the town of Kuna from the south."

Mac watched the A-10s circle the town one last time before lining up on the airport. Chances were they'd been ordered to land to conserve fuel. "Peters is airborne," Sparks told her.

"Good. By the way . . . Where did the Mac's Marauders stuff come from?"

"That's what we call ourselves."

"I didn't get the memo."

Munroe grinned. "No, ma'am. You didn't."

Both of them laughed.

The pilot vehicle left them half a mile farther on, and once the convoy was south of Boise, Mac ordered Garcia to take a right and head for the town of Kuna. It had been little more than a railroad stop back in the old days. But because of Boise's growth, Kuna had become a bedroom community.

However, since Kuna was located outside of the new defensive wall, it was certain to be looted and used as a staging area by any force that hoped to conquer Boise. And judging from what looked like dozens of vacant buildings, people understood that.

After entering Kuna, Mac directed Garcia to lead the column east—into the area located just north of the Snake River Birds of Prey National Conservation Area. What would become of the nation's parks? she wondered. Would people move in, log the trees, and hunt the animals into extinction? There was nothing she could do about it, so Mac pushed the thought away.

She was standing by then, peering over the truck's cab, as cold air buffeted her face. Everything looked the way it had two years earlier. Her sister had been overseas, but her father was in residence, and Mac had been hoping for some sort of reconciliation.

But Bo Macintyre wanted his younger daughter to attend West Point just as her sister had. And the fact that Mac had been accepted into Officer Candidate School and graduated at the top of her class meant nothing to him. OCS was for second-raters, in Bo Macintyre's opinion . . . And being father to the best of the second-raters was nothing to brag about. The long weekend was punctuated by periods of silence—and poisoned by things unsaid.

When Mac left, it was with the conviction that she'd never return. Yet there she was, turning off the blacktop to follow the driveway up and around the farmhouse to park in back. Brown swiveled the fifty around, searching for targets, but there weren't any.

Everything appeared to be normal at first. But, as Garcia killed the engine, Mac realized that she was wrong. On closer examination she saw that some of the ground-floor windows were shattered, and the back door had been left ajar. So what lay within? Had her father been there when the meteors struck? And if so, was he all right?

There weren't any vehicles to be seen, but that didn't mean the house was empty. Mac ordered Sergeant Poole to take his squad in and clear the residence. Once that effort was under way, Mac turned her attention to setting up a defensive perimeter, bringing the Apache in next to the barn, and digging latrines.

That was when Staff Sergeant Emilio Evans approached her. He was second-in-command and, since her platoon had evolved into a company, she should promote him. But how? The army had a process for such things, but that was gone. Mac forced herself to focus on the situation at hand. "Hey, Evans . . . How's it going?"

"So far, so good," he replied. "How did you know about this place?"

Mac felt a pang of guilt. "It belongs to my father."

Evans looked at her. She had put herself first, and he knew it. All she could do was stare back. "Do you have a question, Sergeant?"

"Yes, ma'am," Evans answered formally. "It's about the latrines. Rather than dig them by hand each day, how 'bout we look for one of those mini backhoes? Some of them can be towed. Or maybe we can find a trailer."

"A backhoe would be one more machine to maintain," Mac cautioned. "And it would make the column that much longer."

"Yes, ma'am," Evans acknowledged. "But it would save time and improve morale."

Mac nodded. "That makes sense. Let's be on the lookout for one."

Evans broke the ensuing moment of silence. "Permission to speak freely?"

"Always."

"The house is clear. Go in and take a look around. I'll handle things out here."

Mac looked away and back again. "Thanks, Emilio. I will."

Evans nodded, executed a perfect about-face, and walked away.

It felt strange to pull the back door open and hear the usual screech of protest. Where was Mom? She should have been in the kitchen watching CNN as she fixed dinner. Traces of Margaret were still there, however. The walls were a cheerful yellow—and her apron was hanging from a peg. Not even Bo Macintyre had been willing to take it down.

The rest wasn't pretty. Dishes had been smashed, a swearword was spray-painted on a wall, and the sink was full of trash. Where was Mr. Larson? Mac wondered. Was the part-time caretaker okay? So many people had been displaced. Perhaps he was among them.

When Mac left the kitchen, she entered her father's part of the house. A Confederate battle flag occupied most of one wall. Pictures of Cadet Bo Macintyre, Lieutenant Bo Macintyre, and Captain Bo Macintyre were everywhere. Sometimes he stood all by himself. But more often than not he was with a group of soldiers. All of the images had one thing in common though—and that was an implacable stare directed at the camera. Or at a little girl should she be so foolish as to make a mistake.

Judging from the mess, it appeared that a number of people had camped in the living room. The mantel over the fireplace was scorched, drug paraphernalia lay scattered about, and Mac saw a photo of herself lying on the floor. She bent to pick it up. The girl in the picture was three or four. And there, kneeling beside her, was a young version of her father. He was smiling! Because of something her mother had said? Or because he was having a good time? Perhaps their relationship had been different then—back before the disappointment took over.

The second floor was very much like the first in terms of the vandalism that had been done. And Victoria's room was a mess.

But the trophies were still there, along with her collection of ribbons, and a graduation photo. The uniform fit Victoria perfectly. Mac could remember the way the hats had flown up into the air, and hung there for a moment, before falling back to Earth.

But things were quite different down the hall in *her* room. It, too, was littered with trash. But her mementoes were gone. All of the books, wall posters, and knickknacks had disappeared. Why? *Because he gave up on you,* the voice in her head said. *Because you're the failure that he wants to forget.*

A tear trickled down Mac's cheek as she turned away. What was it her father told her as a child? Soldiers don't cry? Well, some soldiers *did* cry . . . But not in front of the troops. Mac used a sleeve to wipe the moisture away. Then she returned to work.

As the light started to fade, Mac went out to walk the perimeter. Evans and his squad leaders had done well. Fighting positions had been dug as necessary, they were linked to each other, and the machine guns were well sited.

The Strykers were positioned farther back, where they could provide fire support if necessary. The rest of the vehicles were parked at the center of the compound but with enough space between them to prevent collateral damage should one of them take a hit.

As for the civilians, they were safely ensconced in the barn that Mac and Vic played in as little girls. A time so long ago that it no longer seemed real.

Mac gave the go-ahead for off-duty personnel to sleep in the house but chose to put her own bag in the Stryker designated as Roller-Seven, referred to as **IRON MIKE** by its crew. Forward Observer Lin Kho had chosen to spend the night inside the vic as well—and was already asleep when Mac lay down on the bench across from her.

Mac slept well until 0200, when she went on watch. Distant shots were heard shortly thereafter. But other than that, the next two hours were uneventful, and Mac was able to go back to bed for two additional hours.

After getting up at 0600 and taking a sponge bath in the female section of the barn, Mac went to work. All were up by then, civilians included. Breakfast was a haphazard affair in which everyone had to fend for themselves. Except for Mac that is, who would have settled for coffee if Doc Obbie hadn't shown up with one of her favorite MREs.

"Eat it, ma'am," Obbie said with a smile, "or I'll report you to Dr. Hoskins."

"Anything but that," Mac replied as she sat on a tailgate. Sparks was nearby, and she waved him over. "Find Esco," she said. "Tell him to launch the Shadow, and check the highway between here and Mountain Home."

Sparks nodded and left. Mac could see patches of blue sky through the cloud cover for once. Would the weather be better in Arizona? She hoped so. "I spoke to Esco," Sparks said, as he returned. "He's on it."

"Good," Mac replied. "I have a job for you. Mountain Home Air Force Base is located about twelve miles from the town itself. Get on the radio and try to make contact."

Sparks stared at her. "What if I succeed? What then?"

Mac frowned. "What do you mean?"

"They will tell you to come in, and we'll have to take orders from the person in charge. Regardless of what they're up to."

Mac swallowed some coffee. "I have news for you, Soldier . . . That's how it works in the army. We don't get to choose our superiors."

"I know that, ma'am," Sparks replied. "But that's the *regular* army. And they left us to fend for ourselves."

"I read you," Mac said, "but what if the 'regular' army is back online? And there's something else to consider . . . The base is home to the 366th Fight Wing of the Air Combat Command known as 'The Gunfighters.' They fly F-15E Strike Eagles. Guess what will happen if we tell them to fuck off?"

Sparks was silent for a moment. "They'll grease us."

"Bingo . . . So quit exercising your jaw and get to work. That's an order."

"Yes, ma'am. Right away."

Mac watched Sparks begin to put out calls. The conversation was interesting in a couple of ways. First, she knew that Sparks was plugged into what the unit's enlisted people were thinking. And, because he spent every day at her side, he was in an excellent position to feed them tidbits of information. So her comments, or a version of them, would make the rounds during the next hour. A fact of life in the army, and an important reason to keep her guard up.

Second, Sparks wasn't the only person who was worried about being absorbed into a larger command. She was as well. If the "real" army was out there, then good. The unit should rejoin. But what if it wasn't? What if her outfit was absorbed by a group of do-nothings? Or a bunch of crazies like the whack jobs in Yakima? Mac felt the need to protect the Marauders from *everything*, and that included rogue units like her own.

In spite of his best efforts, Sparks hadn't been able to make contact with the air force by the time the column left half an hour later. Mac was riding in Roller-One. The house seemed to shrink as she looked back. Then it was gone. Along with her childhood.

It took fifteen minutes to reach Interstate 84 and turn south. Most of the traffic consisted of pedestrians, people on bicycles, and motorcycles. Some overloaded farm trucks passed the column as well. Mac figured that enterprising farmers were growing vegetables in hothouses and selling them to folks in Boise. Good for them. People had to eat. "Roller-Two-One to Roller-Six. Over."

"This is Six actual. Go."

"The Shadow is fifty miles downrange and circling what was Mountain Home Air Force Base. Over."

Mac felt something cold trickle into her bloodstream. "*Was?* Over."

Esco's voice was tight. Mac could tell that the UAV operator was battling to control his emotions. "There isn't much left . . . Just a crater and a huge field of debris."

Mac remembered the briefing at JBLM shortly after the meteors struck. What had Wilson told them? Something about Chinese missiles and a subsequent apology. Had Mountain Home been targeted? That was the way it appeared. It took a conscious effort to swallow the lump in her throat. "Roger that. What about the town? Over."

"It's still there," Esco replied. "But it seems to be deserted. A pack of dogs is nosing around. But that's all. Over."

Mac remembered Scheemer. The mayor knew, *had* to know about the air force base, but had chosen to hold that piece of information back. *Why?*

*Why not?* The voice in Mac's head countered. *Information is valuable, and Scheemer saw no reason to share. Welcome to post-apocalyptic America.*

Mac had a decision to make as Roller-One led the convoy south. Although the air force base was twelve miles from town, there could be residual radiation, and that would explain why the area was deserted. Maybe they should bypass Mountain Home. The problem with that was the Marauders needed supplies—and a National Guard armory was located nearby.

There was an alternative, of course. She could send two Strykers to investigate while the rest of the convoy went out and around. Under that scenario, the Strykers would rejoin the unit south of

Mountain Home. But dividing her force would entail considerable risk. What if a large force attacked one of the two groups?

With those variables in mind, Mac ordered the column to pull over so she could have a private chat with Dr. Hoskins. He was waiting near the six-by-six and proceeded to clean his wire-rimmed glasses while Mac explained her dilemma. "No problem," Hoskins told her once she was finished. "Fallout radiation fades rapidly. Given how much time has passed, and all the rain since then, the current level of radiation is probably 1 percent of what it was after the blast. So, while I wouldn't want to live there, a one- or two-day visit won't present much risk."

Mac thanked him and returned to the pickup. They arrived on the outskirts of Mountain Home forty minutes later. The Shadow was still up, and since Esco had nothing new to report, Mac took the unit straight in. The armory was located slightly southwest of Mountain Home on a dead-end road. Parched land could be seen all around, with the blast-leveled remains of buildings in the distance.

A sheet of plywood was propped up in the middle of the road. The words, "Gov. prop. Do not enter," had been written on the wood with white paint. Garcia braked, and that caused the other vehicles to do likewise. "Go around it," Mac ordered, and Garcia obeyed.

The ruins of a building could be seen up ahead. It appeared that the structure had been leveled by the blast—and the debris field was pointed north. "I see movement at two o'clock," Brown announced, as he swiveled the fifty around to point in that direction.

Mac looked in time to see a man emerge from the hut located adjacent to the remains of the building. He was dressed in combat gear and armed with a light machine gun. She spoke into the boom mike. "This is Six actual. I'm going to speak with him. I want everyone except Hadley to stay back. If I raise my right hand above my shoulder, shoot him. Over."

There was a flurry of clicks as Mac jumped down off the truck. The ground was hard, and ice crystals glittered in the momentary sunlight. The man allowed Mac to approach him. His weapon was pointed at the sky, but Mac knew the barrel could come down in a hurry. Before she could signal Hadley? Yes, quite possibly. She would die, but so would he.

Mac stopped ten feet away. Now she was close enough to see that the man was a major, or some guy pretending to be a major. "I'm Lieutenant Macintyre, United States Army. And you are?"

"Major Fitch, United States Air Force."

"How do I know that's true?"

Fitch's face had a gaunt appearance, and his deep-set eyes peered out from what looked like dark caves. But he was clean-shaven . . . And even though his gear was dirty, it was squared away. "I could ask you the same question," Fitch replied.

Mac smiled. "Touché. Perhaps we should show each other some ID. But that can wait . . . May I ask what you're doing here?"

"I'm guarding the ruins of this building," Fitch replied stolidly.

"That's one way to put it," Mac agreed. "But I think there's more to it than that. You're standing in front of a National Guard armory. Or what used to be an armory."

Fitch stared at her. "That's why you came? To loot the armory?"

"I wouldn't call it looting," Mac temporized. "We're part of the army, after all."

"*Really?*" Fitch demanded. "Who do you report to?"

Mac shrugged. "No one at the moment. We were cut off."

Fitch looked her up and down. "I outrank you, Lieutenant . . . So you report to me. If you are what you say you are, that is."

There it was. The very thing Mac had been dreading. Here was a superior officer who was either a diehard hero, determined to do his duty no matter how steep the cost, or a mental case. Had Fitch been somewhere else when the nuke-tipped missile fell? Was he punishing himself for being alive? There was no way to be sure.

Regardless of that, Mac faced a choice. Should she take orders from Fitch? Or refuse? Was there some middle way? "I suggest that you put the weapon down, sir. Then we'll talk things over."

"The military doesn't work like that, Macintyre. I'm an 04, and you're an 02."

Mac was reminded of her conversation with Sparks. "That's true, sir," she replied. "But the military you're referring to doesn't exist anymore. If it did, you wouldn't be guarding an armory all by yourself. So put the weapon down."

"Or?"

"Or my sniper will kill you."

Fitch stared at her. At least fifteen seconds ticked by. "I will do as you say," Fitch said finally. "But I'm going to note the date, time, and the nature of our interaction. Then, when the opportunity presents itself . . . I will bring charges against you."

Mac sighed. "Yes, sir. That's your privilege. Please place the machine gun on the ground."

Fitch complied, and Mac thanked him. She wasn't concerned about the threat, but a line had been crossed. After refusing a direct order, Mac could no longer claim that the Marauders were part of the United States Army. They were mercenaries.

She allowed Fitch to keep his sidearm but assigned two soldiers to watch him as Evans threw a perimeter around the shattered building, and Esco sent the Raven up to replace the Shadow, which was running low on fuel.

The Apache arrived, and Mac ordered Peters to land two thousand yards away from the vehicles. Maybe the dust the rotors would stir up was radioactive, and maybe it wasn't. Why take the chance? Mac ordered the pilots to remain in their ship until the air cleared.

Fitch refused to provide the Marauders with any information, but it didn't take a genius to figure out that the supplies he'd been guarding were buried under the wreckage. The next four hours were spent removing debris. Hoskins issued surgical masks for the soldiers to wear, and the rest had orders to stay back.

Eventually, the Marauders were able to recover two dozen assault rifles, four machine guns, and ten thousand rounds of assorted ammo. There were other goodies, too . . . Including crates of grenades, flares, and some pistol ammo. It wasn't a large haul, but it was better than nothing and enough to put a smile on Sergeant Smith's face.

As darkness fell, Mac moved the perimeter over to include the helicopter, ordered the unit to dig fighting positions, and told Evans to establish OPs all around. With Strykers on three of the corners and a pickup on the fourth, she felt reasonably secure.

Mac took the first watch, hoping to get six hours of uninterrupted sleep after that. But her plan went to hell in a handcart when a soldier was sent to wake her at 0512. It seemed that Private Wessel, AKA "the Weasel," had dozed off and allowed Fitch to slip away.

Mac was pissed at Wessel since falling asleep constituted a serious dereliction of duty but was secretly glad to rid herself of Fitch. So she told Evans to place Wessel on latrine duty for five days. And being up, she chose to stay up and prepare for the day ahead.

Mac had been looking for a chance to pull her officers and NCOs together for a command conference. And with no immediate threat on the horizon, and relatively good weather, that morning represented a good opportunity.

So Mac put out the word, and all of the people E-5 and above gathered at 0730. Many had mugs of coffee, and some were eating breakfast. The moving van made a good windbreak, and a fire offered some warmth.

The participants included Evans, Company Sergeant Ralston, Supply Sergeant Smith, UAV operator Esco, Medical Officer Hoskins, and both of the Apache pilots. Mac began by saying that the conference was long overdue—and that she planned to hold one a week from that point forward. The purpose of the sessions would be to facilitate communications, identify potential problems, and devise solutions *before* the shit hit the fan.

"So," Mac began, "let's talk about the next segment of our journey. The way I figure it, we'll get on I-84 and follow it down to Salt Lake City." Much to her surprise, a hand shot up. Company Sergeant Ralston had joined the unit in Pendleton, and Mac was still getting to know him. "Yes, Sergeant . . . Do you have a question?"

Ralston was a burly man and famous for the nonreg walrus-style mustache he wore. An affectation that Mac had been careful to ignore. "Not a question so much as a comment, ma'am . . . Salt Lake City is the obvious way to go, I get that, but it might be best to circle around it."

Mac felt the first stirrings of annoyance—but knew better than to let her emotions show. "Okay, why would we do that?"

"Because the Mormons run Utah, ma'am," Ralston replied. "That includes local government, the fire departments, the police departments, and so on. Plus each family has three months' worth of food on top of what the church has stored away. So while I don't know this for a fact—it's reasonable to assume that there weren't any food riots in Salt Lake City. And by now it's quite likely that a church-sponsored militia is guarding the city. If I'm correct, they'll be looking for looters, bandits, and mercenaries."

Mac felt stupid. Not only was Ralston correct, most of his points were glaringly obvious. Yet she had failed to think of them. Yes, she'd been busy . . . But that was no excuse. It would have been nice to save face somehow—but Mac couldn't think of a credible way to do it. "Holy shit, Ralston," she said. "That didn't occur to me. Thanks for speaking up . . . There's no point in walking into what could be a buzz saw.

"Scratch what I said earlier," Mac said, as her eyes roamed the crowd. "What we need is a route that will take us *around* Salt Lake City as efficiently as possible. Fuel being a serious concern."

Another hand went up. This one belonged to Sergeant Smith. "Yes, Sergeant?"

"I have a suggestion, ma'am. If we follow Highway 93 down to Wells, Nevada, we could do some shopping at the local Caterpillar dealership. Then we could go east and connect with the freeway *south* of Salt Lake City."

It took a moment for Mac to catch on. The Strykers were powered by Caterpillar engines. And it was only a matter of time before the unit would need to replace one of them. Plus, a dealer would have lots of spare parts, too.

Were Ralston and Smith double-teaming her? Both were from Pendleton after all. Probably . . . But that's what senior NCOs do. Often, but not always, for the betterment of their unit. Savvy officers knew when to listen and when not to. "I like it," Mac said, "but let's say we capture some engines. How would we move them?"

Smith didn't have a ready answer but was quick to improvise. "The dealership will have a forklift," he predicted. "As for transport, well, we'll have to liberate a semi from someone." Mac thought the plan was a bit vague—but what else *could* he say?

The conference continued for half an hour and covered everything from the need for field showers, to the maintenance issues related to one of the U-Haul trucks, and the need for Vitamin D supplements. "We aren't getting enough sun," Hoskins told them. "And that means we can't make enough of our own Vitamin D to stay healthy. So please be on the lookout for supplies that we can buy, borrow, or steal."

The convoy was on the road by 0900. After twenty minutes on I-84, they left the freeway for secondary roads that led them around Twin Falls to Highway 93. The surrounding countryside was flat for the most part, unrelievedly brown, and boring.

Thanks to the open terrain, and the fact that the Shadow was out in front of the column, Mac felt she could put Evans on point and ride in Roller-Twelve. The Stryker was the last vic in the convoy, and it was nice to shoot the shit with soldiers from her old platoon.

The first hour passed without incident. Then Esco put out a call for Mac to look at what he said was "some interesting video."

So Mac ordered the column to pull over, authorized a bio break, and went to visit the Humvee. Esco's gear was set up in the back. "Take my seat," he suggested, "and watch the screen. The Shadow is circling Wells."

The Humvee's well-worn interior smelled like the men who rode in it, and Mac wrinkled her nose as she sat down and eyed the screen in front of her. Wells was a small town, and the streets were laid out grid-style. As viewed from above, the town's most prominent features consisted of a well-watered park and adjacent sports field. "Okay," Mac said. "What's so interesting?"

"Zoom in," Esco said. "Tell me what you see."

Mac was surprised by what she saw. The streets were filled with motorcycles! There were hundreds of them. Some were parked in tidy rows—while others were racing down one of the main arterials. "That's Sixth," Esco told her, as he put a grubby finger on it. "See the ramp? Watch what happens."

The ramp was located in the center of town in front of what might be a café or bar. As Mac watched, two motorcycles raced up the ramp, flew into the air, and landed hard. One wobbled and crashed. The other pulled a wheelie and continued on. "So a motorcycle gang took over the town," Mac concluded.

"That's the way it looks," Esco agreed. "And they aren't likely to welcome us with open arms. Of course, Peters and Omata could take them out in fifteen minutes."

Mac could imagine how easy it would be for the Apache to chase the gang members down and grease them. But what if appearances were deceiving? What if the citizens of Wells *liked* having the gang there? Maybe the bikers were better than whatever the alternative was. She said as much to Esco. "I don't think that's the case, ma'am," he replied. "Aim the camera at the athletic field and zoom in."

Mac winced as the scene appeared. Rather than shooting down from directly overhead the drone's camera was at least a mile to the north. That allowed Mac to see the crosses, two rows of them, each with a body tied to it. "It's my guess that the bikers crucified anyone who objected to their presence," Esco said.

That put a different light on things. But Mac was still reluctant to use the Apache, knowing how much collateral damage could result. "Where's the Caterpillar dealership?" she inquired.

"It's on the main drag," Esco said, as his index finger landed again. "Two blocks from the ramp."

"Okay," Mac said, as she rose. "I'll give the problem some thought. Thanks for the heads-up. Do me a favor, Sergeant . . . Keep the Shadow up high, where those scumbags will be less likely to spot it."

"Roger that," Esco said.

It felt good to escape the crowded confines of the Humvee and breathe some fresh air. Mac had a lot to think about as she made her way forward. The Marauders were mercenaries, and mercenaries get paid, so why fight the bikers? But Mac couldn't shake the image of the crosses. Besides, Esco was correct. The gang wouldn't let them waltz into town and take some Caterpillar engines without putting up a fight.

Mac climbed up onto Roller-One and told Sparks to pass the word. "Let's get going . . . We're headed to Contact, Nevada. Tell Peters to meet us there."

It took forty-five minutes to reach Contact. It was little more than a house and a clutch of outbuildings on the east side of the road. There was a turnout on the west side of the highway, and that was where Mac told Garcia to stop. The helicopter was on the ground, and the JP8 truck went out to meet it.

Evans took a squad over to secure the house. Could the people who lived there communicate with the folks in Wells? If so, Mac didn't want them to do so.

Once the area was under control, Mac ordered the unit to hide all of the vehicles with the exception of the Strykers behind the outbuildings. Then, with machine guns positioned to cover the highway and the gun trucks ready to roll, she felt confident the group could defend itself.

Mac still felt qualms, however, since dividing the company in half entailed some risk. But what choice did she have other than to do nothing? Taking civilians and soft-skinned vehicles into Wells would be insane.

Once everything was as good as she could make it, Mac called a meeting. A cold wind whipped her hair around as she explained the necessity of going into Wells, the way the plan was supposed to go down, and contingencies if it didn't. Once all of the questions had been answered, it was time to mount up.

Mac chose to ride in the Stryker designated as Roller-Seven. She was standing in the front air-guard hatch with a light machine gun positioned in front of her as the truck took off. Like the other top gunners, Mac was wearing a brain bucket, sunglasses to keep the airborne grit out of her eyes, and a pair of gloves to keep her hands warm.

It took forty minutes to reach Wells. The ESV was in the lead by then. The vic swayed as it completed a hard right-hand turn, the other Strykers followed, and the column started to accelerate as it hit the straightaway. Mac eyed the scene ahead. There were clumps of trees; low, one-story buildings; and dozens of frozen mud puddles. It would have been better to attack at dawn. But Mac feared that the bikers would get word of the vehicles parked at Contact and have time to prepare.

As Seven followed the ESV into town, the external speakers came to life. Suddenly Mac found herself listening to "The Imperial March" from *Star Wars*. It struck Mac as corny at first, and she was about to order the truck commander to kill it, when she changed her mind. *This is it,* Mac thought to herself, *this is how Strykers are supposed to fight. We're going to kick some ass.*

The town hadn't been fortified, and as far as Mac could tell, the bikers didn't have lookouts. From their perspective, it must have seemed as if the Strykers came out of nowhere. Tires screeched as the ESV led the other vics through a series of turns and onto Sixth. There was a long line of custom bikes parked side by side on the right. Lamm was driving the engineering vehicle and knew what to do. The dozer blade was up and angled to the right. Metal clashed with metal, and the hogs fell like dominoes.

Bikes were parked side by side on the opposite side of the street, too. And that gave the gunners an opportunity for some target practice. Mac fired her machine gun in long, sweeping bursts—and was rewarded by the sight of falling bikes and exploding gas tanks.

Mac felt Roller-Seven slow, swerve to avoid the wooden ramp, and speed up again. The gang had started to react by that time—and bikers opened fire as they poured out of bars, cafés, and other buildings. They were armed with a wild variety of weapons—and Mac could hear the ping, ping, ping of bullets striking armor as she adjusted her aim. A man with white hair and a potbelly aimed an AR-15 at her and jerked spastically as half a dozen 5.56-by-45mm rounds tore his torso to shreds. The chatter of machine guns and the ominous music combined to create a symphony of death and destruction.

But just as Mac was beginning to believe that the battle was over, the situation took a turn for the worse. Not all of the motorcycles were lined up on the main drag. Mac heard a throaty roar and turned to see a trio of hogs accelerate out of a side street and join the fray. Roller-Three was the last Stryker in the column, so they went after it first. But Three was far from helpless. The lead bike went down as a burst of bullets chopped the rider's left arm off, and sparks flew as the hog slid west.

But bikes two and three managed to avoid the wreck and pull up beside Roller-Three. As Mac looked back, she could see that each motorcycle had a passenger. One of them fired a pistol at the Stryker's rear gunner, while the other leaned in to slap something onto the vic's protective birdcage. "Watch out, Three!" Mac yelled into the mike. "They . . ."

The rest of Mac's words were lost as the charge went off. The explosion produced a flash of light and a loud boom. The force of the blast was sufficient to lift the wheels on the left side of the Stryker up off the pavement. They came down with a thump, but the driver managed to retain control, and Three trailed smoke.

Mac had to change her focus at that point as *more* Harleys appeared, and the rear gunner engaged them. "This is Six actual," Mac said. "All units will proceed to the objective and secure it. Talk to me, Three . . . Can you make it? Over."

"That's a roger," came the reply. "We have casualties, though . . ."

"Got it," Mac replied. "One-Eight will respond. Do you copy One-Eight?"

Doc Obbie was riding in the ESV. "Copy," he replied. "Over."

The Cat dealership was impossible to miss, thanks to the huge sign on the roof. Seconds after the ESV pulled in, Sergeant Poole's soldiers surged out to secure the building. Mac's truck slowed and stopped, with the fifty pointed at the street. It began to chug as half a dozen bikes roared past. Obbie ran forward as Three pulled in.

Mac forced herself to switch focus. "Roller-Seven-Six to Flyby-One . . . Clean the streets but avoid structures to whatever extent you can. Over."

Peters's voice was matter-of-fact. "Roger that, Six . . . Pop smoke. Commencing gun run. Over." The Apache came in from the southwest. It was flying just above the rooftops and looked scary as hell. The ship's 30mm chain gun began to fire as Peters followed Sixth, staying south of the red smoke. The shells blew divots out of the concrete, tore already damaged motorcycles to shreds, and pulped a gang member stupid enough to fire at the helicopter with an M-16.

The Apache ceased firing as it roared over the Caterpillar dealership, only to resume on the far side. About twenty bikers had gathered northwest of town and were preparing to attack. When the gunship appeared, they turned, opened their throttles, and took off. That was a mistake. With no houses to worry about, Omata was free to fire rockets at them. The result was two overlapping explosions. None of the gang members survived. Shredded flesh and metal lay everywhere as Peters turned back.

He was hunting now, cruising each street looking for bad guys, but there were few to be found. Finally, after destroying a pickup truck loaded with fleeing gang members, he made the call.

"Flyby-One to Six . . . I suspect some of the hostiles are hiding, but the rest are down. Over."

"Roger that and thanks," Mac replied. "Return to Contact, rearm, and provide security there. We'll call if we need you. Over."

As the helicopter angled away, Mac hurried over to check on the casualties. Like the rest of her Strykers, Roller-Three was protected by slat armor commonly referred to as a "birdcage." The structure's purpose was to detonate RPGs and protect the vic within. Even though the explosive charge hadn't been fired at the Stryker, Mac could see that the steel cage had done its job. The armor was a twisted mess, but the truck's hull was intact. An excellent trade-off for the extra weight.

But even though the birdcage had been able to protect the soldiers *inside* the vic, the top gunners hadn't been so lucky. And as Mac approached the truck, she saw that a half-covered body lay on the ground. Sergeant Poole turned to look as she arrived next to him. "Who is it?" she wanted to know.

"Dinkins," he replied. "He was leaning out over the side, trying to take a shot with his M4, when the charge went off."

"Shit. He was a good kid. I heard 'casualties' plural. Did someone else get hit?"

"Yeah . . . Wessel took a bullet from somewhere—but Doc Hoskins says he's going to be okay. The slug went up into his helmet, circled his head, and fell out! Now Wessel claims that he's immortal."

Mac shook her head in amazement. Wessel the Weasel was one lucky son of a bitch. "Sorry to interrupt," Sparks said, "but we have visitors. Some locals would like to speak with you."

Mac followed the RTO out to the street, where a three-person delegation stood waiting. A man stepped forward to shake hands.

He had a receding hairline, a paunch, and was wearing a Colt .45 six-shooter. "Hello . . . My name is Henry Wilkins. Carol Tice is on my left—Miranda Ivey is on the right. We're all that remains of the city council. The rest of them were crucified. Thank God you came! We thought the government had collapsed."

"I'm sorry to say that it did," Mac told them. "Our unit was cut off—and we're operating on our own."

"Yet you chose to free our town," Tice said. She had long brown hair and dark circles under her eyes.

"What the bikers did to your town is horrifying," Mac said. "And I'm glad we were able to help. But we had an ulterior motive as well."

"And what was that?" Ivey inquired. She had freckles, a pug nose, and green eyes.

"We need Caterpillar parts for our Strykers," Mac replied. "And we knew there was a dealership in Wells."

Wilkins pointed a finger at Roller-Three. "Is that a Stryker?"

"Yes, it is," Mac said. "Who owns this dealership? Could I speak with them?"

Wilkins looked away. "Mr. Vickers owned it. But he and his family were killed early on . . . Before the crucifixions began."

"I'm sorry to hear that," Mac said. "Will you permit us to take what we need from the dealership?"

"I don't think we could stop you," Tice said.

"Probably not," Mac agreed. "But we did take care of the bikers for you . . . Perhaps you'd be willing to give us some parts by way of a reward."

"I'm for it," Ivey said.

"Me, too," Wilkins put in.

"I guess you've got a deal," Tice said. "So take what you want from the dealership, but nothing more. Agreed?"

"Agreed," Mac replied. "We'll bring the rest of our vehicles

down from Contract if that's okay . . . And we'll put some temporary security in place. I would suggest that you gather up all the
weapons that are lying around and organize a militia. Another
gang will overrun the town if you don't."

"We'll get to work on it," Ivey said, "*and* on burying the dead.
Thank you."

Mac looked over to where the body lay and back again. "We lost
one of our soldiers during the fighting. Could we bury him in your
cemetery?"

"Of course," Ivey said. "We'll make a special place for him."

"Thank you," Mac said. "Sergeant Poole will work with you
to make the necessary arrangements."

Once the conversation ended, Mac turned to find that Sergeant
Smith was waiting for her. "We've got what we came for, ma'am,
two Cat engines and a lot of assorted spare parts."

"Thank God for that," Mac said. "We paid a high price."

Smith nodded. "Yes, ma'am. There's a problem, though."

"Which is?"

"We need a vehicle to haul everything with. A tractor hooked
to a lowboy trailer would be perfect."

Mac raised an eyebrow. "And?"

"And I found what we need a few blocks from here."

"See if you can buy it," Mac told him. "Offer some of the stuff
we found at Mountain Home. After what they've been through,
these folks might put a pretty high value on a couple of light machine
guns and some ammo. Not too much, though . . . And it wouldn't
be a good idea to deliver the ordnance until we're ready to leave."

"And if they say, 'no'?"

Mac sighed. One of the reasons she'd joined the army was because
the people who belonged to it were *trying* to do the right thing even
if they failed occasionally. That's what her father claimed, anyway.

Now she was up to her butt in moral ambiguity. "If you can't buy it, then call me. We'd better be ready for a fight if we're going to take it."

Smith nodded. "Yes, ma'am." Then he was gone.

It took the better part of two days for the Marauders to bury Dinkins with full honors, buy the tractor-trailer rig, and catch up on deferred maintenance. Then it was time to get back on the road. Their destination was a base called Camp Navajo, which was located just west of Flagstaff, Arizona. Assuming the information Mac had was correct, a wide variety of supplies could be found there, including fuel for the Apache. The latter was of critical importance because the JP8 truck was running low.

They took 93 south. Then, rather than enter Las Vegas, which was said to be under the control of a warlord, the Marauders went east. After three days of zigzagging across northern Arizona, they wound up on I-40 headed for Camp Navajo. Looted cars lined both sides of the highway, there were crosses on the median, and the overpasses were covered with graffiti.

Rather than show up at Camp Navajo hoping for the best, Mac led the convoy off the interstate north of the base and entered the tiny town of Parks. The Flagstaff area was known for its skiing, but there shouldn't have been any snow this time of year. The evergreens were loaded with the white stuff, however—and there was six inches of it on the ground. That was a disappointment since the Marauders had been hoping for better weather in Arizona. *Maybe it will be,* Mac told herself, *especially at lower elevations.*

About a thousand people were supposed to be living in and around Parks. But they were nowhere to be seen as the Marauders rolled into town and took control of a church.

Evans was busy setting up a security perimeter when Mac went to meet with Esco. "Put the Shadow up," she told him, "and give me all the intel you can. Meanwhile, I'm going to send Brown and Kho out for a ground-level view of what's going on. If the situation warrants, we'll go in. Otherwise, we'll bypass the base and continue south."

Once the drone was up, and scouts were on the way, all Mac could do was wait. To pass the time, she made the rounds and paused to admire the small track hoe Smith had purchased in Wells. Evans was right . . . The machine made short work of digging fighting positions and latrines. That was a definite plus.

Esco called for her an hour later. "Take my seat," Esco said, as Mac entered the Humvee. "Rather than make you sit through the whole mission, I cut some of the footage together."

The UAV operator crouched behind Mac where he could provide her with a running narration. "So here's Flagstaff," Esco said, as the drone circled over the snow-clad city. "Notice the smoke coming out of chimneys . . . That suggests that the power grid is down. And look at the streets. There's very little traffic. Why? Because people are afraid to go out, that's why."

Esco leaned in to put a finger on the screen. "See *this*? And *this*? They're barricades. It appears that the town has been Balkanized."

Esco was correct. Mac could see the way cars, RVs, and piles of junk had been used to seal entire neighborhoods off. That seemed to suggest that the local government had collapsed, leaving citizens to fight among themselves.

"And here's Camp Navajo," Esco added. "It's about thirty miles west of Flagstaff. You'll notice that it's sealed off as well . . . You can see vehicles inside the perimeter. That suggests that the Guard is still there, but nothing is moving. So where *are* the troops? Inside drinking hot chocolate?"

Where indeed? Mac wondered. There should have been lots of activity given the nature of the situation. Maybe the scouts would be able to provide some answers.

A six-hour wait followed the meeting with Esco. Mac knew that

Kho and Brown had been able to reach the base, and were okay, because they had orders to report in every thirty minutes. But the frequencies available to them were available to the local Guard unit as well. That made it necessary to keep the transmissions short and cryptic.

At first, Mac killed time by wandering around, sticking her nose in where it wasn't welcome, and offering unnecessary suggestions. That pissed everyone off. A problem she failed to recognize until Evans told her about it.

The temperature fell as the sun went down and a stygian darkness claimed the land. It was snowing by then—and Mac was worried. Maybe Brown and Kho had been ambushed. Maybe the scouts were lost. Maybe she should send the quick-reaction force out to find them. Maybe . . . "The scouts are back," Sparks announced as he appeared at her side. "And they have a prisoner."

Mac felt a tremendous flood of relief, thanked Munroe, and hurried toward the church. She could see her breath, feel the snow give under her boots, and hear the purring sound the generator made. Half a dozen jury-rigged lights were on inside, it was at least ten degrees warmer, and the odor of cooking hung in the air. Food was another thing they needed more of.

Pews had been moved to make way for rows of sleeping bags—and some of the children were playing a game in the middle of the chapel. All of them were wearing coats. Evans waved her over. "They're in the office," he told her. "Both are fine."

"Good," Mac said as she followed him through a door and into a room equipped with three mismatched desks, some metal filing cabinets, and a bulletin board filled with childish drawings. There were muddy tracks on the floor—and a pile of gear sat where the scouts had dumped it. Brown was standing off to one side, Kho was perched on the corner of a desk, and a stranger was seated on a plastic chair. He was twentysomething and wearing an Indian-style headband. Long black hair fell to his shoulders. Kho smiled. "We brought you a present."

"That's a present?" Mac inquired.

"Yup," Brown responded. "He sure is. Lieutenant Macintyre, meet Corporal Vickers." Vickers continued to stare at the floor.

"A corporal?" Mac inquired. "You're kidding."

"Nope," Brown responded. "This piece of shit is a corporal. It says so on his ID card."

"But he's also a deserter," Kho put in. "Which is how we came across him. There we were, scouting the base, when Vickers cut a hole in the wire and walked into our arms."

"And no one noticed?" Mac inquired.

"Not while we were there," Brown answered. "That's because Vickers was on guard duty—and he left through the section of wire he had responsibility for."

"Wow," Mac said as she looked Vickers up and down. "You *are* a piece of shit. So let's get to it. I want to know everything there is to know about conditions inside the base."

Vickers looked up. His eyes were bloodshot, and arcane symbols were tattooed on his forehead. The letters were uneven and clearly the work of an amateur. "What will you give me?"

"That's 'what will you give me, *ma'am*,'" Evans put in. "As for what we'll give you, how about a bullet?"

Vickers turned to Mac. "Like I said, *ma'am*, what's in it for me?"

Evans was playing bad cop, which left Mac free to be the good cop. "That depends," she said. "*If* you cooperate, and *if* you want a future, there might be a place for you in our unit. Not as an NCO, however. Not yet. You'd have to earn that."

Vickers glanced at Evans, then back. He shrugged. "Okay, but understand this . . . Some bad shit went down on base . . . I didn't lead it, but I was there, and if you plan to go army on me, let's finish it now. Shoot me in the face. I want to see it coming."

Mac felt a sudden emptiness at the pit of her stomach. "Some bad shit went down." What did that mean? It wasn't her job to play judge and jury, however. "You have my word," Mac assured him. "Tell us what you know. And so long as you tell the truth, you can join or take a walk."

It didn't take much to make Vickers talk. He *wanted* to get some things off his chest. And they weren't pretty. The problems began shortly after what Vickers called "the big hit." It wasn't long before some of the unit's junior officers went AWOL, or were MIA, depending on what a person chose to believe.

Meanwhile, one of Flagstaff's city council members tried to take control of the government, one of his peers shot him six times, and the rest of the survivors divided the city into small fiefdoms. Each neighborhood had its own militia—and each was intent on garnering support from the local Guard unit. Because if a council member could secure *that*—they'd be able to seize control of Flagstaff.

The XO wanted the company to align itself with the area she lived in, and roughly half of the soldiers agreed. But after the CO refused to go along, he was found dead of what might or might not have been a self-inflicted gunshot wound to the head. That put the XO in charge.

Her reign came to an abrupt end when troops loyal to the CO shot her and sealed themselves inside a heavily fortified maintenance facility where, according to Vickers, they still were. "So which faction did you belong to?" Mac inquired.

"The CO was a good man," Vickers replied.

"So what's with the long hair and all that crap?" Evans demanded.

Vickers shrugged. "Things went tribal. The XO's people began to dress like cowboys. So we called ourselves the Indians. We let our hair grow, took new names, and went on the warpath every now and then. Some people wanted to leave but had no place to go. Flagstaff is fucked-up, and so is the rest of the country, according to what the ham-radio guys say."

"But you decided to leave anyway?" Mac asked.

"Yes," Vickers replied. "There have been a lot of fights lately, conditions are getting worse, and I was sick of it."

Once the interrogation was over, Vickers was placed under guard, and Mac called her officers and noncoms into the office. After briefing them on the situation at Camp Navajo, she presented her plan. "Based on what Vickers told us, the troops inside the base no longer have unit cohesion, are largely leaderless, and at a low state of readiness. I think we should strike immediately since it's hard to imagine how the situation could improve.

"Rather than do battle with them, I plan to minimize casualties by pinning both groups down. Then, once they're under control, we'll take everything that isn't nailed down! And if some of these folks want to join, then so much the better, so long as it's a number we can handle without compromising security."

Mac's eyes scanned the faces in front of her. "In order take full advantage of what we find, I'll ask our civilians to pitch in as loaders and drivers. The children will be left in the care of two adults, with five soldiers to protect them. That's the plan in a nutshell. Are there any questions, suggestions, or comments?"

There were, but none of them were deal breakers, and after making the necessary adjustments, Mac dismissed the group. There was a lot of work to do before the attack element could depart at 0300, and only four hours to do it in. But, thanks to the processes already in place, they managed to finish on time. The Strykers led the way.

It was snowing heavily by then, which Mac saw as a plus since the white stuff would serve to limit visibility and muffle the sound of the convoy's engines. Because Kho had traveled through the area earlier, she was able to direct the convoy along back roads to the well-fortified main gate. "There's a good point of entry west of here," she told Mac.

And that prediction was borne out. The women were standing in hatches aboard the ESV truck as Kho ordered the driver to stop. "Look to the right," she told him. "See the fence? Can you break through it?"

"Can a bear shit in the woods?" Lamm replied. "Hang on . . . We're going in."

After backing away a bit, Lamm put his foot to the floor. The dozer blade was raised, and Mac felt nothing more than a slight hesitation as steel sliced through the wire mesh. The vic bucked wildly as it passed over a mound of earth and plowed ahead. At that point, they were inside the base, and not a shot had been fired.

Vickers was riding in the three truck and helped to guide them through a maze of low-lying buildings, vehicle parks, and other obstacles. And it was only a matter of minutes before they arrived at the building where his group was holed up. Mac saw snow-filled craters out front, empty fighting positions, and a façade that was pockmarked with bullet holes. It wasn't long before automatic weapons began to chatter, and bullets hit the vics.

That was Vickers's cue to address the defenders over his Stryker's PA system. "Hey, shitheads, this is Vick . . . Stop shooting! We aren't firing on you, but we can . . . I hooked up with a company-sized force that includes three Strykers and plenty of heavy weapons. You can remain where you are, or you can come out. It's up to you. And, if you want to join this unit, the CO is looking for some good people. But if you continue to fire, we'll grease you. You have five seconds to stop."

There were more shots, but not many, and it wasn't long before a dozen soldiers came out with their hands over their heads. A squad was sent forward to search and secure them while Mac, Vickers, and two Strykers departed for building two. It belonged to the people who'd been loyal to the XO—and they saw Vickers as a traitor *and* an enemy combatant.

So Mac spoke to the cowboys over the PA, ordered them to hold their fire, and to remain where they were. It didn't work as first. But they stopped firing once the Strykers opened up on them.

Despite the fact that she could use more troops, Mac knew it would be dangerous to try to integrate potentially unstable soldiers into the unit, because of how much trouble they could cause. Plus, even if the cowboys were able to get along with the Marauders, it seemed unlikely that they'd manage to make peace with the ex-Indians. So the Strykers remained on station while the rest of the Marauders went to work.

As the snow stopped, and the sickly-looking sun rose in the east, it soon became apparent that the amount of material available to the Marauders was beyond Mac's wildest dreams. Weapons, ammo, food, fuel, clothing, and much-needed medical supplies were all sitting on pallets waiting to be taken. That was good. But there was more! The haul included four Strykers, two M35 trucks, and half a dozen other vehicles. Not to mention some additional UAVs for Esco.

But wonderful though the wealth of supplies was, they presented a problem as well. That stemmed from the need to distribute critical materials throughout the convoy lest all of a particular item be lost when or if a vehicle was destroyed. Ammo was an excellent example of that. Fortunately, Sergeant Smith was up to the job and was using a laptop to track everything. Still, it took time to bar-code and load the incoming material, which meant that the Marauders would have to stay in Camp Navajo for a couple of days.

Mac made use of the time by setting up a panel of people to interview the ex-Indians. The committee included her, Dr. Hoskins, and Corporal Cassidy. Their job was to determine if the volunteers would be a good fit or not. In the end, nine of the volunteers were accepted—while the rest were placed in temporary detention. "You'll be freed when we leave," Mac assured them. "And at that point, you can do whatever you choose."

By dawn of the third day, the children and their caretakers had been reunited with the rest of the unit, all of the new vehicles had been integrated into the column, and the supplies had been properly allocated. The convoy was longer now—and would be more difficult to protect. But it was also stronger . . . And better able to defend itself from most criminal gangs.

Mac felt good about that as she stood in the forward air-guard hatch on the lead Stryker and looked back at the convoy. Mac's Marauders had everything they needed now except for one thing, and that was a home.

# CHAPTER 8

||||||||||||||||||||||||||||||||||||

It has been said that democracy is the worst form of
government except all the others that have been tried.

−WINSTON CHURCHILL

**THE NEW MASON-DIXON LINE**

It was just after five in the morning when the rain stopped and a
cold fog appeared. It hovered just above the ground and shivered
as a breeze nudged it. The patriots froze as Sam McKinney raised
a fist. It had been three days and four hundred miles since they'd
departed the relative safety of the Ouachita National Forest. The
group had traveled by car at first. And now, as they neared the
Mason-Dixon line, they were on foot.

Sloan saw McKinney push his hand down and knew that was
his cue to take a knee. He heard voices as the ground fog rose to
envelop him—and his right hand went to the pistol that was hol-
stered under his left arm. A man laughed as dimly seen figures
passed off to the right. Sloan counted six of them. "You've got to
be kidding," a voice said. "What did you say?"

The patrol was gone before Sloan could learn the answer. He

allowed himself to exhale and saw his breath fog the air. Sloan wanted to stand but knew that would be a mistake. McKinney was an ex-Ranger and a harsh taskmaster. He had a sharp tongue and spared no one. "Your *other* right, Mr. President," McKinney liked to say, along with "Keep your butt below the skyline, Howell," and "What the hell's wrong with you, Allston? My grandmother can shoot better than that." But painful though the process was, Sloan felt grateful. Like the others, he had no military training and understood the need to learn.

When McKinney stood, that meant the rest of them could as well. And as Sloan looked back over his shoulder, he could see Howell, Allston, and Jenkins in that order. The latter was an ex–deputy sheriff and McKinney's star pupil.

Sloan turned back to discover that McKinney was already disappearing into the ectoplasm-like fog. He hurried to catch up and position himself fifteen feet behind the ex-soldier. Intervals were important, he knew that now, and didn't want to be on the receiving end of another cutting comment.

Even as Sloan sought to maintain the "situational awareness" that McKinney liked to harp on, he couldn't help but think about where they were, which was just south of the imaginary boundary separating North from South. Except it wouldn't be imaginary for long. Huxton and his cronies were building a picket fence–like barrier designed to keep what they called "the takers" from flooding the South and laying waste to it. Nothing of that sort had occurred, but a constant flow of propaganda assured Southerners that it could, unless they threw their support behind the "New Order."

The ground began to slope up at that point, forcing Sloan to watch his footing. There was a lot of loose rock, and when one of

Sloan's boots sent a chunk bounding downhill, he found himself on the receiving end of a frown from McKinney. Fortunately, the ex-Ranger couldn't say anything without breaking one of his own rules.

Sloan managed to complete the climb without committing any additional errors. As they approached the top, he knew it was time to get down and crawl. After elbowing his way onto the ridge, Sloan heard the sound of a helicopter engine approaching from behind. He was careful to lie perfectly still as the aircraft passed overhead.

As the Apache continued to descend, Sloan could see where it was going. He'd seen pictures of defense towers by then, but always from a long ways off and in the early stages of construction. This one was different. Though not an expert, Sloan could tell that the roughly three-hundred-foot-tall structure was nearing completion. The central column was thick enough to house a cluster of elevators, including one large enough to accommodate the Apache.

The helicopter flared and put down on one of four circular pads clustered around the central "trunk." Once the rotors stopped turning, a tractor towed the helo into the column, where an elevator would be waiting. Then the aircraft would be lowered into an underground maintenance facility.

It stood to reason that a lot of dirt had been removed to make the underground complex possible, and Sloan could see that it had been used to create the berm that surrounded the base of the tower. As Sloan raised his binoculars, he could see that gun positions were embedded in the wall.

"Those are Vulcan Air Defense System guns," McKinney said, as if capable of reading the other man's mind. "They were designed to fire on aircraft but can be used against ground targets as well.

They're no longer state-of-the-art, but each one can pump out a whole lot of 20mm projectiles in a very short period of time."

Sloan tried to imagine participating in an infantry assault on such a well-defended wall and couldn't. "But they *can't* fire on aircraft," he observed. "Not from where they are."

"That's true," McKinney agreed. "But look at the topmost platforms. Those weapons *can* fire on planes."

"What's that boxy thing?" Sloan wanted to know.

"That's a C-RAM," McKinney replied. "It's designed to throw a wall of metal into the air to destroy incoming rockets and mortar rounds before they can hit the tower. The next pod over is a surface-to-surface-missile battery."

Sloan considered that as he turned the binoculars to the right. The sun had risen by then and was peeking through broken clouds. Only a few wisps of fog still remained. Off to the east, Sloan could make out the faint outline of another tower. "What do you think?" he inquired. "Could a strike force slide in between the towers and break through?"

McKinney looked at Sloan with a look of newfound respect. "Very good! You're thinking like a soldier . . . I don't know. It would depend on the range of the defensive missiles, how good their targeting systems are, and whether the Confederates have been laying mines to prevent such an attack. But never say never."

Sloan nodded. "Thank you, Major."

"I was a captain."

Sloan lowered the binoculars. "Not anymore. You're a major now, and my military attaché."

McKinney stared at him. "No offense, Mr. President . . . But I have no desire to be an REMF."

"And what," Sloan inquired, "is an REMF?"

"A rear echelon motherfucker, sir."

Sloan laughed. "I get that. But consider this . . . Assuming we succeed in rebuilding the army, I'll be surrounded by REMFs . . . Some of them will try to blow smoke up my ass. How will I sort them out without your sage advice?"

McKinney was silent for a moment. Then he produced one of his rare smiles. "That would be me, sir . . . Major McKinney, smoke detector extraordinaire."

Both men laughed, pushed themselves away from the ridge, and began the trip down. It was the beginning of a much longer journey that took them up through Branson, Ozark, Springfield, and into the town of Marshfield, Missouri.

After spending some time in the South, Sloan was eager to see how things were going up north. The answer wasn't good. In a marked contrast with cities like Shreveport, Louisiana, the people who lived above the Mason-Dixon line had to deal with frequent power outages. Or no electricity at all. And while there were places where local governments had stepped up to provide local citizens with a modicum of security, the coordination normally provided at the state level had all but vanished, never mind the federal government—which was MIA.

The result was a patchwork quilt of hamlets, towns, and cities, many of which had to compete with each other for scarce resources. All too often, they had fallen under the control of a strongman or -woman who was more interested in taking care of themselves than the population at large. Other communities were under the sway of a single religion. Never mind the legal strictures regarding the separation of church and state or the wishes of nonbelievers.

Each time Sloan became aware of such a situation, he felt a strong desire to wade in and set it right. But the others held him back. "It's too early for that," Allston insisted. "The locals won't listen to you right now . . . But that will change soon. Keep your powder dry."

It was good advice, and Sloan knew that. But it galled him to see so much unnecessary pain, misery, and conflict.

Their ultimate destination was Indianapolis, where, according to ham-radio operators, patriots from all over the nation were starting to gather. But after their car ran out of gas, they'd been forced to hoof it. A mode of transportation that, along with bicycles, was increasingly popular. Even so, it seemed as if there was an unusually large number of people on the highway that day, with more joining from driveways and side roads.

So when they arrived in Lebanon, Sloan expected to see something . . . An open market perhaps, or a street fair, but that wasn't the case. Instead, what he saw was a huge banner that was suspended over Commercial Street. It said WELCOME PRESIDENT SLOAN, and as Sloan drew near, a well-dressed Doyle Besom appeared to grab his elbow. "Right this way, Mr. President," Besom said. "Everything is ready."

A cheer went up as a band began to play "Hail to the Chief," and Sloan felt slightly light-headed. When Besom and Cindy Howell had gone ahead to "Get things ready," Sloan hadn't thought to question the ex–PR man about what that meant.

A wooden platform loomed ahead, and the crowd surged in to surround it as Besom preceded Sloan up a flight of stairs. A generator was running nearby, and the jury-rigged PA system was on. Besom jerked Sloan's left arm up into the air. "Here he is!" Besom shouted into the mike. "*This* is the man who, as Secretary of Energy, was trapped in Mexico when the meteors hit, and paddled hundreds of miles to return home! *This* is the man who was captured, held prisoner, and refused to be a puppet president! *This* is the man who escaped, made his way north, and walked into this town on foot. His name is President Samuel T. Sloan . . . And he's here to put our country back together!"

At least a thousand people were gathered around the platform, with more arriving every second. As they clapped, and Sloan accepted the mike, he struggled to organize his thoughts. "My fellow Americans," Sloan began, as the applause died away, "a swarm of meteorites struck Earth, killed millions of people, and brought our great country to its knees.

"But America has been dealt such blows before and never kneels for long. I am passing through Lebanon on my way to Indianapolis, where a new Continental Congress is going to convene. Once that occurs, we will stand, and not just stand, but stand together.

"Meanwhile, the clouds of war have begun to gather. I have been in the South, I have heard the propaganda, and I have seen the military convoys that are rolling north. More than that, I've seen the defense towers that are being built to keep us from crossing the New Mason-Dixon Line. *Why?* Oil, that's why. Those who control the South have taken control of the oil reserves that rightfully belong to *all* Americans."

That produced a chorus of boos, and Sloan nodded. "As the ex–Secretary of Energy, I can tell you that there are approximately 700 million barrels of oil stored in those reserves. That's enough fuel to run our country for more than two months at pre–May Day levels. Or even longer, assuming we use it wisely. What would that mean? It would mean a jump start while we get shale-oil and natural-gas production back up and running . . . And that, along with wind power, can put us back on the path to prosperity in spite of the persistent bad weather. But there's even more to fight for," Sloan added. "The so-called New Confederacy stole part of our country . . . *And we want it back!*"

The resulting roar of approval echoed between the surrounding buildings. Sloan raised both hands in an effort to quiet the crowd. "I hear you . . . And thank you for your support. But know this . . .

What's coming is nothing less than a second civil war. Brother will fight brother . . . Sister will fight sister . . . And rivers of tears will flow.

"But after the last shot has been fired, and the last body has been buried, our country will rise again. And I want you to be there, standing at my side, as we bear witness to that glorious day. Thank you! And God bless America!"

There was an explosion of applause, which went on and on. Besom had to shout in order to be heard. "Where the hell did *that* come from?"

Sloan waved to the crowd. "Was it okay?"

"*Okay?* It was great! I want you to give the same speech in the next town, and the one after that. Word will spread. There *is* a president—and he has a plan. Now get down there, shake hands, and kiss babies."

It took hours to get out of town, and Sloan was exhausted by then. He remembered the *real* president, the one who had died in Washington, D.C., and how good he'd been at pressing the flesh. "The people's president." That's what sympathetic members of the press called him, and Sloan thought it was true.

Even so, the president had never been consumed by a crowd the way Sloan had been. It was exhilarating, and being the center of attention felt good. *Too good,* Sloan admonished himself. *Be careful, or you'll turn into an egotistical jerk.*

The initial thrill was short-lived. After five minutes or so, the press of the crowd began to feel oppressive. And Sloan was extremely vulnerable. The man he thought of as the *real* president had staff, police officers, and the Secret Service to protect him. So there was a natural desire to wall himself off. But the voice was there to offer contradictory advice. *These are early days, and the citizens of the United States need a leader they can reach out and touch. Be that person, and word will spread. You need their approval. More than that, you need their love. Because in order to do what needs to be done, thousands, no, tens of thousands of your followers will die, and that means the bond with them must be strong.*

It was a sobering thought . . . And as the group marched northeast, feelings of self-doubt began to pull Sloan down. There was so much to do. So much to *be*. Was he up to it? Perhaps someone else would do a better job. That possibility followed him into the town of Rolla, where it haunted his dreams.

The next day began with breakfast at a local restaurant followed by another speech. There were hecklers this time. People who, judging from the Confederate flags they carried, were aligned with the South. The patriots in the crowd drove them away. It was a sobering moment, though, and a potent reminder that the North was far from homogenous.

The group had limited funds. But that didn't present much of a problem because there were plenty of people who wanted to buy them dinner, put them up for the night, or both. That was nice but exhausting as well. Sloan said as much to Besom, who was quick to push back. "Some of these people are wealthy, Mr. President. Even after the disaster. And you're going to need donors."

Sloan frowned. "Donors? Why?"

Besom spoke as if to a child. "The president had served three years when he was killed and replaced by the vice president. That means you'll have to start campaigning in a few months. By that time, at least two or three people from your party will come forward to oppose you, never mind the New Whigs, who have a pro-Confederate bent. So relationships like the ones you're developing now will become critical later on."

Sloan stared at him. "What makes you think that I'll run?"

"The war will still be under way a year from now," Besom predicted. "And you won't want to leave office in the middle of it."

Sloan hadn't thought of that—and realized that he should have. He forced a grin. "Point taken. I will be nice to the wealthy donors."

Dinner was nearly over when a man burst into the restaurant. He was disheveled, as if he'd traveled a long way, and his eyes were darting about. "I'm looking for the president," he said loudly. "I was told that I could find him here."

"He's over there," a waiter said, and pointed at Sloan.

The man nodded and made his way over. "Are you the president?" he demanded, as he stared at Sloan.

Jenkins stood before Sloan could answer and stepped in between them. "Are you armed?"

The man nodded. "Place your hands on your head," Jenkins ordered, "and keep them there. I'm going to pat you down. Or, if you don't like that, you can leave."

"That's right," McKinney said as he held his Glock barrel up.

"I understand," the man said, and placed his hands on his head.

Jenkins conducted a thorough search. In the process he turned up a .9mm Beretta, a wicked-looking knife, and a derringer. All of which were placed on the table. "He's clean," Jenkins declared as he stepped back and out of the way.

"Thank you," Sloan said. Then, having turned his eyes to the man in front of him, "I'm President Sloan. And you are?"

"Captain Frederick Yancy, of the 213th Ordnance Company, Ohio National Guard. The Secretary of Defense sent me to find you. I have an important message."

Sloan was mystified. "*Secretary of Defense?* I don't have one."

That was when Marsha Roston spoke up. "Would that be Secretary of Defense *Garrison*?"

"Yes, ma'am," Yancy replied. "And his message is urgent."

Sloan wasn't sure how to react. Garrison had agreed to carry messages to patriot leaders farther east. Now it appeared that the gentleman farmer and part-time stamp collector had named himself Secretary of Defense! "Please," Sloan said, "have a seat. Would you like something to eat or drink?"

"Yes, sir," Yancy responded. "*After* I deliver the secretary's message."

"Understood," Sloan replied. "Please proceed."

"It's about Fort Knox," Yancy said eagerly. "Secretary Garrison tried to take control of the facility, and the CO, a general named Carol Cox, refused. She believes, or pretends to believe, that the former president is still alive. And she won't take orders from anyone other than him."

"Is there reason to believe that General Cox is pretending?" Roston inquired. "Does she want to keep the gold for herself?"

Yancy shrugged. "I can't say for sure, ma'am . . . But Secretary Garrison believes that's the case."

Sloan was appalled by how much Garrison had taken upon himself. But he understood the stakes, which, to put it simply, were billions of dollars' worth of gold. "Thank you," he said. "Is there more?"

"Yes, sir," Yancy said. "Based on orders from Secretary Garrison, Colonel Foster attacked the fort. But the assault didn't go well. We lost more than a hundred soldiers."

Sloan felt a sudden emptiness at the pit of this stomach. A hundred! Casualties taken trying to wrest control of Fort Knox away from the woman assigned to protect it. What a waste. "And?"

"And Secretary Garrison wants you to return with me," Yancy replied. "He gave me this." At that point, Yancy removed an envelope from a pocket and gave it over. Sloan used his dinner knife to cut it open.

*Dear Mr. President,*

*By now Captain Yancy has told you about the situation here at Fort Knox. I would like to add some advice. As you know, our attack failed. That alone is reason enough for the commander in chief of the armed forces to come here. But I submit that there's a second reason as well. If you are present when we win, people will trust you to take the next step, and that will be an attack on the South. We await your arrival.*

> *Respectfully yours,*
> *Frank Garrison*
> *Interim Secretary of Defense*

Sloan continued to stare at the document after he had finished reading it. "We await your arrival." That sounded like an order rather than a request. And what about Garrison's advice? Was it genuine? Or was Garrison one of the people who would oppose him during the coming election? *No,* the voice told him, *you're too paranoid. Besides, even if your worst suspicions turn out to be true, Garrison is right. Here's an opportunity to snatch victory from the jaws of defeat. Go there, win the battle, and secure the fort. More than that—prove that you're worthy to be president.*

Sloan stood. "Grab your packs," he said. "And let's find some transportation. We're going to Fort Knox."

## ATHENS, OHIO

After a succession of miserable days, the sun was out. And as Victoria Macintyre eyed the highway ahead, she felt free—or as free as any army officer could feel while on duty. The beat-up BMW wasn't much to look at—but the big motor ran smoothly as it carried her north. Vic was wearing goggles, but no helmet, and gloried in the way the air pressed against her face. It felt good to be alive.

The mission was simple: Gather intel, check in with some of the Confederacy's spies, and build relationships with potential allies. Victoria's journey had begun in Texas and carried her up through Kentucky and into Ohio. As she entered Athens, Victoria knew that the town was situated on the Hocking River and was home to Ohio University.

Vic also knew that Ohio had supplied troops and supplies to the Union Army during the first civil war. Did that mean the state would oppose the New Order if a *second* civil war began? Or could the people who lived there be convinced to join the nascent Confederacy? Huxton and newly named CEO Lemaire believed, or *pretended* to believe, that the "Northern rabble" were going to descend on the South like locusts and consume everything in their path. That was possible, of course—but by no means certain.

Victoria believed it was equally possible that the Northerners were too disorganized to attack anyone other than each other. She'd ridden past the devastated farmhouses, seen hamlets that had been savaged by bandits, and circled around towns ruled by warlords. And therein lay what she considered to be the *real* problem. What if a warlord or an alliance of warlords formed an army? And having harvested the easy pickings up north turned their attention to the South. At that point, the dire predictions voiced by Huxton and others might come true.

But as Victoria entered the outskirts of Athens, there weren't any signs of combat. The strip malls had been looted, and abandoned cars littered the streets, but that was to be expected. Where were the people? Outside of foraging dogs, the streets were nearly deserted. And that seemed strange in a town of what had been twenty-four thousand people.

At that point, Victoria spotted the column of gray smoke that was pouring up into the sky. Something was burning? But what? And *why*? Victoria steered the BMW through empty streets to the edge of Ohio University's campus. The column of smoke was rising from a point on the far side of the building in front of her. Rather than ride the bike into the middle of whatever was going on, Victoria chose to park it behind a dumpster.

A knapsack containing a change of clothes and her personal items was on Victoria's back, and a Glock 17 was within easy reach under her left arm as she made her way forward. Then, as Victoria caught a whiff of the smoke, she knew what was taking place. The smell was similar to that of burned pork—and once encountered was impossible to forget.

And sure enough . . . As Victoria rounded the building, she could see fire. It was burning in the middle of a large green, and she could hear the sizzle of burning fat, along with an occasional pop as a skull split open. And when Victoria paused, she could feel the resulting heat.

The fire was already quite large and about to become even larger as a man on a front loader drove the machine forward, raised a bucketful of bodies, and dumped them into the pyre. The force of the impact caused a half-charred leg to roll free of the blaze. The limb continued to smoke as a person in a protective suit stepped in to spear the leg and return it to the fire.

Meanwhile, other people, all clad in white, continued to converge on the scene. They were pushing carts loaded with more bodies—which were taken over to a spot where the front loader could scoop them up. Victoria noticed a figure standing apart from the workers and went over to speak with him. "Excuse me," she said. "Can I ask a question?"

The man was wearing a protective face shield. And when he pushed it up out of the way, she could see the tears on his cheeks. A grubby hand wiped the moisture away. "Sorry . . . But they were my students, and I feel responsible for what happened to them."

"You're an administrator here?"

"The president. Or ex-president. All we can do is burn the bodies to keep the disease from spreading."

Victoria felt suddenly vulnerable. "Which disease?"

"Cholera. The power went out, the water department's equipment failed, and a contaminant entered the system."

Victoria looked around. "And *all* of the students died?"

"No, but at least five hundred of them did. The rest fled, along with most of the city's other residents."

"But you stayed."

"Yes," the man replied. "It was my duty to do so."

Victoria understood the concept of duty better than most—and couldn't help but admire him. "I'm from down south," she told him. "And I just arrived. Is it like this everywhere?"

"No," he replied. "I don't think so. But news reports are spotty, so it's hard to tell. There's reason to hope though . . . We have a president again—and he's going to pull the country together."

The statement caught Victoria by surprise. A new president! Someone to replace Wainwright . . . That was an important piece of information. "Do you know his name?" she inquired.

"Yes, I do," the administrator responded. "Samuel T. Sloan. He was the Secretary of Energy before the meteorites struck."

Victoria was surprised to say the least. According to what she'd heard, Sloan had thrown himself out of a helicopter and died in a swamp. "There are lots of rumors floating around," she said. "Are you sure?"

The man fumbled with a zipper, withdrew a piece of carefully folded paper from an inside pocket, and passed it over. "Here, look at this. Just before the cholera struck, a man in a Revolutionary War costume passed through town. He had thousands of these things in the back of his pickup. I kept mine as a memento."

When Victoria opened the piece of paper, she saw a skillfully drawn likeness of Uncle Sam pointing a finger at her. "President Samuel T. Sloan needs you!" the cartoon figure proclaimed. "Conserve energy, store food, and help your neighbors. America is rising!"

It was an innocuous message in many ways—but Victoria could see past that to a larger plan. The purpose of the message was to reassure the populace, take the first step toward the restoration of civil law, and pave the way to *what*? A government in the North? Or an attempt to reunify a broken nation? There was no way to know—but it was valuable information nevertheless. "Can I keep this?" Victoria inquired.

The man hesitated, shrugged, and waved it off. "Sure . . . I'll find another one." Victoria thanked him and returned to the motorcycle. It started with a roar and carried her away from the campus. Feral dogs had been at work, so there weren't any bodies to be seen. Just widely scattered bones and the occasional empty-eyed skull.

Victoria was no stranger to death, but she had no desire to linger as she went looking for a place to make the necessary call. And when a wide-open soccer field appeared, she rode out to the center of it. A spot well away from tall structures and trees—and one that would give her an 80 percent view of the sky. After parking the bike, she got off and removed the phone from her pack.

The call was encrypted and went through without difficulty. That was a matter of luck in large part but not entirely. The New Order had taken control of all but a few of the country's satellites a month earlier—and was doing everything in its power to disrupt communications up north. That was difficult to do with any precision, but progress was being made. So telephone, TV, and Internet service were extremely spotty outside of the Confederacy.

Mrs. Walters indicated that Victoria's father wasn't available. All Victoria could do was to leave the set on and wait for him to call back. There was food in her knapsack, and Vic took advantage of the opportunity to eat. She was halfway through an apple when the phone rang. "This is Alpha-Four-Niner-Seven."

"And this is Six," her father replied. "How's the boondoggle going? Are you ready to come back yet?"

An image of the funeral pyre blipped through Victoria's mind, but she made no mention of it. "Nope, I'm still having fun. And I have news for you."

Bo Macintyre listened in silence as Victoria told him what she'd learned. Then he spoke. "Sloan's supposed to be dead. So if he's alive, some very influential people are going to fill their pants. Of course, there is the possibility that the real Sloan *is* dead, and some bozo took his place. Time will tell. Can you send me a copy of the flyer?"

Victoria scanned the piece of paper with a hand wand and sent it off. "Got it," Bo said. "Good work. Next, I want you to head over to Indianapolis, where, according to other intelligence assets, the so-called patriots are going to convene a Third Continental Congress in two days' time. That will provide you with the perfect opportunity to confirm the news regarding Sloan. Plus you'll be able to determine if the gathering is for real and look for potential assets. All sorts of people will show up for the gathering—and some might prove useful in the future. Don't hesitate to buy some loyalty if you need to."

The call ended shortly thereafter. There weren't any expressions of affection by either party. That was understood, and something neither one of them needed to verbalize. Victoria finished the apple, tossed the core away, and put the phone back in the pack.

Then it was time to consult a much-folded road map prior to throwing a leg over the bike and taking off. Indianapolis was about 250 miles away—but her immediate objective was to find gas. Had the citizens of Athens left any behind? Probably, but it would take forever to find it. So the most efficient thing to do was to steal what she needed.

Victoria had already done so on two occasions and had a system. The first step was to leave the city via one of the secondary roads that led north. Then, once clear of Athens, Victoria would find a spot where she could hide.

It took half an hour to find the right spot, park, and shut the engine off. That meant it would take a little longer to get going. But the other choice was to let the motor idle and suck gas. So Victoria sat behind a thicket of young hazelnut trees with her eyes on the road.

There was traffic but not much. And when vehicles did pass by, they were generally pickup trucks loaded with people who were armed. They might be farmworkers or paying passengers. It didn't matter. Attacking such a vehicle would be suicidal.

A full hour and a half passed before a likely-looking car appeared. It was an old VW Bug—and coming her way at a relatively low rate of speed. How many people could be in it? Four at the most. But Victoria was hoping for less.

She waited for the car to pass her position before starting the engine. Then she gave chase. Victoria had to keep her right hand on the throttle, so she chose to approach the passenger side of the Bug and fire left-handed. Unfortunately, that would give the driver an opportunity to sideswipe the BMW and send it flying into the ditch.

As Victoria pulled alongside the car, she saw that an elderly woman was behind the wheel—while a man who might have been her husband sat in the passenger seat. Vic pointed the Glock at him, waggled the barrel, and waited for the VW to slow. It didn't.

The woman with wispy gray hair put her foot down, and the man brought a sawed-off shotgun up off his lap. He was swinging the weapon around when Vic shot him in the head.

As the man slumped forward, the woman threw the wheel over in a desperate attempt to sideswipe the big motorbike. Victoria braked, the V-dub missed, and ran off into the ditch. The car was slumped to the right, which made it hard for the old lady to push the driver's side door up and open. Did she have the shotgun? Would she use it? Maybe, and maybe not. But why take the chance? Victoria stepped up to the door and fired three shots at it. All efforts to escape the Bug stopped. A peek through the window confirmed what Victoria expected. The woman was dead.

Victoria knew she was supposed to feel something, but she didn't. Collateral damage was an inevitable side effect of war. And war was a natural part of being human. Bo Macintyre had taught her that, and he was correct. She forced herself to focus. How long before some locals arrived on the scene? Five minutes? Ten? There was no way to tell.

Victoria returned to the bike and rode it forward. She stopped next to the Beetle and got off. The fuel-transfer kit was stored in the BMW's right-hand pannier. She ran the hose from the motor-cycle's tank to the car's tank and began to pump. The gas gurgled as it began to flow. The process seemed to take forever—but all Victoria could do was stand there and wait.

Finally, after what seemed like an eternity, the BMW's tank was full. Victoria hurried to retrieve the transfer kit and stow it away. The bike started with a reassuring roar, and it wasn't until she was half a mile away that Victoria allowed herself a sigh of relief.

The next hour was spent riding north toward Columbus, Ohio. Then as it began to rain, and the light started to fade, it was time to seek cover. Choosing a place to spend the night was part science and part gut instinct. Victoria knew that any house or outbuilding that looked good to her would look good to everyone else and should be avoided.

But old barns, sheds, and looted strip malls were relatively safe places to hole up. The key was to find a spot where she could take the BMW inside and out of sight. So when Victoria spotted the half-burned house, she was quick to turn off the highway and follow a driveway up to an overgrown yard.

The front door was ajar, which allowed Victoria to bump up over a couple of stairs and ride the BMW into a badly trashed living room, where she killed the engine. The next few minutes were spent checking all of the rooms. They were empty.

In keeping with long-established habits, Victoria went about the process of heating water on her Jetboil. Then she poured some of it into a foil pouch filled with dehydrated mac and cheese before making coffee. Once dinner was over, Victoria cleared a place to lie down.

Rather than sleep on the wooden floor, she made a bed out of funky couch cushions—and laid the supercompact Sparks SP1 sleeping bag on top of it. Then, with her water bottle and the Glock close at hand, it was time to remove her boots and slide in. Victoria didn't expect to sleep. So when she awoke to see filtered daylight coming through the shattered windows, it came as a surprise.

Victoria dreaded leaving the bag, and even though she was fully dressed, the cold air made her shiver. She went outside to pee before returning to the house for breakfast. It consisted of instant oatmeal and a packet of Starbucks instant coffee. That was hard to obtain, and she was eternally on the lookout for it. The combination of the two was enough to fill her stomach and make her feel warmer.

Once everything was packed away, Victoria put her one-piece Thermo suit on and rode the motorcycle out through the front door. The highway was covered with a thin layer of mostly undisturbed slush. Occasional snowflakes twirled down out of the lead-gray sky as she cruised along. Victoria knew there would be icy spots—so she was careful to keep the speed down.

Had conditions been better, it would have been possible to reach Indianapolis in three or four hours. But the snow, plus the need to circumvent cities like Columbus, made the trip last longer. Eventually, Victoria found her way onto I-70 just east of Springfield, where she had to share the freeway with pedestrians, fellow bikers, and the occasional bus.

But traffic was light, and that made for an easy ride. There was no sign of military traffic—and Victoria made a mental note to include that observation in her next report.

There was a lot of interesting graffiti, however—much of which was prominently displayed on overpasses. Most of the messages had an anti-Confederate bent. "Down with the New Odor," was one of them, along with "United We Stand," and "Free the South!"

That was interesting because the tags seemed to suggest that, despite the way that the Northerners were squabbling among themselves, they had a shared distaste for the Confederacy. Could Sloan, or the person who was pretending to be Sloan, harness that energy? Victoria figured the answer was yes.

Traffic grew worse after the first hour as hundreds of people poured onto the freeway. Some rode and some were on foot. Judging from the flags they carried, most of Victoria's fellow travelers were patriots—and it didn't take a genius to realize that they were headed for the Third Continental Congress in Indianapolis.

Eventually, the snow stopped, and the temperature rose ten degrees. The procession resembled a parade by then—complete with a bagpiper, a platoon of Civil War reenactors, and a group of high school cheerleaders on a flatbed truck. So when the time came, all Victoria had to do was follow the herd off the freeway, through the streets, and into the Indiana Convention Center's parking lot. The center's modernistic buildings were situated next to Lucas Oil Stadium, and the lights were on! That was nothing less than a miracle in the energy-starved North.

Victoria chained the BMW to a lamppost and joined the swirling crowd. There were dozens of food vendors, and the air was filled with tantalizing odors. Victoria bought a paper plate loaded with grilled sausage, corn bread, and coleslaw—all of which she wolfed down while watching the people around her.

With a full stomach, and the pack on her back, Victoria followed a group of rowdy teens through a maze of tents and into an area where a variety of military vehicles were parked. The menagerie included Humvees, some Bradleys, and a brace of tanks.

Victoria thought she was looking at an element of the Northern army at first. Then she realized that she was surrounded by mercenary units. They had names like the Night Stalkers, the Wolverines, and the Red Ball Express. And, judging from the gear most of them were wearing, they'd been active-duty soldiers or Marines before the shit hit the fan.

Victoria spent the next half hour visiting individual units and chatting them up. Once she told them that she'd been a major in the army, quite a few of the mercs offered to hire her on the spot. It seemed that untrained wannabes were easy to come by, but veterans weren't. And that gave Victoria an excuse to ask lots of questions.

A picture began to emerge. As civil order disintegrated, and military units were fragmented, some soldiers had gone into business for themselves. And with all manner of bandits roaming the land, there were plenty of customers. They were small towns mostly, which would hire a unit or combination of units to protect them, or to attack a neighboring community.

But the people camped in the parking lot knew that change was in the air. What if the North managed to restore the federal government? It would need to defend itself against warlords *and* the Confederacy. And the new structure wouldn't be able to rebuild the military overnight. It would take time, giving the mercs an opportunity to cash in. All of which presented Victoria with the perfect chance to assess the players and look for the kind of assets the Confederacy could use.

But where to start? The answer presented itself in the form of an ex–cavalry officer named Captain Ross Olson. He was a tall man with slicked-back hair, a boyishly handsome face, and hazel eyes. Olson had put together a company of scouts. They were equipped with dirt bikes, armed rat rods, and a platoon of M1161 Growlers. The unit was too lightly armed to battle a warlord toe-to-toe—but just right for intelligence gathering and lightning-fast raids. That meant that Olson's clients would be likely to employ other mercenary units as well.

After some verbal foreplay, Victoria began to probe. They were standing next to the bus-sized RV that served Olson as a mobile command post, drinking coffee laced with rum. "So, what's your preference?" she inquired. "Are you rooting for the North or the South?"

Olson smiled. "Some of my folks are from the South, and some are from the North, so we swing both ways. It's about the money so far as we're concerned."

"That's good to hear," Victoria said. "There are all sorts of opportunities to be had these days."

"Such as?"

"Things are going to get complicated soon." Victoria predicted. "I work for a group of people who would like to establish ongoing relationships with outfits like yours."

Olson took a sip of coffee. "Can you be more explicit?"

"Sure," Victoria answered. "What if we paid you a fee each month? A retainer, so to speak. In the meantime, you would be free to work for the North."

"*Free* to work for the North? Or your employer would like us to work for the North?"

"They would like you to work for the North," Victoria admitted.

"Okay, I like it so far," Olson said. "Then what?"

"Then," Victoria continued, "we'd like to hear from you on a regular basis."

"You want me to spy for you."

"That's part of it," she admitted, "but there's more. The time could come when we would ask you to come south and fight for us. In that case, we would pay you what the North paid you, plus the monthly retainer, plus a hefty bonus for every member of your unit."

Olson produced a low whistle. "That's a very tempting offer."

"And?"

"I need to consult with my team."

"How long will that take?"

"I should know by this evening. We could discuss it over dinner."

Victoria could tell that Olson was hoping for something more than dinner. She smiled. "Okay, when?"

"There's a place called Rosa's a block east of here. Would 1800 work for you?"

Victoria drained the coffee cup and gave it back. "You're on. I'll see you there."

People were filing into the convention center by then, and Victoria followed the crowd. The meeting was scheduled for the largest room that the complex had to offer and every seat was filled by the time Victoria arrived. That forced her to stand in back with the other latecomers while a woman from a little-known rock group sang the national anthem. To her credit, the woman not only got the words right but hit the high notes as well.

That was followed by the Pledge of Allegiance and introductory remarks from the master of ceremonies. He was a state senator and liked to talk. It took him a full fifteen minutes to introduce dozens of dignitaries who were seated in front—and an equal amount of time to explain what the Third Continental Congress was there to do. And that was "to fully restore the United States government, including all the functions thereof, and to put a stop to the second secession." An initiative that would be of considerable interest to CEO Lemaire and his newly formed cabinet.

"But," the senator continued, "before we convene the Congress . . . I have the enormous honor of introducing Reginald Allston, the country's newly named interim Attorney General!" None of the audience had heard of the man, so the applause was muted.

Victoria watched with considerable interest as a good-looking man in a rumpled suit mounted the stage, shook hands with the senator, and took his place behind the podium. "Good afternoon. As many of you know, the former Secretary of Energy, Samuel T. Sloan, was in Mexico on May 1, and was forced to paddle his way home in a kayak.

"Meanwhile, Vice President Wainwright was sworn in as president. But now, in the wake of her untimely death as well as that of many others, Sloan is the next in line for the presidency. It was his intention to be here today . . . But, I'm sorry to say that a rogue general has taken control of Fort Knox, which means it was necessary for our new president to go there to reclaim what is rightfully ours." That statement produced a lot of enthusiastic applause—and Victoria had to join in or look suspicious.

Allston went on to say that other precious resources had been stolen from the country as well, including all of the southern oil reserves, billions of dollars' worth of infrastructure, and the nation's future. Those who were sitting stood to applaud, and Victoria had seen enough. The mood in the room plus the news regarding Fort Knox would go into her next report. But she had more "assets" to recruit. So she left the building and ventured out into the cold. Sleet was angling in from the west, and the Thermo suit was a blessing.

During the earlier stroll, she'd seen a six-gun artillery battery and some support vehicles parked near Olson's unit. What if they went to work for the North? Then, at a critical moment, turned their guns on their employer? Victoria smiled. Her father would love that! She went off to visit them.

With the exception of the convention center and a nearby hospital, the city was dark by the time Victoria finished her last meeting. She returned to the BMW and wiped a layer of slush off the seat before swinging a leg over it. The ride to Rosa's took less than five minutes. Would Olson be there? Victoria felt pretty certain he would. And that expectation was borne out as she entered the restaurant. It was lit with dozens of candles, and Olson came forward to greet her. "There you are," he said. "Can I help remove your clothes?"

It was a joke, or a flirtatious comment passed off as a joke, and a clear indication that Olson had more than business on his mind. What about her? What did *she* want? Victoria wasn't sure yet.

Once the Thermo suit was off, Olson took her to a table where a bottle of wine and two glasses were waiting. They ordered an appetizer, and rather than go straight to business, Olson inquired about her day. Victoria responded with some generalities regarding the Congress and some deliberately vague comments about the meetings she'd had. The last thing she wanted was for the mercs to collude where fees were concerned.

Then it was time to order dinner. And once that was accomplished, talk turned to business. "So," Victoria began. "What did your team have to say?"

"Money matters," Olson replied. "And the devil's in the details. But, assuming we can agree on a price for each component of the deal, we're in."

It took the better part of an hour and most of the meal to pencil out an agreement that was acceptable to both parties. And after Victoria went to the ladies' room, she returned ready to hand over six of the one-ounce gold wafers she'd been carrying in her money belt. Each had been valued at $1,200.00 on May 1. Now they were worth ten times that amount. "There's your down payment," Victoria said. "I'd like a receipt please. Oh, and one more thing . . ."

Olson made the gold disappear—and was reaching for a leather briefcase. "Yes?"

"If you breach our contract, we will kill you. And not just you—but every person in your unit."

Olson looked into her eyes. "Understood. We aren't going to have sex, are we?"

"No," Victoria answered. "But don't give up. Try often enough, and you might get lucky."

Olson laughed and raised his glass. "To the Confederacy, a beautiful woman, and getting lucky." Victoria sipped her wine. The North didn't know it yet—but a battle had been fought and won.

## EAST OF CENTRAL CITY, KENTUCKY

The only vehicle that the presidential party had been able to borrow was a yellow school bus owned by a local church. In order to fill the tank with gas, the pastor had been forced to ask her congregants for donations. Sloan had been there to personally thank each person who gave a gallon, half a gallon, and in one case a Mason jar filled with carefully hoarded fuel.

Finally, after two dozen such contributions, most of the party was able to set off for Fort Knox. The exceptions were Interim Attorney General Allston and Cindy Howell, who were sent north to represent Sloan at the Congress in Indianapolis.

The trip went smoothly at first. Jenkins was at the wheel and managed to maintain a respectable 40 mph as he wound his way through all manner of slow traffic. Sloan was thinking about the past as he peered through the droplets of rain that covered the window. His father had been a Civil War geek—and passed the affliction along to him. So he knew that Kentucky had been a border state during the last civil war. A state so vital to President Lincoln that he said, "I hope to have God on my side, but I have to have Kentucky." And eventually, after the Confederates were stupid enough to attack them, the citizens of Kentucky fought for the Union.

Sloan felt the same way Lincoln had. And there was reason for concern. Kentucky had been a so-called "red state" for many years, and that meant the population had a lot in common with people who lived in bastions of the South like Texas and Mississippi.

And the problem was more than theoretical. If the locals chose to support General Cox, and she were to cut some sort of deal with Lemaire, then 130 billion dollars' worth of gold could fall into Confederate hands! All of which made Sloan feel antsy and irritable as the bus suddenly started to slow. "Uh-oh," Jenkins said, as a sign appeared on the right. "What's up with that?"

As Sloan peered through the beads of rain, he read the hand-lettered sign: TOLL BRIDGE AHEAD. Then, in smaller type: YOU WILL PAY . . . NO EXCEPTIONS. And when Sloan peered through the windshield, he could see that traffic was backed up as people waited to cross. The situation was clear. Bandits, or the equivalent thereof, had taken control of a public bridge and were charging a fee to cross it. Just one of the countless problems the new government would have to cope with. "Let's pay it," Sloan proclaimed. "I need to reach Fort Knox as quickly as possible."

"Maybe we will, and maybe we won't," Jenkins said, as he pulled over. "I think we should eyeball the situation before going any farther."

"He's right," McKinney agreed. "No way are we going to drive into a shit show we might not be able to get out of."

Sloan felt frustrated. "That's bullshit. I'm the president, and what I say goes."

"Not necessarily," Jenkins replied. "Not if what you say is stupid and could get my ass blown off. Thanks to Besom and his people, there are *thousands* of Samuel T. Sloan photos out there . . . What if the people who control the bridge recognize you? What if they take you prisoner? And sell you to the rebels? Or shoot you in the head? Sit tight. We'll take a look."

Once Jenkins and McKinney were gone, all Sloan could do was sit and fume. They were clearly in a hurry when they returned fifteen minutes later. "We're out of here," Jenkins said, as he slipped behind the wheel.

"Damned straight," McKinney agreed. "Those bastards have a Bradley—and it's armed with an M242 chain gun. That sucker could kill a light tank, never mind a school bus!"

Sloan knew he owed them an apology. "Sorry guys, I'm glad you ignored me."

"Anytime, Mr. President," Jenkins said cheerfully. "It was our pleasure."

The group had to backtrack in order to reach the last turnoff, and follow a lesser road to the northeast, where they crossed the river unimpeded.

Then Jenkins turned south, and it wasn't long before they arrived in the town of Rosine, where the bus could get on 62. It led them east to Elizabethtown, the city that Confederate General John Hunt Morgan and three thousand of his men had attacked in 1862. Did the locals remember that? Did they care? Sloan hoped so, as Jenkins took the beltway north and turned onto 31 west.

It was almost dark by the time they passed through Radcliff and ran into a roadblock comprised of two Abrams tanks, half a dozen Bradleys, and a company of troops. A hand-lettered sign ordered them to execute a U-turn and head south. There were two vehicles in front of the bus and both chose to turn back as Jenkins pulled forward. "Stay on the bus," McKinney ordered. "I'll find out who these people are. Then, if it's safe, you can get out."

Sloan chafed at the increasing number of restrictions that were being placed on him, but he knew it was necessary. So he sat and made conversation with Rostov and Besom until the ex-Ranger returned. "They're ours," he announced. "And Garrison gave orders for the company commander to watch for you."

Sloan got up out of the cramped seat, took his pack off the rack above, and made his way forward. "What's the roadblock for anyway?"

"To prevent rogue army units or Confederate forces from linking up with General Cox," McKinney replied. "It appears that Colonel Foster has the area surrounded."

Sloan didn't know Colonel Foster. But it was nice to know that at least one senior officer was on his side and willing to take action. It was cold outside, and as Sloan stepped down onto the frozen ground, flashes lit the horizon. What followed sounded like thunder. "That's artillery," McKinney volunteered. "It looks as if a full-scale battle is under way."

An army officer materialized out of the surrounding gloom. "I'm Captain Pierce," he said. "Colonel Foster's adjutant. Please follow me."

The presidential party followed Pierce through the roadblock to the Humvees waiting beyond. A short ride took them past a well-protected vehicle park to what looked like a mound of dirt—but was actually the roof of an underground command post.

Sentries stood at attention, and the visitors had to stop as a sergeant stepped out to block the way. "Please leave your weapons here . . . They'll be waiting when you exit."

"General Cox managed to get an assassin into the bunker three days ago," Pierce explained. "He shot three officers before an MP gunned him down. That's why no one is allowed to enter the command post carrying a weapon, and that includes me."

A clatter was heard as a small arsenal of weapons was placed on the table. "What you described sounds like a suicide mission," Sloan commented. "I assumed Cox's troops were in it for the gold."

"Some of them are," Pierce admitted. "But General Cox is a very charismatic person. And based on what deserters have told us, a lot of her troops believe the story she fed them. They expect the *real* president to show up any day now."

Pierce led the group through a metal detector and down a flight of wooden stairs into the command center below. A map of Fort Knox was displayed on a large flat-screen. Sloan could see that the base was much larger than the depository and hung from the other end of what looked like a lopsided barbell. The "bar"-shaped corridor served to connect the two facilities. "Come on," Pierce said. "Secretary Garrison is down front."

Pierce led the group past two rows of soldiers all seated in front of glowing screens. They were wearing headsets, and their overlapping conversations combined to create a low-level buzz. "Good evening, Mr. President," Garrison said, as he stood. "Thank you for coming."

"It's good to see you, Frank," Sloan said, as they shook hands. "Where did the Secretary of Defense stuff come from?"

"It's *interim* Secretary," Garrison replied. "Someone had to step in, and I was handy. Or would you prefer to let the military create policy?"

Sloan knew Garrison was right. Someone had to fill the Secretary of Defense role. And, with no other candidate on the horizon, Garrison would do. "You were right," Sloan agreed. "Thanks for jumping in. This is a critical situation."

"That's for sure," a basso voice agreed. Sloan turned to find himself face-to-face with an army officer. He had short white hair, a square chin, and a steely gaze. "It's a pleasure to meet you, Mr. President, I'm Colonel Foster." They shook hands.

"I want to thank you, Colonel," Sloan said. "From what I've heard, you were trying to retake Fort Knox when Secretary Garrison came along."

Foster shrugged. "You're welcome, sir. It seemed like the right thing to do. We're going to need that gold to support our currency—and it would be an unmitigated disaster if the Confederates got ahold of it. Unfortunately, my attack failed."

Sloan looked the other man in the eye and was met with an unblinking stare. "I'm going to ask you a tough question, Colonel. But I need to know the answer. *Why* did that attack fail?"

"It's a fair question, sir," Foster answered. "The first thing you need to know is that my command consisted of the 213th Ordnance Company, the 372nd Missile Maintenance Company, and the 200th Civil Engineering Squadron—along with the Ohio Military Reserve."

"The *what*?"

"The Ohio Military Reserve, sir. It's a lightly armed militia that was formed back in 1803—and serves side by side with the National Guard. And that's where I was going, sir. We were up against a larger and better-equipped force. General Cox commands half a dozen units including the Fourth Cavalry Brigade. And it consists of infantry, cavalry, and some aircraft.

"That said, the responsibility for the failed attack was mine," Foster said. "Simply put, I bit off more than we could chew. Cox had a cordon around the base *and* the depository. I thought we could go in, snatch the general, and end the siege that way.

"Looking back, I realize that I should have focused my attention on capturing the bullion depository. That's what matters . . . And once we have it, we can starve the rest of the mutineers out."

Sloan nodded. "Thank you, Colonel. That analysis was both clear and honest. So, what's our next step?"

"We're going to attack the bullion depository at 0500 in the morning," Foster answered simply.

"Good," Sloan said. "I plan to join you."

That set off a round of protests from Jenkins, Rostov, and Besom. "Don't do it," Rostov said. "You aren't a soldier, and even if you were, there's no one to succeed you."

"I understand that," Sloan replied. "But here's the flip side . . . We're outnumbered *and* outgunned. So it's my hope that if our soldiers see that I'm there, taking the same chances that they are, they'll fight all the harder." *Yes,* the inner voice agreed, *and it will*

*help to build your reputation as well. But you can't say that . . .*
*It would sound calculating.*

"I agree with the president," Garrison put in. "And I have a feeling that Major McKinney does, too."

McKinney nodded. "There's a lot of risk, I grant you that, but the president is correct. This would be a good time to lead from the front. I'll do my best to keep him alive."

Foster looked at him. "And you are?"

"Major McKinney. The president's military attaché, sir."

"Excellent. I'll give you a fire team for support. I'd like to provide a larger force, but we're short of people."

"I continue to think that this is a bad idea," Besom said. "But since we're going to do it, I suggest that you inform the troops *now*. Tell them that President Sloan is here . . . Tell them that he's going to fight alongside them."

Foster turned to Pierce. "Make it happen, Captain—and have someone pull a set of gear for the president."

After eating an MRE, Sloan went to bed. Colonel Foster had a tiny bedroom just off the command and control center, which he insisted that Sloan use. That meant Sloan had the best quarters available. He couldn't sleep, though . . . Not knowing that he might be killed the following morning. Was that how Foster's soldiers felt? Of course it was.

All Sloan could do was toss, turn, and think about the prospect of dying until the alarm next to his cot went off, and it was time to get up. For one brief moment, Sloan considered being sick, or claiming to be sick, but could imagine the contempt that would appear in McKinney's eyes.

That was enough to get Sloan up and out of bed. He brushed his teeth at a tiny sink, forced himself to shave, and put on the uniform Pierce had given him. It was the first time he'd worn one, and he didn't want to sully it. Then he ducked under the combat vest, which he fastened into place. He was still making adjustments when McKinney announced himself. "It's McKinney, sir . . . May I come in?"

"Please do," Sloan replied. "How do I look?"

"Not very good, sir," McKinney said. "Stand still while I tweak some things. There . . . That's better. Jump up and down."

"Why?"

"So the enemy won't hear you coming," McKinney said patiently.

Sloan made a face and did as he was told. Gear rattled and McKinney sought it out. Sloan was ready five minutes later. "Take this," McKinney said, as he gave Sloan a shotgun. "It's just like the ones you grew up with except that the magazine holds eight rounds. If you need to shoot someone, and come up empty, go for the Glock. You can pull that faster than you can reload the scattergun. Copy?"

"Copy," Sloan said. "Lead the way."

General Cox had a number of drones at her disposal, not to mention troops who were equipped with night-vision gear. So the chances of catching the enemy unawares were slim to none. But by sending five Bradleys down Ramey Road and into the base, Foster hoped to divert the general's attention long enough to cut the link between the base and the depository. Once that was accomplished, the actual attack would begin.

Foster had been moving troops around for the last six hours. Some of the movements were necessary, like positioning the Bradleys to attack and placing soldiers within striking distance of the supply corridor. Other troop movements were random and intended to keep Cox guessing.

As Sloan and McKinney left the command center, Sloan shivered and wished he had a pair of gloves. Trucks were waiting, and when Sloan sought to enter the back of a six-by-six, willing hands reached down to pull him in. "Welcome to Delta Company," a burly sergeant said. "We'll show those bastards."

Sloan smiled as he shook the noncom's hand but felt mixed emotions. "Those bastards" were his fellow Americans . . . And the need to kill them ate at him. Yes, some were after the gold, and yes, others had fallen under the spell of what everyone claimed was a charismatic personality. But was there a *third* group? Soldiers who would fight Cox if they could? There was no way to know. Sloan heard a voice via his headset. "This is Delta-Six actual," she said. "Stand by . . . And don't be surprised when you hear something go boom. Over."

McKinney was seated next to Sloan. He leaned in to talk. "After the Bradleys launch their attack, three tactical missiles will strike the supply corridor. That will open a hole for our troops. They will split, turn their backs to each other, and dig in. We expect Cox to attack them from two directions in an attempt to close the gap. That's when we go after the depository. Boom! We're in."

That was the first time Sloan had heard about the missile strike. McKinney made it sound so easy. But the enemy was going to fight back, and good people were going to die. Would he be among them? Sloan feared that he would and hoped his death would be quick.

Even though Sloan knew the missiles were coming, he wasn't prepared for the overlapping explosions that shook the truck and resulted in what seemed like a single flash of light. As the truck jerked forward, he knew that Cox was trying to process the information coming at her. Would she make a mistake? He hoped so.

The trip to the depository didn't take long, and it seemed as if only a couple of minutes had passed before the noncoms began to shout, "Out! Out! Out!" and all hell broke loose.

Had Sloan chosen to remain in the command center and watch the battle unfold, he would've been able to grasp the big picture. But that wasn't the case. Suddenly, his world consisted of muzzle flashes, a loud boom as a rocket hit the gate, and McKinney's voice. "Run! Drop! Get up! Run!"

Bullets snapped past, a grenade went off, and a woman screamed. Geysers of dirt flew up all around them as McKinney zigzagged forward, and Sloan followed. There was no cover taller than a blade of grass. Cox was too smart for that. And her machine guns were sited to put the attackers in a lethal cross fire. Soldiers fell like wheat to a harvester. "Get that machine gun!" a noncom shouted. And Sloan saw a flash of light as a rocket struck home.

They were well inside the fence by then but a long way from the depository, as fresh troops surged out to meet them. Sloan tripped and fell. As he got back on his feet, he realized that the defenders were closer. *Much* closer. McKinney was to the right, firing from one knee. The private to Sloan's left was shooting at targets to *his* left. Sloan realized that he had to hold the center as an enemy soldier charged at him!

The shotgun seemed to fire itself, and the load of double-ought buck blew half of the man's face away. Sloan was thinking about what he'd done, and trying to come to terms with it, when soldiers appeared to either side of him. "We're pulling back, sir," one of them said. "The captain wants you to . . ."

Sloan never got to hear the rest of it as a bullet hit the corporal and turned him around. Sloan caught him and helped the other soldier drag the noncom back to the fence. Bullets buzzed and snapped all around them as McKinney paused to return fire.

The trucks were parked in a line outside the fence—and troops were digging fighting positions behind them. Sloan and the private half carried the corporal around the front of a six-by-six and laid him down. A medic appeared. "I've got this," he said as he went to work.

Sloan was exhausted. He sat down and let his weight rest on a gigantic tire. McKinney came to join him. "What happened?" Sloan demanded.

"We got our asses kicked," McKinney replied.

"Shit."

"Yes, sir. You did good though . . . Word of that will get around."

Sloan felt a momentary flush of pleasure, followed by sorrow. More people were dead on both sides. And all of them were Americans.

A full six hours passed before Colonel Foster was in a position to report. He, along with Sloan, the presidential party, and senior officers were gathered in the underground command post. Foster's expression was grave. "I have good news, and I have bad news. Here's the good news. We cut the base off from the depository. And, in spite of repeated counterattacks, we kept enemy forces from linking up again.

"Secondly, we kept General Cox's forces bottled up inside their defensive positions. And, since they know we can drop missiles on them whenever we choose to, they're likely to stay where they are. Thirdly, we were able to push the forces around the depository back, giving us control of the ground up to the fence. It isn't safe to stroll around in that vicinity mind you . . . General Cox has some excellent snipers."

Foster's eyes swept across the faces in front of him. "Here's the bad news. Our attempt to take the depository failed—and we lost sixty-two soldiers. Another sixteen were wounded, and two aren't likely to survive. What we have now is a standoff . . . One that could last for a long time unless we're willing to drop bombs on them or use missiles. And even though that might be the logical thing to do, it might be perceived as draconian since Cox and her soldiers are American citizens. The last thing we want to do is create another Alamo that the Confederates can rally around."

A discussion ensued. But when the meeting came to an end twenty minutes later, nothing had changed, and Sloan felt depressed. He went back to the tiny bedroom to lie down. He was exhausted, and it didn't take long for sleep to pull him down.

When Sloan woke up four hours later, it was with the sense that he'd been dreaming. But about *what*? An explosion. He'd been in combat, so that made sense. No, there was more to it than that. Something important.

Sloan lay there, staring at the ceiling, trying to remember. Suddenly he had it. The siege of Petersburg in 1864! Sloan sat bolt upright, swung his feet over onto the pea-gravel floor, and hurried to pull his boots on. He had to tell Foster.

The officer was skeptical to say the least. But Sloan was the commander in chief and, for the very first time since becoming president, chose to assert that authority. Foster was forced to capitulate.

It took three weeks to build a temporary structure, bring the drilling machine in under the cover of darkness, and put the Roadheader to work. In his role as Secretary of Energy, Sloan had gone down into a dozen Kentucky coal mines where he'd met hundreds of workers and seen firsthand what their machines were capable of. And that was to bore tunnels like the one Union forces drove in under the Confederate lines during the Battle of the Crater in 1864.

It was a hand-dug tunnel, the purpose of which was to place explosives *under* the enemy troops and kill as many of them as possible. That would open the way for an infantry assault and bring the siege of Petersburg to an end.

Unfortunately, the follow-up attack was a complete disaster, which caused the deaths of 504 Union soldiers and left 1,881 wounded. Some were captured as well.

But Sloan's plan was different. After driving a tunnel in past the enemy's outer defenses, handpicked troops would surge up out of the ground and attack the enemy from the rear.

At that point, the defenders located in, and on top of, the flat-roofed depository would be able to fire at them . . . But not without hitting their comrades as well. In the meantime, they would be taking heavy fire from .50 caliber machine guns and AT4 rockets. A combination that was guaranteed to keep their heads down.

The plan should work. Nevertheless, Sloan felt something akin to a lead weight in the pit of his stomach as the appointed hour arrived, and the Roadheader was withdrawn. A tremendous amount of effort had gone into smuggling timbers in to support the tunnel's ceiling. But there was always the chance of a cave-in that would not only kill the coal miners who were running the Roadheader, but reveal the tunnel's existence. Either possibility would be disastrous. So it was important to use the passageway immediately.

At 0427, Sloan was standing at the back of the command center watching and listening. It had been his hope to go in with the troops, but Foster was opposed, as were the rest of them. Sloan might have dismissed their objections had it not been for McKinney. "I'm sorry, Mr. President," he said. "But you're not good enough for this mission. And if you screw up, it could cost lives. Is that what you want?"

It wasn't what Sloan wanted. So all he could do was stand there and hope for the best as the feint went in, a platoon of Foster's best boiled up out of the ground, and a short battle ensued.

The defenders were caught flat-footed, took heavy casualties, and couldn't withdraw. When the survivors surrendered, that opened the way for one of Foster's Bradleys to roll up the driveway and fire on the heavily armored door with its chain gun. Sloan could see greenish footage of the action on the main screen and could hear the vehicle commander's voice. She said, "Open Sesame," as her gunner blew the doors open.

Shouts of jubilation were heard in the command center—and Besom was there to congratulate Sloan. "Good work, Mr. President," he said. "Here's what I'm going to send out: 'The fighting president strikes again! Based on a plan conceived by President Samuel T. Sloan, the army of the North recaptured Fort Knox, and the 130 billion dollars' worth of gold bullion stored inside.'"

"You might want to wait until the battle is over before you send that out," Sloan cautioned. "And don't forget to give credit to Colonel Foster, his officers, and their troops."

Besom looked resentful. "Of course . . . What do you take me for?" Then he ran off. To add the missing text? Probably.

Sloan wasn't allowed to enter the depository until after sunup. By that time, General Cox had been found with a pistol near her hand and a single bullet wound in her temple.

More than seventy soldiers were imprisoned in underground vaults. Among them were individuals from each unit that Cox commanded, all being held to ensure the loyalty of their comrades, some of whom would have rebelled otherwise.

Once the hostages were freed, and sent into the neighboring base, Sloan figured that their comrades would surrender. Especially if they were offered amnesty, which they would be, so long as they swore allegiance to the North. It was what he believed Lincoln would do, *had* done, via his Proclamation of Amnesty and Reconstruction. And news of the North's even-handedness would help prevent the Southern propaganda machine from turning Cox into some sort of a hero.

As for the gold, it was interesting to look at but held no allure for Sloan. The prize, the *real* prize, was to restore what had been taken. And that included the 700 million barrels of so-called black gold stored down south. A battle had been won. But the war had just begun.

# CHAPTER 9

|||||||||||||||||||||||||||||||||||

Formula for success: rise early, work hard, strike oil.

—J. PAUL GETTY

**NEAR MIAMI, ARIZONA**

It was just after dawn—and the sky was pewter gray. Mac was lying on her stomach on top of a ridge ten miles west of Miami, Arizona, looking down into a canyon. A light dusting of snow covered the ground surrounding the do-it-yourself oil refinery, and half a dozen vehicles were parked around the cluster of multicolored shipping containers used to house the crew.

Five weeks had passed since the mercenaries had departed Camp Navajo near Flagstaff, Arizona, and driven south to Superior. Fortunately, they'd been able to make the journey without taking casualties. Unfortunately, the temperature was only five degrees warmer than it had been in Washington State. And Mac figured conditions would soon get worse. There was no point in whining about it, though . . . What was, was.

As Mac panned her binoculars from left to right, she could trace the path of the muddy maintenance road that ran from one end of the canyon to the other. She knew that the dirt track followed the path of an underground pipeline that ran all the way from Canada down to Tucson. There were hundreds of such lines in the United States, and they went unnoticed unless one began to leak or caught fire.

But after the meteorites struck, and fuel became scarce, the good citizens of Miami decided to tap the pipeline and steal what they needed. The problem was that they had to refine the crude oil before they could use it. That might have put the kibosh on the idea somewhere else. But the citizens of Gila County were a resourceful bunch and had been able to construct their own refinery using tanks, pipes, and valves salvaged from local mining operations.

The process was simple though extremely hazardous. All they had to do was boil the crude and condense the resulting vapor at specified temperatures to produce what was called "straight run" gas and diesel. And that worked for a month or so.

Then a group of banditos called the 711s heard about the refinery, swept in, and took control. The locals attempted to take the refinery back, failed, and hired the newly arrived Marauders to handle the task for them. Now, after a week of planning, the attack was about to begin. "Damn it!" Ralston said. "The bastards are early!"

First Sergeant Norman Ralston was stretched out to Mac's left. Unlike most company sergeants, he rarely swore. So the "damn it" was strong stuff coming from him. Mac turned her binoculars north and saw why Ralston was angry.

The Marauders were supposed to enter the valley from the south. Then, if the 711s were smart, they'd flee north in an effort to escape. But just before they reached the exit point, the locals were supposed to block their path with a couple of graders.

And that's when the Strykers would hit them from behind. Except that the goddamned civilians were early!

And as Mac swung her glasses back to the refinery, she saw that the banditos were boiling out of their shipping containers and taking up positions behind the ten-foot-high berm that surrounded the refinery. Sparks Munroe was lying next to her. Mac spoke out of the right side of her mouth. "Tell Strike Force Hammer to . . ."

But it was too late. The trucks were already nosing their way into the valley, and the Stryker crews couldn't kill the defenders without destroying the very thing they'd been sent to recapture, and that was the refinery.

"Tell the Strykers to withdraw," Mac said. "Then I want you to call Mr. Hanson and tell him to meet me at the FOB."

Sparks said, "Got it," and was still on the radio as Mac turned to Ralston. "We'll use the drones to keep an eye on the situation—but let's leave some observers here as well."

Ralston nodded. "Yes, ma'am."

The forward operating base was a temporary affair, located on a ranch six miles from the canyon. What had once been a house was little more than a pile of charred wreckage. But the forty-two-foot-by-sixty-foot metal shed was intact and being put to good use. It stood on a rise guarded by two Strykers and was surrounded by a dozen well-dug fighting positions.

As the Humvee followed the curving driveway up to the building—Mac could see that Hanson's mud-splattered Ford pickup was already there. As she got out, the civilian hurried over to confront her. Hanson was short, stocky, and overdue for a haircut. Spittle flew from his lips when he spoke. "What the fuck is going on?" he demanded. "You ran! We want our deposit back."

What happened next surprised Mac *and* the soldiers close enough to witness the incident. She was angry, and the pistol seemed to draw itself. Then, with the barrel touching the center of Hanson's forehead, she pulled the hammer back. "Listen, asshole . . . Don't ever talk to me like that again . . . If you do, I'll blow your brains out. Understood?"

Hanson's eyes were huge. He nodded.

"Good," Mac said as she eased the hammer down. "Your people arrived early, tipped the banditos off, and blocked their exit. That left us with two options. We could destroy the refinery or withdraw . . . It was my understanding that option one was unacceptable. If I have that wrong, just say the word, and we'll turn that sucker into a pool of burning sludge by lunchtime."

Hanson's eyes tracked the pistol as it slid back into its holster. "Sorry," he said. "We want to recapture the refinery intact."

"I've said it before, and I'll say it again," Mac replied. "We can seal the canyon off and starve them out."

"Maybe," Hanson allowed. "But that could take weeks . . . And we can't afford to have you sit here for that long."

"Okay," Mac said as she placed a comforting arm around his shoulders. "Let's go inside. We'll have a couple of drinks and work on a new plan."

That appealed to Hanson, who allowed Mac to steer him up the slope and into the metal building. What followed was a two-hour session during which Hanson had three stiff drinks, and Mac took a few sips. And by the time it was over, Operation Fourth of July had been born.

The display of fireworks began at precisely 12:01 A.M. and consisted of illumination rounds fired from an 81mm mortar located a hundred yards behind Mac's position. Mac heard a muffled bang, followed by a short period of silence. Then came a pop as a miniature sun appeared over the canyon and fell trailing smoke as it did so. Harsh light strobed the ground and threw shifting shadows back and forth. And, because the banditos assumed that an infantry attack was under way, they opened fire.

Mac was lying on the same ridge as before, with Ralston on her left and Sparks on her right. She smiled. The more ammo the bozos burned, the better. The plan was to keep the bastards awake, scare the crap out of them, and force a bloodless surrender.

The 711s weren't stupid, however . . . When the attack failed to materialize, they stopped firing. Mac turned to Munroe. "Give Hadley permission to fire."

He did so. But a full five minutes passed before the sniper squeezed his trigger. Mac knew that Hadley and his spotter were on the opposite ridge—and that the marksman was using a rifle equipped with a night-vision device. "Target down," Munroe said, as he relayed the report. "He's lining up on another."

"Good," Mac replied. "Tell the special effects team to turn their lights on."

Once Munroe passed the order along, it was only a matter of seconds before white lights appeared along both sides of the canyon. That gave the impression that soldiers occupied both slopes and were looking down on the refinery. The banditos fired at the lights until someone ordered them to stop. That was when another pair of illumination rounds went off.

Once that display was over, Mac gave the 711s half an hour to marinate in their own juices before ordering the flyover. The Apache arrived ten minutes later, entered the canyon from the south, and passed over the refinery at an extremely low altitude. The roar generated by the gunship's General Electric T700 turboshaft engines bounced off both sides of the valley and made a deafening statement. "Okay," Mac said, "I think we have their attention. Tell Kho to deliver the offer."

Forward Observer Lin Kho and Private Brown had worked their

way in close by then. Kho had a megaphone. "Listen up!" she said. "You are surrounded. We don't *want* to kill you . . . But if you refuse to surrender, we will. So put your weapons down and come out with your hands on your heads. You will be escorted out of the valley and allowed to go wherever you wish."

Part of that was true—and part wasn't. The Marauders *couldn't* kill all of the banditos. Not without destroying the refinery. But they did intend to turn the 711s loose if they surrendered. Would they try to return? Quite possibly. But once the locals had control of the facility, *and* the high ground, the banditos wouldn't be able to roll over the refinery the way they had before.

Having received no reply, Kho repeated the offer, told the defenders which frequency to use, and gave them an ultimatum: They were to respond within half an hour or suffer the consequences. Mac was thinking about the potential cost of an infantry assault when Munroe interrupted her thoughts. "I've got a guy named Pasquel on the horn, ma'am. He wants to talk."

Mac felt a tremendous sense of relief. Thank God! The plan was working. The next fifteen minutes were spent talking to Pasquel over the radio. The bandito said that he and his people were willing to surrender, but not until the sun rose, and they could see their surroundings. Then, if everything looked good, the 711s would walk north. Mac didn't like that but was forced to accept it, and an uneasy truce was born.

But it wasn't long before Mac's initial sense of joy gave way to serious misgivings. In retrospect, the "surrender" seemed too easy. And, according to Munroe, scrambled radio messages were flying back and forth between what he assumed to be the 711s—and some other party. The questions being *who*? And *why*?

Mac wanted to confide in someone. But there was no one other than Evans that she could share her doubts with, and her XO was back in Superior, literally holding the fort. Besides, commanding officers were supposed to be strong, silent types similar to her father.

So all Mac could do was to make sure that the Marauders remained on high alert and wait for the sun to rise. The hours seemed to crawl by. But finally, as a pus-colored sun rose to backlight the clouds, Mac was free to act. She planned to push the 711s out through the north end of the canyon and bring her forces in from the south. To that end, four Strykers were ready to enter the valley on her command. "All right," she said. "Tell Kho to order them out."

Mac kept her binoculars focused on the refinery as Kho spoke. She and her assistant were in a well-dug fighting position behind a pile of rocks. "We kept our part of the bargain," Kho said over the loudspeaker. "That means it's time for you to do likewise. Drop your weapons and come out with your hands on your heads."

That was when the thunder of aircraft engines was heard, an ancient Douglas AC-47 swept in from the north, and two door-mounted 3-by-7.62mm General Electric miniguns went to work. The weapons could fire two thousand rounds per minute, and they were devastating.

Mac knew that ships like it had been used during the Vietnam War to provide close air support—and had been responsible for saving a lot of American lives in situations where units were surrounded by enemy forces. The modern version of the so-called Spooky was the Lockheed AC-130, but some third-world countries were still using the old AC-47s. And the 711s had one of them.

Gunfire raked the top of the ridge as the miniguns opened fire. That forced the Marauders to turn and slide down the opposite side of the hill as the steel rain swept toward them. Mac shouted into her mike. "This is Six actual! All vehicles will disperse . . . All dismounted personnel will take cover! Over."

It was the best she could do. Except for the machine guns mounted on the Strykers, the group didn't have any antiaircraft weapons to call on. And that, Mac realized, was *her* fault. Because rather than consider all the possibilities, she'd been stupid enough to believe Hanson when he described the 711s as "a pathetic street gang."

Now it was clear that the banditos had a backer with a lot of resources and a need for fuel. A Mexican drug lord, perhaps . . . Not that it mattered. All Mac could do was withdraw and hope to avoid casualties. The AC-47 roared past on its way to the south end of the canyon, where the Strykers had been waiting. Mac could hear the rattle of machine guns as the top gunners fired on the plane and could imagine the rooster tails of snow and mud the vehicles would throw up as the truck commanders put their accelerators to the floor.

Mac's heart was pounding as she scrambled back up the hill to the top of the ridge. As her eyes swept the valley, she could see that the banditos stationed inside the berm were pouring out. That didn't make sense at first. The 711s were winning . . . So why would they run? Then it came to her. The banditos were afraid that the Marauders would destroy the refinery! And that was a very real danger since her snipers were hard at work. "Watch your aim!" Mac said sternly. "Don't hit the refinery . . . It could blow."

Rifles cracked, gang members fell, and the AC-47 circled back. Had the gunship been summoned by one of the 711s? That seemed likely. And if the Spooky managed to kill the snipers, the battle would be over. "This is Six," Mac yelled. "Take cover! The gunship is going to make another run!"

The words were barely out of Mac's mouth when the plane arrived over the south end of the valley and opened fire. The pilot was unlikely to know where the snipers were—but could hose the slopes down and hope to get lucky. Columns of snow and mud shot into the air as the miniguns went to work. Then something unexpected occurred.

The sound of the Apache's engines was obscured by the noise the Spooky was making. As the helicopter rose from beyond the east wall of the canyon, it was swiveling to the right. That was necessary because the gunship was carrying point-and-shoot rockets.

Mac watched in openmouthed amazement as Peters fired six of them. Not *at* the AC-47, but *ahead* of it, the way a hunter leads a duck.

Two of the missiles hit the starboard side of the plane. The fixed-wing aircraft exploded into a ball of flame, causing pieces of fiery wreckage to fall everywhere, the refinery included. That triggered a secondary explosion and a geyser of billowing flame. "Holy shit," Munroe said as he looked out over the valley. "Did you plan that?"

"Hell, no," Mac said, as a column of smoke poured up into the sky. "I wish I had."

Roughly four hours later, Mac was sitting in the FOB on the other side of a makeshift table from Hanson and two of his cronies. They were pissed, and Mac understood why. The Marauders had been hired to capture the refinery, not destroy it. So she let them vent.

Finally, after the men ran out of gas, Mac offered her side of it. "Look," she began, "here's the deal. I'm sorry about the way things turned out. We did our best to recapture the refinery and, if it hadn't been for the AC-47, I think we would have done so. And oh, by the way . . . you folks told us that the 711s were nothing more than a street gang!"

Hanson scowled and was about to respond when Mac raised a hand. "Hear me out . . . Both sides signed a contract. It provides for a per diem charge plus a bonus for capturing the refinery. We failed to accomplish the primary mission, so you're off the hook there . . . But you still owe us three ounces of gold per day for twelve days. So pay up."

That set off a round of recrimination that lasted for fifteen minutes. But the outcome was never in doubt. The mercenaries could waste Miami, Arizona, so the locals paid.

Mac spent the trip back to Superior brooding. Once again, she'd been tested, and once again, she'd been found wanting. Or so it seemed to her. What if Peters hadn't taken it upon himself to attack the AC-47 gunship? Would the idea of using his helicopter to attack a plane have occurred to her? Mac didn't think so. *But all of your people are still alive,* the voice told her.

*Because I got lucky,* Mac replied. *What about next time?*

The question went unanswered as the column entered Superior. It was a small town of about fifteen hundred residents. As Mac's Humvee led the rest of the column east along Main Street, there was very little to see other than some old, flat-roofed buildings and vertical cliffs in the distance. Historically, the town was known for two things. The first was its popularity as a location for movies like *How the West Was Won*, *Skinwalkers*, and *The Gauntlet*.

The second was the town's proximity to a major copper mine, which, because of the meteor strikes, was no longer in operation. And that had everything to do with why Mac had chosen Superior as the unit's home. She figured the mine would make a good base . . . And the fact that there *was* a town, no matter how small, helped, too. Because Superior could provide much-needed shopping for the troops and their dependents.

As for Superior's citizens, they were thrilled to host the unit since the mercenaries would have to protect them in order to protect themselves. Not to mention the much-needed cash that the soldiers would spend. So people waved as the vehicles passed by, and that included a squad of Marauders who were out on patrol. Their presence was a sure sign that Evans was doing his job, which consisted of security, maintenance, and training. The latter was of particular importance as new people continued to join the unit.

A short drive took them to the mine. Two A-shaped steel structures marked the entrances to shafts nine and ten. A water tank was perched on a rise, outbuildings sat here and there, and a pile of slush-covered scrap loomed on Mac's left.

Meanwhile, some of the mining company's heavy equipment was being employed to excavate what was to become a subsurface vehicle park and maintenance facility. The company's living quarters were already underground—and impervious to anything less than bunker-buster bombs. And that was important since the unit was large enough to make a tempting takeover target for a warlord.

The company's vehicles were parked in walled revetments where they would be safe from anything other than a direct hit—and that included support vehicles like the fuelers, six-by-sixes, and gun trucks.

Evans was not only expecting the detachment but was there to greet it. He came to attention and tossed a salute as Mac's Humvee came to a stop, and she got out. "Welcome home, Captain."

Mac returned the salute. "*Captain?* Since when?"

"Since you were promoted," Evans said with a smile. "Some potential customers are waiting to meet you—and how many lieutenants command an outfit the size of this one?"

"That makes sense, I guess," Mac said, "although we'll need to chew it over with the troops. But if I'm a captain, then you're a lieutenant. Congratulations, butter bar! You're overdue for a bump. Who are these people anyway?"

"They claim to work for the new president . . . A guy named Sloan. He was Secretary of Agriculture or something."

"There is no government."

"They claim there is," Evans countered. "And they're here to recruit us."

"For what?"

"To put Humpty Dumpty back together again."

Mac wasn't sure how she felt about that. That could be good, if it was for real, but what if Sloan was little more than a warlord? That would mean another step backwards. "Okay," she said. "I'll take a shower and find a clean uniform. Can we invite them to dinner?"

"I'll pull something together," Evans promised.

Mac was ready to meet with the government representatives an hour later. The delegation consisted of Interim Secretary of Defense Frank Garrison and an army major named McKinney. He had piercing blue eyes . . . And Mac feared that he'd see her for what she truly was: a lieutenant, masquerading as a company commander. But it couldn't be helped. All she could do was play the part and hope for the best.

The meeting took place in what had been the mine supervisor's office. A conference table dominated the center of the room, a makeshift bar occupied a wall, and a space heater purred in a corner. Evans was present . . . And wearing the bars Mac had given to him.

After a few drinks, and a discussion of the bad weather, Garrison took charge of the conversation. "Let's get to it," he said. "Here's the situation . . . As you know by now, Washington, D.C., took a direct hit from a meteorite. That was a devastating blow. Our country was left without leadership, and that opened the way for a group of people who want to take over. They call themselves the New Confederacy, and they plan to run their country like a corporation. The president would be replaced by a CEO. He or she would report to a twelve-person board of directors, and citizens fortunate enough to own land would become shareowners. The rest of the population would become disenfranchised.

"But as bad as that sounds to most of us . . . Plenty of so-called haves would vote for a system that puts them on top. That, plus a well-coordinated fear campaign, explains how the so-called New Order has been able to gain traction.

"Meanwhile as the A-holes who run the Confederacy sell their crap to anyone who will listen, they're busy stealing anything that isn't nailed down. Take the Strategic Petroleum Reserve for example . . . According to our sources, they're selling the oil abroad—and using the money to buy voters. In light of these facts, President Sloan plans to restore the federal government, and unify the country."

Mac stared at him. "Even if that means starting a civil war?"

"Yes," Garrison answered firmly. "And that's why I'm here. Military force will be required to stop the Confederacy—and that means we'll need units like this one. Units that shouldn't exist. You and your personnel swore an oath to defend the United States of America . . . Not to steal equipment from the army and go into business for yourselves."

Mac opened her mouth to object, but Garrison raised a hand. "I know, I know . . . You were cut off and looked for a way to survive. I've heard that malarkey before. And we're willing to accept that explanation for the moment, realizing that the government won't tolerate mercenaries forever. Let's talk business. We want to hire Mac's Marauders . . . How much will that cost?"

"No offense," Mac countered, "but how are you going to pay?"

"I guess you haven't heard," Garrison replied. "The Third Continental Congress met and voted to reboot *all* federal agencies. That includes the IRS under the leadership of Interim Commissioner Marsha Rostov. So get ready to pay your taxes."

"And there's another thing," McKinney said as he entered the conversation for the first time. "President Sloan's forces took Fort Knox away from a renegade general a few weeks back."

"So you know him?"

McKinney nodded. "I work for him."

"He's a soldier then," Evans suggested.

"Yes," McKinney said. "Although he has a lot to learn. The troops love him, though . . . Because he fought alongside them."

Mac liked McKinney's style . . . And his frank assessment went a long way toward making her feel better about Sloan.

A civilian entered the room and said something to Evans. He thanked her and turned to the others. "Let's put the business discussion on hold until after dinner. Please take a plate from the back table and follow me. We'll get our food and bring it back here."

The meal exceeded Mac's expectations. Steaks had been cooked on a smoke-blackened barbecue, a pot of baked beans was waiting, and there was plenty of fresh-baked corn bread. Vegetables were hard to come by, though, and nowhere to be seen. But it was a good dinner, with plenty of Mexican beer to wash it down.

Once the dishes were cleared away, negotiations resumed. Mac was unsure of herself. Not only did she lack business expertise, she had no way to know what the unit's overhead would be or what the competition was charging.

But eventually the discussion came down to a charge of four ounces of gold per day, which was one ounce more than the folks in Miami had paid. And that felt pretty good. *But what if there's a more generous client out there?* Mac wondered. *If we take this opportunity, we could miss out on that one.*

When Garrison spoke, it was as if he could read her mind. "I'd like to remind you of something, Captain . . . The time is coming when units like Mac's Marauders will have to rejoin the United States Army or fight it. Which side of that equation would you like to be on?"

It was an important question. Would Sloan succeed or fail? Mac couldn't be sure. *But the unit will be no worse off if he fails,* Mac told herself. *Whereas you could be in a world of hurt if he succeeds and you are on the wrong side of history.* She stood and extended a hand to Garrison. "You have a deal. Let's kick some Confederate ass."

## FORT KNOX, KENTUCKY

The enormous white tent was Besom's idea. It had been purchased from a special-events company in Louisville and erected in front of the Fort Knox depository. That meant any photo of the tent would not only show the modest way in which Sloan had chosen to live but would remind people of the president's recent victory and the fact that the government was sitting atop a whole lot of gold. All of which made sense but meant Sloan had to wear a winter coat most of the time, even though strategically placed space heaters whirred around the clock.

Sheets of fabric had been used to divide the "new White House" into functional areas, one of which was Sloan's office. It was equipped with beat-up campaign-style furniture that was supposed to convey the sense of a general in the field. Sloan was seated behind his desk, reading an intelligence summary, when three people were shown into the "room."

Sloan had interacted with all of them in his role as Secretary of Energy, but never in one place, and the fact that they'd chosen to come as a group was not only interesting—but part of why he'd been willing to fit them into a crowded schedule. Emile Durst represented the Coal Coalition, Joe Cobb worked for the shale industry, and Adele Eakins was a well-known lobbyist for the wind-power people.

Sloan circled around to greet each person, invited them to sit on the canvas director's chairs that fronted his desk, and returned to his seat. "So," Sloan began. "This *is* a surprise. Where are the biofuel folks? And the solar people?"

Cobb was dressed cowboy-style, in a barn coat, khaki pants, and hand-tooled boots. He'd spent a lot of time out in the sun back when it was still visible, and the lines on his face were reminiscent of a road map. "The biofuel people are selling what little bit of corn they have to food processors," Cobb answered. "And the solar people are selling most of their panels to homeowners for pennies on the dollar."

"That makes sense," Sloan allowed. "But I assume you folks are doing well."

"We are," Eakins agreed. "But for how long?" Eakins was a fortysomething dishwater blonde. She looked like a soccer mom but had a master's in aeronautical engineering.

Sloan frowned. "I don't understand," he said. "It's going to take years for us to rebuild, and as we do so, your companies are certain to grow and profit."

"We want to be part of the solution," Durst put in. "But we have some concerns."

*Here it comes,* Sloan thought to himself. *Stick to your guns.* "Okay," Sloan said. "And what are those concerns?"

Durst was wearing a camel-colored overcoat over a suit and tie. His breath fogged the air. "There are rumors that you're going to attack the South."

"What I'm pushing for," Sloan replied, "is the full restoration of our sovereign territory. And that includes the states south of the so-called New Mason-Dixon Line. I hope the secessionists will change their minds and remain with the Union. I sent a letter to CEO Lemaire saying as much."

Cobb looked Sloan in the eye. "And if he refuses?"

"Then we'll take whatever actions are necessary to unify the country."

"And that means war," Eakins insisted. "Don't bullshit us, Sam . . . We aren't stupid."

Sloan struggled to contain his steadily rising anger. "So you're opposed to unification?"

"There would be a lot of casualties," Cobb answered evasively. "Six hundred and twenty thousand men died in the first civil war."

"I'm aware of that," Sloan said. "So that's it? You, as the representatives of your respective industries, came to warn me about the possibility of casualties?"

"War is a complicated enterprise," Durst said. "We need time to ramp up . . . So while unification is important—there might be unintended consequences."

"That's right," Eakins added. "We've read your speeches. So we're aware of your plan to repatriate the petroleum reserves down south."

"The oil in those reserves belongs to the citizens of the United States," Sloan reminded them. "It's my duty to take it back."

"But that could be problematical," Cobb warned. "You were Secretary of Energy . . . Think about what will happen to energy prices if you dump all that oil on the market. Why not wait for a while? What's the hurry?"

Sloan sighed. There it was. The *real* reason why the lobbyists were sitting in front of him. Their clients would profit from the reconstruction process. But they'd make even *more* money while energy prices were sky-high. And *that*, rather than the full restoration of the country's lawful government, was their focus. Sloan looked from face to face. "There could be a price drop," he allowed. "But I doubt it. In fact there's so much work to do that demand could outstrip supply."

"So you're going to push Congress to authorize a war," Eakins said grimly.

"I'm going to push Congress to rebuild this country," Sloan replied. "Whatever that may entail."

The meeting came to an end shortly after that. As the lobbyists left, Sloan knew that a lot of campaign cash was walking out of the tent with them. There were other donors, however . . . And he'd find them. "How did it go?" Besom inquired as he entered the room.

"Not very well," Sloan confessed. "They're afraid that energy prices will drop after we capture the oil reserves."

Besom made a face. "All right, so be it. But I'm taking names . . . And when this is over, there will be a price to pay. Are you ready for the tour?"

"The tour" was another one of Besom's ideas and was set to begin the following morning, with a ground-hugging flight to Virginia. From there, Sloan was scheduled to fly north, west, and back again. The plan was to spend one night in each one of the twenty-five contiguous states that constituted the Union. Sloan was looking forward to the trip and dreading it as well.

Cars came to collect Sloan, Besom, and Jenkins the next morning. In his new role as Interim Director of the Secret Service, Jenkins had assembled a team of five ex–law officers to protect Sloan. They barely knew each other and were learning on the job, but some protection was better than none.

The cars took them to Godman Army Airfield, which was part of Fort Knox. Air Force One was waiting. Except that the post-impact version was equipped with *two* engines—and could barely accommodate Sloan's party. It could fly low, however, below the cloud cover, and land at small airports. And that would be necessary because of the consistently bad weather, and the fact that the North could no longer access the Global Positioning System.

Everything went well at first. Thanks to Besom's advance people, there were welcoming crowds waiting for Sloan at airports, attentive audiences filled the halls where he spoke, and there were offers of support at the dinners he attended.

America is rising, America will come back together, and America will be greater than it was before. Those were the messages Sloan delivered at each stop. And he believed in the first two even if the last one was unlikely to materialize during his lifetime.

City followed city in what became a blur of places, faces, and memorable moments. Those included a standing O in Pittsburgh, fireworks in Detroit, and a clear blue sky in Lincoln, Nebraska. Then the presidential party put down in Cheyenne, Wyoming.

Prior to the meteor strikes, the state had been ranked with Alabama as one of the most conservative places in the country. And, according to what Besom had heard from his growing cadre of operatives, nothing had changed.

In fact, most observers agreed that the only thing that prevented Wyoming from aligning itself with the New Confederacy was the fact that all of the state's neighbors were pro-Union. If only by small majorities. And that was why Besom had wanted to skip Cheyenne.

Sloan had a different perspective however. "We can't win what we don't fight for," he said. "And we need to show the citizens of Wyoming that we care, even if only 10 percent of the population agrees with us."

But when Air Force One landed, it was snowing, the crowd waiting at the airport was waving Confederate flags, and there was no security other than what Sloan had with him. Jenkins and his people hurried Sloan past the hostile crowd and into the second of three black SUVs. The vehicle took him to a hotel, where about a dozen pro-Union people were waiting. Their homemade signs were nearly invisible in the forest of professionally printed New Whig Party placards and at least a dozen Confederate flags.

Sloan knew that, like the original Whig Party back in 1830, the *new* Whig Party favored a strong Congress and a weak presidency. A political structure which, if implemented, would not only be more responsive to lobbyists—but could be used to adopt many elements of the "New Order" that controlled the South. That would require changes to the Constitution, of course . . . But what better time to push for such changes than when the country was on its knees? And people were frightened?

As the security team escorted Sloan into the hotel, he could hear the names they called him, and feel the animus that hung in the air. "Hang the bastard!" someone shouted. A cheer went up. Sloan regretted his decision to visit Cheyenne by that time, but he wasn't willing to cut and run.

The inside of the hotel felt extremely warm after the cold air outside, and Sloan got only a brief glimpse of the comfortably furnished lobby before being escorted down a hall and into a meeting room. It wasn't especially large. Besom knew better than to reserve a room that might look empty in photographs. Union loyalists were seated in the first two rows. But the rest of the room was packed with Whigs. And they were clearly hostile as Sloan took his place behind the podium.

The noise level dropped slightly as Besom gave the usual introduction, but began to increase as Sloan spoke. His eyes searched the room looking for a friendly face. "I come from a farm family," he began, "so it's a pleasure to visit the Cowboy State." That produced a smattering of applause but not much.

"Our country has been through some hard times," Sloan continued, "but I . . ."

"He's an imposter!" a woman shouted. "The *real* president is dead!"

"I *am* the real president," Sloan insisted. "But if you want someone else, then vote in the next election."

"Bullshit," a man said. "I want someone else *now*!"

Sloan saw the pistol come up, heard Jenkins shout "Man with a gun!" and was reaching for his own weapon when half a dozen shots were fired. The would-be assassin jerked spastically as the bullets struck him—and a blood mist drifted away from his head. His body went slack at that point and dropped out of sight. His wife screamed and threw herself on top of the corpse.

There was a roar of outrage as *more* guns were drawn, and people began to blaze away. Sloan brought the Glock up, saw a woman pointing a revolver at him, and shot her in the chest. That was when Jenkins grabbed Sloan from behind and dragged him toward an exit.

Besom was holding the door open, so that Secret Service agents could carry one of their own out of the room, *and* calmly firing a pocket pistol into the crowd. The press secretary didn't seem to care *who* he hit—so long as it was a Whig.

Thanks to Jenkins, the SUVs were waiting out back. The presidential party hurried out of the building and piled into them. It was nearly dark as the motorcade raced back to the airport. Air Force One's engines were running, and the plane was ready to go.

Sloan allowed himself to be hustled on board—but refused to take a seat as the plane started to taxi. A man was laid out on the floor just aft of the cockpit, and three people were bent over him. "Who got hit?" Sloan demanded. "How is he?"

Jenkins got up off his knees. "Agent Castel was killed, Mr. President."

Sloan felt sick to his stomach. "I'm sorry," he said. "It's my fault. We shouldn't have come here."

The wheels left the ground, and Air Force One began to climb. "Idaho will be better," Besom predicted bitterly. "It couldn't be worse." Sloan hoped it was true.

## SUPERIOR, ARIZONA

There were a lot of tearful good-byes as most of Mac's Marauders and their vehicles rolled through Superior, Arizona, on the way to Fort Knox, Kentucky. Would all of the soldiers return? It didn't seem likely . . . But Mac planned to bring as many of them home as she could. Assuming *she* survived—which was by no means certain.

About sixteen hundred miles lay between Superior and Fort Knox. Mac hoped to complete the trip in four or five days, and for good reason, since the unit would remain on half pay until it arrived. The pickup truck designated as Roller-One cleared town first, followed by Mac's Humvee. The column included fifteen vehicles. That left Evans with two Strykers, a Humvee, and an armed pickup truck. That was why the Apache had been left behind. If the base was attacked, the helicopter could make a crucial difference.

The route Mac had chosen was going to take them northwest on Highway 60 to 191 and Interstate 40. They would follow it into New Mexico but stay west of the border with Texas because that area was subject to raids.

The gray clouds were low, and the source of occasional bouts of sleet, as the mercenaries motored up through Show Low and St. Johns. As usual, the Marauders had to share the road with all manner of cars, steam-powered trucks, pedal-powered carts, horse-drawn buggies, and, on that particular day, a motorized skateboard! Its rider was wearing a football helmet and knee pads. He waved cheerfully as he zipped past.

But many of the other vehicles had to be forced into the slow lane by Private Atkins, who was riding shotgun on Roller-One and spent most of his time shouting through a megaphone.

None of which surprised Mac. What *did* surprise her was the volume of traffic. There was more of it, as if the nation's pulse had started to quicken, and things were improving.

Could President Sloan take credit for that? Or had the post-catastrophe shock begun to wear off? Resulting in more activity? The two theories weren't mutually exclusive, however, so maybe there was some truth to both of them.

They pulled into a rest area just after noon to eat lunch. Then, upon returning to the freeway, the Marauders were forced to pass many of the same slow movers they'd overtaken earlier. The convoy was ten miles outside of Albuquerque when Sergeant Esco warned Mac about the roadblock ahead. "Two tanks are sitting in the middle of I-40 with concrete barriers behind them. It looks like some of the traffic is being allowed to enter the city, but most of it is being shunted onto a side road. Over."

"Are there any signs of combat? Over."

"No. Traffic is stop-and-go. But other than that, everything looks good. Over."

"Can you tell who the tanks belong to?"

"No. But the people around them look more like cowboys than soldiers. Over."

"Okay . . . Well done. Follow the detour and see where it goes. Over."

"Roger that," Esco replied. "Over."

The UAV pilot called in fifteen minutes later to tell Mac that the detour was going to take them around the city to a point where they could access I-25 north. It was possible to swing wide and use a secondary road to circumvent the area, but time was money . . . And the Marauders had to conserve fuel. So Mac chose to remain on 40 and deal with the roadblock.

It wasn't long before Roller-One came up on the traffic jam. It was start and stop from that point forward, a fact well-known to local entrepreneurs, who sold all manner of goods and food from brightly painted shacks that lined both sides of the highway.

Doc Hoskins was worried about food safety, and Mac was worried about security, so the Marauders weren't allowed to leave the convoy. It was a decision that was certain to generate a lot of griping—but it was for their own good.

Eventually, after forty-five minutes of incremental progress, the roadblock appeared. A professionally painted sign hung over the freeway. It read WELCOME TO THE NAVAHO NATION and seemed to suggest that Native Americans were in charge of Albuquerque.

The tanks Esco had mentioned were parked so they could fire on the highway, and from where Mac was sitting, it looked as if both 105mm cannons were aimed at *her*.

Two dozen soldiers were standing around burn barrels, assuming that was the correct way to classify the men and women who were dressed cowboy-style and armed with a wild assortment of weapons. Three were mounted on horses and appeared to be on standby, should there be a need to enter traffic and handle a dispute.

A man stopped to talk to the soldiers in Roller-One before making his way back to the Humvee. Mac got out and circled around the front of the vehicle. The local was wearing a flat-brimmed hat, sheepskin coat, and faded jeans. A pair of beat-up boots completed the outfit. Teeth flashed as he smiled. "Are you Captain Macintyre?"

"Yes, sir."

The man looked back along the column. "That's a lot of fire-power, Captain. Where are you headed?"

"Fort Knox, Kentucky."

His eyes were like gun barrels. *"Why?"*

"We're under contract to the federal government. I can show you the paperwork if you wish."

The man smiled. "Why bother? I wouldn't know if the document was real or forged. I hear the North is going to attack the South."

Mac shrugged. "It's possible."

"We'd like to see that," the man said. "The Confederates don't like us—and we don't like them. Will you be allowed to speak with the president?"

"I doubt it."

"Well, if you do, tell him this: You tell him that Chief Natonaba and the Navaho Nation will stand next to him in battle. But if he tries to take Albuquerque, we will fight him to the death. Got it?"

Mac thought about Secretary Garrison. Maybe she could pass the message to him. "Yes, Chief . . . I've got it."

"Good. You have a nice day, Captain. Walk in beauty . . . And remember the old ones." And with that, he turned away.

Mac returned to the Humvee, got in, and gave Roller-One permission to proceed. The detour took them onto Atrisco Vista Boulevard, which led them across arid land and past an airport. Then, after a long and winding journey through some suburbs, the mercenaries were able to get on I-25 and follow it north.

It was late afternoon by the time the Marauders entered the bedroom community of Rio Rancho. Based on the intel provided by Esco, Mac sent Roller-One ahead to inspect a possible bivouac site just east of the freeway, and directly across from a casino. The report came in ten minutes later. The site didn't have access to water but it was unoccupied, and only yards from an on-ramp. And that would make for a quick start in the morning.

The last vehicle in the convoy was towing a M149A2 "water buffalo." That gave Mac the freedom to spend a night without a water source, so she gave the go-ahead. It was her desire to have all the unit's defenses in place before darkness fell. And, thanks to her NCOs, they were.

The night passed without incident, and the convoy was back on the road by 0630 in the morning. The plan was to follow I-25 north into Colorado. Then, near Trinidad, Mac was going to take the unit off I-25 and follow a secondary highway to the northeast.

The Marauders made good progress over the next couple of days. From Rio Rancho they drove to Limon, Colorado, where they spent the night in a deserted RV park. From there it was a five-hour trip to Junction City, Kansas. It was a small town, with an active militia, the leader of which was none too happy about the prospect of allowing a heavily armed group to stay overnight. But unlike Chief Natonaba down in Albuquerque, he found the written contract signed by Interim Secretary of Defense Garrison to be very reassuring. He even went so far as to invite Mac and her officers to dinner in his home.

Mac didn't have any officers other than Dr. Hoskins, so she took Sergeants Esco and Poole along as well, leaving Ralston in command. It was an excellent, home-cooked meal. And Mac felt guilty about dining on meat loaf and mashed potatoes while the rest of the unit ate MREs.

The Marauders were on I-70 just after dawn and entered the outskirts of Kansas City three hours later. A checkpoint sat astride the freeway and was defended by a mercenary outfit called the Devil's Kin. The Devs had six Bradleys. So when one of the mercs ordered

Roller-One to pull over, the driver had no choice but to obey. The rest of the column followed, and Mac placed them on high alert.

If memory served, a hard-fought Civil War battle had taken place nearby. Union forces eventually won and forced Confederate General Samuel R. Curtis to retreat. Was the city still in Union hands? Mac discovered that it was.

After showing her contract to the major in command of the Devil's Kin, she was given permission to continue on. "We've got a contract just like yours," the major told her. "So who knows? Maybe we'll fight side by side one day. Let's drink to that."

Mac was expecting him to produce a bottle of hard liquor, and wasn't looking forward to downing a drink so early in the day. So she was pleasantly surprised when he pulled two cans of Coke out of a cooler, wiped one of them off, and gave it to her. After popping the tabs, and bumping cans, they drank. Mac hadn't had a Coke in months. The ice-cold liquid felt wonderful going down. She was back on the road fifteen minutes later.

There was a lot of traffic, most of which was slow—so it took two hours to creep through Kansas City. But finally, after what seemed like an eternity, the Marauders were able to put the hammer down and log some serious progress. Enough progress to arrive in St. Louis before nightfall. That was when Mac began to believe that there really was a Union Army . . . Even if it was totally fucked-up.

The local military command assigned a specially equipped Humvee to the unit for the express purpose of getting them through the city in a timely manner. Mac was grateful and decided to ride in the Humvee. The man behind the wheel was a sergeant named Taber, and he was a talker. And since Mac was eager to learn whatever she could, that was fine with her. In between burps of sound from the vehicle's siren, Taber gave a guided tour. "See the troops up ahead?"

As the Humvee drew abreast of them, Mac was surprised to see what looked like a battalion of World War I doughboys marching along. They wore Smokey the Bear hats and carried bolt-action rifles. She frowned. "What's up with that?"

"They're volunteers," Taber replied. "Reenactors who dress up and play soldier on the weekends. Some of them are in their seventies. From what I hear, they're going to protect small towns just north of the New Mason-Dixon Line. That will allow the rest of us to go down south."

And there were more volunteers including a gang of middle-aged motorcyclists armed with American flags, a troop of blue-uniformed cavalry who were riding horses, and a float carrying a fifteen-foot-tall Statue of Liberty.

When they crossed the Mississippi at 10 mph, there was time to look down on hundreds of barges and improvised gunboats tied up three or four abreast along the banks of the river. Were they prepping for an invasion? That's how it looked. But the whole thing had an extemporaneous feel. As if someone was throwing things together on the fly . . . And that scared the crap out of her. The last thing Mac wanted was to see a bunch of incompetents piss lives away. Especially the lives that belonged to her people.

Once on the east side of the city, Mac thanked Taber, switched over to Roller-Two, and wished it wasn't so late. That couldn't be helped, however . . . And for once, they had been assigned to a bivouac area just off I-64.

That was the good news. The bad news was that Jones Park was almost full. Other military units had arrived and set up camp, leaving only a small patch of ground just off Argonne Drive. "I want to double the number of sentries we put out tonight," Ralston told Mac. "Chances are that our fellow campers will send teams of scroungers out to steal anything they can."

The possibility hadn't occurred to Mac, who gave the go-ahead. And a good thing, too . . . Because three attempts were made to sneak in and steal equipment during the hours of darkness. The would-be thieves were taken prisoner and left tied to trees when the Marauders departed the next morning.

The trip from St. Louis to Louisville promised to be a straight-ahead affair, followed by a turn to the south. That would put them in Fort Knox by nightfall if all went well. Unfortunately things *didn't* go well. A persistent rain began to fall after lunch, a truck broke down, and it took the wrench turners more than an hour to get it running again. Mac was tired and frustrated by the time they reached Louisville and were forced to stop at a checkpoint, where she was required to deal with some officious bullshit.

It was dark by the time the unit arrived at Fort Knox. Or it *would* have been dark if it hadn't been for hundreds of flickering campfires. "We might as well send the Confederates a message telling them where to drop their bombs," Mac griped, as a motor-cycle rider led the column through a maze of streets.

Private Adams, who was driving the Humvee, chose to re-main silent as their guide came to a stop and pointed into the darkness. "It's all yours," he shouted. "Welcome to Fort Knox!" Then the soldier was gone. Mac swore, opened the door, and got out. The headlights from a passing truck swung across a sea of mud. The Marauders had arrived.

# CHAPTER 10

||||||||||||||||||||||||||||||||||||||||||

Strategy without tactics is the slowest route to victory.
Tactics without strategy is the noise before defeat.

—SUN TZU

**FORT KNOX, KENTUCKY**

Most of the night had been spent moving the unit's vehicles into place, erecting tents, and establishing a perimeter to keep thieves out. That meant Mac only logged two hours of sleep before the noise generated by passing vehicles, the persistent rattle of a power tool, and occasional shouts woke her up.

It would have been nice to stay in the sleeping bag. But at least a hundred things required Mac's attention, including the need to check in. Because then, and only then, would the Marauders begin to collect full pay.

So Mac kicked the bag off and swung her feet over onto the floor. The four-person tent was one of the few perks she permitted herself. It was furnished with a cot, a flimsy lawn chair, a folding card table, a much-abused footlocker, a bulging duffel bag, and a five-gallon jug of water supported by an upended ammo crate.

As Mac crossed the tiny room to the plastic bowl that served as a sink, she could feel the mud under the tent's floor give with each step. None of the external moisture had been able to penetrate the fabric, however, for which she was thankful.

After completing her morning ablutions, and donning her cleanest uniform, Mac made her way to the door, where a pair of mud-caked boots was waiting. She sat on the lawn chair to pull them on. Then Mac threw the tent fly to one side and stepped out into the cold air. That's when she discovered that a sentry was posted outside. Ralston's work? Yes, of course. The private came to attention—and Mac smiled at him. "As you were, Wang . . . You can rejoin your squad now."

Mud sucked at the soles of Mac's boots as she made her way over to the female latrine. That was the moment when she realized that the sun was out! It was visible through breaks in the clouds. The slight increase in temperature was enough to create a layer of mist. It hugged the ground the way a shroud hugs a corpse. Mac shivered and shoved her hands in her pockets.

After visiting the latrine, she made her way over to the cook tent, which, in spite of the name, was little more than an A-shaped awning supported by three poles and some guylines. There was a table, though . . . And a gas-powered stove. Three Marauders were seated on lawn chairs. They stood as Mac appeared, and she waved them back into their seats. "As you were. Where's the buffet?"

Corporal Prevo grinned. "Over there, ma'am," he said, and pointed to a stack of MREs. "There ain't nothing better than turkey chili for breakfast."

Mac laughed, poured some hot water over instant coffee, and ate the Hershey bar that Private Sanchez gave her. After five minutes of shooting the shit with the troops, she could feel the combination of caffeine and sugar enter her bloodstream. With cup in hand, Mac went looking for Ralston.

Thanks to the first sergeant, and the rest of the NCOs, significant progress had been made during the night. And Mac took pride in the fact that their bivouac was well organized even if the surrounding encampment was a gigantic shit show.

The company's scroungers had been able to steal two dozen pallets somewhere. They'd been used to create an elevated sidewalk that ran between the first-aid station and the HQ tent. "Nice job," Mac said. "Now I can wear my high heels to work."

Her voice was intentionally loud so that all of the soldiers working on the project could hear. The line got a laugh, just as it was intended to, and would make the rounds soon. It was easy and made Mac feel guilty.

Ralston was exhausted, and she could see it on his face when he forced a smile. "Good morning, ma'am. We have to show these other outfits how it's done. Fortunately, Sergeant Smith is an accomplished thief."

Smith was standing a few feet away. He smiled. "Thanks, Top . . . I love you, too."

Mac chuckled. "It's time for you to grab some shut-eye, Sergeant Ralston, and that's an order. Sergeant Smith can take charge here. Once I find Sparks, I'm headed for HQ."

"I'm here," Munroe announced, and Mac turned to find that the radio operator was standing behind her. Together, they made their way out to the point where their chunk of real estate fronted George S. Patton Avenue. If the stretch of churned-up mud could be dignified as such.

The duty driver was a private named Isley. He was slouched behind the wheel of a Humvee—listening to music through a pair of earbuds. When Isley saw Mac, he made the buds disappear. "Good morning, ma'am."

"Good morning," Mac replied as she settled into the passenger seat. "Do you know where HQ is?"

"Yes, ma'am."

"Good. Take me there."

As Isley navigated his way through the untidy maze of bivouacs, Mac had a chance to eyeball some of the other units that had been assembled for whatever it was that Sloan had in mind. At one time or another, she saw tanks, a field hospital, com wagons, a wrecker, half a dozen fuel tankers, a clutch of infantry carriers, a pair of medevac vehicles, and a smoke-generator-equipped recon vehicle that was sitting all by its lonely self. The whole thing was FUBAR. Or so it seemed to Mac.

Once they arrived, Mac saw a sign that read: 2ND EXPEDITION-ARY FORCE. She got out, told Isley to wait, and followed a lieutenant inside. Then Mac had to trudge from desk to desk, and from corporal to corporal, showing the company's contract to each one—and answering the same questions over and over. Each stop meant that at least one form had to be filled out, and Munroe offered to pitch in. That was a big help—and cut the process down to an hour and a half.

Finally, after clearing the last desk, Mac was sent into an office with plywood walls. A haggard-looking lieutenant colonel was seated behind a table strewn with paperwork. The hand-printed tent card in front of her read: LT. COL. COLBY.

Colby wore her mostly gray hair in a bun. Her close-set eyes were like chips of obsidian. And she had a cold, judging from how red her long, thin nose was. Mac came to attention, stated her rank followed by the name of her unit. She finished with, "Reporting for duty, ma'am."

Colby blew her nose with a handkerchief and made a face. "It's impossible to find Kleenex anymore," she complained. "And that's a sure sign that the country is going to hell in a handcart. Macintyre, huh? I used to know a general named Macintyre . . . Any relation?"

Mac swallowed. "My father, ma'am."

Colby had overplucked eyebrows. They rose incrementally. "Are you aware that he's fighting for the Confederacy? In fact, from what I've heard, he's one of their most important generals."

Mac *wasn't* aware. Ever since the visit to the house near Kuna, Idaho, she'd wondered where he was and what he was doing. But the possibility that he might side with the Confederacy hadn't occurred to her. It should have, though . . . The New Order's brand of Darwinian politics would appeal to him. Survival of the fittest. That was the essence of Bo Macintyre's personal *and* political perspective. Mac remembered how he had stood, hands on hips, after she took a spill. "Never wait for a helping hand," he told her. "Take care of yourself."

"No, ma'am," Mac said as she stared into coal-black eyes. "I *didn't* know."

"Well, this war is going to divide a lot of families," Colby predicted. "But enough of that . . . Let's get you checked in."

After skimming Mac's contract and reviewing the paperwork the multitude of corporals had prepared, Colby signed two identical documents and handed one to Mac. "There you go . . . Your unit is on the payroll . . . The next step is to visit Major Renky. He'll set up a draw for your company."

"A what?"

"A draw . . . Meaning an account you can use to draw supplies. Payment is due on the last day of each month. Please remember that if you're more than thirty days in arrears, the government has the right to seize all of your equipment, including your vehicles. And, since you have a cavalry unit, you won't be able to fulfill the terms of your contract without them. That would trigger standard clause 32b."

The air around Mac was chilly, but she was starting to sweat. She'd read the contract and knew that Marauders would have to buy supplies, but clause 32b? No, nothing came to mind. "I'm sorry, ma'am . . . Please remind me of what's in clause 32b."

Colby blew her nose. Her thin lips looked even thinner when she smiled. "Clause 32b states that if a unit loses the means to fulfill the terms of its contract, all members of said unit who were on active duty as of May 1 this year will automatically revert to active status in the branch of the military to which they previously belonged. So if you want to be a mercenary, be sure to pay your bills. Do I make myself clear, *Lieutenant*?"

Mac took notice of the way in which Colby had mentioned her *real* rank. An indication that the 2nd Expeditionary Force had at least some predisaster personnel records. "Yes, ma'am. Very clear, ma'am."

"Good. Go see Major Renky . . . Oh, and one more thing."

"Ma'am?"

"If you run into your father, shoot him in the face."

|||||||||||

The Marauders spent the next two days performing deferred maintenance on the unit's vehicles, their bodies, and their uniforms—all of which were filthy. Fortunately, some local entrepreneurs were running an off-base laundry service that offered pickup and delivery.

Mac also held meetings about the need for cost control—and made Smith responsible for staying on budget. Would the supply sergeant send scroungers out to "requisition" "free" parts in the middle of the night? Of course he would. And Mac planned to ignore it.

On the morning of the third day, Mac was sitting in the HQ tent reading the sick-call report when a rain-drenched private entered. "I'm from battalion HQ," he announced. "I have a message for Captain Macintyre."

"That would be me," Mac replied. "Battalion HQ? *What* battalion?"

"The one you're part of," the private answered, as he proffered an envelope. After reading the contents, Mac discovered that not only was she a member of the Scout and Reconnaissance Battalion, she was in command of Charlie Company and expected to attend a command briefing that was scheduled to begin in twenty minutes! And she was supposed to bring her XO.

After hurrying to don a clean uniform and telling Private Isley to "Step on it," Mac and Ralston were still ten minutes late when they entered the large tent. A dozen people were seated on folding chairs, and the major who was standing at the far end of the conference table paused in midsentence. His carefully combed hair was graying, his nose was slightly bent, and his blue eyes were clear. "Well, well . . . Captain Macintyre, I presume."

Mac swallowed. "Yes, sir."

"I know you're a mercenary," the major said, "but I won't tolerate slackness. If a meeting is scheduled for 0900, you will arrive on time or be penalized. My name is Granger. Have a seat. Now, where was I? Ah, yes . . . Our mission.

"The Scout and Reconnaissance Battalion consists of three companies at the moment. That includes a headquarters company under Captain Pearce, a scout company under Captain Olson's leadership, and a Stryker company commanded by Captain Macintyre. Our job is to find the enemy, identify targets, and assess battle damage. The latter is more important than you might think because of the hazardous flying conditions.

"In addition, we'll be called upon to participate in search-and-rescue missions, to support special-operations teams, and to assist the military police if that's necessary." Granger's eyes roamed the room. "Do you have any questions?"

Captain Pearce wanted to know if she would get some additional staff, and Mac took the opportunity to sit down. The chair was next to Olson's. He winked as if to say, "What a load of bullshit." Olson had slicked-back hair, boyish good looks, and hazel eyes.

"What we need is a combination of speed and muscle," Granger continued as he went over to an easel. "So let's review the vehicles we have—and how they can support the overall mission."

The presentation lasted for more than an hour. The plan was for Olson's motorcycles, armed rat rods, and M1161 Growler Strike Vehicles to conduct lightning raids into enemy territory. As they pulled back, the Strykers would be there to support them.

That was fine with Mac, who had nothing to prove and no desire for glory. Her goal was to keep her people alive, make some money, and go home.

Over the next week, Mac learned that although Granger was a stickler for detail, he was fair and determined to succeed. To that end, he asked for and was granted permission to take the battalion out of Fort Knox and into the countryside for a series of exercises. Mac knew that the Marauders were in for some long, difficult days. But if the shit hit the fan, the training would pay off. Work began.

## CHICAGO, ILLINOIS

Sloan was sitting in the spacious green room backstage at the Arie Crown Theater. The 4,249-seat venue was part of the McCormick Place convention center located adjacent to Lake Michigan. Sloan knew that the room was packed with newly elected congressmen and -women, all of whom had been sworn in earlier in the day. Most were members of the Patriot Party, thank God. But Whigs were present, too . . . Lots of them. And because Speaker of the House Duncan was working with a thin majority, there would be trouble in the days ahead.

*But this is now,* Sloan reminded himself. *First things first. Did Lemaire and his so-called "board of directors" agree to our offer? If not, the dying is about to begin.* The door swung open, and Besom stuck his head in. "Interim Secretary of State Henderson is here, Mr. President."

Sloan searched the press secretary's face for any hint of what Henderson was going to tell him. There wasn't any. So Henderson had chosen to keep the information to himself. "Please show him in."

Henderson was balding, jowly, and short. Sloan had chosen him as Secretary of State because he was from the South, understood the culture, and had been the Assistant Secretary of State for Western Hemisphere Affairs prior to May 1. Sloan stood as the other man entered and went forward to shake hands with him. "Don't keep me waiting, George . . . What did they say?"

The pain in Henderson's eyes was obvious. "They said, 'no,' Mr. President. They claim to control a nation called the Confederacy of American States. And, according to them, the countries of Mexico, Cuba, and Haiti have formally recognized their government. I'm sorry, Mr. President. I know this is the last thing you wanted."

Sloan looked away, swallowed, and forced his eyes back again. "Thank you, George. They're waiting for me. I guess I'll have to give them the news."

Henderson nodded. "Tell them we tried . . . Tell them we'll win."

"I will," Sloan promised, and made his way over to the door. Besom was waiting outside. Their eyes met. "Which script do you need, Mr. President? Number one? Or number two?"

"Two," Sloan said. "I'm sorry, Doyle."

Besom shrugged. "I'm not surprised. Don't worry, Mr. President . . . Congress will back you."

"They will tonight," Sloan agreed. "But what about later? When the casualty reports come in? We'll see."

Sloan didn't plan to use the script unless the teleprompter went down but accepted it anyway and followed a stagehand to the point where he could see Congressman Duncan. The Speaker of the House was stalling and thrilled to see Sloan from the corner of his eye. "And here," Duncan said, "is the man you've been waiting for . . . Samuel T. Sloan, the President of the United States!"

A small band played "Hail to the Chief" as Sloan made his way out onto the stage, shook hands with Duncan, and went over to greet the newly named minority leader as well. That wasn't necessary, but it seemed like the right thing to do.

The applause was thunderous, and understandably so, because in addition to members of the House, the Senate, and the reconstituted Supreme Court, more than three thousand citizens were present—all selected through a lottery. That was another one of Besom's ideas—and it was sure to generate coverage in their hometowns. Sloan raised both hands. "Thank you . . . Thank you, very much . . . Please be seated.

"First," Sloan said, as people took their seats, "I would like to congratulate all of our newly elected representatives and senators. Thank you for running . . . We are going to need your strength and wisdom during the days ahead.

"Second, please join me in a minute of silence as we remember the government workers both elected and unelected who lost their lives during the tragic events of May 1."

A hush fell over the crowd as Sloan closed his eyes and counted to sixty. Everything seemed unreal, like a dream, or a nightmare. But when he opened his eyes, the audience was still there. "Thank you." His eyes sought and found the first line on the teleprompter. "I had hoped to bring you good news tonight. Sadly, that isn't the case. Just before I came onstage, I received word that the so-called Confederacy of American States has chosen to secede from the Union."

That produced a loud gasp of horror from the audience, a gabble of conversation, and a shout of, "God damn those bastards! We'll *take* those states back!" The statement was met with a smattering of applause.

Sloan nodded. "I agree with the gentleman in the second row. To paraphrase the provisions of the Insurrection Act of 1807, as amended in 2006, the President of the United States has the power to suppress, in a state, any insurrection, domestic violence, unlawful combination, or conspiracy. And, ladies and gentlemen, that is precisely what I'm going to do!"

Members of the Patriot Party stood first . . . Soon followed by the Whigs, who, though less than enthusiastic about the prospect of a civil war, didn't want to be seen as pro-Confederate. Even though many of them were. The applause lasted for the better part of a minute before Sloan raised his hands, and the politicians took their seats.

"This is not the end of our country's story," Sloan told them. "It's the start of a *new* chapter . . . And one that will eventually lead to a happy ending. Tonight, I will instruct all branches of the federal government, including the military, to take all actions necessary to regain control of those states that signed the articles of secession. And I will direct them to do so with an eye to minimizing casualties on both sides.

"My staff will work with leaders from both parties to initiate, review, and pass the legislation required to support the unification effort. In the meantime, I look forward to meeting all the new members of Congress at the reception later this evening. Thank you for your support—and may God bless America."

The audience stood, and the walls of the theater shook in response to the applause. Sloan waved as he left the stage, hurried past Besom, and entered the men's room. That was where he threw up. He believed that America *would* rise again . . . But he knew that a lot of people would have to die first.

## NEAR MILLERSTOWN, KENTUCKY

The unincorporated town of Millerstown, Kentucky, consisted of cleared farmland, mixed with sizeable patches of timber, all separated by a crisscrossing maze of country roads. There were hills, too, along with lots of streams and rivers. That made the area ideal for war games even if the local inhabitants didn't like to have vehicles churning up their fields and spooking their animals. However, given the extent to which the consistently bad weather had ruined their crops, a timely visit from the battalion's paymaster went a long way toward easing the pain.

A smear of sunlight was visible through a thin layer of bruised-looking clouds—and a cold breeze caused the pennant flying from one-two's aerial to snap every now and then. The Stryker was parked on a logging road that ran parallel to the paved road below and was partially screened by trees.

"War games" was a misnomer, of course. That's what Major

Granger said. He preferred the term "military simulation." And in this case a simulation of what military theorists referred to as "maneuver warfare." The goal was to defeat the enemy by limiting its ability to make good decisions.

Theoretically, that could be achieved by attacking command and control centers, supply depots, and fire-support assets. Under normal circumstances, airpower would play an important role in accomplishing those objectives. But since foul weather was keeping a lot of fixed-wing aircraft on the ground, the Scout and Reconnaissance Battalion would have to fill the gap. Mac's thoughts were interrupted as Munroe spoke. "Here they come," the RTO said. "And, according to Bravo-Six, the enemy is catching up."

Mac was standing near Charlie One-Four's engine and enjoying the heat it produced. She swiveled her glasses to the south. The highway was empty at first. Then she heard the roar of engines, and three off-road motorcycles appeared. The lead bike, the one that Olson normally rode, performed a wheelie as it went by. That was the sort of thing Mac had come to expect of Bravo Company's CO. But somehow, in spite of the fact that Mac didn't like show-offs, the combination of bravado and boyish charm was starting to grow on her. *Focus,* Mac told herself. *Pay attention.*

The next vehicles to pass Charlie Company's position were so-called rat rods which, unlike hot rods, were anything but pretty. Function ruled form, and the function was war. Olson's crudely modified vehicles were armed with machine guns, grenade launchers, and, in one case, an M252 mortar bolted into the bed of a pickup. They were followed by a squad of army Growlers reminiscent of WWII jeeps.

"This is Six," Mac said into her mike. "The enemy is coming on fast . . . Check to ensure that your weapons are clear—and that the safeties are on. Your cameras should be rolling. Over."

Mac heard a flurry of affirmative clicks as she watched the road. The first "enemy" vehicle to appear was a Humvee. "This is Six," Mac said. "Let the Humvee pass . . . Bravo Company will be lying in wait for it up the road. Over."

The next vehicle was a Bradley. It arrived a full minute after the Humvee was gone. "This is Six," Mac said. "Hold, hold, hold. Let's get as many units into the kill zone as we can. All right . . . Fire!"

None of the Strykers fired. But later, when Granger and the rest of the brass reviewed the video, Charlie Company's victory would be obvious. Positioned where they were, the cannon-equipped Stryker MGS M128s would have obliterated the Bradleys. Mac turned to Munroe. "Contact the enemy and tell them this: 'Bang, you're dead.'"

|||||||||||||

It was cold in the barn, but the walls offered some respite from the wind, a place for two-two's mechanics to work on the Stryker's faulty fuel pump. Mac didn't know how to make the repair but had decided to learn, much to the amusement of her wrench turners. There was more to it than that, of course. Her presence meant a lot to them.

The repair was nearly complete when Olson entered the barn carrying two steaming mugs of coffee. He knew all of the mechanics by name, could tell what they were doing at a glance, and immediately offered to hire them. They ate it up.

That annoyed Mac for two reasons. First, good mechanics were hard to find, and she couldn't afford to lose any. Second, how did Olson manage to make everything look so effortless? She felt awkward by comparison.

Mac was wiping oil off her hands as Olson ambled over. "Hey, Robin . . . I brought you some coffee."

"Robin." When was the last time she'd heard someone call her *that*? Back at JBLM, most likely. And why was Olson using her first name? Given that last names were the standard way to address someone in the army? *Lighten up,* the voice said. *It's no big deal.*

"Thanks," Mac said as she accepted the mug. "Come on . . . We can sit in my office." She led Olson to the bench seat that was all that remained of a long-gone truck. It was positioned against a stall.

"Nice," Olson said as he sat down. "I like what you've done with the place."

Mac sat next to him. "Thanks. So what's on your mind?"

"I was up at the house when Granger got the word. This shit is for real."

Mac heard herself say, "I'm sorry to hear that." But was that entirely true? She'd been expecting it. Everyone had. And the sense of foreboding was real. But what about the slight tinge of excitement? Because wrong though it might be—there was part of her that enjoyed combat. A biochemical gift from her father perhaps.

Whatever the reason, Mac didn't feel as sorry as she should have. She sipped some coffee. It was laced with rum. "How do you feel about that, Ross? Do you want to fight?"

The other officer shrugged. "It's what the army trained me to do . . . And it's what I get paid for."

"That's it? You don't care which side you fight for?"

"I *do* care," Olson responded. "I think what the Confederates are doing is wrong. But I'm a mercenary now, and it doesn't make sense to get emotionally involved."

That was similar to how Mac felt. She hoped the North would win but had doubts about its capacity to do so and was trying to remain objective. "Yeah," Mac agreed. "It doesn't make sense."

"So," Olson said, "what's a nice girl like you doing in a barn like this?"

"Is that a come-on?"

"Do you want it to be?"

"No."

Olson grinned. "Okay . . . It isn't." And with that, he got up and walked away. Mac felt as if an opportunity had been lost. But an opportunity for *what*? To be Olson's plaything? Because she was the only eligible woman in the battalion? That was the sort of opportunity she could live without. Mac got up. There was work to do—and lots of it. Mac's Marauders were going to war.

## FORT KNOX, KENTUCKY

Now that war had been declared, Sloan was no longer permitted to live in the big white tent because the Secret Service couldn't protect him there. So he was living underground, two stories below the Fort Knox army base, and just down the hall from the War Room.

There was one advantage, though . . . He could sit in the War Room and stare at the maps, charts, and plans projected on three of the four walls while he ate dinner. It consisted of meat loaf with mashed potatoes, which had been his favorite as a boy. Sloan wished he could go back in time and be a boy again, but that was impossible. This was now . . . And he had a job to do.

According to Article II, Section 2, Clause 1 of the Constitution he was the commander in chief of the United States armed services. Except that the states weren't "united." Not anymore. And he wasn't qualified to be commander in chief.

This was nothing new, since only twelve past presidents had been generals prior to taking office. Yes, others had served. But Ronald Reagan's stint in the army air force's public-relations department during World War II didn't qualify him to run a war.

Of course by that measure, Sloan was even *less* qualified since he hadn't worn a uniform until recently. Yet there he was, eating meat loaf and preparing to attack the South. So which strategy should he choose? The methodical approach that General Whitaker Hern favored? Or the daring "balls to the wall," "deep leap" plan that General "Mad" Mary Abbott was so enthusiastic about?

Hern recommended that the Union Army drive south, make contact with the enemy, and engage them. Then the two sides would slug it out for however long it took.

Abbott's plan was very different. She favored an airborne assault by Army Rangers. They would land in Richton, Mississippi, and seize control of the largely undefended oil reserve located there. And, because the element of surprise would be on their side, the Rangers would have a two-day period of time in which to dig in before Confederate forces attacked them.

Meanwhile, as the Rangers dug in, a task force led by Abrams tanks would lead the invasion force south through Nashville on Highway 65 even as surface-to-surface missiles neutralized the defense towers straddling the highway.

Once a path was cleared, the Northern army would surge across the New Mason-Dixon Line and drive south, killing anyone who got in the way. Then, at the conclusion of a five-hundred-mile journey, the regiment would link up with the Rangers in Richton.

But, according to General Hern, Abbott's plan had a number of weaknesses. First, Hern believed it was going to be more difficult to destroy the Confederate defense towers than Abbott claimed. Second, Hern feared that it might take the defense force a full three or four days to fight its way to Richton. That would seem like forever to the Rangers.

Finally, even if Abbott was successful, she'd have a five-hundred-mile-long supply line to defend. Mad Mary was known for her foul mouth, and called "bullshit" on Hern's criticisms. She planned to resupply the Rangers by air.

Hern scoffed at that and pointed out that the weather would keep Abbott's Chinooks grounded most of the time. And, when the skies cleared, the Confederate Air Force would have an opportunity to blow the lumbering helicopters out of the air. Never mind the fact that the Richton-Perry County Airport was too small for the volume of traffic that Abbott proposed. Point and counterpoint.

Hern had graduated near the top of his class at West Point. Mad Mary had worked her way up through the ranks from private. Both had led troops into combat, both had been decorated for bravery, and both were respected by their peers. So which plan should Sloan choose?

As Sloan prepared to take another bite, he realized his plate was empty. He put the fork down next to the single surviving pea. He was going to go with Mad Mary. *Why?* Because her strategy could cut months if not years off the war and save thousands of lives on *both* sides.

Sloan felt a sense of relief. The decision had been made, and he would share it with his staff in the morning. He stood, removed his plate, and took it away. No one else knew it yet, but the first battle of the Second Civil War was already under way.

## NORTH OF BOWLING GREEN, KENTUCKY

Granger's Scout and Reconnaisance Battalion had been given the "honor" of heading south first. Everyone knew that while the New Mason-Dixon Line lay just south of Bowling Green, the Confederates had attacked and occupied the town a month earlier to give themselves some pad.

Olson's people were on point and likely to make first contact. Mac's Marauders were in the two slot—and ready to provide support. But for *what*? The answer was classified. There were plenty of theories, however—one of which was that General Hern was going to lead the invasion. If so, most observers figured he'd do it by the numbers.

Not that it mattered. Mac was reminded of the famous quote from Lord Tennyson: "Ours not to reason why, ours but to do and die." Strategy had never been the province of mere captains and never would be.

Prior to the Confederate attack, the city of Bowling Green had a population of more than sixty thousand people. Since then, many had gone north, and some told stories about Confederate atrocities. Most of those accounts weren't true but had come to be accepted as fact thanks to the Union's twenty-four/seven propaganda machine. And that helped to turn southern Kentucky against the rebs.

That meant the Scout and Reconnaisance Battalion was traveling through mostly friendly country as it rolled south past communities like Rocky Hill, Smiths Grove, and Oakland. Proof of that could be seen in the fact that people poured out of the tent cities that lined both sides of the freeway to wave American flags as the Strykers passed by.

Mac was riding on one-one, which was in the two slot, just behind the lead Humvee. She was standing in the forward air-guard hatch, and when people waved, she waved back.

But as the column neared the outskirts of Bowling Green, the crowds disappeared. And no wonder. Confederate patrols had been probing the city's northern suburbs, making it a dangerous place to be. That's what Mac was thinking about when the radio came to life.

"This is Bravo-Six actual," Olson said. "We have contact. The freeway is blocked at the Barren River. We're in the trees on the north side. It looks like the enemy has two, repeat *two*, Abrams tanks parked on the south end of the bridge. And they're firing on us now. Over."

Mac could hear the distant sound of big 105mm guns firing—and could imagine the bright flashes as shells exploded in the trees—and sent splinters flying in every direction. But none of that was apparent from the tone of Olson's dry, matter-of-fact report. The scout was brave . . . No doubt about that.

"This is Thunder-Six actual," Granger replied. "Pull back from the river, follow old Porter Pike west to Highway 68, and eyeball the Louisville Road bridge. Over."

"Roger that," Olson replied. "Over."

Then Mac's orders came in. "Charlie-Six, this is Thunder-Six actual . . . Follow 446 to 31 west to 68. Take the old, repeat *old* Louisville Road south and tell me if the two-lane bridge is intact. Over."

Mac acknowledged the order, eyed her map, and saw that the interchange with 446 was coming up fast. A quick check was sufficient to ensure that the truck commander was watching for the turnoff. Then she gave orders for the lead Humvee to fall back. It was thin-skinned compared to the Strykers.

Mac turned to look back. The column was traveling at about fifty miles per hour, and the intervals between the trucks were perfect. That was good. And she was going to say as much when two Apache gunships popped up from behind a hotel and opened fire. Hellfire antitank missiles struck two-two. There was a flash of light, followed by a loud boom, and the Stryker vanished in a ball of flame.

"Take evasive action!" Mac ordered. "And put some fire on those helicopters!"

Mac radioed for help as every machine gun in the column opened fire. "This is Charlie-Six actual . . . We're under attack from *two* Apache gunships. Over."

"This is Bigfoot Five and Six rolling in hot," a male voice said. "We will engage. Over."

The Warthog pilot was as good as his word. Less than thirty seconds had passed when two A-10s swooped out of the clouds and fired rockets at the helicopters. All of them missed. But that was enough to send the Apaches running for cover as Charlie Company continued to speed down the freeway.

Mac was painfully aware that two-two had been carrying an eight-person squad of soldiers in addition to the vic's crew. Eleven people in all. The reality of that hit hard. She couldn't take time to grieve however . . . Not yet.

Mac's eyes scanned her surroundings, looking for directional signs. There weren't any! The Confederates had taken them down. Shit! Shit! Shit! It was too late to count side streets. All she could do was take a guess.

She ordered Lamm to turn off the freeway and found herself on Frontage Road. Damn! That wasn't what she wanted. Wait . . . What was *that*? A sign that said OLD LOUISVILLE ROAD! It seemed that Frontage Road had morphed into Old Louisville Road. And there, visible in the distance, a bridge could be seen.

A Confederate Humvee was parked at her end of the span. It was armed with a .50 caliber machine gun, and it opened fire. Meanwhile, Mac saw two soldiers climb up over the railing on the east side of the bridge and run for the vehicle. Where had they been? *Under* the bridge? Setting a charge?

Mac had to duck for cover as .50 caliber shells hammered the front of the Stryker. One-one was equipped with a 105mm cannon. Mac felt the Stryker lurch as the gunner fired.

Eager to see the result, Mac stuck her head up through the hatch just in time to hear a loud clang as the empty shell casing hit the pavement behind the Stryker. She had surfaced too late to witness the hit . . . But, judging from appearances, the shell had struck the Humvee head-on. That caused the seven-thousand-pound vehicle to do a backflip. Now it was belly-up and on fire. That was when the .50 caliber ammo began to cook off.

So far so good. But that still left the question as to what the soldiers had been doing under the bridge. Planting charges? Probably, because a series of dull thuds was followed by an alert from one of Olson's scouts. "This is Bravo-One-Two . . . They blew the I-65 bridge. An entire section went down. Over."

More explosions were heard, followed by the sound of Olson's voice. "Roger that, One-Two. This is Bravo-Six actual. They dropped the new Louisville Road bridge as well. Over."

Mac's thoughts were racing. Originally, there had been *three* bridges not counting a footbridge. Now there was only one. If that was severed, it would take days, if not weeks, for the Union Army to construct a temporary span across the river or circle around.

The decision seemed to make itself. "This is Charlie-Six actual. Truck one-one and one-two will take control of the bridge. Charlie-Seven will command the rest of the company—and check the underside of the bridge for explosives. Over."

Then, over the intercom, "Hey, Lamm! Put your foot on it . . . Let's cross this sucker fast!"

The truck commander had been listening and understood the risk they were taking. Was a reb watching? And waiting to blow the span with them on it?

Mac felt her head snap back as Lamm stomped on the accelerator. The engine whined, and one-one took off, with one-two right behind it. They had to swerve in order to avoid the burning Humvee. Ammo continued to cook off, and Mac heard a clang as something struck the hull. Her eyes were on the other end of the bridge at that point . . . Where a Bradley was starting to fire on them.

As one-one passed the halfway mark, the 105mm cannon spoke again. Mac saw a bright flash as the antitank round struck the Bradley and heard a burst of 25mm shells scream past her head as the tracked vehicle fired back. It had a chain gun that could fire two hundred rounds a minute—and there was no place for either vehicle to go. Nor could the forces behind them participate in the battle without running the risk of hitting their own people. All the respective commanders could do was fire and keep firing until one of them died.

Mac felt helpless, so she swung the 7.62mm machine gun around and fired short bursts downrange. There was a loud bang as Private Martinez fired the 105 again, followed by a flash at the other end of the bridge, and commentary from Lamm. "You hit his left track! Pound the bastard!"

That was good—but not good enough. Mac ducked as shells smashed into the vic. The Stryker's armor was thick—but not thick enough. It would only be a matter of seconds before the Bradley's 25mm armor-piercing rounds managed to pound their way in.

But by some miracle, the metal held long enough for Martinez to fire one last round. The shell hit the Bradley higher up this time, blew a hole in the hull, and triggered a secondary explosion. Mac didn't see it, but she *heard* it, and stuck her head up in time to see pieces of fiery debris cartwheeling out of the sky. Then she was thrown forward as Lamm stood on the brake pedal. One-one was able to pull around the Bradley (which was hit moments earlier) and chase the fleeing rebs with bursts from its remotely controlled fifty. As that occurred, a squad of infantry deassed the vic and rushed to secure the bridgehead.

Mac heard the machine gun stop firing as she dropped to the ground and went up to inspect the damage. The front right tire and wheel were a mangled mess. But, because the Stryker had *eight* wheels, it had been able to advance in spite of the damage.

The armor plate on the front of the vic was bent, buckled, and torn. One additional burst from the chain gun would have left all of them dead. Mac made a note to pay Martinez a bonus and promote her to corporal. "Well, Captain," a male voice said. "You have some explaining to do."

Mac turned to find that Major Granger had approached her from behind. "Sir?"

"I ordered you to examine the bridge and report what you saw . . . I *didn't* order you to capture it. Your top kick tells me that the rebs left a satchel full of C-4 strapped to one of the support beams. An EOD specialist is removing it now."

So the rebs *were* preparing to blow the span. Mac had been lucky. *Very* lucky. "So charging across the bridge was a stupid thing to do," Granger concluded.

Mac swallowed. "Sir, yes, sir."

The look on Granger's face softened slightly. "It was also a brave thing to do . . . And one that's going to save us a lot of time. I'm going to see what I can do about making you a *real* captain . . . And that might come in handy when this mercenary crap is over."

"Thank you, sir."

"You're welcome. Now, have your people move this wreck out of the way. A platoon of tanks will arrive soon." And with that, Granger walked the rest of the way across the bridge. He was armed with a pistol and an umbrella. The reason for that became apparent when it started to rain. The battle for Bowling Green had begun.

## FORT KNOX, KENTUCKY

General "Mad" Mary Abbott stood a little more than five feet tall and couldn't have weighed more than 110. But the tiny blonde had a personality large enough to fill the War Room from the moment she entered.

Sloan was there, as were General Hern and two dozen other officers, including Major McKinney. All of them paid close attention as Abbott gave her presentation. "Our forces are pushing into the town of Bowling Green," she informed them. "The fighting is heavy, but elements of the 2nd Illinois Volunteers and the Oregon Scouts are about to flank the rebs. Once that happens, the bastards will be forced to pull back."

As Abbott spoke, a red dot hopped from point to point on a huge map. She paused to look around. "But that isn't all," she added. "As the rebs retreat from Bowling Green, we will attack Piggott, Arkansas. We'll stay just long enough to suck a lot of Confederate resources in that direction. Then we'll pull out.

"Meanwhile," Abbott continued, "Operation Pegasus will get under way." A detailed description of how helicopter companies were being assembled at small airports was followed by a discussion of how the Army Rangers would get to the strips, and which units would be in the first wave.

There was a lot of information to take in, and Sloan did his best to memorize it. When Abbott finished, she invited him to speak. Sloan made his way up to the front of the room, where he turned to scan the faces in front of him. "The Confederates not only seceded from the Union, their leaders are stealing oil from the American people and using it to line their own pockets. By taking control of the Richton Storage Facility, we can recover a large quantity of oil *and* send their so-called CEO a strong message. Maybe he'll listen, maybe he won't.

"But even if he doesn't, we'll have a forward operating base in the heart of the Confederacy. And I'll be aboard the third helo to land there."

Sloan hadn't run that idea by his staff because he knew they'd object. But now, as the officers stood to applaud, he was committed. Sloan smiled. "Thank you . . . Don't worry, I won't try to micro-manage General Abbott. This is *her* show, and she'll have the freedom to run it as she sees fit. Besides . . . based on what I've heard, she wouldn't listen to me anyway." Abbott smiled, and the audience laughed.

"Should I fall," Sloan continued, "Speaker of the House Duncan will assume my duties. Those of you who've had the good fortune to spend some time with the Speaker know that he's dedicated to our cause and will provide you with strong leadership.

"Finally, thanks to intensive training received from Major Mc-Kinney, I'd put the chance of shooting any one of you in the ass at no more than 5 percent." That produced a roar of laughter as well as the perfect moment for Sloan to leave the podium.

After the meeting, Sloan went back to his spartan office, where all sorts of issues were awaiting his attention. There were judges to nominate, briefing papers to read, and a stack of executive orders to sign. All of which was enough to make him look forward to leaving for Richton. The wheels of war continued to turn.

# CHAPTER 11

||||||||||||||||||||||||||||||||||||||

We're surrounded. That simplifies the problem.

–GENERAL LEWIS B. "CHESTY" PULLER

**BOWLING GREEN, KENTUCKY**

As Major Victoria Macintyre dashed from building to building, she could hear the distant thump of artillery, the persistent rattle of machine-gun fire, and the occasional crack of a sniper's rifle. A stray dog had latched onto her five blocks earlier and followed Victoria as she crossed a rubble-strewn street. The drugstore had been looted, and she ducked inside.

The black-and-brown mutt followed in hopes of finding food, or collecting a pat on the head. Unfortunately, he wasn't going to get either one of those things from Victoria. She had entered the city of Bowling Green to meet with a Confederate spy—not to care for stray dogs. But, since so much of the town had been leveled, there was no way to know if the operative would be there. Victoria had to try, however . . . Because the agent might be able to shed some light on what the Union Army would do next. And information like that would be of considerable value to General Bo Macintyre and his staff.

Victoria paused to check her map. She was supposed to meet her contact at a bar just off Fountain Square . . . And that was two blocks away. Victoria heard the dog bark as two men entered the store. She figured they were looters, going store to store, ready to grab the things that previous thieves had missed. Both carried shotguns.

One of the men caught a glimpse of Victoria in a mirror and was bringing his weapon to bear when she shot him in the throat. He let go of the pump gun in order to grab the wound. Blood spurted from between his fingers as he backed into a rack of reading glasses and sent it crashing to the floor.

The second man fired. But the blast went wide as the dog bit his right calf. Victoria shot him in the chest. He toppled onto his loot-filled pack and lay staring at the ceiling. The dog sniffed the corpse.

Like most urban pharmacies, the store stocked a little bit of everything, including canned goods. Most had been stolen, but Victoria found a solitary can of stew that was half-hidden under a supply case. She pulled the rip top free, dumped the contents onto a yellow Frisbee, and placed it on the floor. The dog was eating hungrily as Victoria left the store.

Engines roared as an Apache gunship swept overhead. Its nose gun was firing at a target that Victoria couldn't see—and there was no way to tell which side the pilots were on.

Victoria ran, paused behind a dumpster, and ran again. Bodies were sprawled outside a bank. Whose were they? Depositors? Fighting to get their money out? Or thieves shot by the police? Not that it mattered.

Victoria jumped a badly bloated corpse and made her way toward the Mint Julep Bar. One end of the wooden sign was hanging free, and the front window was smashed in. After crossing the street, she paused to catch her breath. Her back was pressed against a brick wall near the broken window. Her contact might be inside waiting for her. Or he might be dead. But assuming he was inside, Victoria needed to warn him or risk taking a bullet. She whistled the first bars of "Dixie."

There was a pause. Victoria heard the same tune from inside the bar. That didn't mean it was her contact. It could be a looter attempting to suck her in. So Victoria entered the bar with the pistol raised and ready to fire. "You're late," a voice said from somewhere in front of her.

Victoria felt some of the tension drain out of her body and glanced at her watch. "Yeah, by three minutes."

She heard a chuckle as Captain Ross Olson emerged from the shadows with both hands raised. "Hello, Major . . . You make those camos look good."

Victoria slid the Glock into its holster. "And you are full of shit."

Olson laughed. "So we meet again." He waved her back. "Come on . . . I brought a picnic lunch."

Victoria frowned. "I didn't come here to eat."

"You're so damned serious," Olson replied. "Just like your sister."

"Robin?"

Olson raised an eyebrow. "You didn't know? I thought you knew *everything*. Robin and I are members of the same battalion."

Victoria took it in. Robin . . . Only a few miles away and fighting for the other side. The *wrong* side. Her father would pretend it didn't matter. But it *would* matter, and that was fine with her. An artillery shell exploded two blocks away. Loose glass fell out of the window frame and made a tinkling noise as it hit the floor. "Lunch, huh? Lead the way."

Broken glass crunched under her boots as she followed Olson back to a booth, where, true to his word, a picnic lunch was waiting. It was romantic if somewhat calculated. Having struck out in Indianapolis, Olson was determined to get in her pants.

What about Robin? Was he trying to seduce her, too? Maybe he had. *Yes,* Victoria thought to herself, *I wouldn't be surprised.*

They sat across from each other as the city of Bowling Green died around them. "We have fresh bread," Olson announced, "some cheese, and a couple of very expensive apples. Oh, and there's *this* . . . It's a nice Chardonnay bottled right here in Kentucky. Did you know that Kentuckians have been growing grapes since 1799?"

Victoria *didn't* know. Nor did she care. But she gave Olson points for doing his homework. And, as it turned out, the lunch was excellent. The wine was a nice accompaniment for the crusty bread, slices of apple, and bites of crumbly cheese.

By the time they were finished eating, Victoria knew everything Olson knew, or *believed* he knew, as the officer's access to Sloan's plans was quite limited. Still . . . given input from a lot of different people, the analysts in Houston would be able to stitch things together.

"Good," Victoria said, as Olson poured the last of the wine into their glasses. "Now let's talk about the *next* step . . . And that's coming over to our side. Our forces are going to pull out of Bowling Green in the next forty-eight hours. That will generate positive press in the North and negative press down south. To counter that, we'd like to announce that an entire company of scouts came over to the Confederacy."

"I see," Olson said as he sipped his Chardonnay. "And then?"

"And then you will use your skills on our behalf, per the contract you agreed to in Indianapolis."

Olson smiled. "That sounds good, Victoria . . . But I was hoping for something more . . . A memory that would keep me warm during cold nights."

Vic nodded. "I get it . . . You want me to strip, lie on the table, and give you a ride."

"That's not the way I would phrase it," Olson replied. "But yes, that would be nice."

Victoria smiled to take the sting out of her reply. "It's tempting, Ross, it really is, but I would find it difficult to enjoy the occasion knowing that a 105mm shell might land on us while we're having fun. So let's put that idea on hold. In the meantime, here's a slip of paper with your orders on it. Commit them to memory and destroy it."

Olson accepted the piece of paper without looking at it. "Roger that. I'll see you soon."

"Yes," Victoria agreed as she slid out of the booth. "You will. Take care of yourself." And with that, she left. The dog was waiting outside.

### ABOARD ARMY ONE, OVER THE STATE OF MISSISSIPPI

Sloan couldn't stop yawning. He hoped that the eight men and two women seated around him would assume that he was sleepy rather than scared but feared that they knew the truth. And the fear made sense. The Sikorsky UH-60 Black Hawk was already deep inside enemy territory. Sloan took a moment to look around. McKinney was aboard, as were Jenkins and eight Secret Service agents. All of them were accompanying Sloan over his objections. "Remember," Jenkins had said two days earlier, "Napoleon had eight thousand bodyguards."

"And not only was the man a tyrant," Sloan had replied, "but he lost the war with England. Thanks a lot." He looked to his right, saw Jenkins yawn, and smiled.

Both of the side doors were open, which allowed a steady stream of cold air to enter the cabin. But, like the rest of the team, Sloan was dressed for it. As the Black Hawk sped through the darkness, he could see the clusters of lights and knew that each marked a town. And why not? The rebs had no reason to expect an attack deep in their territory. That would change.

Sloan leaned back and closed his eyes for what he thought would be a few seconds and woke to find that he had fallen asleep. It was the copilot's voice that roused him. "We're five minutes out," she said. "Check your gear. Lock and load."

Sloan had a thing for John Wayne movies and knew where he'd heard the phrase "lock and load" for the first time. *The Sands of Iwo Jima* had been made in 1949. Now *he* was John Wayne, except this shit was for real.

There was a thump as the helicopter put down in the middle of the LZ established by the personnel on the first two helicopters. The presidential party jumped out, ready to fight. But the rebs didn't realize that they'd been invaded yet. Once the passengers were clear, the Black Hawk took off. Dawn was two hours away. That's when things would get interesting.

## A DAY LATER NEAR MURFREESBORO, TENNESSEE

Confederate troops had been forced to pull out of Bowling Green and retreat to a point just south of the New Mason-Dixon Line. But because the rebs had a firm grip on Nashville, the relief force was ordered to swing east and wait for a swarm of missiles to destroy a defense tower. Then they were supposed to push through the hole and race south and west to Richton, Mississippi. And since

Granger's Scout and Reconnaissance Battalion was on the pointy end of the spear—it was their job to lead the way.

But it soon became apparent what would have been a seven-hour trip for a family on vacation was going to take a lot longer than that. In order to avoid Nashville, the relief force had to travel down Highway 231 just east of Music City. They passed through the towns of Bairds Mill and Silver Hill before they approached Murfreesboro and ran into trouble.

The Confederates knew about the airborne assault on Richton by then, and the effort to send reinforcements south. So although some of their resources were tied up dealing with the fake attack on Piggott—the rebs threw everything they could into the defense of Murfreesboro. And that brought the Union column to a halt.

As Abbott's tanks and the infantry required to support them went forward to deal with the defiant rebs—the lightly armed Scout and Reconnaissance Battalion had an opportunity to rest and regroup. They were camped in and around a middle school. And as Mac made the rounds, she could hear the mutter of cannon fire to the south. It was going to be a long night for the tank crews and the infantry units who were fighting for Murfreesboro.

Mac's thoughts were interrupted by a private. "Excuse me, ma'am . . . But Captain Olson would like to see you. He says it's important."

"Okay, where is he?"

"Room 305, ma'am."

Mac said, "Thanks," and followed the pool of light produced by her headlamp over to a pair of double doors. A flight of stairs led up to the third floor and a wide hallway. The door marked "305" was on the right. She pulled it open and went inside. Most of the furniture had been pushed over against the west wall—but a table was positioned at the center of the room. And there, sitting on top of it, was a cake. Olson looked up from lighting candles. "Happy birthday, Robin."

Mac felt a surge of emotion. No one knew it was her birthday . . . Nobody except Olson, that is, who had clearly done some research. "I won't sing," he promised. "And you wouldn't want me to."

Mac felt a lump form in her throat and managed to swallow it. "Thank you, Ross. This is very sweet of you. Promise you won't tell. If people find out, I'll have to take shit about it for days."

"It's our secret," Olson assured her. "Now come over and make a wish. But, if it involves me, I'm already here."

Mac laughed as she approached the table. The movement caused the flames to shiver. What would she wish for? Peace? Or something selfish? She chose peace.

"Way to go," Olson said, as the last candle went out. "Now it's time for a drink and a slice of cake. Don't worry . . . According to the girl at the bakery, this puppy is only a week old. I hope you like chocolate."

"I *love* chocolate," Mac replied, as Olson held a chair for her.

"Good. Chocolate goes with Jack Daniels. Of course *everything* goes with Jack Daniels," Olson added as he poured two generous drinks.

The cake *was* stale, but good nonetheless. And Mac knew that she would never forget that particular birthday. The first drink was followed by a second plus another surprise.

"No birthday party is complete without dancing," Olson announced. "So I came prepared." Olson's MP3 player was connected to a small speaker. "Unforgettable" flooded the room. And, once inside the circle of Olson's arms, Mac discovered that the man could dance. She allowed herself to relax as they circled the table.

And it was then, as the first song came to an end and another one began that Olson kissed her. It was a *good* kiss and the first in a very long time. *He plans to seduce you,* the inner voice warned.

*I hope so,* Mac replied.

*Why?*

*Because he's pretty, because it's my birthday, and because I may be dead in a few days.* That, it seemed, was sufficient to silence the voice, which wasn't heard from again.

What ensued was slow, considerate, and very satisfying. There was no bed or anything that resembled a bed in the room. So, rather than lie on the floor, they made love standing up. Olson was strong enough to lift Mac, find his way in, and hold her there.

As kisses were given and taken, man-made thunder rumbled in the distance. The pace of their lovemaking increased gradually until Mac found herself at a point from which it was impossible to go higher. The resulting orgasm was not only spectacular but mutual, and that made the experience all the more enjoyable. And when it was over, Mac felt no sense of regret.

After putting their clothes on, they slow danced for a while and had another drink before parting company. There were no declarations of love, and no promises regarding a future that might not exist. What would be would be.

Mac went back to what had been the nurse's office and checked to make sure that her appearance was okay before going out to check on her troops. Then it was time to slip into her sleeping bag and a dreamless sleep.

### RICHTON, MISSISSIPPI

The Richton-Perry County Airport had been transformed into a fort. The maintenance crew's backhoe had been used to dig a deep ditch around one-third of the runway, and by piling the loose soil inside the trench, the Rangers were able to create a defensive berm. And the minute that task was complete, the tractor was put to work digging a large hole at the center of the area that, once it was roofed over, would house the unit's HQ.

Then, if the enemy granted them enough time, the soldiers planned to dig a spider's web system of trenches that would connect the fighting positions together. Some wags were already referring to the base as "The Alamo."

By the morning of day three, 360 Army Rangers had landed inside the perimeter, the newly created berm was surrounded by Confederate troops, and the base was taking a pounding. Thanks to a plentiful supply of FIM-92 Stinger shoulder-launched missiles, the rebel air force had been kept at bay so far. But for how long? And now, as the Confederate noose continued to tighten, General Abbott's airborne supply line was being systematically choked off.

The reality of that was evident as the sun rose, a sickly-gray light crept in from the east, and a heavily laden Chinook helicopter arrived. Ground fire lashed up at it, and Sloan heard himself yell, "Turn around! Go back!"

But the pilot *didn't* go back. It appeared that he, or she, was determined to deliver the helo's cargo of food and medical supplies no matter the cost. So as the Chinook continued to bore in, multiple streams of bullets raked the cigar-shaped fuselage. Smoke appeared as the machine lost altitude. Now the ship *couldn't* turn back. Sloan yelled, "Come on! You can make it!"

And for one brief moment, it looked as though the Chinook *would* make it. Then a rocket-propelled grenade struck the helo, and Sloan saw a flash of light and heard a loud bang. The pilot lost control, and the flaming chopper roared in over the berm, where it flopped onto a mortar pit and killed everyone inside.

Sloan looked on in horror as the fuselage rolled slightly, causing one of the helicopter's thirty-foot-long rotors to hit the ground, shear off, and fly away. The blade sliced a corporal's head off before burying itself in the berm beyond.

Sloan was in shock. He was standing there, trying to process the horror of what he'd seen, when General Abbott appeared at his side. "I think that will be the last one," she said calmly.

Sloan turned to look at her. "And the relief force?"

"They're still hung up in Murfreesboro," she told him. "Colonel Foster expects to break out by nightfall however. At that point, they'll be about 420 miles away."

"Can we hold?"

Abbott looked surprised. "Of course we can hold! We held at the Battle of Shiloh, we held at the Battle of the Bulge, and we'll hold here."

Sloan felt some of Abbott's confidence seep into his body. The relief force could travel 420 miles in what? A day? Two at the most. One of the Chinook's fuel tanks exploded and threw pieces of fiery wreckage up into the sky. A chorus of rebel yells was heard from the other side of the berm. The clock was ticking.

### NEAR MURFREESBORO, TENNESSEE

After a good night's sleep, Mac was in the school cafeteria, pouring herself a cup of coffee, when the runner approached her. "I have a message from the major," she said. "He wants to see you right away."

Mac's appetite disappeared. "Roger that. I'm on my way."

Granger was camped in the coach's office, just off the gym, where Captain Pearce and her HQ people were stationed. As Mac crossed the badly scuffed floor, she could tell that something was up. Pearce's people were packing, and more than that, they were unusually subdued.

Mac knocked on the partly opened door and waited for Granger to say, "Enter." Mac stepped inside and came to attention. Granger said, "As you were," and pointed to a chair. "I suppose you heard." His expression was grim.

Mac shook her head. "Heard what?"

Granger made a face. "Captain Olson took his company out on a mission and never returned."

Mac frowned. "Get serious."

"I *am* serious. But it gets worse. Not only did Olson desert—he went over to the enemy! The news is on all of the rebel radio stations. And you can bet it's getting a lot of play up north as well."

Mac remembered the birthday cake, the dancing, and all that followed. She'd been set up, used, and discarded. Like a piece of trash. She felt dizzy and slightly nauseous.

Some of Mac's emotions must have been visible on her face because Granger nodded. "That's right," he said. "I feel the same way. That's why I want you to find the bastard and bring him in."

"And if he doesn't want to come?"

"He's an enemy combatant. Treat him as such . . . And that goes for the rest of Rat Company as well."

Mac liked her orders. She liked them a lot. But first she had to find Olson, so she went to see Sergeant Esco. The drone pilot and Sparks Munroe were sitting in Esco's Humvee. "We heard the news," Munroe said. "So we were expecting you. Is the CO sending us out to bring the bastards in?"

"That's affirmative," Mac replied. "Assuming we can find them."

"We can, and we did," Esco told her. "The Rats had to keep their IFF (identification, friend or foe) gear on until they entered reb-held territory. And the com people were tracking them. Suddenly, all of Rat Company's vehicles came to a stop. At that point, some of their IFFs went dead, as if the bastards were trying to disappear, but some stayed on. As for *why*, take a look at the screen. I'm using the Raven because it's small and hard to spot."

Mac leaned in to look at the screen. The drone was circling a sports field. Except that the facility was no longer being used to play games. Mac could see what appeared to be soldiers, more than a hundred in all, standing in small groups. Confederates? No, not given the fences that surrounded them and the Humvees positioned to fire on the crowd.

They were prisoners then . . . *Union* prisoners who had been captured during the last three days. "It looks like a holding area," Mac observed. "A place to keep prisoners until the rebs can ship them somewhere else. But what makes you think that Olson's people are mixed in?"

"*This,*" Esco said, as he sent the drone out over the neighboring parking lot. And there, positioned side by side, were Olson's vehicles. Some were transmitting IFF signals. A picture started to emerge. Rat Company had been ordered to report to the lot and meet with someone. Then, while Olson's soldiers were busy turning the IFF transponders off, the rebs took them prisoner! *Why?* Because troops who were willing to desert the Union might desert the Confederacy, too. "Well done," Mac said. "Have you been able to spot Olson? Granger wants that son of a bitch, and so do I."

"No," Esco replied. "I'm afraid the rebs will spot the Raven if I drop that low."

"That makes sense," Mac said. "All right . . . Here's the plan. We're going to go down there, find Olson, and turn those prisoners loose. Esco, you'll operate from here. Sparks, you're coming with me."

"Shouldn't we wait until nightfall?" Esco inquired.

"We can't afford to," Mac answered. "What if the rebs move the prisoners south? It would be impossible to reach them."

Mac left, with Munroe in tow. Then she went looking for Ralston and delivered a short rundown. "We'll take every Stryker we have . . . But leave the rest of the company's vehicles here. I want to roll thirty from now. Oh, and we're going to need six deuce-and-a-half trucks for the prisoners . . . Tell Sergeant Smith. He'll find them if anyone can."

Strike Force Thunder left the school thirty-seven minutes later. The plan was to circle around the worst of the fighting by following Highway 102 under I-24 to Burnt Knob Road, where the trucks would meet them.

The Confederates would notice the convoy needless to say—and throw whatever they could at it. But once Mac told Granger about the prisoners, and he passed the word to Colonel Foster, two Apache gunships were assigned to protect the column.

With the ESV to clear the way, Mac hoped to hit the POW camp before the rebs could figure out what her intentions were. Mac was standing in **MISS WASHINGTON**'s forward air-guard hatch. She could feel the press of air against her face and the adrenaline buzz that preceded combat. Large mounds of garbage blocked the road ahead. The ESV hit one of them blade down and sent trash flying as militiamen wearing old-time Confederate uniforms fired assault rifles at it.

Mac engaged one group with the M60 machine gun mounted in front of her and saw two soldiers fall. Once **MISS WASHINGTON** passed through the gap, the next vic opened fire. The two-lane road was flanked by ranch-style homes, leafy trees, and yards equipped with swing sets. Mac found it hard to believe that she was in a war zone until she saw a burned-out Bradley slumped beside the road.

Half a mile farther on, Mac saw a woman hanging from a tree. Was she a looter? A Union sympathizer? Anything was possible as the ESV swerved to avoid a bomb crater. That sent a flock of crows flapping up into the air. Mac winced when she saw the body they'd been feeding on.

Then the scene was gone, and Mac saw trouble up ahead. It consisted of a one-ton pickup truck with an antitank missile launcher mounted on the back. But **MISS WASHINGTON**'s gunner spotted the threat, too, and fired. The 105mm shell scored a direct hit on the truck, and the explosion threw debris in every direction.

But that was just the beginning. Rebel troops were concealed in the strip mall that bordered the highway. They fired three RPGs at the ESV, and one of them was right on target. There was a flash, followed by a bang, and Mac feared the worst. But as the smoke blew away, the ESV was still rolling! The force of the explosion had been dispersed by the Stryker's slat armor. The truck's top gunner was slumped forward, however—and Mac feared he was dead. "This is Blue-Bolt-Two and -Three," a voice said in her ear. "Stand by . . . We'll tidy up."

Rockets hit the buildings along both sides of the street as the Apaches roared over Mac's head. The ground fire stopped as suddenly as it had begun, leaving the convoy free to proceed. Mac felt a surge of excitement as Strike Force Thunder turned onto Burnt Knob Road. The trucks were there, just as Sergeant Smith promised they would be, all armed with over-the-cab fifties. Mac opened the intercom. "Hey, Sparks . . . Tell the trucks to fall in behind the last Stryker and keep it closed up."

The Apaches were circling a mile ahead, firing on ground targets and clearing a path for the Strykers. "Charlie-Six actual to Strike Force Thunder," Mac said. "We're about two miles from the objective. Remember the plan. I'm going to bail out in the parking lot with Alpha One-Two and his squad. The rest of you will go in hard. Neutralize the Humvees but be careful! A hundred Union soldiers are being held inside the fence, and once you break in, they'll run every which way. *Don't* shoot them. Once the place is secure, load 'em up and meet me in the parking lot. Charlie-Seven will be in command. Over."

Mac heard a flurry of clicks by way of acknowledgments as the ESV took a hard right and entered the parking lot. By prior agreement, **MISS WASHINGTON** and the **BETSY ROSS** paused to let people off. Then they followed the last deuce and a half as the column closed in on the athletic field.

The squad detailed to work with Mac and Munroe consisted of Sergeant Poole and eight members of the first platoon. Mac heard radio chatter and machine-gun fire as she led the detachment of troops into the maze of captured vehicles. Some were in perfect condition, while others were shot up. All of them wore Union markings.

The Raven was circling above, which allowed Esco to see the squad and provide directions. "Turn right," he said. "And follow the corridor west. Take cover behind the Buffalo."

Mac knew Esco was referring to the hulking MRAP or Mine-Resistant Ambush Protected vehicle located directly in front of her. The Buf was huge and would provide the team with a place to hide, while Olson and his people ran from the rescuers and into the parking lot, where their motorcycles and rat rods were parked.

*Why?* Because the mercenaries had broken their contract with the Union and were classified as deserters. All of them would wind up in a federal prison if captured by the North. Plus, they'd need their vehicles to escape. All Mac and her soldiers had to do was wait.

And sure enough, no more than a minute had passed by the time Esco got on the horn. "Here they come," he warned. "About three dozen of them all headed your way."

"Roger that," Mac replied. "Over."

Thirty-six fugitives would've been a lot to handle had they been armed. But that wasn't the case, so Mac figured that Poole and his soldiers could handle the job. She peered around the front of the Buffalo, and there they were, with Olson in the lead. He was running full out. "Wait for it," Mac said. "Wait for it . . . Now!"

The soldiers charged into the open, where Poole ordered the escapees to stop and raise their hands. Most obeyed. But a few of them had weapons that had been taken off dead guards. They opened fire, and Olson was one of them. Mac cursed herself for failing to anticipate such a possibility.

She raised her assault rifle and was going to shoot Olson, when Munroe did it for her. Buckshot from his shotgun hit Olson's legs and dumped the mercenary onto the pavement. His weapon skittered away as Mac went forward to stare down at him. Their eyes met. Olson's face was screwed up in pain. "Robin? Hey, hon, how 'bout some first aid? I'm bleeding to death."

Mac nodded. "That's too bad."

Olson spoke through gritted teeth. "You're a stone-cold bitch . . . Just like your sister."

Mac frowned. "You know Victoria?"

Olson had freed his belt by then—and was wrapping it around a thigh. "Yes, I do. She paid us to come over and double-crossed us when we did."

Mac smiled thinly. "That sounds like my big sis."

Olson made a face as he pulled the tourniquet tight. "Give me your belt," he demanded. "For the other leg."

"Sorry," Mac replied. "I need my belt. It's holding my pants up."

Olson's face was contorted with anger. "I screwed your sister."

Mac nodded as she brought the rifle up. "And *she* screwed you."

There was a loud bang, and half of Olson's face disappeared. "I saw that!" one of the Rats yelled. "You murdered him!"

The blood drained out of the man's face as the weapon swiveled around to point at him. "Not so," Mac replied calmly. "My rifle went off by accident."

"That's how it looked to me," Munroe confirmed.

"I'll have the company armorer look at it," Poole put in. "Maybe you need a new trigger assembly." His soldiers chuckled.

Mac waited for the wave of remorse. It never arrived. She felt empty . . . sad and empty. An engine roared as one of the Strykers pulled up next to her. Sergeant Ralston jumped down. "The prisoners are on the trucks, ma'am. We took two casualties. Doc Obbie says both of them are going to make it."

"Good. Search the prisoners for weapons and load them up. We need to get out of here pronto."

Ralston responded, "Roger that," and went to work. The Apaches continued to circle overhead as Mac returned to MISS WASHINGTON and climbed aboard. *Victoria*. They would meet one day . . . And one of them was going to die.


RICHTON, MISSISSIPPI

The President of the United States was sleeping in a ditch six feet away from General Abbot's unburied corpse. His eyes flew open as cold raindrops hit his face and trickled down his cheeks. A flash of light was followed by a loud boom as something struck the center of the compound. Lightning? Thunder? No. It was an incoming 81mm mortar round. The rebs fired one at the same spot every fifteen minutes. The purpose of the ritual was to prevent the Rangers from sleeping, and the plan was a success.

Sloan eyed his watch. It was 0947 on the fourth day of hell. General Abbott had been killed the day before, leaving Major McKinney in command. All because Sloan had been stupid enough to believe that he could use a shortcut to win the war. General Hern was correct . . . There was only one way to whip the Confederacy . . . And that was to push them back foot by bloody foot until they were ass deep in the Gulf of Mexico.

Sloan forced himself to roll over and stand. Sheets of rain were falling by then, and his uniform was covered with mud. He barely noticed as he followed the trench toward the bunker. Sloan heard the crack of a rifle shot as a Union sniper fired—followed by the rattle of machine-gun fire as enemy bullets raked the top of the berm. He was too tired to look back.

A ramp led him down into the stinking hole where the battalion surgeon and his medics were laboring to save as many lives as they could. Everything was in short supply—and that included blood volume expanders, dressings, and painkillers. Sloan heard a man groan as he followed the dangling flashlights past the aid station to the command center beyond. Mud sucked at the soles of his boots as he entered the room. McKinney was sitting on an ammo crate with a handset to his ear. He looked up, nodded, and pointed to a chair. "Yes, sir . . . Tomorrow by 1500. That sounds good. We'll save some rebs for the relief force to shoot at. Over."

And with that, McKinney gave the handset to his RTO. "Good news, Mr. President . . . Colonel Foster believes the lead element of his relief force will arrive by midafternoon tomorrow."

Sloan was sitting on a lawn chair with the assault rifle laid across his knees. "He *believes*? Or he *knows*?"

McKinney shrugged. "He believes that he knows . . . How's that?"

Sloan chuckled. "Can we hold on long enough for that?"

McKinney nodded. "Of course . . . This is *our* shit hole, and we're going to hold it until we're ready to leave."

Sloan was reminded of what Abbott had said in response to the same question. He shook his head in mock despair. "You're one crazy son of a bitch."

McKinney grinned. "Look who's talking, sir."

A mortar round landed above them, and dirt showered their heads. Both of them laughed.


### NEAR MURFREESBORO, TENNESSEE

"We broke through. The rebs had to pull back." That's what Major Granger told Mac when she returned to the school. Captain Pearce and her staff had finished packing their gear and were loading it onto a truck as the two of them spoke.

"That means we can send a convoy south," Granger continued. "Except that it isn't a relief force anymore. General Abbott was killed in action, and there's no way in hell that her plan will work. So we're sending an extraction team instead. But the opportunity to pull our people out of Richton won't last for long. Confederate reinforcements are on the way . . . And in a day, two at most, they'll roll over the airhead and erase it. That's where you and your people come in. I'm sorry to send you out so soon—but Charlie Company is all I have to work with at the moment."

Mac felt a sense of relief. Granger was all business. If the major knew about Olson's fate, which he almost certainly did, he'd chosen to ignore it. And that was fine with her. "Yes, sir," Mac replied. "You can count on us."

"Good," Granger replied as he opened a map. "Here's how it's going to work. The relief force will rely on speed and brute force to get through. Wheeled vehicles can travel faster—so they'll take the lead. You'll have two Buffalo Cougars on point. They'll trigger any mines or IEDs that have been planted along the highway. Your Strykers will come next, followed by transportation for the Rangers.

"The heavies, including a company of tanks, will bring up the rear. Their job is to protect your line of retreat. But you'll outrun them pretty quickly. Then you'll be on your own."

"Why not bring the president out by air?" Mac inquired.

"For the same reason we can't resupply the airhead," Granger answered. "The airport is surrounded by AA batteries. Plus, the president said that if a helo managed to get through, he'd refuse to board it unless all the Rangers come with him."

"The airborne idea was stupid," Mac observed, "but he's staying with the troops. I like that."

Granger nodded. "The president ain't perfect, but he's worth saving, so get your butt in gear."

That had been four hours earlier. Mac's temporary command consisted of two Buffalos, six Strykers, a tanker loaded with twenty-five hundred gallons of fuel, and six M35 trucks. Fifteen vehicles in all. Since the convoy's departure US Route 231 had been "prepped" by A-10s and Apache helicopters. That allowed the quick-moving column to thread its way through a maze of still-smoldering vehicles even as they took sporadic fire from rebel troops.

Rather than give them a target, Mac chose to ride inside one-three's mostly empty cargo bay. She could hear occasional pings as bullets flattened themselves on the Stryker's armor. That didn't bother her but would scare the crap out the people in the unarmored tanker and the M35s. It couldn't be helped, however . . . All she could do was hope for the best.

Even though the truck commander swore that they were doing a steady 50 mph, which was damned good given the conditions, Mac wanted to go even faster . . . And it took a lot of self-discipline to keep from checking on the convoy's position every five minutes. So it came as a relief when the TC announced that Shelbyville lay just ahead.

Mac ordered the fueler to the front of the column before telling all the other drivers to pull over. "Top off your tanks," she instructed, "and pull forward. Make sure that at least one weapon in every vehicle is manned," she told them. "Pee if you need to, but don't go more than twenty feet off the highway to do it. And pee quickly . . . We won't be here for long. Sergeant Poole, meet me at one-three, and let's get to work."

Mac had the footlocker open by the time the ramp went down, and Poole arrived with two privates. "Grab some spray paint and flags," Mac told them. "It's time to redecorate."

The idea had occurred to Mac when she saw Pearce's people stuffing trophy flags into a garbage bag. By covering all of the Union designators with beige paint and flying Confederate flags from every antenna, they might be able to convince the rebs that the convoy belonged to them. And why not? Both sides were using the same kinds of vehicles and were dressed in nearly identical uniforms.

Once the changes were made, Mac ordered everyone to "mount up," and the convoy got under way. Shelbyville had a population of sixteen thousand people. And as the "Confederate" military vehicles rolled through, the locals came out to wave. "Smile at them," Mac said over the radio, "and honk your horns."

They did, and the column of vehicles was able pass through town without being shot at. The good luck held as the convoy snaked through Fayetteville and across the border into Alabama. Then, in order to avoid Huntsville and the Redstone Arsenal located nearby, Mac ordered the lead Buffalo to turn west. The extraction team rolled onto I-65 south with flags flying.

Meanwhile, based on the reports that Munroe was receiving, the heavies had been able to establish a firebase just north of the state line. But tanks and the soldiers sent to protect them were attracting so many rebs that they might have to pull back. If that occurred, Mac's line of retreat would vanish.

Mac forced herself to ignore that possibility as the blood-red sun arced across the sky, and the column continued south. Everything went smoothly until Munroe received a message from HQ. Based on video captured by the Predator drone that was scouting ahead of them—a Confederate roadblock was blocking the freeway north of Birmingham. Perhaps it was a routine affair—or maybe it had been set up to stop the convoy. The reason didn't matter.

What *did* matter was the need to break through, and the fact that if they managed to do so, their disguise wouldn't work anymore. *But all good things must come to an end,* Mac told herself, as she stuck her head and shoulders up through the hatch. *It had to happen.* "This is Six actual," she said, over the radio. "Shoot anyone who fires at you. Over."

The checkpoint was a well-organized affair, with two lanes for civilians and an express lane for military vehicles. On orders from Mac, the first Buffalo began to accelerate as Confederate MPs sought to flag them down. The fifty-six-thousand-pound truck collided with the back end of a Humvee and sent the vehicle flying end over end. It landed on its roof, and sparks flew as it screeched to a stop. The Buf blew past. Rebel troops opened up on the rest of the vehicles as they followed. Mac and the rest of the gunners fired back. The engagement was over less than a minute later.

Mac knew what would happen next. The rebs would pull out all of the stops to block the convoy. And, since they were still 230 miles away from Richton, it was going to get hairy. A knot formed in her stomach.

They were doing 60 mph as they left Birmingham on I-20/59. Mac eyed the lead-gray sky. They had no air cover other than the Predator. And she was well aware of the fact that a single A-10 could grease her tiny command in a matter of minutes. But the ceiling was low, and that might keep planes on the ground. Luck would play a big role in what happened next.

Fifteen minutes later, word came in that two tanks and a whole lot of infantry were waiting for them in Tuscaloosa. And there was no speedy way to bypass the city. "I have two Hellfire missiles hanging on my Pred," the drone operator told her. "I'll take care of the big stuff. The rest of it belongs to you."

As they entered town, Mac saw thick columns of black smoke ahead and knew the pilot had kept his promise. After passing the burning hulks, the convoy came under small-arms fire. What sounded like hail rattled against the Stryker's hull as Mac fired back. Empty brass flew sideways, bounced, and hit the road.

But the rebs had something more serious up their sleeves. The officer in charge had placed AT4 teams on overpasses, where they could fire down on the Union vehicles! Mac swore as a rocket struck the lead Buffalo's windshield and exploded. With no hands on the wheel, the enormous vehicle careened across the freeway and slammed into a concrete embankment. Fuel spilled and went up in flames. Mac shouted into her mike. "Those are unguided missiles! Take evasive action!"

**MISS WASHINGTON** swerved left and right, a rocket flew past, and Mac heard rather than saw the resulting explosion. There was no time to think about it as six motorcycles entered the freeway. Each bike carried *two* riders. A driver and a gunner. The gunners were armed with stubby M320 grenade launchers. They were single-shot weapons—but one hit from a high-explosive round could destroy the fueler.

"Protect the tanker!" Mac ordered. Working as a team, two Strykers pulled forward to shield both sides of the vulnerable fueler. Grenades exploded as they struck the birdcages that protected the trucks. The motorcyclists paid a heavy price as the convoy's gunners fired on them. Mac saw a bike tip over, slide, and block another machine, which did a complete somersault. The driver landed on his head.

Then, as quickly as they'd entered the trap, the Union soldiers broke free of it. Mac's thoughts were on the soldiers in Buf one, and their families in Arizona. How many of her Marauders were going to die? It didn't bear thinking about.

"Sparks . . . Get Richton on the horn. Tell them that we're three hours out—and to package the worst casualties for transport in the Strykers. The rest of the Rangers will ride in the trucks. They can bring medical gear, personal weapons, and ammo. Nothing more. Got it?"

"Yes, ma'am," Munroe answered. And as he went to work, Mac's thoughts turned to the task ahead. The airport was surrounded . . . How could she break through the Confederates? And do so quickly? What she needed was a club. A *big* club . . . But *what*? Then the answer came to her . . . Would the brass authorize it for *her*? No, probably not. But would they do it for the President of the United States? Hell yes, they would. Mac smiled.

# CHAPTER 12

||||||||||||||||||||||||||||||||||||||

No battle plan survives contact with the enemy.

—GENERAL COLIN POWELL

**RICHTON, MISSISSIPPI**

Sloan and those who still had strength enough were enlarging the bunker by hand. It was a team effort. One Ranger would use a pick to break chunks of mud off a wall, another would load them onto a shelter half, and a third would drag the load up the ramp for disposal. There were four teams, and it was hard for them to stay out of each other's way.

Meanwhile, the rebs continued to probe various sections of the perimeter and drop mortar rounds into the compound. Sloan didn't wonder *if* he was going to die in Richton. The question was *when*. And the sooner, the better. He was swinging a pick when the order went out: "Pull back from the berm! Get into the bunker! Cover your heads!"

Sloan didn't have to enter the bunker since he was already in it. He turned his back to the wall and sat in the mud. Men crowded in around him as McKinney and his officers sought to pack everyone into the underground retreat. A lieutenant called out a number as each person entered. That was followed by a crisp, "Everyone is present or accounted for, *sir*!"

"Roger that," McKinney said, from somewhere nearby. "Incoming! Cover your heads!"

Nothing happened. Ten long seconds dragged by. The chaplain was praying. "'Yea, though we walk through the valley of the shadow of death, we fear no evil: for thou art with us; thy rod and thy staff they comfort us.'" What was happening up above? Were rebs preparing to enter the compound? Sloan hoped so.

Sloan felt the earth move as the first of what was to be *six* submarine-launched Tomahawk cruise missiles landed outside the berm. All Sloan could hear was a muted thump as the thousand-pound warhead detonated.

The bunker's roof consisted of wood salvaged from an outbuilding and covered with two feet of dirt. Some of that soil filtered down to dust the tops of their heads as *more* missiles left their tubes out in the Gulf of Mexico, arched high into the sky, and fell at a steep angle.

Taken together, the resulting explosions were calculated to create a 360-degree swath of destruction around the firebase, thereby opening a hole for the extraction team. A cheer went up with each additional strike, and after the last impact, McKinney spoke. "Let's hear it, Rangers! Three cheers for the United States Navy!"

The response was a heartfelt, if not entirely respectful: "Swabbies! Swabbies! Swabbies!"

"All right," McKinney told them, "the first platoon will go up and reestablish the perimeter. The second platoon will stand by to load casualties. The extraction team is due to arrive five from now. Go!"

Sloan followed a Ranger up onto the surface, where he paused to inhale some moist air. It was pitch-black, so he couldn't see the destruction the missiles had inflicted, but there was no incoming fire. Not a single shot. That spoke for itself. A distant voice could be heard calling for a medic . . . And that meant some of the rebs were still alive.

"Here they come!" someone yelled, and Sloan saw headlights approaching from the west. They were taped, to reduce the amount of light they threw, and seemed to wander as the column made its way through what resembled a moonscape. A spotlight came on as a vehicle with a dozer blade hit the berm and pushed its way into the compound. The evacuation had begun.

Sloan took one end of a stretcher and helped carry a badly wounded Ranger toward a large vehicle with eight wheels. A female army captain was directing traffic, and when Sloan tripped, she moved in to support him. "Careful, Private . . . Watch where you step."

That was when McKinney appeared out of the gloom. "The private is the President of the United States, Captain Macintyre."

"Sorry, Mr. President," the captain said. "But watch where you step."

Sloan grinned as Macintyre helped load the patient onto GLORY BOY. Once the task was accomplished, they stepped aside to let another stretcher pass. The wash from a cargo light fell across her face. And as Sloan looked at Macintyre, he was struck by the thick mop of brown hair, the officer's steady eyes, and her softly rounded features. She didn't *look* like a warrior—not to him anyway. But her name had been mentioned more than once during the last twenty-four hours, and Sloan realized that he was face-to-face with the officer in command of the extraction team. "Thank you," he said. "Thank you very much."

"You're welcome," Macintyre responded. "I hear they call you 'the fighting president.' That's good, because we'll have to kick some ass in order to make it home." And with that, she was gone.

||||||||||||

The evacuation was supposed to take thirty minutes, but the better part of an hour had elapsed by the time the last Rangers were pulled back off the berm and loaded into trucks. Mac was standing near the back end of an M35, talking to Sergeant Ralston, when Major McKinney appeared. A taillight threw a reddish glow across McKinney's face. "There you are," he said. "I have orders for you."

Mac felt mixed emotions. She liked being on her own in many ways. And orders, *any* orders, would limit her freedom. Of course, orders could protect her as well. Especially when the shit hit the fan. "Sir, yes, sir."

"Here's how it's going to work," McKinney said. "Shortly after the column departs, it will split into three elements. Here's a list of the vehicles in each element—and the routes they're supposed to follow.

"You'll be in charge of Element Alpha," McKinney said, as he gave Ralston a piece of paper. "Your orders are to go back the way you came, hook up with the heavies, and accompany them back to our lines.

"I will lead Element Bravo up Highway 15," McKinney added, as he turned to Macintyre, "while you take the president north on Highway 45."

Mac frowned. "Permission to speak freely, sir?"

"Go for it."

"Does dividing our force by three make sense? Wouldn't it be better to keep everyone together?"

"Normally, I would say, 'yes,'" McKinney replied. "But there's nothing normal about this situation. Our most important objective is to get the president home in one piece."

Mac felt a rising sense of anger. "So you're going to use the Rangers, and most of my command, as decoys."

"In a word, 'yes,'" McKinney replied. "We're at war, Captain . . . And the president's life is worth more than mine, yours, or Sergeant Ralston's."

Mac looked at Ralston. She knew his wife *and* his children. He nodded. "I understand, sir."

Mac felt a lump form in her throat and struggled to swallow it. "And the president? What does *he* think of your plan?"

"He doesn't know about it," McKinney answered evenly. "And that's the way it's going to remain until the elements part company. Then, when you think the time is right, you can tell him."

"Excuse me, but that's going to be a problem, sir . . . According to what I heard, Sloan prides himself on being with the troops. He'll have you court-martialed."

McKinney frowned. "Do you think I give a shit? I left the army, and I came back to serve my country. It *needs* Sloan. Yes, following General Abbott's advice was a mistake. But that's how it goes. Lincoln placed his trust in McClellan, and we know how *that* turned out. Lincoln won the war, though . . . Besides, who among us hasn't been fooled by someone?"

Mac thought about Olson. "Sir, yes, sir."

"Good. You have a talent for war, Macintyre. The fact that you're here proves that. So I'm counting on you to get Sloan home. For our country. Do you read me?"

Mac was taken aback by the intensity in his eyes. "Yes, sir. Five by five."

"Excellent. I'll see you up north. And you, too, Sergeant Ralston. I'll buy the beer."

They parted company at that point. According to the orders Mac had been given, she was to command **MISS WASHINGTON** and the **BETSY ROSS**. And sure enough . . . She returned to find that neither truck was carrying casualties, their tanks had been topped off, and the President of the United States was chatting with Munroe. It seemed that both of them were worried about the impact the war would have on professional baseball.

Sloan turned to look as Mac entered the cargo bay and the ramp came up. "We meet again . . . Are we about to leave?"

"Yes, sir," Mac responded.

"Where's Major McKinney? And Director Jenkins?"

"In other vehicles, sir. It doesn't make sense to put all of our senior people in one truck."

Sloan nodded. "Right. You'll keep me informed?"

"Yes, sir."

"Good. Thank you."

Mac put her helmet on, stuck her head and shoulders up through the forward hatch, and gave the necessary order. "This is Charlie-Six . . . You have your orders. Let's roll."

Then, sure that Sloan couldn't hear, Mac spoke to the **MISS WASHINGTON**'s truck commander via the Stryker's intercom. "Hey, Fuller . . . We're going to split off from the main column when you come up on Highway 42. Follow it to 45 and hang a left. The *Betsy Ross* will take our six."

"Yes, ma'am," Fuller replied.

"And keep that to yourself," Mac said. "Do you read me?"

"Yes, ma'am. Lights on? Or lights off?"

Mac thought about it and decided that it was best to look as normal as possible in hopes that the locals would assume the vehicles were on their side. "Lights on," she told him. "Thanks for asking."

**MISS WASHINGTON** lurched through a series of craters before finding smooth pavement. Mac could hear the parting comments from other vehicles as the convoy split up, but Sloan couldn't. And she planned to keep him in the dark for as long as possible.

It didn't take long to hook up with 45 and turn north. The highway took them through Battles, Chicora, and up to Waynesboro, all without incident. Fuller had to pass heavily laden trucks every once in a while, but traffic was light, and the trucks were doing fifty. Everything looked green to Mac, who was wearing night-vision gear.

Their luck continued to hold all the way up to Meridian, where Highway 45 passed the city a few miles to the east. Then they came up on something Mac hadn't anticipated. A Confederate convoy! It happened so quickly that they couldn't avoid it, and Mac was trying to formulate a plan, when Munroe tugged on her pant leg. "What's going on up there?" he wanted to know. "I've got a rebel lieutenant on the horn. He wants us to identify ourselves."

Mac's mind was racing. "Tell him we're members of Bravo Company, from the Austin Volunteers, and we're headed to Columbus. Ask him if this is Highway 15."

Mac didn't know if there was such a thing as the Austin Volunteers and figured the lieutenant didn't either. She ducked down into the cargo bay and removed her helmet. The president was staring at her. "What's up?"

Mac held up a hand as Munroe said, "Yes, sir . . . Thank you, sir. I'll tell the captain. Over."

Munroe looked from face to face and grinned. "He told me to tell you that we're on Highway 45, but it will still take us to Columbus, and we're welcome to tag along."

"That's outstanding," Mac told him. "Talk about lucky . . . Good job."

Then she turned to Sloan. "We ran into the tail end of a reb convoy, sir . . . And they allowed us to join up! All we have to do is follow them to Columbus and find a way to fade."

Sloan's grin turned into a frown at the mention of Columbus. He produced a much folded map and began to examine it. "Columbus? What the hell? You came down through Birmingham. Where are we?"

Mac ran fingers through her hair. "We're on Highway 45, Mr. President. We passed Meridian awhile back."

Sloan's anger was plain to see. "That isn't the route we were supposed to take. Get Major McKinney on the radio! I want to speak with him now."

"Sorry, sir," Mac replied. "I can't do that. The major is in command of Element Bravo. They're rolling up Highway 15, and I have orders to maintain radio silence."

Sloan frowned. "McKinney lied to me!"

"Yes, sir . . . He sure as hell did."

"I'll bust him to private."

Mac shrugged. "He doesn't care, sir. None of us do." And, somewhat to Mac's surprise, she discovered that the statement was true.

Sloan's eyes grew wider. "Oh, my God! The troops . . . Element Bravo you said. Tell me what's going on."

Mac did so. And when she was finished, Sloan looked away. His voice cracked when he spoke. "He's using them as decoys."

Mac nodded. "Yes, sir . . . And he's with them. The same way that you're with us."

Sloan's eyes came back to make contact with hers. He forced a smile. "And there's no place I'd rather be. What happens now?"

"We'll let the rebs lead us into Columbus," Mac replied. "At that point, we'll give them the slip and follow Highway 45 into Tennessee. Somewhere right around Jackson, I think we'll run into trouble."

Sloan's eyes narrowed. "Yeah? Why's that?"

"Because at that point we'll be about 190 miles away from our lines. Assuming that General Hern has been able to push south, the rebs will have to retreat, forcing us to pass through an area where it will be hard to tell friend from foe."

Sloan's face was covered with grime and three days' worth of beard. He scratched it. "That makes sense, Captain . . . How do we prepare?"

"I'm not sure that we can," Mac answered. "Other than to grab some sleep. There's a perfect example of what I'm talking about." She pointed at Munroe. Munroe had fallen asleep during their conversation. His headset was on, and he was snoring.

Sloan grinned. "I'll do my best."

Mac returned topside after that. Cold air washed around her face, Confederate taillights led the way, and the moon was playing peekaboo through the clouds. She thought about Sloan. The man was sincere . . . and pleasant. Bit by bit, she was coming to like him.

||||||||||||

After a delightfully boring trip to Columbus, the Strykers were able to separate themselves from the convoy with a simple, "Thank you." Outside of a pit stop just south of Aberdeen, the Strykers drove nonstop up through Tupelo and into Selmer, Tennessee. The trucks were running on fumes by then. When Mac spotted a brightly lit gas station, she ordered the truck commanders to pull over.

Such convenience stores were typical of what she'd seen in the postcatastrophe South. The so-called board of directors was very good at providing their "shareowners" with fuel and keeping the price down. By using oil from the reserves? Possibly. But regardless of that, it was a good way to build support and keep it.

After **MISS WASHINGTON** came to a stop, Mac jumped to the ground and entered the store to speak with the attendant. No customers were present—and that wasn't surprising at 0246. The kid behind the counter had an unruly thatch of blond hair and a skin condition. "Activate pumps three and four please," Mac told him.

The kid pushed some buttons. "Okay, ma'am . . . I'll need cash or a government voucher."

"Well, that's the thing," Mac replied. "I don't have enough cash—and I'm out of vouchers. But no problem . . . I'll give you an IOU."

"I can't take IOUs," the teen replied, and was going to turn the pumps off when Mac drew her pistol.

"Sorry," she said. "But I must insist . . . Come out from behind the counter and lie on the floor." Munroe had entered by then and helped hogtie the kid with a couple of extension cords. "How 'bout some candy bars?" he inquired.

"No can do," Mac answered. "That wouldn't be right."

Judging from the expression on Munroe's face, the RTO couldn't see any difference between stealing fuel and stealing candy bars. But he couldn't say that and didn't.

They were back on the road ten minutes later. Would the local police look at the surveillance footage? And try to chase the Strykers down? Mac hoped not. But she was ready to respond if they did.

Fortunately, there was no pursuit. But, consistent with Mac's fears, the situation on the highway began to change. The southbound lanes of the highway were jammed with cars trying to escape the fighting to the north. The scene was reminiscent of what Mac had seen in Washington State after the meteor impacts.

The northbound lanes were relatively clear by contrast although the Strykers had to pass slow-moving military vehicles from time to time. No one challenged them, however, since they were speeding *toward* the front lines, not away from them.

As they pulled into Jackson, all of the traffic was forced to leave the freeway and funneled through city streets. There was no obvious reason for the detour—and the incoming vehicles added to the congestion in the city's streets. Mac was standing in the front hatch when an MP signaled for the **MISS WASHINGTON** to stop, and Fuller had little choice but to obey. The MP climbed up onto the birdcage so that Mac could hear him. "Good morning, ma'am . . . Where are you headed?"

"Up to Martin," Mac answered. "To kill us some Yankees."

"Yes, ma'am," the MP agreed. "I'd take 45 east if I was you . . . Some A-10s caught one of our convoys on 45 west just before sunset yesterday. Kick some ass for me."

"Roger that," Mac replied. "And thanks for the intel."

The soldier jumped to the ground, and Mac ordered Fuller to proceed. Then she ducked down into the cargo bay, where Sloan was waiting. "We're close, sir . . . Only seventy miles out. But here's the problem. We're flying a rebel flag, but when the sun comes up, I'll have to take it down. Either that, or run the risk of taking fire from Union forces. But, because we won't be broadcasting a reb IFF signal, *they* might attack us. That's why I want you to gear up and be ready if we have to bail out." Mac pointed to the assault rifle propped up next to him. "Do you know how to use that thing?"

Sloan offered a slow smile. "You'll notice that I'm alive—and that it's clean."

Mac grinned. "Point taken, Mr. President. Did you get some sleep?"

"No. Did *you*?"

Mac laughed. "Hell, no. But Munroe is fully rested. I'll keep you in the loop."

It took the better part of an hour for the Strykers to clear the traffic jam, bypass a roadblock, and crash through a fence onto the highway. The northbound lanes were completely empty, and that suited Mac just fine. The Strykers were doing about 50 mph, and every mile they put behind them was a victory.

The southbound lanes were another story, however. They were filled with reb vehicles, trucks loaded with soldiers, and pathetic-looking civilians, many of whom were on foot. What did that imply? The rebs were pulling back, that's what . . . And the battle lines were being redrawn back behind them.

That's what Mac was thinking when the mine went off under **MISS WASHINGTON**'s armored belly, flipped the Stryker onto its right side, and threw her into the ditch next to the highway. Mac hit hard and struggled to breathe. Finally, after sucking some air into her lungs, Mac managed to stand. The **BETSY ROSS** came to a stop just short of the wreck. And that was Mac's impetus to move. The rebs had mined the northbound lanes of the freeway—and would probably do the same with the southbound lanes once their forces turned to fight. That's why northbound traffic had been forced off the road and into Jackson. Shit, shit, shit!

The sky was starting to glow in the east, which meant there was enough light to see by. As Mac arrived at the wreck, Sloan crawled out of the air-guard hatch. He was clutching his rifle and wearing a fully loaded vest. Once on the ground, he turned to assist **MISS WASHINGTON**'s gunner.

As Munroe appeared, Mac saw that he had a cut over his right eye. He passed his radio, shotgun, and a bottle of water down before wiggling out. *"Fuller?"* Mac demanded, as the RTO stood. "Where's Fuller?"

Gunner Cissy Roper was on her feet by then. Tears were streaming down her face. "He didn't make it, ma'am . . . The mine went off under his seat."

Mac wrapped an arm around Roper's bony shoulders. "I'm sorry, Cissy . . . Munroe? Take her to the *Betsy Ross.* Mr. President, follow me. We've got to keep moving."

The ramp was already down when they arrived at the **BETSY ROSS**—and the TC took off before the hatch was up and locked in place. Mac took a quick look around. Sloan had applied a dressing to Munroe's cut—and Roper was hunched on a bench, with her head in her hands.

The TC was a corporal named Anders. Mac went forward to speak with him. "Take it slow, Andy . . . Watch the surface of the road for anything that looks suspicious. And drive on the shoulder when you can. That's a gamble, needless to say—but it's a chance we'll have to take."

Anders kept his eyes glued to the LCD screen in front of him. He knew how Fuller had been killed, and he knew that the same thing could happen to him. "Yes, ma'am."

Mac went back to sit on the bench opposite Roper. Her mind was racing. Speed versus safety. That was the calculation. Even though the truck had been forced to go slowly, it was still moving faster than they could walk.

On the other hand, the **BETSY ROSS** constituted a very visible target. For both the rebs *and* Union forces. Unless . . . She turned to Munroe. "Try to get ahold of somebody senior . . . someone on Hern's staff."

Munroe went to work. After a dozen attempts, he shook his

head. "I can't get through . . . Someone is jamming all the frequencies."

Mac swore. The "someone" could be working for either side. She turned to find that Sloan was smiling. "Welcome to *my* world, Captain. A decision has to be made, you're the one who has to make it, and you have zero intel."

Mac made a face. "Screw you, sir."

Sloan laughed.

"Okay," Mac said, as she glanced around. "Grab anything you need. And don't forget to bring water. We're going to bail out."

Mac passed the word to Anders, he pulled over, and all of them were clear three minutes later. She would have used a demolition charge to destroy the vehicle if one had been available. But there wasn't, so Mac ordered Roper to drop two thermite grenades in through a hatch. Odds were that the resulting fire would find some ammo and set it off. Then it was time to run.

Mac took the point. She had an M4 carbine acquired from the **BETSY ROSS**, a fully loaded tac vest, and her pistol. They were off the highway, and crossing the fence next to it, when the Stryker blew. Mac heard the explosion but didn't turn to look. Thick brush blocked the way, and it was necessary to shoulder her way through it.

A wide-open field lay beyond. It was pockmarked with overlapping shell craters. What remained of a Black Hawk helicopter was sitting in the middle of the field, with bodies sprawled around it. Treetops were visible beyond the crash site. Some had clumps of foliage, but most didn't, and the rest were jagged stumps. Fingers of smoke probed the sky in the distance—and the rattle of machine-gun fire could be heard. Maybe, if they moved quickly enough, the party could find a way around the fighting. Mac waved the group forward.

She dashed to a crater, went prone, and waited for the others to catch up. Then it was time to do it again. They were coming up on the Black Hawk's shot-up carcass when Mac heard a grenade go off and saw what might have been fifty soldiers, all backing out of the tree line. They were firing toward the north . . . And clearly under pressure. Rebs then . . . Left behind to try to slow the enemy down.

No sooner had *that* realization sunk in, than the Confederate soldiers turned and charged straight at her. Mac had two choices. She could fight or surrender the President of the United States to the enemy. Mac ran to the helicopter. It was teetering on the edge of a crater as a wisp of black smoke dribbled out of the engine compartment.

Mac had to climb up the blood-slicked deck, and step over a body, to reach the pintle-mounted machine gun. Then, with both hands on the grips, she opened fire.

Bullets kicked up columns of dirt in front of the oncoming soldiers and wove a trail of death in among them. Some appeared to trip, others were snatched off their feet, and one man was forced to perform a macabre dance before falling to the ground.

But there was incoming fire, too . . . Mac heard dozens of pings and felt something tug at her jacket as Sloan yelled, "Kill those bastards!" He was firing short, well-aimed bursts from his assault rifle, and even more fire lashed out at the rebels as Anders and Roper joined the fight.

Fully half of the enemy soldiers were down by that time, but the survivors were desperate and continued to elbow their way forward. They were getting close, and Mac was about to run out of ammo when some red smoke drifted past the door.

"Don't fire on the helicopter!" Munroe shouted, and Mac was about to ask, "*What* helicopter?" when the Black Hawk swooped in and began to circle. Mac gave thanks when she saw the Union markings on the aircraft's fuselage.

Most of the surviving rebs had taken cover in shell craters. But the helicopter crew could see them—and the door gunners opened fire. A brave reb stood, aimed an AT4 at the helo, and staggered as a stream of heavy bullets put him down.

The Black Hawk circled the area one more time, failed to draw fire, and swooped in for a landing. The rotors continued to turn as black-clad troops jumped out and came rushing forward. "President Sloan!" one of them shouted. "Identify yourself!"

Mac watched Sloan go out to meet them. He was hustled toward the aircraft as six of the heavily armed rescuers stood ready to shoot Mac's team. "Back away from the machine gun!" one of them ordered. "Place your hands on your head!"

Mac did as she was told while Sloan turned, or tried to, only to be stripped of his carbine and hustled away. Once Sloan was inside the helo, the rest of the rescue team returned to the Black Hawk.

Mac lowered her arms as the engines spooled up, and Army One took to the air. The engine noise began to fade as the Black Hawk flew north. Munroe appeared in the doorway. "I got through," he said.

"Yeah," Mac said dryly. "I noticed that. Good job."

"So what now?" the RTO wanted to know.

"We'll do what we can for the wounded," Mac answered. "Put out another call . . . Maybe we can get some medics in here. And a Mortuary Affairs team as well."

Munroe nodded, and Mac began to tremble. The mission was over—and she was alive.

|||||||||||||

As the Black Hawk took off, Sloan ordered the crew to turn around and retrieve the others. "Sorry, Mr. President," one of the operators said. "Our orders are to bring you back as quickly as possible. Not to mention the fact that there isn't enough room for them."

Sloan aimed a cold stare at him. "Give me my rifle."

The man made no effort to obey. Sloan pulled his pistol and aimed it at the man's face. "Give me my rifle, or I will blow your fucking brains out!"

"Give the president his rifle," a familiar voice said. "I taught him to never part with it. And he's been through a lot."

Sloan turned to find himself eyeball to eyeball with McKinney. The soldier nodded. "Welcome back, Mr. President . . . Don't worry about Captain Macintyre. A second bird is on the way to pick her up."

Sloan put the pistol away, slumped back in his seat, and accepted the rifle. It was part of him by then—something he could trust. "Good. Captain Macintyre is an amazing woman."

McKinney raised an eyebrow. "Sir, yes, sir."

Army One crossed the New Mason-Dixon Line shortly thereafter, and two dozen reporters were waiting when it landed. The attack on Richton had been a monumental failure. But, thanks to Doyle Besom's efforts, it was being portrayed as a magnificent initiative gone tragically wrong. Or what Besom referred to as, "Part of the brave journey."

And photos of a dirty, disheveled, but combat-ready president getting off a Black Hawk were worth a thousand words. Maybe the assault had gone poorly . . . But the battle for the hearts and minds of America's voters was going well.


## MURFREESBORO, TENNESSEE

After being flown to a rest area outside Martin, Mac and her soldiers were loaded onto a school bus, which took them to a small town named Union City. It had been the site of a minor battle during the first civil war—and was home to a graveyard full of unknown soldiers.

Forward Operating Base Cleveland occupied about a hundred acres of farmland and included landing pads, a field hospital, and a supply dump. The bus dropped Mac and her people off in front of a tent marked PROCESSING CENTER, and spewed black smoke as it roared away. Thus began three days spent trying to find out where the Scout and Reconnaissance Battalion was quartered. But it was an opportunity for them to take hot showers, draw new uniforms, and get some sleep.

Once contact was established, and their orders came through, the group managed to hitch a ride on a southbound helo that took them to a base near Murfreesboro, where the mission had begun. The battalion was headquartered on the grounds of a defunct warehouse complex by then—and Granger was there to meet them as the Chinook landed. "It's good to have you back," Granger said warmly as he shook hands with each person.

That was followed by an awkward moment as Granger cleared his throat and looked away. When he turned back to them, his expression was grave. "I have some bad news to share . . . I'm sorry to say that Element Alpha, the one led by Sergeant Ralston, was attacked by enemy aircraft. There's the possibility that some of our people survived and were taken prisoner, but there's been no confirmation of that."

There were expressions of grief all around, and Roper began to cry. As many as nine of Mac's people had been killed—along with what? Two dozen Rangers? Probably.

In keeping with the contract the Marauders had with the government, a large payment would be made to each soldier's family . . . But nothing could make up for the loss of a husband, father, or lover. "And Element Bravo?" Mac inquired.

"They got lucky," Granger replied. "They were halfway home when a Chinook swooped in to pick them up."

"Good," Mac said. "What about the Strykers?"

"They were destroyed," Granger replied. "So the enemy couldn't use them. That's the bad news."

"There's good news?"

"Yes," Granger replied. "I think so . . . The government decided to cancel the mercenary program and buy out the balance of your contract. And that means you'll receive a large lump sum. But," Granger continued, "another decision was made as well. Effective 1200 hours yesterday, every single one of you was reactivated at your previous ranks. Except for *you*, Macintyre . . . Your captaincy was confirmed. Congratulations."

Mac wasn't surprised. The mercenary thing had been a stopgap measure . . . a way to protect what remained of the Union while the federal government got back on its feet. And, after meeting Sloan, she felt glad. He was a good man. And if anyone could put the country back together again, he could. "Thanks, I guess," Mac said. "So here we are . . . We have a headquarters company but very little else."

"True," Granger agreed. "But not for long . . . New vehicles are on the way. They're supposed to arrive in a week or so."

"I'll believe that when I see it," Mac replied. "But I hope you're right. Is there anything else?"

"Yes," Granger replied. "Follow me to my office. I have something for you."

Mac accompanied Granger across what had been an employee parking lot, to a small outbuilding. The hand-printed sign read, BAT. SCOUT & RECON, HQ.

Mac said, "Hello," to the unfamiliar sergeant seated behind the reception desk and followed Granger into his office. He closed the door. "The things I'm about to share will be announced tomorrow. First, I'm going to name you as the battalion's executive officer *and* Bravo Company's commanding officer."

Mac was both surprised and pleased. That in spite of the fact that the XO slot would come with lots of extra work. "Thank you, sir . . . I'll do my best."

Granger smiled. "I know that. And, there's this."

Mac accepted a manila envelope, opened the flap, and removed the sheet of paper within. According to the title at the top it was a Presidential Unit Citation for Charlie Company, First Scout and Reconnaissance Battalion, 150th Infantry. Which was to say, *her* company.

"It's rare for a unit smaller than a battalion to receive such an honor," Granger informed her. "But it seems that the president wants to recognize Charlie Company, and I agree with that decision. And there's something more as well."

Granger offered her a burgundy-colored case. And when Mac opened it, she saw a Silver Star nestled within. Mac knew it was the country's third highest decoration for valor . . . What would General Bo Macintyre think of that? Would he be proud? Of course not . . . Not so long as she was fighting for the wrong side.

There was something else in the case as well . . . It was a much-folded piece of paper that, when opened, proved to be a handwritten note.

*Dear Mac . . . That's what the troops call you behind your back, and having been part of your command, I feel that I rate that privilege, too. I wish I could pin this medal on you myself. But things are a bit harried at the moment. So, rather than wait, I ordered the Secretary of Defense to make sure that you receive it now.*

Mac could read between the lines. The president was afraid that one or both of them would be killed. She continued to read.

*I guess that's all, except to say that I will never forget your intelligence, bravery, and foul mouth.*

> *Respectfully yours,*
> *Samuel T. Sloan*
> *President of the United States*

Mac could see that Granger was curious, but she chose to tuck the note into her breast pocket without sharing it. "Thank you, sir."

Granger nodded. "You'll receive the medal tomorrow. Dismissed."

The sun threw light but no warmth as Mac left the shack. Her right hand went up as if to touch the note before falling to her side. It was cold, but Mac felt warm, and there were things to hope for.